NO LONGER PROPERTY
OF ANYTHINK
RANGEVIEW LIBRARY
DISTRICT

THE
SOUND
OF

Steadfast
Love
2

THE
SOUND
OF

RACHELLE REA

WhiteFire
Publishing

This is a work of fiction. All characters and events portrayed in this novel are either fictitious or used fictitiously.

THE SOUND OF SILVER

Copyright © 2015, Rachelle Rea
All rights reserved. Reproduction in part or in whole is strictly forbidden without the express written consent of the publisher.

WhiteFire Publishing
13607 Bedford Rd NE
Cumberland, MD 21502

ISBN: 978-1-939023-62-9 (digital)
       978-1-939023-61-2 (print)

To my grandmother, Sarah Rosalie Detwiler.
For being there and being you and showing us all how to rise above.
Thank you for being my Rohesia.

Dirk

Chapter One

Barrington Manor, Northampton, England
September, 1566

The mystery of her survival soared within and around me until I was aware of naught but her. Her and that smile as she asked me about her rosary and spoke about marrying the man that she loved. The candlelight flickered on the wheat-colored strands of her hair.

I stopped at the foot of the stairs that would carry us out of the dark dungeon of her uncle's castle and up into the keep and tightened my hold on her. Distant voices reached my ears, but his did not—her uncle, the man whose madness had driven him to holding Gwyn captive. I listened only long enough to ascertain Cade and Gerald reassured Ian, Margried, and Agnes that Gwyn lived. When Gwyn's smile grew, making her eyes glitter a brighter green, I decided not to join the others just yet.

What had she asked again?

Would you be disappointed in me if I did not wear my rosary anymore?

That she had asked me that spoke of just how far she had come. That rosary meant much to her, judging from the way she had clung to it ever since I had taken her from the Dutch convent. That she would be willing to set it aside after wearing it daily…was she now willing to become Protestant?

I opened my mouth and said the first words my mind found, hardly hearing myself. "I would not be disappointed in the least. But I would be upset with you if you did not wear it on your wedding day."

She tilted her head. "And why would that be?"

I stared down into her eyes. What had I just said? I shook my head to clear my thoughts. "I changed my mind. I care not what you wear. As long as you marry me."

She pressed a hand to her throat. My mouth dried.

"Are you asking me to be your wife?" Her steady gaze chased away the last cloud of fear that lingered from my confrontation with her uncle, Oliver.

I had been so afraid I would find her dead. And then, when I had found her locked in that dungeon, that she would die in my arms. "Aye, milady, and that was not an answer."

"How is this for an answer?" She came closer and feathered gentle lips to the scar on my face, the scar that served to remind me of all I had once been, all I could become again if not for the blood of Christ.

Once more, my arms tightened around her back and beneath her knees. I would never allow myself to become that man again. To do so would endanger Gwyn. I refused to entertain even the notion of that.

So I kissed her. I laid my mouth over hers and infused every ounce of tenderness she inspired in me into that kiss, trying to tell her I accepted her answer to my question, trying to tell her this kiss was to be different from her perception of our first. For this time, I in no way wished to keep her quiet. I wished only to quiet both our souls.

When I pulled back, her eyes remained closed. She rested her head on my shoulder, and I tucked my cheek to her temple. She had been through so much. It was time to see to her safety and security above all else. "Gwyn?"

"Aye?" She sounded drowsy. I clenched my jaw, suddenly aware of how solitary was the hall in which we stood, of how close I had gathered her to me, and how very soft her voice had become. Dare I to hope that the lioness had been tamed?

I hoped not.

A weight in my cloak pocket reminded me. "I trust you will never do that again."

Her eyes popped open, and a flicker crossed her face. "Do what?"

I set her down close to the wall and stayed near enough she could lean on me should the need arise. After all, I had just saved her life. The woman was allowed to be wobbly.

I whisked her glasses from my pocket and held them out to her close enough for her to see. "Do not ever leave your glasses behind."

Her fingers took them from my palm, leaving soft circlets of heat on the skin she had touched. The eyes that stared up at me from behind thin lenses seemed mournful. I studied the paleness of her face before scooping her into my arms again. "What did you think I meant? Just now?"

Did her chin tremble? "I thought you wanted me to never kiss you again."

My eyes closed. "Gwyn."

When her head rested on my shoulder once more, the fear that had vanished at her laughter mere moments ago resurfaced. She should have broken into a Spanish tirade, not taken such a ludicrous command from me seriously. "Why would you ever think that?"

"I know not." Tears had found lodging in her whisper.

I began to move toward the others. Our few moments alone in the cold stairway, that one kiss, would have to be enough for now. Gwyn may have just agreed to become my bride, but she had also just been rescued from a dungeon, from darkness, from a discarded key that had left her trapped. I needed to tuck my bride-to-be into a warm bed as fast as I could find one.

Before I could allow that thought to wander any further, Cade and Ian came into sight.

"Gwyneth!" Margried, the postulant who had come from the burning convent with us a fortnight ago, rushed over to us first. Her eyes brimmed. "You are well."

I shot a look at Cade, but he was already joining us. Though I set Gwyn down, I stayed close. She and Margried embraced for a long minute that contained more than a few soft whispers and, if my ears did not deceive me, at least one muffled shriek that seemed to originate from Margried.

I watched from two paces away, on guard lest Gwyn's strength fail her. Her eyes testified to her weariness with the circles beneath them, even as she closed them in joy at being reunited with her friend. It had not been the proper time to ask for her hand. She was fragile now. But the words had tumbled out, and I would not take them back—as if I would ever wish to.

When the women released each other, Cade wrapped an arm around Margried, inspiring a shy smile on the woman's face. Agnes came forward with halting steps. Gwyn smiled and hugged the woman. Agnes's eyes closed for a brief second before she opened them again and stepped away.

I picked up Gwyn again. I was taking no chances of her plunging to the cold stone floor on which we stood. I opened my mouth to stifle her imminent protest, but she merely rested her head on my shoulder. That was odd.

Gerald, the gatekeeper to whom I owed my life, cleared his throat and motioned with his head. I glanced toward the corner and saw the dark forms in the shadows—Gwyn's uncle, Oliver Barrington, and his henchman, Arthur. Both dead.

Agnes sighed loudly from the center of the room. Ian looked my way and tossed his gaze to the ceiling before sending a pointed glance at the disgruntled older nun. I had neither the energy nor the leisure to laugh. I looked down at Gwyn. "Best we find you a place to rest."

"I would like that."

The fear multiplied when again she offered no protest. Bed. Now.

"But wait." Something in her voice made me look at her. She stared up at me with eyes too trusting. "Where is my uncle?"

I turned my back on the others to afford us privacy. I had thought that she had understood, while she still stood barred within her dungeon cell, that he was dead, that he had made his own death a condition of my saving her. A sigh punctuated my low whisper of her name. "Gwyn."

She must have read the truth in my eyes, for she swallowed. Her chin wobbled. A quick nod and that glazed look I hated took over her gaze.

"Gwyn, I am sorry. So sorry."

Her deep breath caused her whole body to shudder. I laid my forehead against hers.

"Where?"

"Gwyn—"

"Where?"

I sighed. "Here."

Her head turned in Margried's direction. She looked at Agnes next. I knew the moment she found the shadowed corner where they lay, for her entire face turned ashen and tears glistened behind her glasses.

The breath left my stomach. "Do you want to—?"

"*Nee.*" She used the Dutch her mother had taught her, the Dutch she always fell into when upset.

Leaving the others to follow, I steered my boots toward the stairs. Of a sudden, I could feel the burn in my gut from Oliver's stab. A graze, I knew, hardly more than skin-deep. And hardly more important than taking care of Gwyn now. I would see to it later.

Footsteps behind me assured me the others came. At the top of the stairs, I turned in the direction of the room to which the maid had taken Agnes and Margried the night before—and to which I had in turn taken Gwyn.

"Dirk?"

I looked down at her, trying to tell from her features what she needed, but the shadows stole that privilege from me.

"I am frightened."

I flicked my gaze to hers, taking in the look on her face, willing my eyes to deny what my ears had heard. Her tears had fled, but her pallor confirmed her words. How had she grown even paler than before? Or was it merely the shadows?

"You are well, Gwyn. Whole. I am right here, and I will not allow anything"—I kicked open the door to the room that had been my destination—"to harm you." I stifled a wince as my side protested.

Agnes clucked from somewhere behind me. "You could have waited. I would have lifted the latch for you."

Gwyn shivered. "I know. I trust you. It's just that…"

I stepped within, stopped, and stared down into her emerald eyes, the need to know what caused her distress swamping my insides. Gwyn was a fighter, a lioness, a lord's daughter as noble as the Queen herself could claim to be. Why, then, this trepidation?

Her gaze roved the ceiling. She drew in a deep breath and spoke in that same small voice. "'Tis dark in here."

"I will light a candle." Movement behind me reassured me someone would see to it.

"'Tis cold."

I tightened my arms around her. Then realized I had been doing that a lot lately. I loosened my hold. "I will fetch you a blanket."

"Aye, but…"

Passing the bed and, upon it, the crumpled blue gown I had slashed during our swim in the sea, I strode to the window to give us more privacy. Rustling behind me meant blankets were being prepared. Yet, if need be, I would keep her in my arms forever. I was determined to erase that panicked look from her eyes. So help me, if Oliver had done anything to dampen or destroy the fire in her spirit, I would—

"This place…"

"What is it?" I gentled my voice for I did not wish her to think—

Her gaze flicked to mine. "I am being silly. I am sorry. I should not think such things." Her words sped past her lips. The bodice of her dress heaved with hurried breaths.

She was panicking.

I forced my face to conceal my reaction. I winced at her thinking she had anything to apologize to *me* for. "Tell me. I want to know what has your skin pale and your eyes wide."

Her throat worked as she swallowed. "It is just that…"

I placed a kiss on the top of her brow and tucked her head beneath mine. "Tell me, Gwyneth-mine."

"I have not spent a night here since the night my parents died."

My eyes closed, and a moment's pause magnified my lack of response. What to say?

A woman's hand touched my shoulder. "Lord Godfrey?"

I turned. "Call me Dirk, please, Margried."

She nodded. "She is weakened. She needs wine. Bread."

Gwyn's brows collided. "I am fine."

I frowned down at her. "Nay, you are not." Of course. How could I have forgotten? She had just spent hours in a dungeon, locked away with, she believed, no way of escape. Even Oliver had mentioned only an hour before, when we first came bursting in, that she might need refreshment. All because I had not been there, alert to her, when she needed me, and Arthur had abducted her. The pain of the truth cut deep, but there it was.

How I had failed to think of it before, I did not know. But I thought of it now. Of the scene that had surely taken place. Arthur appearing at our camp in the dark of night, snatching her from sleep. While I slumbered mere feet away. How she must have struggled, sought in vain to awaken me.

"I will fetch some then." Margried's words forced me back to the present. She turned away with a smile, but it was a sad smile.

I faced the room again and watched Cade follow Margried out the door. What would I have said, if she had not interrupted with her insight?

Gwyn shifted in my arms and nodded at me. Such a noblewoman, tipping her head in thanks for the service of my arms. I set her down with reluctance banging at my ribcage. What could I say to comfort her? This place was synonymous with death for her. As if she did not have enough trouble with sleep already.

I studied our surroundings. The long chamber held one large bedframe, two large windows, and sundry furnishings. Agnes turned down the blankets on the bed—her gaze flicking to Gwyn and me. Her brows pinched together, and her mouth formed a thin line as she looked up at me.

I raised an eyebrow.

She turned her attention to Gwyn. "Milady, you must want to…" Her voice trailed off as she glanced at me again. I narrowed my eyes, not catching her meaning. I watched Gwyn walk toward the bed and grasp the bedpost. She peeked back at me.

Right. Whatever they wished to discuss, they did not want me there to overhear. I gave them each a curt nod and strode from the room. With great restraint, I refrained from touching Gwyn's shoulder as I passed her. Refused to allow myself to brush her fingers with my own. Though I longed to touch her, to feel her realness once more, to reassure myself she was alive... her wide eyes were so mournful.

And the horror of the thought that I had allowed this to happen made my blood run cold.

I shut the door behind me, closed my eyes, and forced myself not to open the door again, not to go to her. I set out to find Ian and Gerald. They had not followed us into the chamber earlier. Had they even followed us up the stairs?

I took one step toward the stairway and stumbled. Wincing, I put a hand to my side. Time to see to that gash gained at Oliver's hand during the struggle that had ended his life but brought Gwyn back to me.

Gwyneth

Chapter Two

I watched that good man leave the room and took a deep breath. For, despite what I had long thought about him, he was a good man. And he wanted to marry me. I swallowed and let my eyes rove around the room to take in the space I had visited many times before.

The high windows, the wall coverings, the rushes on the floor, even the counterpane on the bed all looked so familiar. Yet different somehow, because I was different. The events of the last weeks had challenged my soul and taught me about faith. I was both grateful and amazed at how my perspective of even a simple room could change. This place looked lighter, airier now.

Sister Agnes snapped a corner of the blanket she had been fiddling with for far too long, drawing my gaze to her. "What are you not telling me?"

Everything. "Please, not tonight, Sister Agnes."

I could not yet piece the words together. She must be tired tonight, too. No use in frustrating both of us by marching into a discussion over my "coming to God," if that was even the right term for it, with this stalwart Catholic nun. She was still in a dither over Margried's recent conversion. The sudden longing to have Reverend Joseph here to inquire of tore a sigh from my throat—surely he would have answers. He always did.

I took another deep breath and let myself sag against the bedpost to which I clung. On the morrow, I would sort through it. On the morrow, I would think about it. On the morrow, I would tell the others everything. Dirk and Margried needed the details. Sister Agnes needed to know. For now, I planned to sleep the day away, if sleep would have me.

I looked at her again. Her face had changed, softened. Compassion resided in her eyes. She straightened, finished with the blanket. "Are you well?"

I smiled. "I am just fine."

She cocked her head, and I heard the disbelief echoing in her mind. But she moved on, and for that I was thankful. "Would you like a bath this morn?"

"Was that what you did not want to ask me in front of Dirk?"

Her fingers again reached for the blanket as she frowned. "He hovers over you."

I did not want to delve into *that* subject. "I will fetch Joan and ask if she can draw some water and see to the tub being brought up."

I released the bedpost and took one step toward the door. Swayed. Returned to the bedpost. Blinked until the room ceased to spin. Sister Agnes came to my side.

"Mayhap the bath can wait until this afternoon." I forced a smile.

She stared at me. "If you want a bath, a bath you shall have."

"'Tis an awkward request for Joan and the other servants to have to tend to, what with all the commotion going on in this house all night." They surely had other tasks to occupy their time, I realized. Like burying two bodies. My stomach lurched as my mind conjured the metallic smell of blood that had wafted through the hall and followed Dirk and me up the first few stairs earlier. Then, I had focused on blinking away the tears and breathing through my mouth until I could detect the odor no longer. Now I waited for my stomach to settle.

I would *not* retch.

"Nonsense." Sister Agnes turned toward the door, a wrinkle between her eyebrows attesting to her worry. "They will be happy to see to your needs. I will return in a moment."

The door clicked shut behind her. Just like that, I was left alone. But I was not. Alone. *God, You are supposed to be a friend. That is what I have been told. That is what I believe now.*

So I would just remember to believe it. I opened my eyes and moved away from the bedpost, to the window, willing someone to bring up the tub, pails of water, anything, anyone, and soon. My deep breath shuddered between my ribs.

Being alone had its advantages. I could now allow the events of the night to seep in. Though I was not sure I could fully fathom them yet, I could try to make sense of them. I watched the first tendrils of dawn embrace the sky stretched above Barrington land.

Dirk had come back for me.

Despite my prayers that he would not, despite what he must have thought when he woke and saw me gone, he had returned for me. And he had been wounded for me. He had tried to hide it, but I had seen. Tears filled my eyes. Although I blinked to wash them away, they persisted in blurring my vision.

He loved me. Truly. A single tear slipped down my cheek. My limbs turned to sand, and I sagged against the wall even as I stared out into the beginning day, bright with light. He had defeated my uncle, and my uncle had been killed. Dread filled my stomach for both Dirk and me—for surely this third death in my family would cast further stain on my beloved's name.

And it had orphaned me.

Orphaned. I had been forced to make peace with that word many months ago, but now it was much worse. The last of my family was gone. Why had Oliver turned so wretched?

A knock on the door caused me to turn. I swiped at my cheeks. "Come in."

Joan, my maid since I had lost my nursemaid eight years ago, entered. My shoulders sagged. "'Tis you. How are you, Joan?"

She blinked. "The more pressing question is how are you, milady?"

I waved away her politeness as I watched her enter with a bucket on each arm. "I think we can do away with the pleasantries for one morn, at least. Are you well? Did—" I choked on his name, "the lord hurt you?"

"Nay, milady. And it is sorry we are that we could not free you sooner. Good thing Lord Godfrey arrived when he did." Joan's eyes held kindness. A touch of uneasiness darkened her expression, but it faded just as quickly as it had come.

"Indeed, it is." I watched her set down the buckets of water and head for the door. "Who is 'we'?"

"All of the servants, milady." Joan smiled. Then, instead of disappearing through the door, she opened the portal wide. Two young men lumbered inside, the tub between them. They set it down and bowed. I inclined my head but did not miss the blush that climbed both their cheeks. Two more maids then took their place and filled the bath with the water from the buckets on their arms. Joan moved to do the same with the buckets she had brought.

"Thank you all." Each of them looked up in surprise at my words. I did not blame them. I had not often appreciated all that the servants did for me during my lifetime of living at Barrington Manor.

The truth struck me, then. I stood staring as the agitated water calmed and the steam rose from the tub.

My uncle, the lord of the manor, was dead. And he had left no heir. This house, this entire estate, would become the Queen's.

She could have it. Too many painful memories resided in this place for me to mourn it, though the thought that I was now homeless wrenched a knife in my back.

The last of the maids departed, clicking the door shut behind her. Sister Agnes then opened the door and entered the room before I could even begin to fret about having been alone. She paused, looked at the tub, then stared at me. "Are you feeling up to a bath?"

I took a deep breath. The warm air encased my lungs. "I—I am, aye, thank you."

She raised her eyebrows. "Then why are you so pale?"

"Will you help me from this gown? Joan must have forgotten…" But she had not forgotten. The echo of her asking if I needed help undressing resurfaced in my mind. I had never answered, had not even registered her words.

I was glad when Sister Agnes stepped behind me and began attacking the buttons at my back. Minutes later, I stepped into the tub, steaming and scented with lavender that promised to chase away the metallic smell. My skin pebbled beneath the warm water; I relaxed.

"Milady…" Sister Agnes's voice trailed, leaving worry threaded through the air.

"Please. Not now." I shook my head, closed my eyes, and breathed deeply of the warm air, not opening them again until I heard the door close once more. Forcing the events of the day—and all that they entailed—from my mind took little effort. I just wanted to forget for a moment all that had happened—and all that it meant.

When the water cooled, I stepped out and donned my shift and the dressing gown Joan had left on the bed. Then I flung myself back onto the soft coverlet and lay there. *God, I…*

How to pray?

I am an orphan. I suppose You knew that before I did. But I do not want to be. Did You know that?

I put a hand to my pounding forehead. This was not how it was supposed to be. If my parents had lived, we would all have still been living here, *Moeder* just as timid as ever, but at peace, Papa filling the halls with laughter. My other hand rose to my face. *Nee*, this was *not* how it was supposed to be. My parents were gone forever.

I swallowed. I would not allow myself to venture down that road. The tears could fall, but my heart would not break nor give in to the temptation to hate. Faces flashed through my mind. Margried. Sister Agnes. Ian. Cade. Joan.

Dirk.

I might not have any family left, but I had friends. A future with them. With him.

I struggled to fathom the fact that he had come back for me. Although I supposed I shouldn't have been surprised at that. He always came back for me. That was one of the reasons I loved him. And now I was to be his bride. There. Something else I struggled to fathom.

The door creaked open. A small white hand snuck through and clung to the frame. I propped myself up on my elbows and smiled a half-smile. "Come in."

Margried ducked through the portal, face solemn. "I hope I did not wake you. I did not realize the door could be so loud."

I waved her words away and sank back onto the bed, suddenly lacking the strength to support my own body. "I was not sleeping."

"Trying to sleep, then?" Margried's voice held a wince.

"Trying not to think."

"Ah, I see." She lay down next to me. For some odd reason, her nearness made me smile. We lay there, not touching, not talking, for moment after moment. At the same second, we turned our heads toward each other. Was this what it might have been like if I had grown up with a sister?

Margried's black hair swirled around her face. Her cheeks held a blush, her eyes a sparkle. I raised one eyebrow. "Cade?"

Her blush deepened. "Aye."

I chuckled. "I am happy for you, Margried." After living a life of such sorrow, Margried deserved such happiness as this. Her mother had died years ago. Her father had attempted to betroth her to my uncle. She had run away from the loveless match, taking refuge at the same convent where I arrived broken after my parents' deaths. She had suffered at the hands of the Dutch rioters who had burst in the same night Dirk did, and now she was in love with Dirk's best friend.

Her smile widened. "And I am happy for you."

Once again, we lay there, content to be silent and think of the men who had captured our hearts. This was new, this feeling of being in love, of being in love *together*. "What is it about a man that can infuriate and enthrall at the same time, Margried?"

She laughed softly. "I imagine they might be asking the same thing about women."

"Mayhap. You were right, you know."

"About what?"

"About it being what the man does not do, just as much as what he does." That dark night in the monastery, when Margried had acknowledged that her first impression of Cade had been as tainted as mine had been of Dirk, she had confessed that her opinion had eventually been swayed as much by when he refused to act as when he acted. How right she had been. Dirk had never given me cause to think him a murderer. 'Twas simply a case of my assuming the most logical explanation and denying the need to probe deeper.

But then I had seen a side of him I had never imagined existed. A caring, compassionate side. A side I believed portrayed his heart. "Dirk's first words to me were 'Fear not.'"

Margried tipped onto her side to face me. "I did not know that."

"'Twas before we took you and Sister Agnes from your chamber."

"Cade's first words to me were 'I have you.'"

My brow furrowed. "How—?"

She smiled. "You were unconscious at the time. Dirk carried you through the doorway of the convent, and Sister Agnes waved a kitchen knife at him."

"She what?"

Margried chuckled. "A kitchen knife! I could scarcely believe it, either. Then, when she was satisfied he meant you no harm, she moved to return it to her pocket, but I lost my balance. Cade caught me. *I have you*, he said."

I smiled. "That is kind."

"Cade is kind."

I laughed. "I am not sure he would agree should he hear you say that."

An image of the confident Cade, so witty yet grave, failed to coincide with the word *kind*. However, I was not his Margried. No doubt with the shy and tender girl, he had indeed proven himself considerate, gentle.

Much to my surprise, she failed to laugh with me. "I was not sure how he would feel when I told him."

My laughter died, as well, for I knew exactly to what she referred. Her previous betrothal. How had he taken the news? *Tread gently, Gwyneth.* "You told him?"

She nodded. "I explained it all while we rode to Barrington Manor last night, the first time."

"Then he knew…"

One corner of Margried's mouth lifted. "He knew when we arrived. He knew when he saw your uncle. He knew when *I* saw your uncle. While I shook with fear, he shook with anger. Every moment I wondered who would burst first, me into tears or him into fisticuffs."

I sat up to face her and shook my head. "I sat there wondering the same thing about Oliver and Dirk, waiting for either or both of them to give in to their anger."

"Both of our men seem to have great self-restraint."

Silence settled over us once more, and I contemplated that amazing trait in Dirk. While I all too often allowed myself and my emotions to spill onto whomever was near, he weighed the situation, the options, the consequences of his actions. 'Twas a far wiser way than mine.

I glanced around the room, taking in the tub and the lavender scent still permeating from the bath. Somehow the space seemed smaller without him in it.

"He did not blow up that night at the convent," I whispered. "I tested him time and again, refused to go with him. He did not leave me. He could have."

"Cade did not like sitting across from the man who wanted me for what my father would pledge in dowry, but he did not take a swing at your uncle. He could have."

I snorted, remembering how tense the group of us had been the night before, amused by the image in which my mind indulged of Cade breaking Oliver's nose. I fought the stab of pain that reminded me my uncle was gone. The truth was he had been gone long before last night…he had changed and for a long time had not been the uncle I knew as a child. I pulled in a breath, praying that in death he could do no more damage. That Dirk would not bear the blame for his demise as he did for my parents'.

Margried sat up on one elbow and reached to lay a hand on my shoulder. "I am sorry, Gwyneth."

"I am sorry, too. We both suffered at his hands."

"But I did not know him. You…" Her features twisted as she searched for the right words.

"I trusted him."

Her blue eyes pierced mine. "This mustn't make you doubt the trust you invest in others."

I sat up too quickly, waited for the room to stop spinning, and stared at her. "What do you mean?"

She studied her hands. "When my father informed me he had arranged a match for me, I was only hopeful. When he told me your uncle's name, I was devastated. I fled. I wonder now what would have happened had I stayed."

Margried's story had shocked me once. Her story of pursuing freedom in the Low Countries hardly fit small, quiet Margried. Yet it did fit her somehow. Her courage was of the quiet sort. Just because the flame burned without fanfare did not diminish the brightness or the warmth.

"What advice are you giving me, Margried?" My tired mind slogged through her story, searching for the gem she sought to give.

She grasped my hand. "I nearly missed the gift God has given me in Cade because I did not wish to trust him. I did not wish to risk being hurt again by a man who thought he knew better than I what I wanted, what I needed."

My eyes widened. "You think because of what my uncle has done..."

"I do not want you to miss the gift God has given you, Gwyneth. In Dirk."

One corner of my mouth tipped up. "I do not fear such a thing. If anything, my trust in Dirk has only grown this day. He saved me from my uncle for the second time."

Relief entered Margried's blue eyes. The smile I had not allowed myself bloomed on her face. "I am glad. So glad."

I lay back on the bed, examining my heart to see if what I suspected was indeed true. "I am glad, as well. I feel sorrow. And uncertainty. But I am glad, too."

Margried nodded and settled beside me once more. "It is nice being glad, together. Even with the sorrow mixed in."

I sat straight up again, an alarming thought tugging the gladness away before I had the chance to fully exult in it.

"What is it?" Margried mimicked my movement and peered into my face.

"Do you think...*he*...doubts me?"

Her brow furrowed. "What?"

"Dirk. He knows Arthur took me? He knows I did not run off on my own last night? I did not return to my uncle of my own free will? Because I told him I would go with him. I would never have fled. Not now. Not after what I know of him." My thoughts and words jumbled together, tripping over each other in the air between us.

Margried shook her head, causing her black curls to sway. "Nay, nay,

21

Gwyneth. He knows. The men deduced what happened right away. I have never seen Dirk look so haunted as when he knew Arthur had taken you."

My lips tightened at the thought of that look. I had seen it before, when he had stood before the window of this very chamber mere hours ago, with me in his arms. The light of daybreak had illuminated the concern on his face as I rambled on, unable to squelch the fear that had strangled me. It had been foolish to allow my emotions to gallop ahead as I had. "It warms my heart that he loves me so, but pains me that I cause him pain."

Margried patted my shoulder. "You cause him joy, as well."

"Do I? What have I done to make him smile, to make him laugh, to make him happy?" Though she opened her mouth, I did not want to hear the stutter in her voice, so I continued. "I told him I would become his wife, but beyond that I have been naught but a burden."

Margried's face turned serious. Her voice lowered until she sounded motherly. "You must not entertain such thoughts—"

"It is true." I balled my fists. "I want to do something for him. Something to make his eyes light with a smile."

The motherly voice disappeared, and in its place a timid whisper came. "Well, I do not see the harm in—"

"But what could I do?" I stared out the window. Morning had taken full reign of the land visible on this, the west side of the castle. My hands ached because I had been clenching them so tightly, so I released them. I reached for my hair and fluffed it with my fingers to aid its drying.

When I caught the idea and gasped, Margried startled. I had been silent so long she must have become lost in her own thoughts.

The sorrow of the night still pulled at my soul, but the fear and despair I had experienced failed to dampen my eagerness. A corner of my heart tucked away the idea that had just come to me, deep inside, where I could revel in the possibilities. I would bring a smile to Dirk's face by giving him what he wanted most: his good name. Godfrey would once again be a name that rang with honor.

Surely I could see it done. I would need help, of course, to make it happen, but I knew just the man for the task.

Dirk

Chapter Three

After I left Gwyn, I found Cade and Ian walking through the Great Hall in the direction of the stairway I descended. Both looked haggard. Ian's young eyes looked pained. Cade's expression was closed, but the way he shook his head made me look to the empty corner. Oliver's and Arthur's bodies had been removed. I met Ian's gaze first, then Cade's. Neither man said a word.

My friends were not known for being talkative, of course, which was one reason we got along so well. Cade had been a friend since childhood; he had turned prodigal with me and weathered my father's death at my side. After that, we had both turned to God. Then we found Ian.

"Where is Gerald?" The gatekeeper had saved my life and led me to Gwyn, and that made him the most to be trusted among the deceased lord's servants.

Cade grasped the railing in his hand, though he did not move a boot to the first step. "Putting away the shovels."

I nodded. I would ask later about where they had buried Oliver and Arthur. I turned, intending to return to Gwyn's room, if only to stand outside her door.

"Dirk." Ian's puzzled tone made me twist my neck slightly to acknowledge that I heard him. "Are you injured?"

"Nay, this blood is mere decoration." Putting a hand to my side, I winced and growled, "I am sorry. That was unfair."

Cade clasped a hand to my shoulder as he climbed the steps and passed me. "Go easy on the pup."

"I am no pup!" Ian closed the distance between him and our backs.

"I said I was sorry." I glared at Cade and followed him up the stairs and into the chamber across from the women's. On the morrow, I might see about more rooms for all of us. The women's chamber only had one bed for the three of them. Ours had two.

As Ian entered and shut the door behind him, I shook my head. We did not need more room. This was the safest arrangement. The women were across the hall from us and, therefore, easy to watch out for. I shook my head again and sat on the nearest bed. What did any of it matter? We would not be staying long.

"Cade." I need not have called the man. He already approached. He lugged the basin from the corner, set it on the floor at our feet, and sat on the bed beside me.

"Ian, fetch that toweling." Cade lifted my arm. I sent him a glower for treating me like I could not get my arm out of the way myself, but he had already slid off the bed. He knelt at my side to get a better look at the wound.

He was trying to help, and I was sending him looks. I must be tired.

Cade ripped my tunic wide open right over the gash, the brickbrain.

"What did you do that for?"

"It was ruined already."

Ian snickered as he came close with the toweling. I sent *him* the fierce look I wanted to give Cade. Ian backed up a step, face sobering. That was better. At least I still scared the youngest of us.

Cade shoved my shoulder, sending a spike of pain down my side. I sucked air past my teeth but did as he bade, twisting to the side so he could better see.

"'Tis not deep. It could use stitches or it could go without."

I weighed the options. If I voted for stitching up the gash, Cade would probably fetch one of the women. They would be gentler than he in tending my wound, but I reddened at the mere thought of having them attend me. "I'll go without."

He swabbed and cleaned the area, which made me groan once before I bit my lip. After that, I used Ian as a distraction. The man's face paled, then turned green, which was most entertaining.

Gwyn had a sensitive stomach, as well. Did she rest? Had she found sleep? Or had sleep found her—distressing her as was its wont? The image of her lovely face burdened with a troubled expression twisted my gut more than the pain from Cade's ministrations.

He wrapped it sparingly and sent Ian after our packs—and a new shirt for me. The younger man looked glad to get away.

"There. You should live. You're welcome."

I snorted and stood. "You should become a healer. Many a man would be glad to have your tender hand at the ready."

Cade smirked. "I should, indeed."

I rolled my eyes heavenward. He would find some occupation to busy him and provide for Margried once he wed her. Cade was a second son, as I was. His father's estate would go to his elder brother. My father's estate had gone to my own elder brother one year ago when my father died. And now it belonged to me.

"What are your plans?" Cade leaned against the wall, arms crossed against his chest, eyes trained on the door.

I flicked my gaze in that direction and saw naught save the closed portal that bespoke Ian's continued absence. Where was he with my shirt? I needed to be clothed so I could check on Gwyn. "You never have much desire to hear my plans."

Cade leveled me a look before turning right back to stare at the door. For what did he wait? Ian's arrival? "So you do not know what to do now."

I growled. "We ride for Godfrey Estate tonight."

"That is not enough time. We must allow the women to rest."

Realization swept through me. *That* was why Cade watched the door. He was thinking of the women. Margried, in particular, if I had to wager a guess. "How long do you suggest?"

Ian opened the door and tossed me a bundle. "Gerald says to tell you he will keep the gate closed."

I raised an eyebrow as I lifted the shirt, ignoring the pain in my side. "Does he fear someone's coming?"

Cade chuckled. "Do you not fear the same?"

I slid my arms through the sleeves. Of course. I had forgotten in the melee. We were in England now. As soon as rumor spread that I was here, we would be on the run again. I groaned, more from the expectation of the flight we would have to make from here to Godfrey Estate than the discomfort of Cade's bandaging.

"One day." Cade pushed away from the wall.

Ian's brow furrowed, and he stopped in the center of the room.

Pulling my shirt over my head, I watched Ian. "We will stay one day, then, and leave on the morrow."

"Only a day?" A tone not quite resembling a whine invaded Ian's voice.

"Will you start questioning me now, too?"

Ian shook his head. "It's just that the women—"

I tossed up a hand. "I am well aware of how hard we have pushed them and what they have endured, but we have not yet reached journey's end. They are not safe here."

"And you think they will be safe at Godfrey Estate?" Cade's playful chiding had ceased. Hope and doubt warred in his words.

I met his gaze. "Godfrey Estate is more easily defended."

It was true, and we all knew it. A stronger gate and swarms of men protected the inner keep and bailey of my childhood home. Barrington Manor, with its thinner outer wall and minimal manpower, could never hope to match it.

Ian crossed his arms. A weight settled over his face. "I hadn't realized... it didn't work."

I took a step toward him, the guilt and shame of the scheme I had asked them to help me with washing over me. They had agreed to help me abduct a woman to clear my name of her parents' murders. They were better friends than I deserved.

"It was never going to work. I should never have suggested such a foolhardy plan in the first place. We put all of the women in danger." Gwyn, most of all. And she had suffered much because of my desire to see my dream realized.

Cade ran a hand through his hair. "Godfrey Estate will not stand forever, Dirk."

I returned his knowing glance. "It need not."

Ian blinked. "What do you mean?"

I laid a hand on his shoulder. "I am a wanted man once more. Nay, I always was. That has not changed. But what has changed is that *that* will never change." I dropped my hand and stared at the ceiling. "What I mean is my reputation is thoroughly destroyed. I have no hope of ever seeing it restored. I will forevermore be the man who murdered Gwyn's parents—in the eyes of all men, anyway."

Ian shook his head. "But you are not."

My whisper matched his. "I cannot prove my innocence, not after all this time, not after casting this last dubious escapade of abducting her onto my already soiled name."

Cade stepped forward until we formed a circle. "*She* does not believe you did the deed."

I nodded. "Nay, praise God, she does not."

Ian grinned. "She will be your proof, then. She can shout it from the rooftops, tell everyone her uncle murdered them, not you. She will do it for you."

I smiled at his eagerness even as my heart sank like a stone. I had been foolish. So foolish. I had asked for her hand, offered her my name when I had not one to give. "She is a woman. An extraordinary woman. But a woman, nonetheless. None will believe her or take her word as weight enough. And that I have abducted her...they will think I bribed her or worse."

Ian's face fell. Cade's thoughtful eyes stared at the floor. I nudged him with my opposite arm, not wanting to jar my bad side. "Speak."

He shook his head and sighed. "You are right. No one will ever believe her."

Ian's head reared back. He looked beyond frustrated. "Is there naught to be done, then?"

Cold numbness stole through me, and the chamber seemed to shrink around us. The wall coverings and even the bed took on a menacing air. "For me, nay. I will understand if you part with me here and now, return to your family and save your name before it is tarnished by being linked with mine."

Ian scowled. "You know I have no family to go back to."

"That is what you say—"

Ian glared at Cade and interrupted him. "It is true." He looked at me. "I stay with you."

I swallowed. "Then there is but one last thing to be done." Cade and Ian's eyes met mine; Cade's filled with determination, Ian's with resolve. "We must get the women to Godfrey Estate...and leave them there."

Gwyneth

Chapter Four

"What is wrong?" Margried touched my arm to show her concern; my gasp must have been audible enough for her to notice. Whereas this bedroom seemed both foreign and familiar, the memory of the old friend I had been thinking about brought only the nostalgic awareness of times gone by. He was a friend and always would be; I knew that, therefore I trusted him to help me.

I grinned at her. "If you were Sister Agnes, right now you would—"

A knock at the door preceded Sister Agnes's entrance. "I heard that. I would what?" Sister Agnes closed the door behind her, leaned against it, and quirked an eyebrow. I could not decide which seemed less characteristic of her—forsaking her perfect posture for the sake of slouching or waiting patiently for me to explain.

Margried looked at me, a giggle in her eyes.

There was no escaping it, then. "I have an idea that Margried wishes to hear. I was just about to say that if she were you, she would be demanding I tell her."

Sister Agnes's head cocked to the side, the chestnut bun at the back of her head never wavering.

I interpreted that look and smiled softly. "I know. You are not demanding now. Is it because you do not wish to know?"

"It is because you will tell me if you wish, and there is nothing I can do to persuade you otherwise if you do not wish."

I took a moment to consider the best way to tell them. I moved from the bed toward the tub and dipped in my hand. Shaking my head, I turned back to the nun. "You both no doubt wish to bathe. I will call Joan for warm water. I am sorry I did not think to call you after I finished."

Sister Agnes shook her head, her face solemn. Displeased. But about what? With whom? Had she guessed what had gone on within my soul in that dark dungeon room?

"No need." Sister Agnes sat in a chair and folded her hands in her lap.

Margried stood, her brow furrowed, her gaze transferring from Sister Agnes to me. "You have not distracted either of us. I still wish to know your idea."

The moment had come to an end, and I decided to be direct. "I am going to help Dirk restore his good name."

Margried blinked at me, stared, then grinned. "Do you need any help?"

A good woman stood before me. "You most certainly may aid me, but I have in mind that I will need even more willing friends. I am going to enlist the help of a man I have known for years."

Sister Agnes's eyes had drifted closed but at that they popped open again.

"He is like a brother to me. He saw me to the *Kanaal* after..." I swallowed. Suddenly, the weight of grief that had hung over me like a heavy cloud descended once more. It had lifted while Margried and I reveled in the new feeling of having two good men to love. How I wished now that it had stayed away.

Margried was at my side, her arm around me. "Enough, then. You can tell me the rest later. Speaking of rest, you need yours."

I glanced at the only bed in the room. Never had it looked more inviting. But Sister Agnes...her eyes had closed once more. I could not just let her sleep in that chair.

Her eyes opened as if she had sensed my gaze. She remained silent—so strange.

"Come." Margried rose, tugged me to the bed, left me standing, and pulled the coverlet back.

I shook my head, not wishing to sleep. I never wished to sleep—because of the nightmares. But especially on this day, I did not wish to sleep. And Sister Agnes... "*Nee.* Sister Agnes, you are drifting away even now. Come."

One corner of the nun's mouth lifted. "I will sit here while you rest."

Sighing, I acknowledged that I would receive no escape from that quarter. I met Margried's gaze. "You must be exhausted."

She laughed, a lovely, merry sound. "None of that now. I know there are other rooms in this grand castle of yours. I will find my own bed. No need to care for me at the moment."

I climbed onto the bed.

Margried let out a breath of air and smiled. "Still, 'tis nice to have people caring for me. For us. Is it not?"

My eyes closed against the tears pricking behind my lids. *Oh, Uncle Oliver, what made you stop caring?* I breathed past the tears that found lodging in my throat. After holding onto the hope of family all this time, all these many months, something inside of me shattered to find it had never been quite as real as I had thought.

And how real was that? During my childhood, my uncle had been the co-conspirator in all my schemes. He had been my first real friend—the only one who had not had to be the parent or grandparent as well as a playmate. Where had he gone wrong? *God, I want to understand.* Mayhap I never would.

Margried put her hand on my head. "Shh, Gwyn. Are you well?"

I reached up a hand and found tears on my cheeks. "Nay." The word was a croak.

I did not understand. How could he have changed so much? How could he have hated my parents so much that he wanted—ensured—their deaths?

Margried helped me lie back. The tears kept coming, but these tears were different. Silently they tracked down my face. I squeezed my eyes shut to ignore their existence even as I knew a small seed of hope at being able to cry in front of Margried. 'Twas a sign of great trust for me that I let her see me weep.

Still, the only one I had allowed to see me really weep—great wrenching sobs that shook my own ears in their fierceness—was Dirk. I gasped, a piercing pain igniting my chest at the image of his face appearing before my mind's eye. I whispered his name.

A swish of fabric. The click of the door. Footsteps in the hall. I opened my eyes to find that the sun had hidden behind a cloud. The room seemed darker than midmorning should allow.

I tasted salt. Burrowing my head deep into the pillows, I shut out the darkness, the questions, the overwhelming knowledge that I was alone.

The door again. More footsteps, deeper ones. A whimper escaped me from within my tunnel of softness. If the sun could decide to hide, then I could, too. Just this once I could let the sorrow pour through the cracks in me.

Just this once.

Dirk

Chapter Five

"Leave them?" The first to break the silence that had settled over us was Ian, voice cracking.

It had probably been close to an hour since I said those words, but they had not left my mind in all that time. Apparently, they had not left his, either. I pushed away from the bedchamber wall and punched him in the arm. "I thought you were beyond the voice-changing grief."

His cheeks reddened, and he scowled.

Cade smirked from his seat on the bed. The remains of what he had used to bandage me littered the blanket. "Ease off the pup."

Ian stood straighter. "Aye, ease off—hey!" He glared at Cade, who grinned back. When Ian returned his gaze to me, I could see he had not forgotten, would refuse to drop it.

So I answered before he could repeat himself. "We *must* leave them. 'Tis the only way to protect them."

"Did you not just ask the woman to marry you?" Ian asked. I ignored him.

Cade sighed. "I do not like it."

"And you think I do?" I bit back a roar, dragging my hand down my face instead. I needed sleep. The call of oblivion was a siren's song. Only after I had allowed peace to seep over me would I cease snapping at these men who stayed beside me despite my foolishness. And what foolishness it had been, my plan of bringing Gwyn back here to set the record straight about the man I was.

I did not regret it, not for a second. Of course I did not. She might have died that night at the hands of the rioting villagers had I not been there. The mere thought poured ice through my veins, paralyzing me.

But she had not died. Not that night, nor the next when the thieves

31

attacked, nor the next when she had slipped from the deck of Tudder's ship. And, God help me, she would remain safe and sound for the rest of her days. For as long as I had breath in my lungs, I would protect her.

If only that did not mean leaving her behind.

"You said it yourself, Cade." I glared at him, certain he would know I was not angry with him so much as with the truth staring me in the face. "Godfrey Estate will not stand indefinitely. No place will. None of them are safe as long as they are in company with me. We will take them to my mother—and then I will leave."

Silence settled as Cade and Ian swallowed this.

I laid a hand on Cade's shoulder. "You will marry Margried." I turned to Ian. "And you will find your own way."

Ian's brows furrowed. Trepidation entered his eyes. "I have no home to go back to. You know that."

"You cannot come with me. Any who do will be branded as criminals."

"You do not think we already are?" Cade crossed his arms over his chest.

I ran a hand through my hair. Oliver and Arthur had been the only ones who would spread the malicious rumors that Cade and Ian had thrown in their lot with me, and dead men told no tales. "The only ones who have seen you with me are dead—and Joseph would never betray me."

Ian stared at me, his expression unreadable. "I will go with you."

Expelling a ruffled sigh, I decided not to argue.

I looked at Cade. "Stay at Godfrey Estate. My brother is gone, and I cannot stay. You could protect them."

He opened his mouth to answer, his face solemn, when we were interrupted by a knock. A hurried knock. And a call. "Lord Godfrey! Dirk!"

I lunged for the door at the same time as Cade. I got there first, pulling the portal open, only catching it a second before it banged into either or both of us. "Margried?"

The poor girl looked frantic. Her eyes took up half her face. "Come quickly. Gwyn needs you."

I bounded across the hall, narrowly avoiding bowling her over. I glanced back as I put my hand on the latch of Gwyn's chamber. Cade had his arm already wrapped around Margried.

"What is wrong?" No sounds came from within. What would I find?

"She weeps."

My brows unknit as worry swamped me. I opened the door and saw her. Bundled in the blankets on the bed, she seemed so small that I hesitated. Shadows bathed the room as if the sun refused to shine. Agnes sat asleep in a chair across the chamber.

A whimper stole from beneath the pillows into which Gwyn had tunneled. I went to her, wordless, helpless to find the right words. She wept, Margried had said. I had seen this woman cry before; never had she been so silent, so unassuming about it. Did she stifle herself for Agnes's sake, to give the woman peace as she slumbered?

When I gathered her into my lap, she turned her face into my neck. Her grip tightened. *Beautiful girl.* Refusing to give full vent to her tears for another's sake—it was so like her. And yet…these tears seemed different somehow.

Into her ear I whispered words of hope and reassurance, words I believed wholeheartedly, words I wanted her to believe.

We sat there for a long time, and somehow I knew Agnes would sleep right through it and Cade and Margried would be there in the hall, peeking in on us. I played with her hair and stroked her back. She smelled sweet, and I credited that to the tub sitting in the center of the room.

As I tangled my fingers in hair the color of sunshine, the fingers of the light crept into the room, over the window casing, across the rug, up the bed. "Look. Here comes the light."

The shudders calmed to shivers and the shivers to a gentle shaking every few moments. She still had not opened her eyes, and I found myself longing for that more than anything. A glimpse of her green eyes meant more to me now than sleeping, leaving, getting her to Godfrey Estate. Hang all that. All that mattered was that she was on her way to healing. Well. Whole.

The tears had ceased. "Gwyn?" Her hair had dried around my fumbling fingers. She shifted against me, and I swallowed hard at the feel of her soft, sweet self. It would be a good idea to get off this bed as soon as possible, but I was not leaving her yet.

A stab went through my core at the thought that I *would* leave her, eventually. I must.

"Dirk?" Her voice sounded hoarse, not unlike the night she had screamed after hearing the truth of her parents' deaths.

"Are you well, Gwyneth-mine?"

She kept her head tucked in my neck as she answered, "*Nee.*"

I pulled back and put a hand on her cheek, breathing deep of the scent of her. "You will be."

Her eyes glistened with the hint of a sad smile. "I think I will."

I smiled as she emerged. On her forehead a wide mark proved she had pressed herself against my jaw. I winced.

The smile disappeared.

I kissed her temple to erase the thought from her mind—the thought that I found her weepy face less than beautiful. I kissed her cheek next, then her nose.

The smile reappeared as she took a shaky breath. "I miss him. It makes no sense, but I do. I miss him, my uncle. And them. And all of us, all at once."

"I know."

"How could he have done that to them, Dirk? They loved him. They did not understand each other sometimes, but they loved him. And he did not love them back. How could he have not loved them back?"

Smoothing the hair from her face, I shook my head. "I know not."

"It makes no sense. He makes no sense. Their deaths make no sense."

"I know." I almost tucked her head under my chin again, but I settled for brushing my fingers against the mark on her forehead. It was fading. If only her pain would do the same. One day, I prayed, it would.

"When will it stop hurting so much?" Her words were whispers.

I stared into her eyes. "I know not. But I know you. You are strong. And you are full of hope. You will heal."

"How can you be so sure?" The spaces between her blinks were growing short.

"I just am." I rose up, lifting her against my chest, and stood beside the bed. "Do you see that, Gwyn?"

I had no fingers free to point, but I nodded my head and watched her look toward the window.

"The light comes." I lowered her gently toward the bed, drinking in the sight of her. "You *will* taste it again and see how sweet it is."

I stood, watching over her until her eyes roved back to me. I smiled. She closed her eyes, giving in to sleep at last. Staring down at her, I fought against the constriction of my chest. *She will never be mine.* Swallowing the roar only worsened the pain.

"Dirk." Cade's voice.

Then Margried's low "I will stay with her now."

I shook my head. "You are as exhausted as she. You should rest."

Cade's hand fell on my shoulder. "As should you."

I sank from his grip onto the edge of a chair at Gwyn's bedside, a smile quirking at one corner of my mouth. If she knew how we all hovered above her, she would be awake inside a second. A frown recaptured my mouth as I realized she should be awake from the sound of our voices alone—she must be sleeping hard.

It was when she slept the deepest that the nightmares raged the hardest. Decision made, I settled into the chair. "I can sleep here."

"See that you do. Sleep, that is." Cade's tone and features immediately gentled as he took Margried's arm. "Come, we can venture into one of the other unclaimed rooms and find a bed. For you." He cleared his throat.

I grunted to cover my laugh. I could not have bumbled that sentence any better. By the look Cade sent me, he knew it.

"But I can stay here. There is another chair." Margried attempted to pull away from him.

Cade refused to let go and steered her toward the door. "A proper bed."

"I can share with Gwyn—"

"You would not rest, and it is already scandalous enough that Dirk insists on staying."

Margried scoffed as he led her out into the hallway. "That is not true, and even if it were, the threat of scandal has not been enough to stop you these last few days…" Her voice trailed off as she and Cade began searching the hallway for a door that led to another empty chamber. A door banged, convincing me that even straining to hear the end of that sentence—much less the rest of the conversation—would be futile. A pity.

At first I conjectured she had meant "you" plural. If she had, indeed, she was correct. We had escorted three women from the Low Countries, across the Channel, and to England with hardly a remnant of respectability. Then I grew convinced she meant "you" singular, as in Cade alone. I chuckled to myself at how he might have put that thought in her head, remembering how the door to Margried's and Gwyn's chamber in the monastery had slammed in my face after Cade entered, after we had just learned Margried no longer wished to be a nun.

Gwyn did not so much as stir. Tangled in blankets, she lay facing the window. I rose, leaned over her, and tugged a corner of the blanket to form a soft hill just in front of her face to act as a shield against the sunlight. Her breath fanned my hand. I pulled back reluctantly, but not before the sweet scent that was hers met my nose.

My heart galloped. She was safe, I reminded myself. No one in this keep wished to harm her and, depending on how I wished to tally us, five to twenty people wished to see her remain safe.

Unbidden, the image of her standing in that dark dungeon below, bars denying me the sight of her face, rose in my mind. She had been so certain there was nothing I could do, but I had freed her. If only I had been able to spare her from ever being thrown into that pit in the first place…but I had slept too soundly the night before, slumbered straight through her abduction. Terror's fist clamped my gut. I would not be so foolish again.

My eyes drifted down once, twice. I reassured myself this castle was clean of any with unsavory intentions and put my trust in, at least, Ian, Cade, and myself, who would protect her with our last breaths.

Only then could I allow myself to sleep.

Agnes's snort woke me. A quick glance confirmed the nun still slept, although she would probably wake soon. Next, I assessed the sunlight. Mid-afternoon, nearly evening.

My gaze flicked to the bed. A sound midway between a sigh and a groan tumbled from my mouth. I stumbled from the chair and headed for the door. Where had the woman gotten herself off to now?

I left the house to find the sun bathed the bailey. With all this light, Gwyn's glasses would cast a glare and impede her sight. All of my senses heightened. The urge to find her, to reassure myself of her safety, intensified. *God, I am trying to trust You where this woman is concerned, but she is making that endeavor most difficult.*

She would, of course. She was Gwyn. Difficult ran in her blood.

"Hallo." A seven or eight year old lad stared up at me, clad in rough clothes.

"Aye?" I stared down at him, smiling at the serious look on his face.

"Are you the knight?" His freckles danced on his nose when he scrunched his eyes to avoid the sunlight. "Because I heard the lady talking about a knight."

Gwyn. "Lady?"

"That's what I heard Rufus call her."

I nodded slowly. "You hear a lot of things, eh…?"

"Alfie, sir." He touched his head even though his thatch of hair was devoid of a cap.

I nodded again. "Now if you would show me where the lady is…"

"Oh, sure, sir, sure. Though I don't think I should show you." He leaned in, and I stifled a smile. His crop of freckles reminded me of Titus, Tudder's son, but this boy appeared a couple of years older, maybe eight. Alfie grinned. "She did not know I was there, y'see."

My brow rose again. "Were you spying on the lady?"

Alfie swallowed. "Nay, sir. I wasn't, sir." His hands drifted up, then down, then up again as if he did not know what to do with them. "It's just that, well, sir, I had finished mucking the stall beside her and heard her. I wanted to know if she was well, then she started talking about a knight, and I wanted to hear the rest of the story."

"'Tis not right to listen in on ladies when they do not know you are there. But thank you for staying until you knew she was well." I nodded at him and strode away.

He came up beside me, and I slowed so he could match my steps, even though my eagerness to get to Gwyn now pulsed. She had been talking of a knight, had she?

Alfie almost tripped but righted himself just before I reached out to steady him. "I did not tell you where she is yet."

I winked at him and paused in the dimness of the stable door. "If you could point me in the direction of the stall beside the one you mucked?"

He grinned and pointed. "Way at the back there."

I thanked him. Letting my eyes adjust to the sudden dimness, I took small steps. The last thing I wished to do was startle her. "Gwyn?"

A blonde head leaned out of a stall. I could not help the grin. She smiled back.

Then a frown found my face. "Where are your glasses?"

"I forgot them." Still, she leaned out, neither coming closer nor retreating.

"That is not like you." My footsteps brought me slowly to her side.

"Mayhap while travelling. But here at home I know my way around well enough."

I felt a prickle of unease; anyone could sneak up on her anytime, no matter how well she knew her way around. But I silenced that warning for now. Mayhap I was being too careful of her. I pushed that concern to a place where I could find it later and closed the distance between us. She stood in a stall with a massive beast as fair as she. The horse had a darker coat, but the mane matched Gwyn's hair in hue.

"Who is your friend?"

Gwyn patted the horse's neck. "His name is Charger, but he has always been Char to me."

I opened the gate, earning my first full glimpse of her. "Gwyn. Your hair." I had not noticed it at first, but now—

"Oh." She tossed a hand to her head. "I forgot to put it up." She bundled it in one hand and twisted it.

I winced. Did that hurt? "Nay." I reached out but stopped myself. "It…" She turned away.

How to tell her it was not the sight of her looking as if she had just risen from bed that concerned me…? For that was far from the truth. Surely she had no idea how she affected me, how her touch blazed fire through me, how one look sparked every sense within a second. "You are beautiful."

She blinked and laid her other hand on Char. She did not believe me.

I let my hand reach the rest of the way and stop her nervous coiling. She stilled. I studied her golden head, the softness of her locks, trying to decide what to address first. How the sight of her unbound hair dried my mouth or that more than just Alfie had probably seen her looking as lovely as this? I reminded myself that she had grown up here, that many of those same men had probably watched her grow up and would therefore be as intent on protecting her as I would.

Well, mayhap not quite as intent as I.

I gave in and slid my fingers over the golden mass she had gathered in one hand. She let go, and her hair tumbled free about my fingers. I had seen it unbound before, of course, but never on the day after she had agreed to be my wife.

Her eyes widened, and I was tempted, very tempted. But a more rational part of me refused to kiss her while she stood in a dimly lit stable stall, her hair cascading over the shoulder of her—was that a dressing gown? I groaned inwardly. I definitely could not kiss her now, half-dressed as she was.

Laying my hand on the horse—Char, I reminded myself—I cleared my throat. "Is he yours?"

She straightened and patted Char's neck. "He is. Has been ever since I was twelve. Since Grandfather died, Char has been the only one to ever really listen. We have had many adventures together."

"So when you told me you rode your horse against your mother's wishes…"

She looked down, then back up. "Char."

"Why Char?"

One shoulder lifted. "Charger always sounded too violent."

I leaned against the short wooden wall, more to get away from her sweet, dressing-gown clad self than anything else. God forgive me, I could not help but ask, "What about *knight*? Is that too violent a word?"

She narrowed her eyes. "What do you mean—?" She gasped. "Were you spying on me, Devon Godfrey?"

I blinked. "You know my Christian name?"

A huff escaped her pert nose. "You think I would have agreed to marry you if I did not know the full name I would be taking?"

"*I* was not spying on you. You have an admirer, a lad not yet old enough to croak who said he heard you sounded upset. He heard your story of the knight." I pushed away from the short wall, leaned toward her, and slid my hand from Char's neck to his shoulder, where her hand lay. "What story were you telling your horse?"

Her eyes flashed as she injected a bit of a highland accent into her voice. "Oh, an inane tale of an annoying man who never knows where his lady fair may be."

Her accent was impeccable. The momentary speck of admiration that arose in me for her way with languages evaporated, though, when the latter part of her statement rang too true. I had lost her now twice, slept through Arthur's abduction and missed completely her leaving the chamber this day. Guilt stabbed.

The overwhelming desire to gather her into my chest and never let her go stormed through me. The tempest spun until I could not take a breath, and I clenched my jaw to keep her from seeing. Never would I have expected love to be this powerful in its draw to protect her.

But was I not proving myself unequal to the task?

Gwyneth

Chapter Six

I whispered into the dimness of the stables, "You're looking at me like I'm about to break."

"Are you?" There was a new vulnerability in his eyes, something I was unused to seeing in him.

I studied him, torn between scoffing at his question and sighing at being cared for by him. Could I look forward to a lifetime of this? "*Nee.* I wager I am stronger now than I have ever been before."

His eyes narrowed. "Why do you say that?"

How to tell him about what had transpired in the dungeon? "Because I am betrothed to a wonderful man, and because I gave my heart to the Lord last night." I smiled up at him.

He had been so intent on finding the key that my admittance last night must have fallen on deaf ears. His features froze, then a look of such joy crossed his face that he took my breath away. "Gwyn."

When he took me in his arms, I chuckled. "I told you I am stronger. Just yesterday I could not have stood an embrace such as this."

He put me away from him, and I pouted, sorry for what I had said. But he stood near enough that my eyes, even without my glasses, could savor the elation in his own. I blinked up at him, took a step closer, and laid a hand on his chest. "But if I did break, you have proven most adept at piecing me back together." Did his breathing just stutter? "You want to know whom I meant when I mentioned a knight in my story?"

Those brown eyes darkened.

I watched in wonder. Was I doing that? I leaned closer. "The story the lad overheard?"

His heart pounded beneath my hand as he waited for my answer.

For a moment, I just stood there, awed by my own power to sway his focus, command his attention, occupy his every thought. I rose up on tiptoe and put my mouth close to his ear. "I was..." Abruptly I dropped down and flashed a grin. "...not talking about you."

I ducked under his arm and scooted out of the stall, already giggling. He whirled and charged. I squealed and ran. Slipping in the hay, my feet found their footing after a moment and steered me to the back of the stables. Heavy footfalls thundered at my heels. If I could just make the door—

His roar filled my ears. My heart thudded to a stop. The convent. The Dutchmen. The torchlight. My shoes scraped at the hay covering the floor but failed to grab the ground. Fear arced through me. Strong hands settled on my shoulders. I cried out, lurched away, and seemed to watch myself turn to face him.

This made no sense—this irrational reaction to his playful growl. I pasted on a smile.

But the damage was done. I had reacted and wrung away from him. He had noticed.

"Gwyn." The short word came out a prayer. He held out both hands to me.

It was then that my back registered the rear door of the stables. The laugh I forced sounded false. "You have backed me into a corner."

His eyes flicked between mine, making warrior deductions, calculating my every breath. "I frightened you."

"*Nee.*"

"I made you fear me."

"Dirk."

"I barreled behind you like a drunken lug. Idiot."

"Never."

"Stop making excuses for me. I give you far too many opportunities."

That sounded far too final. I stepped close and buried my face against his shirt, savoring the scent of him mixed with the mustiness of our surroundings. My arms crept around him, and his did the same.

"I have hurt you," he whispered. "I have always hurt you."

"You sound like me."

He pulled back to stare at me, his eyebrows low.

My laugh rang genuine now. "This is why we are so good with each other. We are both hurting but looking for healing. This is why we belong together. We are finding that healing in God and in each other."

That very morning, I had been disappointed to discover the nightmares summoning me from slumber before I wished to awaken. I had hoped coming to God the night before might release me from them, but alas. Not yet. If only I could sleep one night—just one night—through without being beckoned from my bed by the terrors. Always the same old dream, soft and lovely, like lace…always ending the same terrifying way. Although, even acknowledging that I had just thought *not yet* spoke of my hope—that someday I would be free of them.

He brought me close again before I could decipher the dark look that entered his eyes, but not before I discerned that I did not like what that look might mean.

"Have you seen Sister Agnes, Margried?" I passed through the door, still positioning my glasses on my nose.

Margried's hands wove in and out of her silky black locks as she braided it over her shoulder. She sat, humming, in front of the window in the chamber that sat adjacent to the one I had occupied. "She slept in the chair."

I did not bother saying what we both knew—that she no longer sat there.

Margried's fingers flew. "Do you think she might have gone to the kitchens?"

I cocked my head, doubtful. "I was just there. She does sometimes seek a quiet place to pray." Of course, it seemed like ages since we had sought and found a quiet place for prayer. The last opportunity would have been the morning of the day the Beeldenstorm came to the convent. What a day that had been. Dirk had burst into my borrowed nun's cell to save me from the raiders intent on destroying everything Catholic about the convent. We had left the place behind, burning.

After leaving Dirk in the stables this morning, I went to the kitchens, where I finally decided it was time to tell Sister Agnes what happened to me the night before in my uncle's dungeon. I had given God everything. To me, surrender sounded like peace. But I feared my nun friend would feel betrayal.

Margried rose from the window and came toward me, fingers still working to finish her braid.

"I saw that Dirk also slept in my chamber." I kept my face blank on purpose.

She nearly dropped her braid, looking worried. "Cade tried to talk him out of it, but Dirk was determined."

I draped an arm over her shoulders. "If you stood in my place, would you be upset?"

She smiled as we walked out of the room. Tidying the end of her braid with a loop of leather, she lifted her chin. "Where do you think she might have gone for a bit of quiet?"

As we came to the top of the staircase, I took a deep breath, staring down at the expanse of the first floor visible from where we stood. "I could not say."

Margried started down the stairs, leaving me behind. "You must know of some tranquil nook."

I followed her with tentative steps. "When I was younger, I searched out the noisier places." Much to my mother's dismay, the stables and anywhere bustling with visitors—few as we had—or even servants drew me more than stitching or books ever could.

Margried looked around. "I enjoy finding pools of peace in the midst of prattle."

I bit back a laugh. If I did not already know Margried was a lover of words, the ones she had just chosen would have stamped her.

The thump startled us both. Margried's shoes slapped the stone stairs seconds ahead of my own. We burst onto the main floor and into the small bower across from the Great Hall. Sister Agnes scooped the book off the floor and looked up at us, face serene.

If only I was not about to shatter that serenity with my news. Could it be called a secret, only hours old? It mattered not. What mattered was that she would see it that way.

Sister Agnes returned to her seat on the horsehair couch draped with a rich, warm blanket. She and Margried exchanged words, but I failed to hear them. Instead, I came close and detected on that blanket the lavender my mother always wore.

Tucked into the corner of the hallway, the bower remained my mother's room even after her death. It appeared as if my uncle had not touched the space—and had ordered the servants not to, either. A bunch of wildflowers sagged, wilted and shriveled, against the neck of a vase, and I felt a rush of tears. For my father had given her those. He often brought her wildflowers.

I swallowed and reentered reality. "I hope you slept well, Sister Agnes." I eyed the book in her lap but could not discern the title.

She nodded. My words fled. Margried sauntered deeper into the room and settled onto a chair. Then she smiled at me in encouragement.

"Are you going to tell me or just stand there stewing about it?" Sister Agnes's lips looked pinched as soon as the last word left her mouth, as if this were as painful for her as it was for me.

I fastened my gaze on the sunshine streaming through the window. I should sit. *Nee*, it would be better to stand. And I did not feel like moving. "Something happened to me while I was in that dungeon…. I came to faith."

She sucked in a breath and stood from her chair.

I winced, bracing.

"You—!"

Margried rose, hands outstretched. "Now, Sister Agnes."

I stepped between them. "'Tis well, Margried." My whispered words spun straight into Sister Agnes's darkened eyes.

"'Tis not *well*, Lady Gwyneth."

I fought another wince. "But it is. I was full of so much fear before. So much hate. And now…I feel free, cleansed from all that, as if all my sins are naught. *Nee*, because all my sins *are* indeed naught. Washed away."

Sister Agnes was shaking her head. "You sound so…Protestant. You who have been Catholic all your life. Lived in a convent for months. What made you think you were sinful?"

"I hated a good man. Even had he been a terrible man, that hate crippled me. All my sins crippled me. And I could not rise again, not with them as heavy as chains around my neck."

She slumped back into her chair. She who never slumped. She who never raised her voice, either. I almost wished she would here, now. It was how I acted whilst angry. Angry I could handle. I struggled to know how to carry this calm, cool fury emanating from her.

"All your sins?" she asked.

I dropped my gaze. "Hate. Fear. Selfishness."

Her chest rose and fell. "If this is about confession, about England no longer having priests to hear your sins…"

"But it is so much more than that." Margried spoke from behind my left shoulder, respecting my need for space but willing to defend me. Why could I not be sweet like her?

Sister Agnes straightened her habit. "I do not understand."

I waved a hand in the air. "It is much more than confessing my sins. It is about absolving me of them, forever. And going directly to God with them. Not needing any intermediary, not even a priest."

Sister Agnes looked all the more dubious.

"Sister Agnes, do you remember when I first came to you?"

Her eyes softened. "You carried yourself like a queen."

A queen. My mind traveled to my uncle and his plans for me. The mad man had actually schemed to make me a queen. 'Twas the very scheme that had started all of this trouble. "My mother taught me how to be a lady." I knelt at Sister Agnes' feet. The surprise in her eyes made me smile. "Albeit timid, she was a wonderful woman. You would have liked each other."

"I am sorry for your loss."

I nodded. "What stole her—them—from me...Sister Agnes, when I thought that Dirk was to blame, when I saw his hands red with blood..."

She pulled my hand into hers. "You were grieving."

Banishing the ghost-scent of blood from my nose, I shook my head. "*Nee*, I never grieved. Not properly. Not rightly. I hated Dirk. I hated that night. I hated that my parents were gone from my life forever. I hated that I had to leave my home—my life—behind."

I glanced over my shoulder to find that Margried's smile held sorrow—and encouragement—again. "Sister Agnes, I should never have allowed myself to walk down that road. But I would neither stop nor turn when once I had glimpsed that path."

"Lady Gwyneth, 'tis normal."

"Mayhap." I conceded that, at least. "But just because 'tis normal does not make it right." I glanced at Margried again. "I experienced tragedy, but others have as well. And not all choose to travel the path that I did. Some come through it shining like the brightest sunny day."

Tears glistened in Margried's eyes.

Sister Agnes's face turned to stone, even as her words remained gentle. "What does this have to do with your time in the dungeon?"

I smiled at her. "Everything."

Her expression wrinkled with worry.

"I allowed my soul to waste away in hatred and pain and sorrow. But no more. I have been shown a better way."

She shook her head. "But what does it *mean*? What appeal does the faith of Godfrey and Reverend Joseph hold for you that *my* religion could never give you?"

"Freedom."

"Because you no longer need celebrate the hours with prayers, light candles, or recite Our Fathers?" Her tone turned scoffing.

I understood how hard this must be for her. After all, I had only recently been there myself, teetering on the edge between doubt and belief.

"Because He loves me."

"Godfrey?"

"No. Yes." I blushed. "I speak of God. He loves me, Sister Agnes, and loves you, too."

Sister Agnes glanced at Margried. "This better way is yours now, as well?"

Margried's head dipped. "It is worth even the pain that brought me to it."

Was it shock that made Sister Agnes's hands shake over mine? "Did that man put you up to this?"

I could not be sure to what man she referred—Dirk? Joseph? No matter. I was losing her. "No one put me up to this."

Margried stood and took a step forward, into the sunlight. Her dark hair blazed two shades lighter. "Faith cannot be bartered or shoved or forced."

Sister Agnes's throat worked as she swallowed.

"Neither man forced me into anything," I continued. "Not even the pain of losing my parents was enough to throw me into God's arms. It was the dungeon, Sister Agnes. 'Twas the thought that I might never be free from that dark place."

I stared at her hands covering mine, the wrinkles crisscrossing the skin, the spots that spoke of many hours in the sun, working in gardens with her beloved plants. "It was the hunger for freedom that made me ask the Lord for healing. It was the realization that naught else could save me that made me see only He could."

She stared into my eyes, intent.

"He set me free from the hate. He loves me and willingly, gently came and gave me faith to believe it." The sun stretched past the floor where I knelt. It reached up to kiss her face and caress her hair, tightly pinned in a knot at her neck.

Suddenly she jerked to her feet, clasping her hands, unclasping them. "Does this mean you are no longer Catholic? That you have converted as Margried has done?"

I stood, too. "I know not whether this means I am less Catholic than I ever was or a truer Catholic than I ever hoped to be. All I know is my heart is new."

Sister Agnes turned away. How alike we were, for not so long ago I had turned away, too. So many times. But over and over, I could see now how God drew me back again.

Margried reached out to Sister Agnes. I stayed still.

Then she fled from the room, running from the truth she could not yet accept.

How alike we were, indeed.

When we woke the next morn, Margried looked around the room, then at me, and sighed. Noticing Sister Agnes's absence, I echoed the sound. "She was worse than this when I told of her of your conversion. Mayhap she is becoming used to the shock."

Tossing her gaze to the ceiling, Margried groaned. "What could be worse than running away?"

I laughed. "Running away to impale a certain monk, a certain knight, or both." I sat up in the bed and reached to scoop the hair off my neck, remembering Dirk's reaction to seeing it loose the day before.

Leaving the bed, I crossed the room and sat at the vanity table. As I reached for the brush, I looked at Margried's blurry reflection in the mirror then turned my attention to taming the tangles that had taken up residence since the last time I had been near a brush. Which had been too long ago, from the rebellious way my hair snagged at the bristles.

I struggled with the brush, yanking and wincing at turns. "I have never been patient—with—my—hair." Tugs punctuated my words.

Margried's head dipped to the side as she smiled at me. "I would offer to help, but I would be no quicker."

"You would be gentler." I held out the brush and watched her approach in the mirror.

"I would, indeed." Cool fingers combed through the mass of hair as she grasped the brush in the other hand. The ends drew her attention first.

"You are at most things." I smiled.

"And you are stronger. 'Tis why we make good friends."

My nose scrunched. "Yesterday I fear Dirk thought the opposite."

Margried's face popped up over my shoulder from where she had bent down to minister to my hair. Shock widened her eyes. "He said we do not make good friends?"

I snorted. "*Nee*, of course not. He—he asked me if I would break. And I feel he expected me to do just that."

She yanked. I yelped. She winced, meeting my eyes in the glass. "I am sorry." She went back to her brushing. "I think he fears for you yet."

I smiled. "He is overprotective. What need has he to fear now?" My

47

smile died, and my hands met in my lap. "My uncle is dead. No other wishes me harm."

Margried stopped brushing.

I looked up from my hands. "What is it?"

"Do you not know, Gwyneth?"

I raised a brow. That expression looked fine on my face in the mirror. "Know what?"

The brush stood still in her upraised hand, a witness to my ignorance.

"Tell me." I swiveled on the seat, bringing my fingers to rest over hers. "Margried."

"Well…you are *nearly* right. No one wishes *you* harm."

I raised my other brow to match the first and squeezed her hands. "What are you saying?"

"Naught has changed, you know."

I leaned forward to hear her.

She blew out a breath and waved the brush in the air. "You asked them once—when we first arrived back in England—if we were on the run. The answer Cade gave you then is the same he would give you today. Dirk is still a wanted man."

I turned again, but the mirror mocked me, denying me the chance to hide my face as I wished to do. So I masked my emotions instead, as I had never masked them before. Of course I had forgotten that very thing: Dirk was indeed a wanted man. "I know that."

I had wanted to restore his reputation. What I had forgotten was the danger while he still bore *murderer* on his back. And now that my uncle had perished here in his own home on the night Dirk rescued me… He may not have been the one to do the deed, but did it matter?

I had said he had done it once before.

My eyes followed the brush as Margried raised it high. But I saw Dirk as he had looked on that night, kneeling over my parents, knife in hand. I slapped my hands on the vanity table. "It is all my fault."

The brush plummeted as Margried jumped, startled. "Gwyneth?"

My heart galloped above my lungs, quickening my breath. "I said he did it. I said he murdered them. Because I thought he was guilty. But I was wrong. And now he runs…my fault." My hands slid from the desk into my lap, and I stared at my face in the mirror. The circles beneath my eyes seemed to widen, deepen, as if the knowledge pulled me down.

Margried laid the brush in front of me. "You must not say that. He would not."

A pocket of silence passed, as Margried searched for words to reassure me, words that would fail. For the blame lay squarely on my shoulders. A knock sounded at the door.

Margried looked that direction and stepped away. "That is probably Sister Agnes, returned to fetch something. Or perhaps…to hear more?" The hopeful lilt in her voice betrayed her heart.

I shook my head, for I knew who it was. But I did not want to see him, see his eyes, so drawn with sorrow and pain, and know that I had caused that grief, that burden. My feet melded to the floor even as my mind sent the signal to them to move to intercept Margried, but when I finally rose… he stood before my chair. All man—as strong and steadfast as ever, like the warrior he was. He looked straight at me.

"I need to talk to you."

Margried stepped toward the door as if to leave. I held up a hand to her. "Stay." She did.

I trained my gaze on Dirk's chest. "I fear I am really quite tired." Despite the fact that we had only just awakened. "Later?" That last word I fairly choked out, wishing it back. How could I look at him ever again, much less talk to him?

His shoulders lowered—I could tell, for still my gaze had risen no higher than his neck. "A moment, if you please."

"I do not wish to fall asleep on you." I winced.

His boots approached the hem of my dressing gown. His hand reached for mine, and I could not pull away. "I would not mind a whit. I will sit with you."

I crossed to the bed, releasing Dirk's hand in the process, and sat down. Now Margried would have to stay. As a chaperone.

Dirk followed and took the chair in which I had found him yesterday. "I need to tell you something, Gwyn. And you are not going to like it."

What if I told you I am the source of all your troubles? What if you realized that the very reason you worry over me is of my own making?

"We are leaving today," he said. The breath left my stomach, for the "we" included me.

My gaze met his, then flicked to Margried. *Make him stop,* my eyes tried to tell her.

But he did not stop. "I am taking you to my mother and sisters. With them you can recover. You will like Godfrey Estate." He grasped my hand. Something about his grip… "I must leave you there, Gwyn."

I turned over onto my stomach and pressed my face into the pillow. My head throbbed even though I had only worn my glasses for the last few hours of the day.

All six of us had supped in silence. Sister Agnes had excused herself first, not bothering to explain what we all knew: her destination was the chapel. Margried and Cade had mumbled some excuse and sought solitude. Ian had left the table next.

When Dirk had reached for my hand at the table, I had fled from him. He had tried to follow; I had shut myself in my chamber. His intermittent knocking had stopped after an hour. Now it was nigh unto midnight, Margried had long been slumbering, and still I lay awake. Moonlight crept in through the window, at turns taunting and inviting me. _Come,_ it whispered. Clouds hid it every so often, teasing me into thinking I was finally to be left alone.

Slipping from the bed in which Margried still slept, I donned the dressing gown that had seen far too much use this day. I could not believe I had gone all the way to the stables the day before in naught but my shift and this meager covering. 'Twas hardly proper. _Moeder_ would be disappointed in me.

But this was different. This was the middle of the night, and my mind swirled with what I had to do. I crept out the door, tossing one last look at Margried, who slept soundly. Sister Agnes had chosen a chamber farther down the hall, while Margried had insisted she would stay with me. I had pondered returning to the chamber I had called mine since childhood, but the thought of venturing into the hall introduced the possibility of Dirk finding me. So I had stayed.

I tiptoed now down the stairs, thankful I had remembered to step into my shoes. At the foot of the stairway, I hesitated. Yet the call of the moonlight proved stronger.

I did not enter the courtyard. Instead, I walked the long path to the Great Hall but passed the room by. I had not stepped a foot inside alone since the night of my parents' murders. I had no desire to do so now.

A breeze caressed my face when I opened the back door and scurried into the silvery swath of light descending from the sky. My gaze remained trained on my destination: the hill where my parents had taken me to talk. Here they told me about the grandmother I never knew. Here they told me there had been a brother who had not lived past infancy. Here they told me my grandfather and aunt had the plague and I could not see them. Here they gave me the rosary.

Now I climbed that hill, steeling myself for the lonely sight that would greet me. Yet how does one prepare for the pounce of grief? My legs burned by the time I reached the place where I could finally see…nothing. I sank to my knees, willing myself to breathe.

Never before had I climbed this hill to find myself alone.

Tears cascaded down my face. I swallowed the shrieks that wanted to be free of my throat and pressed my sleeve to my face. Such a small, empty space when once so much life had happened here. Now it seemed a graveyard. I nearly gagged over the loamy scent of the ground. Sister Agnes once told me that the fragrance of dirt was the fragrance of all life. How could that be true when beneath lay the dead?

"Oh, *Moeder*, Papa." They had taught me how to be a lady. But the decision to discard all of that decorum came easily as I abandoned propriety and stretched out on the dying grass. Autumn's kiss rested in the brown tips on the grass stalks. They crackled beneath my sleeve and tore between my fingers. I slapped the ground. September was meant to be a month of harvest. Instead, winter had come early. Death reigned. Winter's chilling touch refused to let me be. Clouds covered the moon again, dousing the light, confirming my thoughts.

God, I do not understand. Just when You breathe life into me, I feel dead again. I stared into the moonlight, remembering all they had been, mourning all they would never be.

Images cascaded through me. My parents' worried faces as they scolded me. Their smiles as I looked at them in awe, my diamonds around my neck for the first time. Their embrace. They would never again hold me, never again smile as I touched the rosary they had given me, never again chide me for being rebellious. They would never see me on my wedding day or exclaim over the babes I bore.

I would never see their hair silver or their hands wrinkle. I had never before looked ahead to the time when my parents would age and leave me, for I had always thought such a thing was far in the future.

I had been wrong.

Their old age had been stolen from me. I slapped the ground once more, relishing the resulting sting. Then I gathered grass in my palms, crushed the stalks, only to reel back my hand in shock. Dismayed by the fact that now not only was I mourning the death of two persons once living and so very much alive—I was aiding in death. I smoothed the stems of grass beneath my skin.

"Ik hou van jou." A breath shuddered through me. *"Te quiero."* My eyes squeezed shut against the tears—and failed. *"I love you."* I whispered the words again and again until I could only mouth them through the sobs.

Dirk

Chapter Nine

After an hour of tapping on her door every few minutes to beg her to open up to me, I gave up and wandered across the short width of the hall until I found myself in the empty room Ian, Cade, and I shared. Time passed as I waited and prayed, but neither God nor Gwyneth answered my pleas.

All through supper, I had contented myself with the thought that the others would surely leave and allow us a moment of privacy. But she had pulled away from me, and my heart had sliced open. I'd followed her to her chamber, but she'd shut the door. I had released a sigh and let my forehead drop to the wood. My tongue had longed to plead with her, but I remained silent, not out of pride, but out of confusion. What could I say to her to make her open the door? If she would just allow me to speak for one moment... Yet what could I say after telling her I must leave her?

Footsteps in my chamber made my head turn.

Cade's smile looked strained as he came to stand beside me. "Margried said you upset Gwyn."

Another sigh pulled from me. "I told her we were leaving on the morrow. She did not take it as well as I hoped."

"Nay, you told her you were leaving her at the Godfrey estate. Have you not yet learned that our women require the truth in small doses so as to allow it to sink in?" Cade grasped my shoulder and steered me toward the bed. "Margried will be up in a moment to see to her. You need to let go and rest tonight."

"Where is Margried now?"

Cade sighed. "She went to the chapel to talk to Agnes."

My brows rose, then ducked again as I shot one last glance out the door before Cade closed it behind him. "I thought there was tension between those two."

Cade nodded. "Margried refuses to give up on making her see that her story of God's grace is true—and could be true for Agnes, too."

"Agnes still struggles with guilt over what happened in the Low Countries?"

"Aye. It bothers Margried."

I plopped onto a bed, my elbows finding my knees. "I bother Margried." I snorted. "Did she tell you she tossed me out earlier?"

Cade's eyes went to the ceiling, and his features stretched taut as a cocked arrow. "Aye."

I raised a brow. "That's all you have to say?"

He leaned a hand against the wall. "Nay."

I waited.

His breath became a huff. "Your timing is always impeccable."

I rolled my eyes. "I know."

"Margried found your insisting on talking to Gwyneth in their room disconcerting. She was uncomfortable enough with your staying by her bedside yesterday."

A corner of my mouth quirked. "She sounds a bit like Agnes."

Cade glared.

I held up both hands. "Sorry. I know you struggle to like that woman." To be honest, Margried *should* berate me for discarding propriety—she was the only one who could. Agnes had still slept when I left the room and probably did not realize I had ever been there. "Margried is right. It was improper. It was also necessary."

Cade tossed his hand toward the sky, took a step toward me, then leaned back again. "Why do you always have to think that?"

I gave him a grimace. "Think what?"

"You think that everything you do is—" He stopped, let out a breath, then sank onto the other bed in the room.

I rose and walked to the opposite wall. Heavy curtains blocked out the light from the only window in the chamber. Throwing them back proved futile. Night had descended. Leaning an elbow against the window, I stared out, straining, hoping to see the faintest glimmer. How long I stood that way I neither knew nor cared.

At last Cade spoke again. "'Tis nearly midnight. I am going to find Ian. He should have returned by now."

I did not move. "Nay. You are going to tell me what you were going to say."

He exploded again. "That is exactly what I am talking about!"

I faced him. "What is?"

"Everything you do is necessary. You assume every single word or action is justified by your situation."

Our eyes met. Anger poured from his. I stared back. "Are you calling me proud? Because I will be the first to admit that, even after all the times I have been humbled, I have failed to learn the lesson."

Cade shook his head. "Do you ever stop to think that mayhap there may exist a better time, a more suitable circumstance, a gentler way?"

I raked a hand through my hair.

"You love her." Cade's words brought my gaze to his.

"I do."

"Then do not try to hide it. When you do, she knows all the more." A smirk stole across his features.

I smiled. "I should extend the same advice to you."

"I asked for the hand of the woman I loved first." He glared, but the anger had left his eyes. "You care for her well. But in your eagerness to see she is well cared for, you trample her trust."

I swallowed hard.

"Just…" Cade shook his head again and moved toward the door. He opened it. Looked back at me. "Just realize that merely because you think a route is right, does not mean it is."

I spun away and stared out the window as I listened to the door close.

The clouds had torn away from the moon, and a glimmer of light shone down on a lone figure on the hill.

Gwyneth

Chapter Ten

When his hand closed over mine, I did not flinch. I did not jerk. I did not pull away. Guilt circled my heart, a hawk above prey, for I had ruined him. My accusation—as justified as it might have seemed—had been the catalyst for everything. And though it had brought us together, it was also now ripping us apart.

The ground proved a hard place to lay, but I remained still against the dirt, black and cold. The night had only become deeper, so I could barely see him, even when he reached down for me and turned me in his arms.

"Oh, Gwyn." My name on his breath nearly undid me. Did he not realize that I had made his life what it was? Did his love for me conceal the truth? Or had he forgiven me—was such a thing possible? If anyone's heart could hold such mercy as that, of course it would be his. But that failed to alleviate my guilt or make a way for us to be together.

I let him set me on my feet but sagged against him. I wiped five grass-stained fingers on his jacket.

He chuckled. "Decided to take a nap in the dirt?"

I wiped my other five fingers on him. "Want to join me?"

He hummed. "Do not tempt me."

At that, I stepped away.

His strong hand caught my wrist. "You should not be out here alone."

"I am fine. This is my home."

He touched my bare nose. "I know. You can find your way around, even without your glasses."

"Have you come to take me inside?"

His gaze flicked toward the gate. "I came to see if you needed someone."

I thought I had spent all my tears.

He saw. How he saw in the meager moonlight I would never understand.

But he saw my tears, and he squeezed my hand. "I am sorry I could not save them, Gwyn."

Blasted tears.

"I never told you that before, but I will regret until the day I die that I did not get there sooner."

Beautiful man.

I reached for him, wrapping my arms around his waist, resting my hands on his back, breathing in the scent of near-winter and wind. "I do not blame you."

My breath hitched, for my own words were what I longed to hear from him. Yet still the guilt remained. On the very night we spoke of, both of our lives had changed forever.

And they would never be the same again.

"Dirk?"

"Aye?" His voice sounded gruff.

My heart sped up. In the stables, my soul had filled with such wonder at how my nearness affected him that I had not had the time to notice how *he* affected *me*. But he did. Oh, he did. "I wish this moment could last forever."

He wrapped his own around me. "But then we would not grow beyond this."

Frightening thought, indeed.

He cupped my face in his hands, something he had never done before. I quite liked the way this allowed me to stare into his brown eyes. Until those brown eyes stared back and I saw my heart reflected in his.

I slapped my hand against his chest. "I have already wept too much tonight."

He smiled. "Good thing it's midnight—and that makes it morning."

I glared.

He grinned.

I chuckled.

He laughed, and his laugh made my hands rumble against his shirt and made me feel safe at the same time.

"You are dangerous, Dirk."

He sobered, but his eyes remained playful. "You are dangerous, Gwyn."

I raised both brows. "Why is that?"

"You explain first, milady."

"You trick me into thinking all is going to be well." I expected him to smile or laugh again. I expected him to call me daft and remind me all *was* going to be well. What I did not expect was for him to grip me close, lift me up, and trudge down the hill as if it were not midnight and he could probably barely see where we were going. But that was what he did.

"And you are dangerous, Gwyn—" He pressed his face to my hair. Definitely could not see where he was going— "because you make me think sleeping in a chair beside your bed, barging into your chamber when you are weary, and standing on a hill with you in the middle of the night are all acceptable."

"You are wrong."

He skidded to a stop.

"It is midnight. And that makes it morning. So it *is* acceptable to stand on a hill with me." *Especially when, without you, I cannot stand.*

He brought me to my door and I waited behind it, listening to him cross the hall and slip through his own. It was then that I realized he had never told me all was indeed going to be well.

Dirk

Chapter Eleven

We were to depart in the morn. I sent word to my mother of our imminent arrival, slept the night through, and woke to find both Cade and Ian stirring. We said not a word. The women did not break the silence, either, when we descended to find them already seated and breaking their fast. All save Gwyn.

My whispered question to Margried rendered the fact that Gwyn had left for the library. After navigating the winding halls and finding the room, I stepped into a space stacked with bookshelves. Gwyn sat at a massive desk that leveled her above-average height and lent her the look of a little girl. She had tamed her hair, bidding it to stay balled at the back of her neck. I missed the freedom she had given it yesterday. Ensconced in papers, she did not look up.

"Gwyn?"

"Good morrow." Her gaze met mine before dropping once more to the desk. Her fingers grasped a quill pen. The steady scratching of ink against paper ensued.

"Are you ready to leave?"

She looked up again and set the quill aside. "I am not going with you."

I stepped closer to her. Her face appeared just as serious up close as it had from several feet away. "Let me explain what I said—"

"There is naught to explain. I said I am not going with you. I cannot."

I circled the desk. She rose and backed from my reach. I shook my head. "You said naught of this last night."

"You did not ask." She was backing out of the library now.

I followed. Once before we had engaged in a similar dance. She had stepped away from me in the cabin on Tudder's Sea Beggar ship. Then she had squinted, and I had stepped closer to allow her to see my face. That encounter had nearly ended with a kiss.

Mayhap I should try that now.

"I have much to do, Dirk. This place—" She swept her arms wide. "This is no longer my home. It belongs to the Crown. I must see to it when the Queen's men come to claim it."

"Listen to me." I spoke slowly. "Allow me to take you to my mother."

"I know you believe we can grieve together, she and I, but you do not understand."

Frustration mounted. "Make me understand then."

She sighed, but stopped. *Thank You, God.* We stood in a hall lined with pictures of Barringtons past. Her ancestors stared down at us with stoic features. Hardly the best place to explain. I considered taking her hand and dragging her outdoors, into the fresh—albeit slightly cold for this early in the autumn—air. But if I did and the presence of other people stole from us the privacy we had here, she would not confide in me.

"Gwyn?"

She squeezed her eyes shut. "I cannot go with you."

I laid a hand on the wall. "If you do not go, we do not go."

Her eyes popped open. "That is ridiculous."

"But true. If you refuse to go, Agnes will refuse to go. If Agnes refuses, Margried will do the same. And if Margried stays, Cade stays. Ian and I may as well stay, too." We would not, of course. I would not put the rest in danger by remaining here, and Ian was determined to go with me. But I assumed the sober, determined, pleading expression that I once counted upon in my wilder days. It was time to take Cade's advice and temper the truth.

This was *not* deceit; it was for her own good.

"That is not true." Her weak voice contradicted her statement—and her words, my thoughts.

"You know it is. And you know you want to be far from here." I had seen that much last night. She could not stand another day in the place where her parents had died, of passing by the room where she had seen their lifeblood spill. She thought I had not seen; mayhap she did not see herself. But she needed away from here—for healing.

Her glasses rested on her nose this morning. Her green eyes shone behind the lenses. "What will your mother think of me?"

Of all the things I had braced myself to hear pouring from her mouth, I had not prepared for those. "Whatever do you mean?"

"She will not want me there."

"Gwyn…" Why would she say such a thing?

She turned and walked away. All the way past the Great Hall, to the entryway, where the others stood. The aroma of the morning meal wafted through the air. I gently took Gwyn's arm and led her a few feet away to afford us some privacy. "Tell me why you think such a thing, and I will tell you why you are wrong."

"I am right, and you know it." She pulled away and stalked toward the others, who were doing their best not to stare—except for Ian, who gawked.

I glared at the man before turning my stare back to Gwyn. "My mother is a kind soul. She will welcome your presence."

Her eyes bore into mine before she skittered her gaze to Margried and Agnes. "If she knew who I am, she would not."

I looked at Cade and Ian, echoing Gwyn's look of *leave, now*. "Explain."

Cade shoved Ian out of the room. Margried tugged on Agnes's arm. The nun glared at me, but I locked my gaze on Gwyn again. Her mouth opened. Closed. "I cannot."

"There, now. We are alone. Aye, you can."

A deep breath caused her chest to rise and fall. She spun away from me, sleeves swirling, skirt ballooning. When she faced me again, I saw the look on her face and cringed.

The onslaught of Spanish flew from her mouth, leaving me spellbound by the power of the language, by Gwyn's command of every word. She looked the lioness with her hair aflame, with the sunlight breaking into the entryway. I fell in love with her all over again.

When I stepped toward her, she followed cue. Still chattering away, she stuck her finger in my chest. Ah, I had forgotten she liked to do that. I grabbed it and, before she could guess my intent, brought it to my mouth and kissed it. It smelled of ink. "Gwyneth-mine, you know I cannot understand a word."

"I should teach you. I am really quite eloquent."

I took her whole hand in mine. "I am sure you are, and I would like that."

"Repeat after me. *Idiota. Estúpido. Estúpido sin filo.*"

I did, even though I knew she was insulting me.

The hardness in her face cracked. She threw back her head and laughed. In that moment, I could see the change that finding God's love had made in her.

Then she slapped me with her free hand and swiveled away. But I still had the other. "Come with us, Gwyn."

Her eyes stared into mine, the smallest hint of a waver my only hope.

Then she pulled her hand away and stepped through the doorway.

I turned and followed her, scooping her hand into mine again. Cade walked toward us, eyebrows raised. "The horses are ready."

Gwyn made an unlady-like sound. "I am not, so we are not leaving yet."

I shot her a smile. Because she had said *we*.

Gwyneth

Chapter Twelve

Sitting in bed, I picked at my food. Margried pushed my plate back toward me every time I shoved it away. She finally gave up after the fifth time. Then she grasped my shoulders in a quick hug, and we stood from the bed together. The kitchen maid took the tray.

In the chamber I had adopted as a replacement for my own, Joan helped me into a somber traveling gown that my mother had once loved. Little had she known that I would wear that suit the day after she died, when Uncle Oliver had allowed me to run off to her homeland.

How often had she told me stories of that land, of how tulips grew tall and the language we shared flowed free? How often had I begged her to consider taking me there, the place where she kept part of her heart, even after nearly two decades of living in Elizabeth's England? How often had she chided me for asking?

I looked down at myself, frowning at how the gown hung on me. Joan apologized, and I shook my head. Just as the gown failed to fit perfectly now, so had my mother's Low Countries. I had seen little of the beauty, too much of the heartache and religious rage.

So did this place fail to fit me now. I had grown up here, had never known anywhere else as my sanctuary. Yet I had not returned to the Great Hall. Even more significant, I had not returned to my bedchamber. Why? Why did I wilt at the very thought of facing that place?

Without really knowing why, I touched the diamonds I had tucked into my pocket after Joan finished. Mayhap because when my parents gave them to me, they had promised me that the two of them would be with me on the day I pledged my love to the man I married. Too many memories torn by tragedy.

Nodding my thanks to Joan, I stopped her before she would have opened the door for me. "Take this. Have it sent to the Earl of Lansberry." I held out the letter I had been composing in the library earlier when Dirk had found me. "Please."

Joan hesitated. "You wish to send it to him by courier, milady?"

I nodded. "Would you mind taking care of it for me?"

She looked surprised that I had asked. "Of course not, milady." Confusion lit in her gaze, but that was to be expected. After all, the man to whom the letter was addressed lived closer to Godfrey Estate than Barrington Manor. Logic dictated I should wait until we arrived at Dirk's home to send it. But I did not want Dirk to know.

Not until I knew my old friend would come.

Before I left the keep, Gerald approached me. "Lord Godfrey said you wanted to see me."

Considerate, as always. "Do I recall aright that you can read, Gerald?"

He dipped his head. "Aye, milady."

"Excellent. With Arthur dead, there is no steward to see to things. I leave the Manor in your capable hands until it is claimed, Gerald."

He nodded his head. The responsibility I laid on his shoulders was great, but I had no doubt he would prove equal to the weight. When he turned to go, I called him back. "Do not wait too long to tell Joan how you feel."

His expression bordered on shock, but no confusion twisted his features.

Merely because I wore glasses did not mean I did not see.

Sunlight warmed my face as I stepped outside. Today would be one of the last autumnal days. A good day for traveling. Margried approached me, hugged me. Cade came to her side, and she deserted me—I cursed the jealous streak running through me. She put her hand in his elbow.

Then she turned back and reached for my hand. I took it. Sweet, sweet Margried. So unlike me. Dirk was there then, leading Char. He looked more handsome in the sunlight than he should have. *Mercy, God, mercy. I beg of You.*

I *was* going to make this right. To do that, I would need to explain my idea. But not now.

I shied away from his touch, and the hurt look on his face unraveled the threads holding me together. I started to turn toward him again in a silent plea for his help in mounting Char, but, before I could, he waved at Ian; I let Ian lift me, hating the tension radiating from the man.

As soon as everyone mounted, we left through the gates. Dirk nodded to Gerald as we passed through. I wondered at their silent understanding but did not ask.

The desire to run raged through me. I could give Char a swift kick, turn him west, and be hidden by the forest inside of an hour. Dirk would never find me. I knew those woods—with the help of my glasses—as well as I knew the planes of his face.

I sighed. He may never find me, but he would never cease to look, either. My fingers reached out to pat Char's neck in silent apology for not being able to give him his head. Mayhap another time.

After this was all over. *God, may this be all over soon. May it end.* And end mercifully. With Dirk still in love with me, still desiring to spend his life with me. *Hold to hope,* I reminded myself. There was still a chance. Still a thread of possibility that my plan—and Anders Revelin—would ensure Dirk, even after he recognized the truth, would still want to marry me, that he would not leave me as he said he would.

We settled into an easy rhythm, heading north toward Godfrey Estate. Of course, I was soon to meet Lady Godfrey and her daughters, Dirk's sisters. Best not to give Char his head, even for a moment. It would not do to regress to the habits of my youth—such as claiming Char's back in a flurry of petticoats—when very soon regality would be my mantle once more.

How I dreaded meeting Dirk's family! What would they think of me? Surely they blamed me. *God, I am going to need You.* And I would be staying with them, for I was not only orphaned but homeless. *I am going to need You for quite a while.* Dirk's words rose in my mind, although in truth it seemed they had never left. *I must leave you there, Gwyn.*

My heart seized. Mayhap the reason for his planned abandonment was that the truth had sunk in at last—that I was the cause of all his troubles, that my accusation had ruined him. After all, had I not once thought the same of him—that one deed of his had spelled the end of life as I knew it? And what had I done?

Hated him for it.

I studied the imposing outer wall boasting a potential threat to those who may wish to do harm to any within Godfrey Estate. Dirk called out a greeting, a grin already resting on his face, albeit one that did not quite reach his eyes. I blinked at the heavy patter of footsteps required to open the gate and allow us entry.

During this dying season, England was ugly to any eyes but the most romantic—and mine had never been accused of such rosiness. Brown grass put up no fight beneath our horses' hooves; the stalks merely lay down and succumbed to the trampling as we traversed the miles to Dirk's home. Brown leaves hung limply from tree branches, as if eager for the first breath of winter to come and carry them away.

It would not be long now before the air turned chill and snow fell. Winter's mark lay on the land, the stamp of ownership evident even though the cold had not yet made good on the claim. My heart clenched. He would be far away from here by the time winter came to collect her yearly prize.

My eyes widened at the expanse of the courtyard. Twice the size of my childhood home, this place loomed large, light, and airy. My shoulders lowered of their own accord. Odd. Peace enveloped me as I took in my surroundings. People—mostly men—strode across the courtyard, looking young, strong, and formidable. Godfrey Estate boasted many more men than Barrington Manor.

I swung my gaze to look at Dirk. He watched me already, a tense expression riding in the lines around his mouth. His twenty-three years sat heavy on his features today, even as the sunset behind his head cast his red hair on fire. Pulling my thoughts away from the attraction tethering us together, I acknowledged that he had not brought me here for the purpose he had expressed.

He had deceived me; he intended for me to find healing here, aye, but he also trusted this place to protect me. More than the convent hidden away on the shore of the Low Countries, which ultimately proved a deadly place for Catholics among Protestants. More than Barrington Manor, my own home, which hid the worst danger of all: a murderer among my own blood.

I stared at Dirk, wondering at the weight that shrouded him. Leaving me here made him miserable, too. I tore my gaze from him, the pain of doing so almost audible in my ears. Or was that the sound of my heart breaking?

Ian stepped beside me and reached up. Once on the ground, I settled my skirts around my feet, pressing my lips together at the wrinkles residing in the folds of my dark gown. I smoothed my fingers over the gold braiding at the waist meant to distract from dust and wear.

I intended my deep breath to fortify. It failed.

She came in a cloud of laughter.

Dirk's answering laugh and open arms confirmed the identity of the woman in black. I found myself smiling; she did indeed snort when she laughed. She launched herself into his arms with a dainty decorum I immediately envied. Her red hair, the same shade as Dirk's, boasted silver streaks that caused aging to look gentle. "Devon, son, nearly a year! I have missed you!"

Two more women raced into the courtyard on feet swift but somehow lady-like. Dirk took each of them into his arms in turn, cupping their faces, exclaiming over them with that smile I loved—though the wolf was nowhere to be seen in it. Not here, now, with his sisters.

A certain smugness welled up in me, and I swallowed hard. So that smile he shared only with me.

I shook my head. *Forgive me, God.* Somehow, though I now questioned whether I knew what would truly please the Lord, I was certain jealousy and pride would not.

"Lady Gwyneth."

My limbs froze as Rohesia Godfrey came to stand before me, in mourning garments that reminded me she still felt the loss of her eldest son. I still stood where Ian had helped me to the ground, but I noticed Char no longer supported my back; someone had led him away. I dropped a curtsey. "I am most pleased to meet you, Lady Godfrey. Your hospitality has earned my gratitude."

She smiled sincerely and took my elbows. "You are most welcome, young one. I see you have stolen my son's heart."

I flicked a surprised glance at Dirk.

Lady Rohesia Godfrey laughed, a snortless one this time. "I have eyes."

Could she tell that I loved him in return?

Her smile widened. "Your thoughts are easy to read, my dear. You have an expressive face. And a beautiful one."

When she released me, I could feel the beginnings of a blush. She turned to Dirk, and her movement caused me to realize my line of vision extended several inches above the top of her red and silver head. I thought Dirk had told me she was tall as well?

"You are sure to tell her that often, Devon, am I right?"

Devon's smile slipped for but a moment. "Every other hour." His gaze seared straight into me.

Rohesia bounced to turn back to me. For an older woman, she possessed a great amount of energy. "Make it every hour, son."

He nodded, his face serious. "Gwyn, meet my sisters." He gestured to the taller one. "This is Millicent." She dipped her perfectly-coiffed head, her face expressionless. Dirk's hand swept to his other side. "And this is Susan."

Smiling, Susan walked up and hugged me. A mite unprepared, I hugged her back more out of necessity than desire—she was a head shorter than I; mayhap she was accustomed to it. I leaned forward to soften the difference. The girl, however, looked nonplussed at only reaching my shoulder. The scent of rose-water met my nose as she pulled back. "I can tell I am going to like you," she whispered. Her dimple winked at me.

Before I could tell her I thought I would like her back—even though I was only partially sure about that—she took two steps back to stand beside her mother. Rohesia clasped the hands of Margried, who looked to be resuming the role of noblewoman with ease in one of my dark-colored gowns.

Sister Agnes held back, standing with Ian. Both looked decidedly uncomfortable.

"She is a kind-hearted woman." Dirk's whisper in my ear almost caused me to jump.

"So you said. So she seems." That came out harsher than I intended. I looked up at him. Strangely, his eyes seemed to say he knew I had not meant that as it sounded.

I watched Rohesia greet Cade, Sister Agnes, and Ian, playing the perfect hostess, making all seem welcome. Susan seemed a great deal like her—both had a way about them that put the others at ease. Millicent held back. "Your sisters seem kind-hearted, as well."

Dirk's soft sigh sounded happy, as if he were relieved to be home. "They are beautiful women, albeit prone to tears."

I could not stop my laugh. "Is that a shortcoming in your eyes?"

He started to nod, stopped, and looked askance at me, wary. "There cannot be a right answer to that question." His face softened, and his hand reached for mine.

Remembrance stole over me with all the suffocating effect of a blanket on a sunny summer day. Refusing his hand, I stepped away. I had ruined his life. How dare I stand here and flirt with him?

Pain sliced through my heart. For how much longer would he be here? He planned to leave me here and go wherever he planned on going. Without me, the woman he had asked to wed him. The chasm between us widened and threatened to swallow me whole.

"Come, come, all of you must be tired, ready for refreshment and rest." Rohesia waved for everyone to follow her into Godfrey Estate.

I watched Cade take Margried's arm and stepped further away from

Dirk, just in case. Susan came to walk beside me, the rose-water swirling into my nose again. "I am delighted about your coming to stay with us, Lady Gwyneth."

"Please, call me Gwyneth."

Her grin widened. "I would like that. I think we shall be good friends."

I smiled in return—hesitant, hopeful.

"We can talk about my brother until the dark watches of the night." Susan leaned forward as she walked, meeting the gaze of Dirk, who had come to stand beside me. He had not taken my arm, but he stood close enough to belay suspicion in case Rohesia looked back. She would wonder why I did not lean on his arm, but she would not worry about us being separated by several feet. As we would have been had I had my way. Once again, Dirk's wisdom outweighed my own. I had thought only of getting away from him. He had thought of how that might look—and had wanted to save me the embarrassment.

Infuriating man.

"What do you like best about him?" Susan's question jarred me back to her. I had missed most of several sentences extolling her brother's virtues. Here was an admiring younger sister.

I hesitated too long.

She giggled and took my arm. She somehow still managed to seem noble even as she acted so young. Her giggle tugged on my smile. "You cannot choose, can you? I expected you to say his red hair. I know not of another young Englishman with hair so fiery."

I glanced at Dirk. "Indeed."

He looked amused, annoyed, and embarrassed all at the same time. 'Twas a look I had not seen on his face before. I found it hard to look away.

Rohesia led the way inside, with Cade and Margried following her. The three of them had been deep in conversation, although I could not tell what about.

Susan and I entered next. My throat caught at the beauty of the entryway. Tapestries and paintings lined the walls. Not so many as to be cluttered. Not so few as to make the great space seem bare.

The manservant who stood at the door closed it after Sister Agnes, Ian, and Dirk entered. Dirk's indulgent, brotherly expression had vanished, replaced with a glare at Ian.

I hid my mouth behind my hand when I realized why. Ian stared at Susan with an awed look on his face.

"Devon." Rohesia's word brought my attention back to her. She stood, hands clasped, staring at her son with a soft smile. "Should you and your guests prefer to refresh yourselves first, Alyce and Paul will see you to your rooms. Supper is ready in the Great Hall."

I forced myself to keep my attention firmly placed on Rohesia. This awareness of Dirk's every move, every expression, had to end. He would be leaving soon.

Alyce and Paul, servants as kind as their mistress, came forward. The excitement of the introductions drained away, and my weariness returned. I could tell by the way Margried stumbled on the stairs that exhaustion claimed her, as well. Cade caught her easily, and she turned a grateful look his way.

Dirk's hand touched my elbow as he appeared at my side. My whole arm heated. "Do you wish to retire or go to the Great Hall?"

I wish to hear you say you forgive me. I had made a mistake—blamed him when it was logical *but wrong* to do so. "The Great Hall would be fine."

He steered me in that direction. My gaze took in the furnishings, the beauty Rohesia had brought to what otherwise might have become an intimidating edifice.

Rohesia and Susan had disappeared—now I knew where they had gone. Susan looked up from where she stood talking with her mother. Her hands moved when she spoke.

Cade called Dirk's name, and Dirk's apologetic look was the last thing I saw of him as he turned the corner.

Susan came to me, obviously intent on seeing us become friends, after all. She saw to it that I sat next to her, and I sank into the seat, aware of how tired I was. A long time had passed since I had ridden Char for an entire day.

I smiled and sipped wine stronger than the ale that had been the staple at the convent. I nibbled at the cakes and dainties Susan pressed toward me. We talked of the journey, of Dirk, of the weather—nothing too serious. I learned Susan was genuinely bubbly, her mother kind, Millicent quiet.

A sudden longing to spend an hour in Char's stall, just leaning my head against his strong side, overtook me. I covered it well, I thought, calling on all the etiquette I possessed and acting the lady I had not been in a long time.

My head began to swim before I sampled half my plate, but I kept on, answering Rohesia's questions, surprised to find that not one of them seemed either superficial or false. Meanwhile, the thirst I had mentioned to Dirk, oddly, failed to be satisfied.

Susan distracted me by interjecting sporadic comments, but mostly she smiled up at me with sincere joy in her eyes. I wondered where Millicent was and where Dirk had gone.

I gasped and took another sip of my wine to hide it. What if he had already left?

"You are welcome to stay here for as long as you wish," Rohesia said.

My hand shook as I laid my goblet on the table. I forced my eyes to focus through my lenses as I squinted at her. Strange. How had my wine goblet emptied so fast?

Rohesia frowned of a sudden, a tight expression on her face I had not seen before in the…how long had we sat here talking? Her whisper cut through the buzzing in my head. "Susan?"

Her daughter looked up and lifted her brows.

"Did you refill Gwyneth's wine glass?"

Why did she…? Oh. I had asked her to call me by my Christian name.

Susan covered a yawn and nodded her head. "She mentioned to Devon she was thirsty, and he told me to see to it she had all the cider she wanted. Oh no! Cider!"

Rohesia's lips thinned. Susan fastened her gaze first on the goblet in front of me, then on my face. "Mama, I did not mean—"

Rohesia rose from her chair and morphed into two Rohesias. I blinked, but they refused to meld into one.

"I know, dear. All will be well. Fetch Devon." Her voice sounded higher than it had a mere moment ago. Of course, that could be because there were two of her. I suddenly wanted away from both of them.

"What is wrong?" I slid from my seat onto unsteady feet. My heels hurt, and I wanted to shift my weight from hip to hip for relief. I found I could not do it. "I would like to go to my chamber now, if you would not mind, Lady Godfrey."

She came close, took my hand. "Call me Rohesia."

"Oh, I could not do that." I ducked my chin, demurring, still dismayed that I could not seem to make my feet move. Why not? I heard a hitch in my breath.

"Gwyneth, all is well." Rohesia was so much like her son. That was exactly what Dirk always told me when fear gripped me.

And I was afraid now. Without knowing why. I wanted to know why. Now. Tears filled my eyes, further obscuring my vision. I finally closed them, surrendering, taking off my glasses.

"Mother?" A strong male voice that conjured images of muscled arms

71

and tender kisses filled my ears. I strained toward it even as my hands clenched my glasses. I swayed, my balance unsure.

Muffled whispers from Rohesia. I did not hear her words. I did not care to hear her words. I wanted away from her, away from all else—save for him.

"Dirk?"

Those arms I had just been dreaming about wrapped around me. My eyes opened, and my hands fell away. Twin tears slipped down my cheeks. He brushed at them and hoisted me high. His soft smile filled my vision, pouring peace through me. "Gwyneth-mine, I am right here, and I am taking you to your chamber so you can rest."

I did not respond. Why was he smiling? If he was smiling, all must indeed be well. What he always liked to promise me, then, was coming true.

At the word *promises* ricocheting through my thoughts, the pressure increased. I put a hand to my head. A whimper broke free. "Dirk. Hurts."

Climbing. We were climbing. The staircase spun as he answered, "What hurts, Gwyneth-mine?"

One corner of my mouth lifted. "I like it when you call me that."

"Will she be well?" Susan's worried call burst into my brain. I winced and tried to lay my head on his shoulder, but the steady ascent of the stairs jostled my head forward again.

Dirk's red curls bounced as he turned back to me.

"You should consider a haircut." I reached up to touch one. "Nay, never mind. I like it this way."

A worried line appeared between his eyes. I smoothed it away as a door opened behind me. Dirk laid me back in a bed. A soft cocoon of cushions and blankets sighed as I settled in. He tunneled his arms out from beneath me, but I caught his hand before he could pull away completely. "*Wacht.*"

"You have not told me to wait in a long while." His smile again. Soft and tender. I wanted to see the wolfish one. It had been a long time since I had seen it.

I was about to tell him so when I realized how large his hand was compared to mine. I examined it, releasing it, turning it over, threading his fingers through my own. I looked up at him. "You have strong hands."

"Thank you." He leaned down and kissed my forehead.

I frowned. Did he not usually kiss my mouth? I strained my neck up toward him, breathing deep of the scent of near-winter and wind that hung about him. All man.

He leaned forward again. Ah, finally, a kiss. But he only kissed my

Gwyneth

cheek, whispered, "Goodnight, Gwyn," and turned to go.

I cried out, and he spun back, his gaze everywhere at once, checking, fearful for me. He released a breath that sounded like a sigh—a relieved one—and gently grasped my head in his hands. "You are safe here. No need to fear. No need to fear ever again."

My lashes fluttered closed of their own volition. My mouth felt thick. "Do not..." I forced the words out even as I sank further into the bed. "...leave me."

Darkness swooped in and took me far away. So, I suppose, I was the one who left.

73

Dirk

Chapter Thirteen

For a long moment, I leaned over her, her face in my palms. My arms looked massive beside her small body, encased in the softness of the bed. Her flaxen hair fell over my skin. Once I knew she slept, I tensed, waiting. I had never witnessed this part of the process before.

I had never watched the nightmares come.

My thumbs stroked her temple, smoothing back the tendrils soft as eiderdown and light as sunshine. Slowly, gently, I pulled my hands free, though I would have stood there the entire night if only I could ensure the nightmares would never arrive. I spied her glasses in her hand, pried them free as gently as I could, and laid them on the nearest flat surface. She would want those upon the morn.

Then I crossed to the windows that opened over the hills behind my home and tugged the curtains closed against the view. The soft light of twilight intruded little into the chamber Mother had set apart as Gwyn's, but I wanted nothing to disturb her.

Especially not the nightmares I knew she feared. She had never mentioned them to me, not once. A pang in my chest told me that hurt, that sliver of distance she kept between us. Why had she never trusted me with them? What were the nightmares even like? I shuddered to think, for I could well imagine what scenes haunted Gwyn's dreams. They must be terrible, indeed, if she never spoke of them.

I raked my hand through my hair, remembering with fondness the look on her face as she touched a curl earlier and bade me not to cut it. The frisson of joy fizzled when I realized that moment had hardly been real. Or could it be more real than the distant way Gwyn had acted earlier this day?

She was drunk.

I wanted to laugh and roar about the knowledge. I had no one to blame but myself. I heard her say she was thirsty and had bid Susan see to it she was satisfied. Oh, Susan. She always went over and above what was called for. Thank God Mother had discovered what was happening before Gwyn had become ill.

When I had laid eyes on her, her hands shook, and she had removed her glasses. That alone spoke of her confused state more than anything else could. Her gaze had been unfocused on the stairs, and I knew the discomfort behind her temples would only increase by the time the morn came.

I took her glasses now and gently adjusted the arms, slightly loosening them. Mayhap that would prove to be of some relief to her.

Her cries, however, had undone me. Ripped at a place in my heart reserved only for her.

I braced a hand against the wall and watched her, willing the nightmares to try to claim her now, while I was here, while I could comfort her. Let them come and try to take her. If need be, I would wrestle them to the ground and bury them there in the dust of Godfrey land.

She did not stir or squirm. She did naught but slumber.

After I crossed the chamber and clicked the door closed behind me, Susan launched herself into my arms. "I am so sorry, Devon," she whispered into my chest, straining on her tiptoes to even come that far. "I never meant to—"

I put a finger to her lips. "I know, Susie. You did just as I bade you. The blame lies at my feet."

She pushed my hand away and pouted. "I never even thought—"

I raised a brow and fought a chuckle. "I know."

Mother came out of a door across the hall and smiled at the sight of us. But tension reigned in that smile. "Sister Agnes is settled." She took in the way Susan's head nestled against my shirt. "Oh, Susan…"

Susan sniffed.

I hugged her tighter. "Time was I could tuck you into bed with a story, and, no matter what had happened that day, all was sunshine to you."

She frowned up at me. "I'm all grown up." She left the circle of my arms and twirled, then smirked up at me. "Well, grown *older*."

I grinned. "Aye, I think the *up* may be over for you, Susie."

She giggled, and I knew all was sunshine again. Mayhap the years betwixt the bedtime stories and now weren't so many after all.

Mother shook her head at both of us. "'Twas an honest mistake, and no one is angry with you over it."

Susan bit her lip. The sunshine had spotted a cloud. "Do you think she will be?"

I chuckled. "No chance. She will be upset with herself and suffering from a headache, but she would never blame you. ''Twas I who drank it,' she'll say."

My impersonation of a female voice brought both my mother and sister's hands to their mouths. Their matching gray eyes sparkled with mirth.

I sobered and glanced at the door at my back. "Mother, she..."

"Did you put her to bed, son?"

"Aye." My hand reached toward the door latch.

"Did she fall asleep straightaway?"

"Nearly so." My fingers hesitated.

Mother nodded. "She will probably sleep better than she has in weeks, the poor girl. Mayhap God will use this to give her blessed rest."

My hand fell back to my side. Because of those words, I could leave her. Besides, Agnes slept across the hall, Margried resided only two doors down, and my own chambers were but one wing away. If she needed me this night, I would be there.

The deep breath I had just invited into my lungs left again.

For now.

"We will leave on the morrow."

Ian stopped pulling on his shirt. His eyes widened as he looked up at me, disappointment arcing across his features. Mayhap because he would be leaving Susan behind. A growl threatened to release from my throat. I had seen the way the man looked at my sister when we arrived.

Ian was an honorable man I would entrust with my sisters' lives if need be...that did not mean he was worthy of either of them.

"Very well." He turned back to his bed, shrugging his shirt from his shoulders. No complaints. No questions. No concerns. Ian would make a good partner on my mission.

I nodded, my esteem for the man growing as I shoved aside the brotherly thoughts. I shut the door to his chamber and groaned. Three more people needed to know, and none of them would be as easy to tell as Ian had been. They would voice complaints, ask questions, express concerns.

I charted my course for the boudoir, knowing I would find Mother and Susan there, expecting that Millicent had joined them as well. The sound of their voices wafted from the room. I stopped just outside, before they could see me, and just listened to the music of their conversation. My mother sounded beyond thrilled to have so many occupy her home. She had always been happiest when surrounded by people.

Susan, still slightly glum and contrite over the wine incident, did not speak as much as usual. But, then again, Susan was like the sky. She could thunder one moment and shine warmly the next. Ian had better…I shook away that thought before I could finish it.

Millicent's voice cut in. "I am not sure about her, Mother."

"Whatever do you mean, dear?"

My ears perked up as Millicent went on. "She seems sullen and rude."

"How so?" Susan. "I found her ever so kind." Sweet Susan.

Millicent sighed. "Something about her voice, her eyes…rang…false."

I clenched my teeth and entered the room. Millicent's eyes widened.

"Devon?" Mother stood. So she had read the look on my face.

Noticing that Susan had gone pale, I schooled my features. "Lady Gwyneth Barrington is the truest soul I have ever met." I looked Millicent in the eye, knowing I was being harsh, accepting that there was no other way to make her see. Millicent and I were so much alike—hardheaded and stubborn and that elusive adjective that Cade had tried to alert me to while still at Barrington Manor. "She has seen tragedy and has thrown herself into the arms of God for healing and hope. She is the woman I love. You will not speak such of her again, Millie."

Millicent nodded, but her eyes sparked anger. She would have preferred a more private upbraiding. She may have even been contrite had I sent Mother and Susan out or called her away with me for a moment.

Instead, I had acted exactly as Cade had warned. I swept a hand down my face, feeling the beginnings of a beard. "I am sorry, Millie."

"Your words were warranted, Devon." Mother scoured me with her gaze. "What I am concerned with now is the look on your face that says you are leaving."

Susan squeaked.

Lord, help me. I had rushed into dressing down Millicent like a child and humiliated her needlessly. Was now indeed the right time to tell them of my plans?

Silence.

"Devon?" Mother's eyes said she wanted to hear with as little delay as possible the reason for the shuttered expression I wore. Sometimes God answered prayers in different ways...

"Ian and I will leave upon the morrow."

Mother sat again. I went to her and knelt. Her hand reached out for my head.

"Why?" Susan's voice lodged tears.

I took them all in with my gaze. My joy at seeing them again was overshadowed by the absence of my father and, now, my brother. My father's death marked the night my life changed forever, my salvation had been stamped sure, and my home became once more Godfrey Estate—the night I foreswore the prodigal lifestyle I had lived for two years.

But after the murder of Gwyn's parents, I went on the run again. Avoiding those who wished me dead or could see me tried for a crime I had not committed remained my sole purpose until I stumbled onto the news of Gwyn's travelling to the Low Countries, the land of her mother, a land hostile to all she stood for. I had latched onto a foolhardy plan to save her—and myself. If only I had known how it would have to end.

While I had been busy failing at that, my brother had died.

And now I would be leaving my sisters and mother, too. Indefinitely. "How can I stay?"

Their voices filled the room, arguing that I had *just arrived* and needed to *rest*, had not seen them in *months*, and had not even told them about Gwyn yet.

I shook my head and raised a hand, pleading for silence. "I refuse to put you all in danger by remaining here. Word will get out that I am back in England, that I am here. This is the only way to secure your safety. I would be apprehended here."

Mother shook her head. "Devon, you are acting without heed once more."

"This is my only choice, Mother."

Millicent spoke next. "Where will you go?"

I smiled sadly at the sister who knew it was fruitless to argue or try to dissuade, who had already mentally moved on to asking the practical questions. We were much alike. "I intend to return to Joseph first. To Tudder, eventually."

My mother sighed. "How I wish you were home for good."

A slice in my heart widened at the word *home*. For I did not have one anymore. Not truly. I was destined for a vagabond life. No hope remained of my ever clearing my name, of my ever managing the estate in my father's and brother's stead. I was effectively leaving my mother, sisters, and Gwyn to the mercy of the next male cousin who would inherit Godfrey Estate. But was that not better than having a murderer as their provider?

Susan's tears glistened on her cheeks. "Devon. Please stay."

"I refuse to put you in danger, Susie. Any of you." I met the eyes of each woman in the room, stopping short of embracing them all again. I would bid them farewell upon the morn. No need to rouse additional emotion now.

"For just a little while? A few days?" Susan begged now, her eyes pleading with me to reconsider.

"Devon, you only just arrived," my mother said. "You need to rest. You have not slept in a real bed, eaten real food, in how long?"

I patted her hand. "We spent two days at Barrington Manor."

Her face darkened. I looked to Susan and Millicent. Both faces boasted drawn, uneasy looks.

"What is it?" The words came out low.

"Mere gossip." Millicent tugged at her perfectly-coiled hair.

"Tell me." I flicked my gaze between Mother and Susan, my tone making evident my demand.

Susan spoke first. "There have been rumors that Lord Barrington has mistreated his servants in recent months. He has exhibited signs of…rage and madness."

"He is now dead."

Quiet gasps echoed in the silence that followed my words.

"So Gwyneth…" Susan's tears ran freely again.

I nodded and rose from where I had been kneeling at my mother's seat. I immediately regretted the move, for I did not wish to tower over all of them. "She is an orphan."

My mother's eyes watched me with far too much intuition. I knew this conversation was not over for her, but she would refrain from asking more while in the presence of my sisters.

Millicent's face attested to her shock. Mayhap she realized the woman she had ridiculed needed compassion, not censure or criticism. Every ounce of the woman I loved was true as a sea breeze.

"Millicent, take your sister to her chamber." My mother's order swung through the air, delivered with a tone that would brook no argument.

Susan opened her mouth anyway. Mother pierced her with a look equal parts love and determination. Millicent placed her hand on my shoulder as she passed.

I sat in Susan's empty seat after the door closed behind them. The rosewater my sister loved hovered around me. I breathed deeply, wondering. I had known Gwyn only in the most desperate of circumstances, I realized as I closed my eyes. When she did not have cause to fear for her life, what suited her fancy? What kind of luxuries made her happy? Did she indulge in perfumes as my sister did?

On the night that I had met her, she had stood on the stairs and stared down at me with a steely gaze laced with pride and fire. What scent had surrounded her that night? I had not been close enough to know.

My heart seized. I need not know. I would not be returning from this mission as a normal betrothed man would—arms full of gifts for his beloved. I leaned forward, letting my elbows rest on my knees. I might not return from this *mission*, as I called it, at all.

"Devon, did you kill him?"

I sat straight up, seeing Gerald standing over Oliver. "Nay, Mother, I did not."

Relief loosened her shoulders. Her chin dropped to her chest, and I knew she prayed, thanking God for one less sin on her son's shoulders. "You know I love you, son."

"And I love you, Mother."

"I know you love that young woman, too."

"More than my own life. She has…run away with my soul." I had not planned on revealing so much.

"Then why do you insist on breaking her heart?"

I sucked in a breath. "I am trying to mend it."

"By leaving."

"By protecting her." My voice turned hard.

"You are tossing her away."

"That is not true."

"She will see it that way."

Unwilling to believe it, I shook my head. Gwyn must see… "Her eyesight is poor, but her heart sees further than anyone I have ever known. She will understand."

Mother remained silent, taking me in, chewing on the words she wanted to say, deciding which ones would arrow straight to my core and achieve the purpose she meant for them. That was my mother: careful, considering. All I had learned of verbal sparring—that served me so well in Gwyn's case—I had learned from her.

"I…"

I waited, letting her have all the time she needed.

"You will not understand what I am about to say, Devon, but please listen."

Staring into her eyes, I gave her my silent promise that I would.

"I bade your father farewell on the same night you did, knowing what his leaving meant to you, what it did inside you."

"God saved me that night."

She nodded, tears already glistening in her eyes.

"Do not cry, Mother; you know what it does to me."

She smiled softly and stroked her hand across my forehead. The silence of night had descended over the estate. Such quiet that I took a deep breath, enjoying the peace, enjoying the knowledge that all I loved slept safe beneath this roof. Gwyn's image rose in my mind, and I breathed a prayer that she did indeed rest peacefully. My fingers trembled with the sudden desire to check on her.

"Your thoughts have gone to be with her."

I nodded, shamed.

"No need to apologize, son. 'Tis as it should be. But I was not finished, you know." She smiled.

I nodded again.

"On the night your father died, I lost the one I loved as you love Gwyneth. Then, on the day Harold died…" She took a shaky breath.

I clenched my fists in my lap.

"Yet, when your brother died, I know the strength that came to your soul."

Blinking, I stared at her. How could she have known? Cade and I had asked Joseph to code his letter, saying naught of my presence much less of my comfort…

Her smile turned sad. "I know because I prayed for it and I see it even now in your haunted eyes. On that day, I lost my firstborn. No mother should have to know such pain."

I bit back a groan. If only I had been home…with them…I could have done something.

"Something happens in a woman's heart when she loses someone, Devon. We can find new strength, aye, that's true, especially if the name of the Lord flies to our lips soon thereafter."

The sound of Gwyn's screams that night at the monastery resurfaced between my ears. And I thought of the new spirit of joy that had clung to her these last few days, even through the unidentifiable tension she insisted on keeping between us.

"But losing someone…it sits heavy on a woman's wounded soul, in her eyes, within her empty arms." She stared at the floor as if seeing the faces of my father and brother there.

"I am sorry, Mother." My words came as a croak, and I stood, reaching for her.

She melted into my outstretched arms. She clutched my shoulders and spoke into my chest. "Gwyneth has lost so many, Devon. Her parents. Her friends from the convent. Her uncle. Listen to me." She pulled back and took my face in her hands. Her steely gaze bore into mine. "You must think hard about whether she can survive an even greater loss than these combined. You must consider what your walking away will do to her."

My chest ripped open and accepted the knife she plunged deep inside. Then it closed again, to bury the bloody wound, never to be healed. "Mother, I must."

She pulled in a deep breath and nodded. "I feared that would be your choice."

My eyes stared into the solemn knowing in her eyes. "You know me too well, Mother." No humor lingered in the words.

A small smile rose on her face even as a tear slipped down her cheek. "You are too much like me."

"To my credit."

She brushed her hand over my forehead again, and I closed my eyes for a moment. Then I looked down at her.

"Do me proud, son."

"How can I?" The words fled my mouth before I could bid them back again.

Her smile was radiant. "Be you."

She did indeed know me too well. She knew I was never coming back. I gathered her close again. Her hands skimmed my back, and she returned the embrace with a mother's devotion.

As I pulled away from her, as I clutched close the look in her eyes, left the room, closing the door behind me, my own words thundered through my brain. The declaration of what they meant trampled all the hope I had nurtured when I had held Gwyn in my arms and kissed those lips that had just received my offer of marriage. *I must… I must leave her.*

She would survive. I knew she would. She would see.

But would *I* be able to live without *her*? Because as surely as I knew my mother spoke true, I knew the reverse was true, as well.

Something happens in a man's heart when he loses someone. It sits heavy on a man's wounded soul, in his eyes, within his empty arms.

What would saying goodbye to her do to me?

It was then I decided not to say goodbye.

Gwyneth

Chapter Fourteen

The raging headache little compared to the shame marching through me. Drunk. I had become drunk last night on offered wine, had swayed and whimpered and cried out in irrational fear. I remembered most of it, too. That would have been embarrassing punishment enough, except for the black patches of space betwixt the moments I could recall.

What had happened during the minutes—I gasped...hours?—in which my memory had deserted me?

I knew I had risen from the table and taken off my glasses...then I remembered the sweet words Dirk had whispered as he smiled down at me. But what had transpired in between? How had I found myself in his arms?

I knew he had laid me in the bed, kissed my forehead and then my cheek...my thoughts and words then made me blush. But what might have I said before then, whilst he somehow transported me from the Great Hall to my chamber? I groaned just considering it.

Then I turned over and retrieved my glasses. After I placed them on my face, the vision before me made my breath catch. I reached for the unruly bunch of wildflowers, my fingers trembling.

Precious moments later, I waved the maid away, grateful for her help fastening the many buttons to my crimson gown, but eager to go down. My fingers absently played with the string of pearls draped across my bodice.

"If you wish to break your fast, milady, Cook will be glad to fix a tray for me to bring to ye, or you can come to the Great Hall, if you wish."

I looked at her and blinked. "I missed the meal this morn?"

She shuffled her feet and looked to the floor. "You slept, milady."

My body froze, then I moved woodenly toward the door. In the hallway at last, I reminded myself to breathe. Down the stairs I went, then into the courtyard.

Everyone stopped to stare. I saw not one familiar face. My heart jumped into my throat, then sank to my feet. Cold acknowledgement wrapped its icy tentacles around every inch of me.

He was gone.

Though I knew, I asked anyway, my voice high. "Lord Devon Godfrey. Where is he?"

A knobbed finger pointed out the gate we had entered last night. I glanced at it in horror before a warbly voice called me back to the finger's owner. A man with kind eyes and straggly hair held his cap in one hand and pointed with the other. "He left a little while ago, milady. You just missed him."

I am missing him even now. "Bring me a horse. Bring me Char." A puzzled glance from all around. "The mount I rode yesterday. Darker coat, lighter mane. Bring him to me."

One man nodded and darted away. The door to the castle opened behind me. Margried and Rohesia exchanged worried glances when they saw me. "Gwyneth." They said my name together.

"He left." The two words fell like stones from my mouth. "I know."

Margried stepped forward. "He wanted to wait for you."

But at the same time Rohesia said, "He did not wish to wake you."

I turned away from both of them. "You could have woken me, Margried."

She touched my arm. "I know. But after I heard what happened last night…"

I could scream at the flush I knew claimed my face.

"Milady." The man I waited for led Char my way. He was all I had now. I should pack, if I was to do what I meant to do. But if I had just missed him, as the man had said, I needed to leave now in order not to lose my head start.

What stopped me from bounding onto my horse's back right away was Rohesia's voice. "Open the gate."

A murmur rippled through the crowd of men who had gathered to watch the mistress of the manor and her guests. Several faithful feet flew to their task in obedience to her order.

"Thomas, go with her." In response to Rohesia's command, a tall man parted the crowd, leading a horse. "He went east," Rohesia said to him.

I looked into her gray eyes. She came toward me, her features stiff. I recognized the look as one that meant she restrained tears behind taut cheeks. Her hand reached out to me. I looked from the pouch in her palm back to her eyes.

"Take it. It should be enough to see you to the continent or beyond or wherever you go."

I flung my arms around her, clinging tight to this woman I planned never to see again. She knew. She knew I intended to lash myself to his horse's mane if that was what it took. I was not coming back.

Infused into my embrace was my farewell to her, to Susan, to this house I would have loved living in because Dirk's presence seemed evident here.

But I could not stay here without him. I could not *be* without him. She knew that. So she gave me the silver.

I pulled back from her embrace and clutched the coins close, hearing them sing to me as they clinked together. If hope sounded like diamonds, surely truth sounded like silver. Like this silver. The truth of a promise of a new life. A different one, aye. But one with him.

After tying the pouch to my side, I nodded at Rohesia, words failing. I could see it then. The resemblance. It went far deeper than the auburn hair. This woman had given birth to the man who held my heart, had cared for him and raised him to have the warrior-heart I loved. Which made her a warrioress in her own right.

And us kindred spirits.

I pulled Margried close, then turned away and pitched myself onto Char's back. The gates creaked open, but I had already commanded Char to gallop.

God, lead me to him. Char took the invitation to run with all eagerness, but my heart flew out in front of us, searching the land for any sign of the man to whom it belonged. *Help me find him. Please. Help me find him.*

Dirk

Chapter Fifteen

Every mile tore free a piece of my heart and soul until I was nothing more than a hollow shell of a man. That should have made the parting easier, but instead I could not increase my pace for anything. Ian and I ambled along, each of us silent and somber, lost in our own thoughts. He no doubt allowed the sight of Susan to rise in his mind. Unlike him, though, I did not have the luxury of what-ifs. I knew there was no other way.

Ian sighed at last. "'Tis broad daylight, Dirk. We are inviting any and all to find us."

My lips smoothed into a thin line. *Let them come.*

"Too many want your arrest for us to travel by day without speed."

Let them try and take me.

"We must make haste to St. Benet's."

What did it matter now? Without her, my life meant naught. The sound of the voice I had waited for the night prior, while standing in my mother's boudoir, thundered through my thoughts. A new strength surged through my apathy. I mattered to God. *For what, Lord? What good can I possibly serve, what value can I possibly be to you now, a wanted man? For I am destined to be no better.*

But Ian was right.

"Go on, then."

A second before his heel struck his horse and spurred the animal into a run, we both heard it. Hoofbeats behind us, heading straight for us. I swiveled around, trying to get a glimpse of our pursuer.

Ian put a hand to his baldric, over the blade attached there. I palmed my own dagger. Then I froze.

"Wait!" I held out a hand to Ian, at the same time returning my dagger to my baldric. I turned my mount and ran to the one running after me.

Her hair shone ivory in the sun, streaming behind her like a stroke made with a painter's brush—and a gifted one at that. Char carried her toward me until at last mere feet separated us. She halted. I halted.

Oh, Gwyn.

Thomas rode behind her, sent no doubt by my mother to guide Gwyn straight to me. I suddenly regretted and rejoiced that I had told my mother the direction I was taking.

I dismounted, walked to her, and held up my arms. I could not think. I could not breathe. I could fathom naught at the moment. Except holding her, reassuring myself she was well after the fiasco last night, and relishing the sight of her whom I had thought to never see again.

She accepted my help, stood on solid ground, reached up, and slapped me.

I heard a snort. I turned my head enough to gift Ian with a glare.

Spanish filled my ears, and I heard the words she had taught me. "…*Idiota…*" I stared at her, mesmerized by the way her hands moved, her eyes sparked, her hair swung as she gestured and moved. "…*Estúpido…*" She walked around, came back to me, drew back, came close again, close enough to poke her finger in my chest.

I did not even try to respond, calm, or console. What could I say? I was all she called me and more. More than she could ever know. More than I could ever overcome—even for her. I was a murderer in the eyes of England. And I refused to lash her to the life I would need to lead because of that unearned condemnation.

"…*Estúpido sin filo…*"

When she stopped at last, her eyes poured green fire and her chest heaved up and down.

To fill the silence, I said, "I am glad to see you fully recovered from last night."

Her mouth dropped.

"I—I meant that I am relieved you do not suffer any ill effects from the…inebriat—" I gave that sentence up for lost and stared down at her. This might be the last time I ever saw her.

She slapped her hand to my chest and left her palm there. Mayhap she guessed my thought, for next she flung her arms around my neck with quiet desperation. The lioness had departed in favor of Gwyn, all Gwyn, only Gwyn. Her fingers sank into the hair at my neck and drew my head to hers. I rested my forehead on her smooth white one for a moment.

Then she completely surprised me—she kissed me.

Gwyneth

Chapter Sixteen

I had naught left to lose. My family, my home, my life lay in tatters all around me. He wanted me to stay with his mother and heal; this I knew. This I had accepted yesterday morn when he had begged me to come, refused to leave me at my childhood home, which truly did not feel like home anymore.

But I did not accept it now. Not like this. Not without him. What did feel like home was right here, right now, out in the open in the middle of a forest path, with Ian looking on, the whole world given a view of my desperation.

I cared not. I cared only for him and for kissing him like my life depended upon his knowing every single ache and hopeless corner inside me. Because, in a way, in every way, all did depend upon him.

"Dirk." I broke away for a second to breathe.

He shuddered and drew me closer as if he feared I was done and pulling away. Far from it. I ran my fingers through the red curls that had captured my attention last night on the staircase—ah, so that was how he had gotten me to my chamber—and allowed him to kiss *me*.

"Gwyn." Then my worst nightmare came true, and he did pull away. "Ian," he growled. I opened my eyes to see Ian turning away obediently, then closed them again because Dirk was kissing my jaw, my throat, my cheek.

"Take me with you."

He ceased. Inside the swirling maelstrom comprised of naught but the two of us, our love raged. Here was my chance. *God, give me the words.* "Please, do not refuse me." *I need more words than that.*

He grasped my head in his hands. He had done this last night, too. "Gwyn—"

89

"I—I do not care where you are going. I do not care that you dared to leave without saying farewell."

"I could not—"

I shoved his chest, disproving my words, swallowing the sobs that sought their freedom. "I brought Char. I will ride behind you. I will cause no trouble, make no complaint. Just, please, Dirk…" I buried my face in his jacket, clutching him with both hands, breathing him in. "Take me with you." I was begging and unashamed.

A rumble against my ear sounded like a groan. He was giving in; my heart leapt.

"Nay." He put me from him. "Go back, Gwyn. You cannot come. I do not want you to follow me. Just go back."

For a moment, the shock of it poured through my veins. Then I realized what he was doing, and I started trembling. "Do not do this, Dirk. I see right through you, just as you see straight through me. You are trying to deceive me."

"I am doing nothing of the kind." His hard voice nearly killed my courage; never had he spoken to me in such a way. Not even at the convent, when my stubbornness and refusal had nearly cost us our lives. He had always been the epitome of gentleness with me—until now. "I am being truthful. If you have any shred of respect for me, you will leave and return to the others. Obey me in this, Gwyn, and I will remember you fondly."

Lies. All lies. I could scream from the fury. "You are being cruel and heartless to drive me away."

"Nay."

I ignored his denial. "But it will not work. I am going with you, whether you approve or not. I will ride behind you no matter where you go or how you try to lose me."

He stepped forward and grabbed my shoulders. I knew he knew I meant it. He pulled in a shuddering breath and let it out just as I inhaled.

We could stand this close for always, he and I, breathing the same air, facing together the world that had broken and betrayed us. Forever. "You know I am right."

"You are right." His admittance sounded more like defeat. "I did not mean those things. You do see straight through me. As you have from the moment I met you." He smiled—a sad, wistful smile.

I smiled, too. "I thought you a nuisance the first time I saw you."

He grunted. "Have I ever risen above that?"

I rose up on my tiptoes and kissed him. "Far above. You are everything to me."

"As you are to me."

I smiled, sure of his answer now. "Then let me come."

"I cannot."

I melted.

"Do not follow me, Gwyn. I beg of you."

"I *will*."

He held me to him. We stayed there a long moment, before he started speaking into my hair. "I love you, Gwyn."

"I love you, too."

"I would have been honored to spend the rest of my life with you by my side."

"You *will*."

"I cannot. Consider our betrothal broken."

"How can you say that?" I pushed away. The urge to scream overcame me again.

"What choice do I have? I have no life to offer you!"

His bellowing shout threw me back a step, but then I took a fistful of his shirt in my hand. "Your choice is this: let me go with you. The life you have is the only one I want."

"A vagabond's life? A prodigal's life destined never to be restored? I could never allow your fate to be such, Gwyn." He leaned down, his earnest eyes boring into mine.

"We will go far away from here. Iceland. The New World. I will not be a burden. I have packed nothing. I need nothing. I need only to go with you."

He whispered, "You could never be a burden" at the same moment as I pulled his mother's pouch from where I had tied it at my waist, the only thing I had brought with me.

Holding it out to him, I watched the emotions cross his face. Understanding. Resignation. Determination.

"I do not need—"

He would not take it, so I placed the pouch inside his coat myself. "We need each other."

"God knows I do need you."

I laid my head on his chest. "We will be together, and that is all that matters to me."

He shook his head. "You are a lady. You deserve more."

"And what about you?" Anxiety swam in my words. I could hear it; he was giving up. And if I did not dissuade him, he would leave me today, and I would never see him again. He would never let me follow him. I would never be able to keep up.

Or he would merely take me back to Godfrey Estate. I would fight it with all that was within me, but the moment I fell asleep or let him out of my sight for one innocent minute, he would be gone, scattered to the four winds, never to return.

I could not breathe. "What about you? You are a lord's son. The estate is yours now."

He raked his hand through his hair. "I am a murderer. I am nothing."

Because I said you were. The pain of having caused this ultimate sorrow in his eyes slashed me afresh. What had I done? If only I had known, that night my parents had died at my own uncle's hand, that this was where it would lead us. I would have stayed silent. I would have never breathed his name.

Dirk glanced up at the sun. It shone down with intensity, a last effort to assert its authority before winter stung at September's end and encased us all in cold. Except my bones already complained of a chill.

"Go back to Godfrey Estate, Gwyn. You and my mother…find comfort in each other."

I glared up at him. "Is that your farewell?"

He put inches between us, took my hands, lifted them to my shoulders, threaded them through with his fingers. "Nay." His gruff voice resurrected my tears. "This is."

The kiss was one of sorrow. Of complete and utter sadness. And mourning. Mourning for what once had been and what could never be again.

My choked sobs ended it. I inhaled, trying to stop, trying to step toward him. But my feet had cemented themselves to the ground. Dirk had turned away. He turned back again, and my heart gasped in hope for one moment before I realized his intent to see me atop Char again. Having seen me safely seated, he stared into my eyes. I could barely see him. Did his eyes glisten as mine did, or did I imagine that in order to comfort myself?

"Come back to me." I reached for him, but he slapped Char's rump and sent him careening down the hilly path. My last glimpse of him was of him sinking to his knees.

Dirk

Chapter Seventeen

After I slammed several tree trunks and bloodied my hands, Ian and I rode against the wind. Nothing held me back now. My chest had turned to stone, and my heart with it. When we stopped to water our horses at a small river, I acknowledged I had driven the animals too hard. They panted and drank, and we had to hold them back lest they make themselves sick. Guilt assaulted me.

I pushed back the image of her face, stained with tears, of her hand, reaching back for me. The trees above me swayed in the wind. I wished for rain. I wished for a storm. I wished for snow, for sleet, for hail. Any kind of foul weather would be welcome now. Any sort of distraction I had to push against to arrive at my destination would be a balm to my soul.

Lord... I could not pray. I had no words. And I heard silence in return.

We released the horses to drink again. I stood staring over the expanse of the water, aware of Ian slowly, methodically rummaging in his saddle bags for the provisions my mother had made us pack.

She had asked me again this morn if I was certain about what I was doing. She had not asked me with the same words, in the same way, as she had last night. But the undertone was the same. And so was the effect.

Gwyn was strong. I knew I had hurt her. I cursed myself for doing so. But the deed was done. She was safe. Or would be as soon as she got back to Godfrey Estate and ensconced herself within my mother's loving arms. No outside force would get to her; no threat would make it past those walls.

And I had procured Cade's solemn promise to that end, as well.

For all the times my mother bade me stop and think, for all the looks she gave me, begging me to go and bid Gwyn farewell, even if she was not yet fully awake, Cade had remained silent. For once, we agreed. No argument about my pride or need to have it my way stepped between us.

Ian was confused; Margried was angry; Agnes had refused to see me off. But Cade understood. It was as if once again he and I were the brothers we had been when wildness had raged in our chests.

I knew I had no choice but to leave; he knew I had no choice but to leave. So I left. And he stayed. I left to protect them. He stayed to protect them. When I had glanced back at my home, mayhap the home I was leaving for the last time, he had stood with Margried in his arms. His hand had lifted to wave to me. The acceptance in that movement had buoyed me.

Mayhap it had buoyed my strength too much. The similarity of Cade's wave and Gwyn's haunting reach assailed me. The fact that one person understood I could do naught else but leave had supported the slap to Char's rump that sent Gwyn back.

Ian handed me food. I took it and ate without looking, tasting, or thanking.

Doubts rained down on me as we approached St. Benet's. I should have let her come. She could be in front of me in the saddle right now. For there was no chance I would have let her ride Char. Not after that kiss. Where had she learned to kiss like that? My neck flamed when I realized *from me.*

I should go get her. Fetch her. Bring her with me. She would come. I had no doubt of that.

Stop it, Dirk. This torment must end.

A mere mile to go before we reached St. Benet's and temporary refuge. I harbored no illusions that the former monastery would prove a safe place for us permanently. If that were the case, Gwyn would be in my arms as I rode.

Nay, no place would ever be safe for me again. Not even Iceland or the New World. *Oh, Gwyneth-mine.* But I could not ask her to go into banishment for me. The wilderness was no place for her.

My heart groaned as the great walls of the monastery loomed above us, tall and imposing. In this place, Gwyn had fought for her life against the lung fever intent on taking it. She won by the grace of God.

I drew my hand across my forehead, amazed at how the memory of the way she had woken up just a few mornings later and flung porridge in my face warmed me. I wanted to laugh and shout at the same time.

We rode up. This time I did not have Gwyn in my arms. This time she did not thrash and cry out, suffering from the fever. This time what I would not give to have her here, not suffering, but surrendering her life to spend it with me.

I lowered my forehead into my hand, struck anew by the pain of her absence. Was this what I was destined for then? A lifetime of looking around, always wishing I'd see her materialize out of the tree line, doomed to never have my wish granted?

A voice called out from behind the closed door. "Who goes there?"

I swallowed and said, "Travelers journeying past, desperate for food, drink, and care."

The creaking of the door announced him before I could glimpse his face. I dismounted, and Ian did the same.

Joseph stood, solemn, waiting.

We stood there, staring at each other. I had no words he would accept, for I saw the intensity burning in his eyes. He could read the agony in me and answered with compassion in his silence. I did not bother to give an explanation, and he required none.

He swept his wide sleeve toward the door, yawning open, and saw us inside.

Once within the hallowed halls, I saw her image in my mind, breathed her name, and collapsed. The last thing I knew was a stinging in my hand. It had to be because it connected with the stone floor—or did it have anything to do with a slap to a horse's back that sent her away from me forever?

Gwyneth

Chapter Eighteen

When Char brought me through the gate, I lay across his neck, gripping his mane in both hands, my eyes closed against the pain. I knew I looked a fright, but why should I care?

I heard shouts. Margried's gasp. Rohesia's sigh. Cade's hands reached up and pulled me down. I sank against him before I found my feet, wiped my eyes, and stepped away. "I thank you, Cade."

He grunted. I flashed a perfunctory smile at him, appreciating the lack of platitudes.

Silence hovered. I pressed my hands to the circles beneath my eyes, which felt strangely heavy. Sister Agnes reached me first. Her broken face brought the tears back. She opened her arms, and I clung to her.

We were so very much alike, she and I. If ever Sister Agnes decided to tell me the story of her life before she came to the convent, I imagined it would sound as tragic and simple as mine. For it did seem as if my life had been simple enough. Grew up. Lost parents. Ran away. Returned. Betrayed. Found God.

Except, of course, for falling in love, everything fit in a perfect order, a neat pattern.

She said nothing. I appreciated that, too.

A few moments passed before I heard Susan's anxious voice from the other end of the courtyard. It sounded different, out of breath, which at first I shrugged off. Her brother had left today after only hours at home. She should be distressed, if not mourning him as I was.

But that was not all that was in her voice. I opened my eyes to see her form shuffling beside another, taller figure. Of course, many were taller than Susan, but… I pulled away from Sister Agnes's embrace.

"Gwyneth, you should know…" Margried's worried tone sounded low

96

in my ear. As if she intended no one to hear but me.

"Know what?" The form had not yet come close enough for me to tell, but I...

"He came shortly after you left, and he insists you summoned him, but..."

"I did."

"You did?" Cade had stepped beside me. I glanced up at him. Of course. *Dirk*. He had seen to it that I would not be without a protector. I wanted to roll my eyes and weep again simultaneously.

"Before leaving Barrington Manor, I had Joan send a missive." My whispers became swift.

"Why?" Cade's question came just as the form came close enough for me to see.

I smiled through the lenses of my glasses at the fair-haired man approaching me with a knowing look in his eyes, a confident swagger in his step.

"And who is he?" Margried whispered into my shoulder just before he stopped in front of me.

"Good morrow, Gwyneth." He bowed and tipped his head to smile at me. "You sent for me?"

He arrived earlier than I had thought to expect him. But Anders always seemed to know what I needed. I had known him longer even than I had known Char. In fact, Char had been his idea. I remembered the cool spring day Papa had brought the horse home. Shy, hesitant, I had held back.

"Go on. You know you want to." Anders, visiting from his estate as he often did, nudged me in the direction of the horse. "And you always get what you want, Gwyneth."

My ten-year-old self shied away mere steps from Char.

"Meet Charger." Papa patted his nose.

"His hair is the same shade as yours. Do you see that, Gwyn?" Thirteen-year-old Anders had pointed out.

The horse's brown eyes had looked into mine, and that had been it. I was Gwyneth; he was Char. We were friends. Just as Anders and I had always been friends. Born to recusant Catholic families, we shared a bond. Our religion was illegal, although many of us continued to practice. Recusant Catholics, we were called, because we did not attend the Protestant prayer services.

Anders knew me better than just that bond, though.

I shook my head, banning the memories from surfacing. Today bore no time for distractions. In the center of the sunny courtyard of Godfrey Estate, Anders took my hand and kissed it.

"You know this man?" Cade growled.

"Anders Revelin, Earl of Lansberry." He nodded to Cade, a smile arcing on his mouth. His gaze fastened on me again. Wind tore at his hair. "The lady's oldest friend and fellow recusant."

Margried startled me by placing her hand on my arm. Sister Agnes seemed to hang on his every word. She would—he was Catholic, after all. Properly Catholic.

Rohesia stepped forward. I had nearly forgotten she had been present when Cade fetched me off Char's back. "Come, my lord. You must be eager to rest after your journey."

Anders offered his arm, ever the elegant gentleman. "'Twas hardly arduous, milady." He looked at me over his shoulder. "Lady Gwyneth calls. I come."

I shook my head at his foolishness. But an ache in my head—leftover from last night?—lingered, and I snatched my glasses from my nose, clutching them in my hand. Dirk was out there somewhere, running from a reputation I had ruined, unable to rest because I had falsely accused him of murder. But I would set things right. I would see his name restored.

And Anders would be the one to help me.

Anders's perfect answers seemed to satisfy Rohesia. Cade, however, wore his concern on his face like a soldier wears armor. I noticed Margried patting his hand and exchanging glances with him as we sat in the Great Hall and sipped wine—well, I pretended to sip. I had no desire to repeat the events of the night prior.

"When did you receive Lady Gwyneth's missive?" Rohesia responded to Anders's lead and called me by my title when referring to me, even though I sat just across from them.

"This morning, milady. I called for my horse immediately upon reading it."

"You were at home when it arrived then, Anders?" I sent him a look that said he was not to disclose the contents of my message. Not yet. Joan's words revolved in my mind: The county of Lansberry was closer to our present location at Godfrey Estate than Barrington Manor. I cocked my head, deciding to inquire of Anders later if he had ever met Dirk. After all, the two men had grown up closer to each other than to me.

"I was. And glad I am, too, so that I could answer your call straightaway." His expression turned compassionate.

I took a deep breath, glad to have him as an ally. This man knew me. He had been there for me when Char scared me. He would be there for me now when my greatest fear was losing Dirk forever.

Cade leaned forward. "How do you two know each other?" His voice icy, he gestured between Anders and me.

Margried's hand crept up, toward Cade's arm, then settled down again. So she disliked the question as much I did. Cade sounded like a concerned older brother.

I gave him a placating smile full of meaning. "I have known Anders since I was small." I laughed lightly, diffusing the moment. "Is that not correct, Anders? Why, I cannot recall our first meeting, so long ago it was."

The mirth in his smile put me at ease that he had not taken offense at Cade's tone. "I recall it."

My laugh died away. I blinked at him.

"Let us hear the tale." Cade shifted his shoulders to appear more relaxed, but the lines around his mouth failed to smooth. What had the man so on edge?

Mayhap 'twas the same thing that had me so on edge. The absence of his best friend and brother in arms. The sudden longing for Dirk swamped me, and I took a reluctant sip of my wine just to have an excuse to tip the goblet and hide my damp eyes. I blinked again and looked up.

Anders watched me, studied me with an expression on his face I could not decipher. That was different. I had always been able to read Anders.

I nearly gasped. Of course. His image was blurry because my glasses lay in my hand. I glanced around, taking in my fuzzy surroundings, amazed that I had allowed myself to go without them for so long in this foreign environment.

Anders had made me so comfortable that I had failed to realize my blindness. I had taken them off when he said, *Lady Gwyneth calls. I come.*

"'Twas midwinter. Late morning. My father took me with him on a trip to visit Lord Barrington."

"Which one?" I asked. *My uncle or my grandfather?*

"Your grandfather, Gwyneth." His voice went soft.

I smiled, the image of the man I missed rising in my mind at the mere mention of his name.

"The men had business to discuss, and I was left to myself. The courtyard was a perfect playground for a ten-year-old boy."

I looked away, shaking my head. I did not recognize this tale. He spun a piece of fiction, crafting one of his stories meant to amuse and entertain.

"I came around the corner of the stables and saw you. Your gown was golden, and you were looking away from me so that I could see only the profile of your face."

My eyes narrowed.

"You were singing. Innocently. Purely. Completely oblivious to the two men talking politics mere feet away and the little boy staring at you in fascination. You had the voice of a bird on the first day of spring, eager to come out of hiding and express joy in newfound life."

I flicked my gaze to my left, where Margried's hand rose to cover her lips. Rohesia's mouth had drifted open. Neither woman was more surprised than I.

He told the truth.

Anders was not spinning fiction or crafting a story. I remembered the day vividly. The memory had been stamped onto my seven-year-old brain with an indelible mark, but one that had been incomplete until now, for I remembered not Anders's presence. The day had been my birthday, and my father had asked me how I wanted to celebrate. *Moeder* had laughed at him and warned him I would answer with all manner of requests.

But I knew better than that. I had not asked my father for what I truly wanted: a frolic on the little pony, Char's predecessor, on which I had learned to ride. Instead, I asked him to take me to the stables. There I had sung for him.

And for Anders. Unknowingly.

The man looked straight at me.

Cade's long, low exhale was the only sound. I pondered the man before me as tears filled my eyes, conjuring one of the sweetest memories I had of my father and twisting it with an added truth I had never before seen.

He had been there, all along, and I had never even seen him.

"Did we meet that day?" My brows drew together as I struggled to remember.

A fraction of the light in his eyes blew out. "Nay, not that day."

I felt compelled to apologize. "I—I was so young."

He waved away my words. "You were. But you were not."

My brows rose at that. He chuckled.

Rohesia folded her hands in her lap. "He is right, Gwyneth."

I looked between her and Anders, glad they were getting along. I hoped that Cade would soon see the brotherly connection Anders had with me—and tone down the protective instincts Dirk obviously assigned him to sharpen. "What is he right about?"

The light reappeared in Anders's gaze. "You have always been, will probably always be, innocent and pure and seemingly young. But you, Gwyneth Barrington, have an old soul that sees much and possesses wisdom beyond your years."

I drew a deep breath. I had an old soul, Anders said. I was wise. Then why I had done such a despicable thing to the man I loved? I was not wise. I was foolish. The most foolish girl alive.

Dirk

Chapter Nineteen

Strains of voices invaded my sleep.

"Did you make it to Barrington Manor?" Joseph's voice.

"Aye." The emphasis belonged to Ian alone. "We returned her to her uncle, but then, ah, complications arose."

"What kind of complications?"

Shuffling ensued. Almost as if footsteps—but not quite normal treads—receded from me, then returned. The voices were softer now, as if Ian and Joseph stood closer but did not wish to disturb me. And why did they not wish to disturb me?

"Her uncle killed her parents all those months ago, Reverend Joseph."

"Go on." A groan infiltrated Joseph's voice.

"The man had one of his best follow us. 'Twas the same man who followed us at the docks—I don't know if Dirk told you about that. But he took Lady Gwyneth back to the manor with him while we slept."

I struggled to move. Why could I not move?

Joseph grunted. "He went after her."

"We all did. Lord Barrington and his steward died in the ensuing scuffle. Dirk rescued Lady Gwyneth, and we stayed there two days."

"Why only two days?"

Darkness filled my vision. Why could I not see?

"He wanted to take her to his mother as soon as we could travel, as soon as she had recovered."

"The danger to her was gone, but his presence put her at risk." Frustration leaked into Joseph's tone.

Ian was quiet a moment. Enough of a moment that I almost drifted away. Then, "Aye."

"What of Lady Godfrey? I have a hard time imagining her approving his leaving again."

A sigh from Ian. "She did not look at all pleased when we rode away. Although her reaction was naught compared to…"

Joseph gave up any claim to a whisper now. "To…?"

I tried to open my eyes, but they refused to obey. I tried to move my hands, but all I could do was clench between my fingers some of the bed upon which I lay. But why did I…?

"Lady Gwyneth."

Joseph chuckled. My fingers clenched harder.

"She came after us."

Joseph mumbled something that sounded suspiciously like "good girl."

Ian's frustration stole his whisper, as well. His voice bounded through my brain. "And then he sent her back. We left her behind, Reverend. Why did he do that? Why would he leave her behind?"

A groan pulled my chest, one I did not intend to be free. The voices stopped. I tugged against the darkness. It was time for me to wake. It was time for me to explain, once again, this time to Ian—and Joseph—why this was necessary, why my abandon—

Ice poured through my veins.

Abandoning her…was necessary?

I raged against my immobility. I needed to slam something around, if only my own head. I *had* abandoned her, hadn't I? Abandoned her…the one act I had promised never to subject her to again.

Sleep, oblivion, unconsciousness, sweet darkness invited me in. I accepted.

I woke, gasping for air. Heat clung to each pore, but a blanket stifled my movement. Why was I covered in blankets if sweat doused every inch? I roared, angry at whatever it was that held me here.

"Oh, be quiet."

I turned toward the voice. Joseph calmly poured water from a pitcher into a clay cup and came toward me. Toward my bed. I lay in a bed, then. Why could I not remember getting here?

Well, I remembered getting here, to Joseph. But I most certainly did not remember a bed. Or getting into it. Or piling blankets on top of myself until I bathed in my own sweat. I flung the covers away, instantly agitated by the way my arm shook afterward.

Joseph sat, out of the trajectory the blankets had taken. "Impressive throw."

I scowled at him. My arm had disappointed me, merely plunging the blankets off the opposite side of the bed and onto the floor. Why was Joseph being sharp? He only became that way when he was tired.

He was a lot like Gwyn in that way.

A sharp pain lanced my chest so that I nearly grabbed my heart. Gwyn. Her wheat-colored hair shining silver in the moonlight. Her emerald eyes reflecting joy, love, pain, sorrow. Her rose-colored lips searching for my own.

"Coming back, is it?" Joseph held up the cup and swirled the liquid contents.

I suddenly very much wanted that water.

"Here." He handed me the cup.

My scowl deepened at the shaking of my hand. I brought my other hand to help his brother. Together, all ten of my fingers struggled to keep the cup steady as I satisfied my thirst. I drank the cup dry and held it out to Joseph. One corner of his mouth lifted in a smirk. My arms shook from holding the empty cup out to him.

Finally, he took it and retraced his steps to refill it once more. "You have slept for nearly three days."

My head fell back against the bed. Three days. I should have been rested, reinvigorated. Instead, I felt weak.

This time Joseph did not turn around and sit back down. "I am going to be calm about this, Devon." He faced away from me, staring out the small window carved into the wall of the cell in which I lay.

I watched his monk's garb shift over his back. He was not built like a warrior, like a fighter. But what muscles he had contracted as he chewed on the words he was about to say.

"I am going to be calm about this, and I am going to listen to you tell me what is going on. I promise you both those things, but I cannot promise you that I am going to like it." He returned to my side, to his seat, and handed me the water.

I studied the ceiling, considering how the boards fit together side after side after side. What I had to tell him was far from so neat and orderly—more like tangled and beyond sorting out.

My hand reached for the cup again. I forced myself to hold it in but one hand while I drank.

Joseph took it back from me. "Well?"

"What do you want to know?"

He snapped the cup to the nearest flat surface. "All." A vein pulsed in his neck.

So I started from the beginning. "I heard Ian tell you much of what happened after we left here."

"There are holes."

"I will fill those in if you prefer."

"Later. I am much more interested in *why* you are here."

I sighed, but he stopped me with a hand in the air.

"Nay. I am much more interested in why you are here *alone*."

"Ian—"

Joseph glared.

My anger overtook me. "I left her. Ian was right. He told you true. Every word. I left her behind."

"And she followed you."

I closed my eyes, images of her flying through my mind, but I willed them to slow so that I could savor them. Her hair a streak behind her as she rode. Her settling on the ground in front of me, staring at me as if she had not seen me in years. Her kiss. Her begging me to allow her to go with me. The look on her face when I refused, when I sent Char off, when I hit my knees. The last glimpse of her red gown as she disappeared into the distance.

"Devon." Joseph reached up to touch his cap, squeezing his eyes shut as if in prayer. I hoped that was the case. Mayhap God would listen to him.

Joseph tried again. "I can see the agony painted on your face. You love her."

"Could you not see that when we were here before?"

"Clear as day. That is why I fail to understand why you are doing this."

I had thought that Joseph would understand. Of all the many who begged me to do what could not be done and stay, I had thought that Joseph would see my reasoning and acknowledge there was no other way for me than to leave. "Do you not see? I have to do this. My goal in seeing her from the Low Countries was to procure her safety. I have done that. There is no better place for her now than Godfrey Estate."

Recognition lit Joseph's eyes. Or mayhap it was merely the flicker of the candlelight that attempted to light the dim, hazy chamber.

I kept on anyway. "But there is no worse place for me. Because of who I am."

Joseph sighed.

"In the eyes of all England, I am a murderer. I could not shake off that stain on my name now if I tried."

"What do you plan to do?"

I closed my eyes and tilted my head back. When I opened them again, I saw the ceiling, the boards in a neat, orderly row.

They mocked me.

Gwyneth

Chapter Twenty

"Gwyneth."

I looked up, pleased by the awed look on Anders's face as he stood at the foot of the staircase. He appeared every bit the adoring adopted older brother in that moment. I was thankful he had come. Still, my soul reached out to a man miles away, a man as stubborn as his red hair seemed to require.

I slid my hand down the banister as I descended. Finally, I stood before Anders and met his gaze. He stood only a few inches taller than I was, so it was no effort. "I am grateful you are here."

'Twas what I had said to him in my missive. *I have returned to England. I will be at Godfrey Estate. I would be grateful if you came.*

His head cocked, causing his wavy blond hair to shift. In our childhood—when we had really only had each other to befriend, recusant Catholics as we were—a lock of his hair had always fallen across his forehead and made him look young. He seemed to have tamed that now. A pity. "Grateful? Not glad?"

I took his offered arm and let him lead the way. "Both, then." *But more grateful.* He merely did not know why yet. He would soon, though. Now seemed the perfect time. He seemed receptive, at last.

After his arrival three days ago, Rohesia had been most gracious about my inviting him to her home. She had assigned him a room in the wing with Cade's. He had taken dinner with us each night since—modest affairs, as the house was still in mourning for Harold.

At dinner, my heart clenched every time I looked at Millicent. Seeing her blank expression only reminded me of who was missing from the table. He should have been there, would have been there, if not for me. I tried to smile at her once, just to assure her I did not mean to ignore her, but she had looked away. I had not had the strength to try again.

"Something weighs heavy on your mind." Anders had led me to the Great Hall, quiet this time of the evening.

Finally. At last he acknowledged me. For the last few days, every time I had tried to tell him why I had called him here, he had changed the course of our conversation. I was determined not to let him leave my presence this night without him knowing my purpose for summoning him. Now was the time.

"Yes." These last few days had given me plenty of time to think about how I would approach this subject, but not enough time to choose which one was best.

Anders turned me toward him. "Is that all you are going to say? Yes?"

"*Nee.*"

He smiled and pulled me into his embrace. Stiff at first, I accepted it for what it was—comfort—and leaned in before softly pulling away. His embrace felt different than Dirk's.

He touched my elbow, saw me settled onto a seat, and knelt at my feet. I shook my head, releasing a light laugh. "Sit."

He obeyed, choosing a seat across from me. "I am anxious to hear what has stolen the light from your eyes." The teasing glint in his gaze disappeared, and he became serious. "Tell me what worries you, Gwyneth."

What worried me? That every morn since Dirk had gone, I had reached for the bouquet of wildflowers I hoped he had returned to leave for me. And each morn, my hand came up empty.

His smile seemed genuine, but his eyes looked more than concerned. Compassionate.

My shoulders relaxed. "Anders, I trust you."

His smile reappeared. "As well you should."

"Thus I am about to tell you something that means a great deal to me."

He studied my face, attention focused on naught but me. I swallowed, wishing the tears would have held themselves at bay a while longer. Opening my mouth, I tried to speak, but it proved futile.

Anders took my hand. I squeezed my eyes shut, felt the stiff frames of my glasses. I tugged them off and held them in my other hand. Then I opened my eyes, staring down at Anders's strong fingers wrapped around one palm and my spectacles in the other. There seemed to be some significance in that I failed to grasp.

"Gwyneth…what is it?"

I looked him straight in the eye. "Do you know Dirk Godfrey?"

He nodded slowly, returning my gaze. "Second son to the late Lord Godfrey, in whose Great Hall we sit."

"I accused him of—"

"No need to say the words, Gwyneth. I know."

"I *do* need to say the words." When he remained silent, I continued. "I accused him of murdering my parents months ago."

Anders's hand tightened around my own. "Then you sought refuge in the Low Countries, in the quiet of a convent."

"Not so quiet, after all."

His eyes narrowed, and he waited.

"The Beeldenstorm found us."

He stiffened.

"Something…happened. About two months after I came to be there…"

The rest of the story released in a rush. That horrific night. Margried's injury. What Margried had told me about Sister Agnes and the kitchen knife. The highwaymen the following day. My lung fever and waking up in St. Benet's. Returning home only to discover the man I thought would be my safe place had betrayed me from the start.

Only I did not tell him all. I left out Dirk's words at the riverside. And the ocean. I kept to myself the way he had flung porridge on me by accident—and I had returned the favor on purpose. I did not share the stolen kiss I thought was to buy my silence—or the way he asked for my hand.

Some things are meant not to be shared, but to be treasured.

Then I told him Dirk had left. "You arrived after I returned from going after him."

Anders listened to it all without flinching. I had expected him to erupt in rage at certain points and reach out to me in concern at others. He did neither. He only listened.

His lack of response concerned me.

When I finished, I sank back slightly and waited for the storm to break. But this was Anders, not Dirk. Where Dirk would have long since reacted, Anders—patient Anders—sat back and studied me. Impatience tugged. "Are you going to say anything?"

"What do you want me to say?"

"I know not. Just say something."

"I am glad you are rid of him."

I stood. "I wish you had not said that."

He lifted both hands, remaining in his seat. "You asked me to say something."

"I did not ask you to be rude." Towering over him was not as much fun as I thought. I sat again.

"I am glad you confided in me."

"That is better."

He chuckled. Then he tipped back his head and studied the ceiling.

I had forgotten about this: the way Anders could belabor his words for hours before speaking them.

I put my glasses back on.

He grinned at me. "You are beautiful."

My eyes flooded, for Dirk had told me the same in the stables mere days ago. And now he was gone.

Anders's eyebrows drew together. "Gwyneth." A tone of warning entered the word near the last syllable.

I blinked and drew a deep breath, swallowing the temptation to snap at him.

"Gwyneth, you did not. Tell me you did not." He leaned his face into his hands, then stood and strode away from me.

I raised my eyebrows. "What are you talking about?"

He turned back. "Tell me you did not come to care for the man."

I stared.

He put a hand on his head and examined the ceiling once more. "Gwyneth, what were you thinking? Is this some sort of ill-fated timing? Was he just there when you needed someone?" He closed his eyes. "Oh, God, I should have gone with you."

Stunned, I sat in silence. But not for long. "What was I thinking? Ill-fated timing? There when I needed someone? Of course he was there when I needed someone. But it took me a while to see what I needed all along was *him*."

Anders's eyes widened, and he came to me, his movements slow, controlled. He gripped my shoulders. "Look at me. He is a prodigal. A rogue. Do you even have any idea what he has done, the kind of life he has led?"

I shoved him away. "Dirk is—"

"You do not, do you? Your parents never told you; your uncle did not have the time."

I flinched, but he continued.

"Forget about him. Forget you ever knew him. Forget you ever admired him. This—this is not love." He threw his gaze heavenward. "This is manipulation or contrivance on his part. You are innocent, as you always are, but..." He shook his head. "He was a liar, a thief, a drunkard, and much more."

I stood. "I will listen to no more."

He held me fast. "You need to know the truth."

"*Nee*, you need to know the truth!" My chest heaved once, twice. I controlled the volume of my voice. "And the truth is this: Dirk may have sinned in his past, but so have I. We are forgiven by a merciful God. But his honor is marred in the eyes of men because of *my* sins—because I accused him of a crime he did not commit. I believed what I thought I saw, when I had not seen the truth at all."

Anders stared at me.

I poked my finger in his chest. "And you will help me absolve him."

His blank stare lasted a moment too long. I finally turned away from him, intent on leaving him there to ponder my words and return when he was willing to hear me out and help me. I swept out of the room, not bothering to look back at Anders, and nearly collided with Sister Agnes.

"Lady Gwyneth, Lady Godfrey requests your presence in her boudoir."

I nodded at the nun, who fell into step beside me. A moment passed before she said, "I want you to know something."

I paused mid-step outside the boudoir. The scent of the rushes on the floor attested to the cleanliness of Rohesia's household. My shoe swirled them around now as I waited for Sister Agnes to speak.

Finally she said, "I am not leaving. As much as I dislike Lord Godfrey, I dislike even more that he left you here. I will not leave you stranded."

She nodded, serious, duty done, and turned to enter the boudoir. Reeling from the abruptness of her statement, I followed a second later, unsure whether I was offended for Dirk's sake—or grateful to her, for mine.

Dirk

Chapter Twenty-One

"Why does Reverend Joseph call you Devon?" Ian had been quiet all morning; I should have known it would not last.

"He knew me before I was Dirk."

Ian chewed on this a moment. Then, "How did you acquire that moniker?"

I ignored him and slung the paddle through the trough of water in front of me. The trough came to my waist. The wash swirled and eddied beneath the bubbly surface. I had been a fortnight abed and today was my first day back on my feet. This was the only task Joseph had consented to assign me. I was grateful, I reminded myself, as I winced down at the water.

Ian managed his own trough a few feet from me. The lye mixed with the water filling our troughs. That and the motion of our paddles meant clean clothes and linens at the end of this stage of the washing process. Or so I hoped. Staring down into the dark concoction, I wasn't so sure.

I looked up, studying the sky. Ah. It was about the ninth hour, so Joseph must be in the chapel. Though he would no longer call them mid-afternoon prayers like he practiced while a Benedictine monk, Joseph still clung to a few of his monastic habits. In this way, he was similar to a few of his compatriots, Marian priests, who served as parish clergy but retained traditional Catholic practices even though Catholicism was illegal.

Yet Gwyn had stubbornly pledged allegiance to that religion until recently.

Joseph came out of a side door, interrupting my musing. He came straight toward me and motioned for me to hand him the paddle. I raised a brow, refusing. I heard Ian chuckle and shot a glance that silenced him.

"Devon, you will overtax yourself."

I harrumphed. "I slept through Michaelmas. I am quite recovered."

"You had a vicious fever."

"I have lain abed these last days out of respect for your knowledge of healing, but I am recovered."

He folded his arms, sleeves ballooning. "Your head aches. Your eyes are weary. Your hands shake."

I bit back a growl and flung the paddle. Then I closed my eyes at the stab of pain rolling through me. Her face was never far from my thoughts. How could I miss someone so much whom I had only truly known a matter of weeks? Less time had passed since I had last seen her, but it had stretched on like an eternity—an eternity without the scent of her hair, the touch of her hand, the sun of her smile.

Joseph caught the paddle. I let him. Running my hand through my hair, I looked up at him.

"And your eyes are tortured," he whispered.

I nodded, unable to speak. What would I say?

"What of you, Ian?" Joseph turned to the younger man suddenly.

Ian looked up, eyes wide. "I feel well."

"Do you?" Joseph glanced from me to Ian. "Your eyes are nearly as anguished as Devon's."

A stone wall barricaded Ian's features. I had never before seen the like—not on the face of the young pup Cade and I had picked up like a stray. He had always been as open as a peasant man's pockets. I stared, amazed at how he shuttered himself now.

"Enough." Joseph tossed the paddle away from him, though it stayed in the water. The long wooden handle swayed in the remnant of the circle Joseph had been creating before it simply stopped spinning.

Ian's paddle was soon apprehended, as well. Joseph motioned toward Ian and me. I followed him, beginning to feel the effects of lying for days on end abed, ill, and then rising to push wash around a trough for hours.

"Where is he taking us?" Ian leaned in to whisper the question as we trailed after Joseph through the narrow hallways of the monastery.

"I am not sure." And that was the truth. But I had one suspicion. I had been down this way before. That suspicion was confirmed when Joseph turned a corner and I saw the steps—and watched Joseph troop down them. The cutaway stone that indented the floor brought back Gwyn. She had taken the first two steps before I had spoken and alerted her to my presence. I had offered my hand while she climbed the last two.

"You should not accost maidens in a monastery."

I smiled at the memory. *"Is that what I am doing? Accosting you?"*

"What do you call it?"

With that one simple question she made a mistake—invited me to say, *"I would call it most anything save such an unsavory word as accosting. Mayhap flirting."*

And she had blushed.

"Enter." Joseph held open the door to the scriptorium. Ian, I saw, had already entered. I trod down the steps and slipped through the door, leaving the memories behind me. I had not been in this room in over a year.

Since the last time Cade and I alone had sought refuge at Joseph's expense. The poor man must wonder at times what we would do without him. Mayhap he even entertained a wish or two that we had never met him. I rubbed my hand over my eyes, remembering those dark times with reluctance. The wrong choices. The gambling. The debts. The brawls. The running—ever running.

And every time we needed a warm place to sleep or a plate of food to devour, we went to Joseph. All because he had offered when we had first met—and we believed him from the first. I thanked God we had.

"What is this place?" Ian's question seemed too loud in the room.

Joseph smiled. The man was in his element, surrounded by the tools of his trade. He went to stand by the desk. "This is my home."

Ian raised a brow.

"And my workplace."

Ian inched closer. I followed, well aware of the purpose of each of the instruments but willing to listen again. The first time Cade and I had come here, I had asked the question still revolving in Ian's eyes. Joseph had answered then as now—with joy on his face. The sun streaming in through the window behind the desk added to the effect.

Joseph pointed to a small pot. "Ink for writing." His finger drifted toward a small blade close at hand. "A knife for scraping off mistakes." His hand hovered over a square stack. "Paper." He continued to point out the various accoutrements necessary for his work.

Ian and I stepped closer, examining the proof of his labor, the purpose of his life. Though Gutenberg had invented the printing press, still Joseph clung to the old ways in a certain sense.

"What are you copying now?" I glanced at the sheets lying on a corner of the desk that remained untouched by the sunlight. The letters faced him, and the ache in my head dictated I not try to decipher them upside-down.

"The Gospel of Mark."

Ian leaned closer. "Do you only copy the Scriptures here?"

Joseph shook his head. "Since the Rule of Saint Benedict requires that all brothers are to have books, I read for two hours every day."

Ian looked betwixt us.

"Reverend Joseph has converted, Ian—he just hasn't abandoned all his old habits."

Joseph raised his eyebrows. "Better, I suppose, than if you hadn't abandoned yours."

We shared a laugh, but mine ended prematurely. For thinking of the past sent my thoughts to Gwyn. And thinking of Gwyn shortened my patience. "Why did you bring us here?"

"I thought Ian might like to see my work. And I wanted to pull you away from sending yourself back into sickness by overtaxing yourself."

I glared at him. "You had another reason."

He pasted on an innocent look. "Did I?"

Ian folded his arms, clearly bored by the exchange. His interest in Joseph's vocation had fizzled. "If you do have a purpose for bringing us to this room, you had better get on with it before Dirk implodes."

Joseph and Ian grinned at each other; their amusement failed to spread to me.

At last, Joseph let out a breath and leaned to place a hand on either side of his desk. He stared down for a moment at the instruments that occupied his days. I admired the man. He was the singularly most interesting man of the cloth I had ever met. And I wasn't alone in my admiration of him.

Conversations with him had been enough to send both Margried and Gwyn to thinking further about their faith. Margried had come to faith soon after speaking with him. Gwyn had taken longer, but his influence played a part in her taking God personally. I would be forever grateful to him for that.

And he had cared for me when Cade and I had been one step above rogues—and that barely. Never judging, always loving, he had taken us under his capable care as an older brother might. As our own older brothers had been honor-bound not to do; where they could never be seen consorting with us, lest that be misconstrued as their giving their consent to our reckless behavior, Joseph had stepped in and saved us from ourselves too many times to count.

"I brought you here..." Joseph's pause stretched overlong. When he looked up, sincerity shone in his eyes. "Because I am worried about the both of you. This is the place where I go to divest of my worries; I brought you here so you could divest of yours."

Ian looked at me, and I stared back. He remained silent, so I asked the question on both of our minds. "This is the place where you let go of what worries you?"

Joseph blinked back at me.

Ian touched the desk, his finger alighting on the side that hosted the sunshine. "Not the chapel?"

After a moment of silence, Joseph nodded. "So…which one of you wants to go first?"

I raised a brow. Oftentimes Joseph possessed wisdom that simultaneously put my spirit at rest and made my head hurt. This was not one of those times. Neither Ian nor I were ready to let go of what haunted us; neither Ian nor I understood fully what haunted us.

Facing one's demons is only possible after feeling their breath on one's back. I had not yet slowed down enough to recognize the heated stench. Neither had Ian, apparently, for we both turned around and left Joseph behind his desk.

I slept late the next morning. Not by intention, but I acknowledged the reality when I rolled from the hard cot to find sunshine on the floor and on my feet. A sigh pulled from my mouth. A short while later—after making use of a cloth and the basin of water in the corner, as well as raking a hand through my hair—I strode out into the corridor to find chaos.

Ian collided with me, pulled back, and failed to apologize. "We must go. Now."

Not used to taking orders from the younger man, I narrowed my eyes. "What is happening?"

"Men are here."

I let my head roll back, feeling the tension radiating through my shoulders before the last word had fully left Ian's lips. I followed him back into the monk's cell. "When?"

"Just now. Not a minute ago. Reverend Joseph, in the garden, heard them riding up."

That surprised me. They had been heard approaching. So they were traveling loudly—which meant one of two things. They were either in a hurry and being sloppy. Or they were cocky and did not mind making an entrance. Mayhap both.

Either way, 'twas enough.

Ian tossed his things into a satchel.

"Did you get a glimpse of any of them?" I mimicked his actions, gathering what little I had brought with me from my mother's house. And the pouch Gwyn had pressed into my hand.

He shook his head. "Just heard they were on their way and ran."

Ran. The word echoed in my mind like the swing of a sword just before it slices skin. I rubbed the scar beside my right eyebrow.

Joseph appeared in the doorway of the cell; his eyes said it all. Others were here, others we could not trust, whatever their business with him and St. Benet's.

Joseph I could trust. I knew he never told that I had been here or where I was going. Of course, the latter I made easy for him—I never told him where I was going. I hardly ever even knew myself. Now I nodded at him. "I thank you, old friend. As always."

Ian, bag in hand, mumbled an echo and looked at me.

And we were off.

Gwyneth

Chapter Twenty-Two

Anders left the next day.

After reading his note, in which he promised to return but said naught else, I tore up the paper, hoping he meant his words. If he did not come back, what would I do? How would I help Dirk?

When I thought of a way, I went to Rohesia and explained. I could not expel the stable boy at Barrington Manor from my mind. When I mentioned Dirk had told me of Alfie, she ordered two men, including Thomas, to accompany me there. Cade insisted on going. Margried kissed him goodbye early the next morn, before the sun even rose.

I embraced her. "We will be back by nightfall." Or so I hoped. Foolhardy: that was what this was—leaving the place where I felt safest for the one where I felt the most grief.

When we arrived hours later, Gerald met me at the gate, a smile on his face. "What brings you home, milady?"

"The quickest of visits. I came to speak with young Alfie, the stable boy." Although I would do more than merely speak to him if he would let me.

A light in Gerald's eye sparked my interest. I dismounted with Cade's help then moved so that Gerald and I possessed a measure of privacy. "What has put such joy on your face?"

The man's face reddened, and I knew before he even said, "Joan has accepted my suit."

"That is wonderful news." Indeed it was. But their apparent happiness somehow sharpened my own pain.

It only occurred to me after he left for the stables how sudden all this was. Alfie's name had rolled around in the back of my brain since Dirk had mentioned him to me, but the pressing need to see him only arose half a day before. The swift adventure felt more akin to Dirk's impulsiveness than my own—and made me miss him all the more.

From the shadows of the stables, Gerald and Alfie emerged. Alfie's head hung down as if fearful of what this summons meant. I motioned for Cade and the two riders Rohesia had sent with us to remain behind while I stepped forward to greet him.

"Alfie," I said softly.

He glanced over at Gerald, who gave him an encouraging nod. Then he bowed and looked up at me. "Milady."

I smiled. His hair needed cutting, his face, washing. He stuck his hands in his pockets, but I imagined they sported callouses from the work he did morning till night. Surrounded by servants such as he as I had been all my life, what drew me to this boy in particular? Something invisible but strong. Mayhap it was the fact that Dirk had spoken with him. Mayhap it was the Spirit of God reaching out to another.

"Alfie, you know who I am, but I do not know who you are."

His face creased in puzzlement. A couple years older than Titus, a sense of weariness hung around his shoulders. Whereas Tudder's boy had leapt into my arms, this one hesitated to even speak. "What do you want to know, miss?"

"I am not sure. Where is your family?"

"Died in the plague." Said so matter-of-factly, the words failed to stun me. Still, deep sorrow penetrated. He knew the very sorrow I had endured.

"I am very sorry to hear that, Alfie."

One shoulder lifted. He became braver, lifting his gaze to take in Cade and the others behind me. "What else do you want to know?"

I took a deep breath. "I want to ask you a question that may sound silly."

His gaze leveled with mine, and I wondered again why I was doing this, what compelled me. All I was certain of was that this was right, ridiculous as it was. I could only hope he thought the same.

"This place is no longer my home, Alfie. I will never live here again. I will most likely never return. Everyone will most likely need to move on once the Queen takes possession. I will not be taking even my lady's maid with me." I glanced at Gerald and smiled at his look of relief. "But I was wondering if you wanted to accompany me to my home for the time being—Godfrey Manor."

I might have said more except he interrupted me with, "Is there a stable?"

"Yes, Alfie." At my answer—at the news that something with which he was familiar would be present in this foreign place I invited him to—he smiled.

I bade my childhood home farewell again, tearless, and we rode through the night to return to Godfrey Estate with Alfie. When I dismounted, Margried pulled me aside and whispered in my ear, "He is back."

For one agonizing moment, I thought she meant Dirk.

"Are you quite sure about enlisting his help?" Margried pressed—unusual for her.

Calming my heartbeat, I studied her face. Concern stole the smile that had lit her face when Cade had pulled into the moonlit courtyard moments before. "What burdens your mind?"

"Only that he seems…unsteady."

"Anders?" I nearly scoffed at her. "A raging storm could not move him."

"But might you want him to move?" She shrugged her shoulders and turned from me to walk with Cade into the manor house.

Following them, I thought on her words. Confidence that Anders would help me, out of loyalty, if nothing else, eventually won out.

When I entered the inner keep, Anders stood at the foot of the stairs. Almost as if he had never left. My eyes widened when I saw him there, but I was swiftly learning to hide the looks that had always gotten me into such trouble with Dirk.

"Surprised to see me?" He leaned close to whisper the question in my ear.

I looked away on pretense of examining a dark corner of the castle. "I send for you; you come." The tease was intended to get a rise out of him. It failed. I sighed. "Anders, when are you going to commit to helping me?"

"Milady." He only called me milady whilst he was angry with me. Although angry was not the right word with Anders. *Irritated* fit better. "I *am* helping you. I have just returned from the Earl of Cushborough's."

I gasped and took hold of his sleeve. "You did? And?" I scarce could take it in; the man had said naught about his destination in the brief note he had left for me. Now, realizing that he had gone to speak to a nobleman on Dirk's behalf—and waiting in suspense until Anders told me the outcome of the meeting—I had to remind myself to breathe.

Anders looked down, paused a moment, then looked up at me again with sorrow and something akin to determination in his eyes. "He is not favorable to your cause, I'm afraid."

My heart sank into my stomach, but I steeled my spine. Mayhap Anders' pleas on Dirk's behalf had proven insufficient, but I could add my voice to the cause and write to the earl myself. Deciding not to confide this to Anders lest I hurt his pride, I patted his sleeve. "That you lobby on Dirk's behalf means much to me. We will not give up until we see him absolved of my accusation."

That I now had Anders on my side buoyed my hope. And sometimes, I had learned, hope was all I needed.

"Gwyneth, your mind has wandered, dear." Rohesia smiled at me from her seat across from mine.

I took a deep breath and settled back into the cushioned seat I had been occupying for close to an hour, my eyes roving over the empty boudoir. The muscles in my back seemed inclined to protest to such a long time with no movement, but I had hardly noticed the passage of time. Well, until a moment ago, when my mind had wandered to Anders and the nobleman he would visit this morning on Dirk's behalf. I would write another letter, similar to the one I had written to the Earl of Cushborough.

"I beg your pardon, Lady Godfrey. Do forgive me. What were you saying?"

She pointed again to the passage of Scripture we had been studying. "We were discussing patience being one of the fruits of the Spirit."

I allowed my gaze to rove over the page we had come to this morning. Patience indeed occupied a place in Paul's list. "But if every believer is to be faithful—another of the Spirit's fruits—in the good deeds the Lord has given him to do, how is he to be patient, as well? How can one wait while one works?"

Rohesia's hand eased over the holy words. The Godfrey family possessed a Tyndale Bible. I had hesitated when Rohesia had called me to her boudoir—the day I had first told Anders of my plan—and offered to allow me to read it. Sister Agnes had left the room when she heard, her disapproval all too clear. But I was drawn by Rohesia's generous offer to counsel me in knowledge of it.

I had tried to dance around the discomfort I felt at her offer—I wished to be polite, to keep from rejecting her outright. Then she had said Dirk had confided in her about my coming to God.

"What did he say?" I had asked, breathless.

"He said you have known tragedy and that you have thrown yourself into the arms of God for healing and hope."

When the tears had filled my eyes, I had said yes. Now I lived for these hours where we talked of God.

Rohesia twisted her mouth to one side and looked at the ceiling. "I believe you are confusing patience with idleness."

My brows drew together. "Patience, I thought, meant waiting for something." In a whisper, I continued, "Something Anders does well."

Rohesia raised a brow. "He does patience well, you say?"

"He waited to tell me he supports my…" I let my voice drift off, unwilling to confide in Rohesia just yet about my plan to absolve her son. But something in her voice made me ask, "You disagree?"

A wry smile lifted a corner of her mouth. "Patience does not necessarily mean sitting idly by, vacillating over a decision."

My jaw dropped at how serious she seemed. Twice now a trusted friend had come to me with doubts about Anders: first, Margried, and now Rohesia. Surely they were wrong. I had known him longer than they. And now he was on my side.

Her nod tossed free one auburn curl at the nape of her neck. "Patience can mean remaining still while God works. It can also mean realizing that what one wants now is inferior to what one will receive if one waits."

I reread the passage. Rohesia waited. *Patiently.* I had come to learn about how the life of a believer was to be lived just as much from her example as from the hours we spent studying the pages the Godfreys treasured as a sacred gift. Letting my tongue recite the words in silence to myself now, I agreed with them. 'Twas a sacred gift, indeed.

"Is that what Paul means when he mentions 'crucifying the flesh with its passions and desires' here? That a believer is to recognize the value of waiting for…" I collected my words. How ironic that the instruction I received from *Moeder* in how to conduct polite, but intelligent, conversation could fail to stand up to the heavy thoughts piling up in my mind now.

How badly I wanted to discuss with Dirk all I was coming to learn.

"The value of waiting for…?" Rohesia smiled in encouragement.

"…for what is better instead of seizing what is good as soon as is possible?"

Gwyneth

Rohesia's gaze reflected joy. "And more than that, each believer is to be patient, even unto receiving what seems to be far from better."

What I thought I had at last understood fled from me again. "I am sorry. I am confused."

Rohesia laughed. "Let me tell you a story."

I settled in to the horsehair couch, leaning back against the forest-green covering. Rohesia did love telling stories. Almost as much as Anders did. I bit my lip lest it curl in frustration at the thought of his name.

"When I first met my husband, Harold, his sister disliked me."

I could not imagine anyone not immediately adoring Rohesia. She was…like Margried. Instantly relatable. Even in her dark gowns that bespoke of her widowhood, she exuded warmth and light.

"I knew not why she disliked me so, but she went out of her way to ensure I knew of her distaste. I tried everything. I avoided her. I went out of my way to show kindness to her. I bought her gifts. I ignored her. At last, I did what I should have done from the beginning."

I waited.

"I talked to Harold about it." One corner of Rohesia's mouth rose. She no longer looked at me. Instead, she stared past my shoulder, as if she could see her late husband, hear what he said to her all those years ago. "And do you know what he said?" Her smile grew. "He told me to wait. He told me Marian was jealous because I was to become a bride before she was—she was older than he, you know."

I nodded as if this knowledge was not new to me.

"Two years later, after I bore our son and her distaste for me had seemed to grow—I assume because not only was I married before she was, but I was also a mother first—she married a wonderful and wealthy nobleman. After that, we could tolerate one another with a degree of kindness. We have never been friends, but the tension eased."

"Where is she now?"

Rohesia looked at me once more. "In Bristol. With her husband, three sons, and four grandchildren. We get along better than ever now." She leaned forward as if about to tell me a secret. "I believe she is happy she has more sons than I do and became a grandmother first."

I shook my head, amused at Rohesia's flippant but gracious assessment of a woman who had caused her pain.

A flash of sorrow crossed the woman's face. "I suppose I crossed the threshold of widowhood sooner than she. I pray she does not envy me that."

Intent on veering her from her sorrow, I sat forward and touched her arm. "Patience, Lady Godfrey?"

"Oh!" The sorrow disappeared. Or, rather, it faded to the background. "Marian caused me discomfort in those early years after I joined the Godfrey family. I thought the only thing that could possibly redeem the suffering was if God performed a miracle in her heart, changed her, and we became friends. I prayed daily that such a change might occur."

Rohesia clasped her hands in her lap. "That never happened. Only years later, when I finally accepted that we would never be as close as sisters, did I realize that God had answered my prayer in a way I never expected." She lifted her hands to reach out for mine. "He made my heart far more compassionate and kinder than it would have been had I not had to suffer what I did. Instead of changing her, He changed me."

I looked down, studying the pattern in the rug that covered the stone floor of the library in which we sat. My fingers played with the green covering of the couch. "You thought you were waiting for the better thing… but the Lord gave you something different?"

"Nay, Gwyneth."

Our eyes met.

"I was waiting for what *I* thought was the better thing. And God gave me what was truly best."

I closed my chamber door behind me, holding a letter in my hand. Anders had returned with another unfavorable response. This nobleman, too, had not believed in Dirk's innocence. I had adjusted my letter accordingly and planned to post it without his knowledge. When I looked down, a small note caught my eye.

After I read the contents, I smiled. Anders was gone again. Breathing a quick prayer for his safety and success, I found a manservant to post the letter for me. Then I turned my footsteps toward the stables, intent to see how Alfie was settling in. Margried entered the hall and paused, a broad smile on her face.

"What has you so happy?"

Her smile became a grin. "Cade is taking me on a ride." She blushed and looked down. "I am glad I found you. I wanted to tell you where we would be."

Sweet Margried. She wished me to hear from her own lips where they had gone lest I worry I had been abandoned again. I pasted on a smile. "Have a lovely time."

Her smile dropped, and she looked at me with her heart in her eyes. I saw in that moment how much she loved that man—and I hoped he knew how blessed he was. To have her—'twas a treasure. Though we had not been friends all our lives, I felt as if we had. And it was new—this aching inside of me. For even in just a thousand little ways, I was losing her to him.

When I needed her most.

"Gwyneth. Have you been weeping?" Her whisper slipped past the defenses around my heart.

I swiped under my eyes. "*Nee*. I am merely tired."

She studied me once more and shook her head. "You *have* been weeping." Her voice hardened. "You have been weeping over him, have you not?"

I took a shaky breath. I had been. Ever since I finished this second letter. Ever since Millicent snubbed me this morning, walking past without a glance at me after I called her name. *Foolish girl.* I should never have spoken. I meant only to wish her good morrow, but the blank face had sent rage running through me with the force of a summer gale. How dare she? How dare she walk around this place and live when it was his absence that made it possible? He left to save us. And she did not have the decency to grieve with me.

Then Susan had mentioned him in the Great Hall when we broke our fast and I had barely made it through until the end of the meal. At my first opportunity, I walked sedately from the room only to collapse in this borrowed bedchamber, my sanctuary, to give the pain in my heart some release. Only none had come. After all those tears, none had come.

"Have a good time with Cade, Margried."

She refused to receive my dismissal. Her black brows came together. "Why could he not have just stayed? Or taken you with him as you asked him to?"

Sometimes I wondered if I should have confided to Margried the details of my going after Dirk. I had not told her I had kissed him or that I had begged. But she knew that I had asked, and I was glad I had not told her all, for she was embittered enough over him turning me down.

"He is doing what he does best, what he promised me he would always do." *Protect me.* Although, in the process, he was breaking the other promise he had made me. That he would never abandon me.

Margried blew out a sigh. "Protecting you, he claims. But what good is protection if he can never see you again, or you him?"

I swallowed. Indeed. "He thinks this is best…"

She folded her arms and muttered to herself about Dirk's lack of sense, wisdom, or courage.

At that last one, I intervened. "Margried, please."

One look at my face, and she ceased. "I am sorry, Gwyneth." Coming close, she embraced me. Her head rose just above my shoulder. I let myself rest there for a moment, but there was really only one embrace I wanted.

And he wasn't there to give it.

I pulled away. "Go with your man. Pay close attention. I want to hear all about it when you return."

A smile lit her eyes even as sorrow remained there. "I could stay, if you need me."

Her compassion overwhelmed me. "I will be well." I glanced out the window. "This may be the last day you have to enjoy only mildly cold weather. Go. Love him." Those last two words escaped without my consent.

Margried looked at me and said nothing, but I heard. Oh, I heard. She hated this—this being in love while I had lost mine. She slipped away, reluctance in her movements. I loved her for that.

Margried would ride through the countryside this day, not caring that the view was drab and brown this time of year. Winter's cold clutches had taken possession of England, and the result was the loss of the beauty of summer. It echoed the loss of the love Dirk and I shared.

Margried would sit by the riverside, in the open meadow, or on a rock overlooking whatever view Cade chose for her. They would talk and laugh and share a long kiss. Then they would return home just before dusk captured the land.

No longer up to my visit with Alfie, I returned to my chamber and moved to the window, watching Cade and Margried ride away together, longing for that to which I had bid farewell forever.

For a brief time I allowed myself to imagine. Imagine what it might have been like if I had never done to Dirk what was proving so very hard to reverse. Imagine the life we could have lived here if he had been a free man, an honorable man whom all others knew to be honorable. Mayhap he would have planned an outing such as this for me.

He would come to fetch me from my bedchamber or the library where I studied Scripture with his mother. I would have no idea what he had planned. He would tell me naught but that I was to follow him. My hand in his, he would lead me to the stables, where Char would be waiting.

And we would run. Together. Free. We would give the horses their heads and run to the very edges of his family's land, our laughter the only sound for miles. We would arrive at wherever we wished to stop, eat, talk, laugh, and hold each other.

A sob tore from my throat. Soon. If Anders and I proved successful—and we had to—then soon those dreams could become reality.

And that was when the idea came.

Dirk

Chapter Twenty-Three

We arrived at the docks in early morning on our borrowed horses. I thanked God we had been able to procure our mounts from the monastery's stables. Having horses made the journey much swifter. Still, several days had passed with naught but riding and thinking. Mostly about Gwyn. And the men who had come to St. Benet's. Mayhap they had brought Joseph news, supplies, or merely sought to visit—old friends. Whatever their business, it would have been too great a risk to stay and see.

As Ian and I galloped over the English country, charting a course to the coast as winding and twisted as possible, I prayed hard that the slab of stone in my chest would soften. Not so that I would care again. But so that hardness would not lead to harshness that would lure me back into the wild ways that had consumed years of my life.

We avoided the known roads as much as possible and rode mostly at night, sleeping when the sun rose and rising when the moon took its place. We stayed in no place longer than a day and made our presence known only when we needed bread or other supplies. And Ian did all the talking when we needed to barter for those things—I spent none of the silver my mother and Gwyn had given me. I hung back, not wishing to be recognized.

Because of the path we chose, it took us much longer to reach England's edge than it should have. Neither Ian nor I cared. We were two men running from the law, with no purpose in mind except to seek out an old friend and keep ourselves from being caught and captured. For that would spell certain death for me and almost as certain death for Ian. A murderer and his companion too often acquired the same swift sentence.

After less than a fortnight had passed, I gave up trying to convince Ian to turn back. He didn't even respond anymore; he had stopped refusing and settled for just looking at me, watching me with much the same haunted look I knew resided in my own gaze.

That was what I failed to understand—his own sorrow, his own shame, the expression that seemed to say he was no young pup, that he had seen as much as I had and more. But I did not try to chip away at the mystery. Night after night as we rose to ride farther east and, morn after morn, as we bedded down in a hollow or cave or thick copse of trees, silence reigned more and more.

The chill from the water collided with the wintery wind, as brisk as it was blustery. November would soon arrive in all of its cruel, heartless glory—I tucked my curled fists close to my face and breathed into them at the mere thought. Then I held close that prejudiced view of November, for it meant I still cared about something.

Joseph warned me to take care of myself, claimed my body had been spent by the travail of the last few months. That was why I had collapsed when, at last, I had deemed myself to be in a safe place. I knew he was right, but at the same time I could think of little else but arriving at the coast and leaving her behind for good.

"Do you think he will be here?" Ian's voice sounded rusty in the eerie silence of the morn. From the cold or from disuse?

"Tudder?" My voice grated, too. I needed to see Tudder. I was in a bad way. I knew it. And I also knew that if I did not speak with the friend who had nearly pulled me back from the chasm once…I would cease to care. And if I ceased to care, I might as well turn myself in. For nothing would mean anything anymore. I could not allow that to happen. Though I could do nothing else for her—could never even see her ever again—I must do that for Gwyn. Live honorably.

I almost laughed at the irony. That woman inspired me—*me*—to live honorably.

"What if Tudder is not here?" Ian asked.

I did not answer. The sudden thought that my captain friend might not be here had not occurred to me until now, which shamed me. Only losing Gwyn could do this to me—disarm me in such a way.

We stabled the horses some distance away and took the usual route through the crustier side of the docks. The smell of saltwater mixed with the strong stench of spirits as we cut behind the tavern.

A man ducked out of the back door, releasing bawdy music and rowdy laughter. The pewter tankard in his left hand tipped, spilling, when he wobbled once. He sneered at us and took a sip. I put one hand at my hip, over the knife hidden there. Ian's fingers twitched toward his blade as well.

The man's expression shifted from one of amused arrogance to disgust. He promptly leaned over and vomited. Then he collapsed back onto the tavern's threshold. I stepped over his body, noting the steady breathing and the slump of his shoulders against the closed door. He would have a horrible ache in his neck by nightfall, but he would live.

By the time ships materialized through the fog, I had realized the inevitable chance we were taking. Tudder might not even be here. He could be in the Low Countries or off the coast of Spain, hunting galleons heavy laden with gold and New World treasures. He could have left yesterday; we might have just missed him.

I dragged a hand down my face and thought of the coins my mother gave me. We could rent a room in the tavern for a night, purchase passage across the Channel, lie low in France for a while…

"Dirk. I have been expecting you."

At the sound of the Dutch accent, Ian and I spun around. The sight of my old friend sent peace cascading through every corner of my soul. All save that one corner marked off for Gwyn.

"Tudder." I reached out; he returned the gesture. We clasped arms.

"Took you longer than I thought."

I narrowed my eyes, watching his face as he and Ian greeted each other. "How did you know I was on my way?"

"You saw her to safety. Now you are running again." Tudder's eyes narrowed. "Are you well?"

I will never see Gwyneth again. Of course I am not well. "Weary. That is all." The lie came too easily.

He did not seem convinced. Well, that made two of us. "Come." He motioned for us to follow. "The *Rijke Ziel* awaits."

Tudder led us through back alleys past other dens of questionable repute where the fog seemed especially thick. I thanked God for the shady shelter wafting from the Channel this time of year; it proved more than adequate cover. Which reminded me… "How did you know we would be here?"

Tudder turned around and grinned at me. "You were studying the ships, trying to see which one was mine, just as you always do."

That was all he would say. Well, he was almost right. No need to tell him I had not been looking for his vessel—I had been too busy planning what to do if it weren't there.

One of Tudder's men rowed us out to the *Rich Soul*. Though I doubted the man knew English, I kept a still tongue in my head. Naught but the chop of the water and creak of wooden hulls serenaded our brief trip. Tudder climbed the ladder first and was soon out of sight, causing the hemp rope to snap back against the dark belly of the ship. Ian held back a moment. "How do you think he knew we were on our way here?"

I grasped a rung in my hand. "I intend to ask him that very question again before the day is old." Boot after boot, I climbed, mulling over that very mystery.

As soon as we had boarded, Tudder beckoned us below. The hazy dimness of the lower decks made me squint, and I thought of Gwyn. Did she wear her glasses faithfully, and had my loosening the arms eased her headaches? Or did she now know Godfrey Estate well enough to go without them?

I drew in a deep breath at the longing that punched me.

In the captain's cabin at last, I glanced around. Tudder's astrolabe and other maritime instruments sat on his desk in disarray, bringing to mind a flicker of the image of Joseph's desk. The blankets on his bunk looked tousled. The porthole appeared smudged with fingerprints.

I looked at Tudder anew, my eyes seeing him with a fresh sort of sight— the sight of souls bound by the same inexplicable loss.

For the cabin looked in need of a woman's touch. I knew Mary had gone on a few voyages with him—the ones he deemed safe, anyway— before Titus had been born. This space spoke of her presence—and now her absence.

Tudder knew my sense of loss.

If he saw the look on my face, he ignored it in the determined way he strode to the desk and opened a drawer. He did not need to rummage around; he found what he was looking for straightaway. He turned back to face me, a stony look on his face, holding the paper aloft.

"This is how I knew you would be coming. What took you so long?"

I raised a brow, noting the fact that he had not laid what looked to be a letter in my hand just yet. "We were detained."

"St. Benet's?" Tudder knew Cade and I sought sanctuary there when we had no place else to go.

"Aye." Ian answered before I could. "Dirk took ill."

I sent him a swift glare before latching eyes on Tudder again. "May I see it?"

"So that is why you look horse-whipped."

I stepped forward and snatched the letter from his hand. As soon as I held it, however, I gentled my hold. The paper...it was expensive. I flipped it over fast and recognized the writing. My mother's. I lifted it to Tudder's eye-level. "When did this arrive?"

He crossed his arms over his chest. "Twelve days ago."

My eyes shut. We had left St. Benet's a fortnight ago. If we had not tarried so long to twist our trail…

"And I have been waiting for your arrival ever since."

I jerked. "You read it?"

Tudder pivoted, reopened the drawer from which he had pulled the letter in my hand, and fetched another piece of paper, identical to mine. "I read this one."

I reached for that, too.

He let me snatch it. "That one is addressed to me, so yes, I read it. The one in your hand was enclosed and is yours. It is still sealed, brother."

I scanned my mother's words to Tudder.

> *Lady Rohesia Godfrey, by the grace of God to Captain Mathieu Tudder of the merchant vessel* Rich Soul, *presumed Hemsby, her most kind greeting.*
>
> *I pray you are well, nephew. I have prayed for you since learning of your recent tragedy. I beseech thee, if the whereabouts of your brother are known to you, request that he reply to my letter.*
> *Yours, Rohesia Godfrey*

I looked up at Tudder, a small smile on my face.

He nodded. "Your mother is sly."

"She is that. Calling you her nephew." I shook my head.

"And you my brother."

"How is that sly?" I gave Tudder an innocent look and handed the missive to Ian, whose curious look was amusing.

Tudder laughed.

What we left unspoken? His *tragedy*. Mary, his wife, deceased these past five years.

I fingered the other letter, sliding my fingers over the name on the outside. *Devon.* No last name. No nickname. Only the Christian name she and my father had christened me with at my birth. So like her to succumb to subterfuge when penning a letter to Tudder—a letter that had little chance of falling into the hands of Tudder's enemies. Though the Lord knew Tudder had made many enemies, captain of a Sea Beggar ship as he was. He and his fellow captains championed the Protestant Dutch cause of independence against Catholic Spain.

So like my mother to do away with subterfuge when it came to a slip of paper addressed to her only son. My throat caught at the *only*. If Harold had lived, mayhap he and Gwyn would have gotten along well together.

I did violence to that thought before it could go further.

Tudder clapped a heavy hand on my shoulder. "I will leave you to it, then." He and Ian left the cabin.

Though I had not tried to hint that I wanted to read the letter alone, I realized now that I did. Sinking down onto Tudder's bunk, I wondered absently if Titus slept in here with his father or in the crew's quarters with the others.

I unfolded the letter, shoving aside the pang that shouted no letter from Gwyn accompanied my mother's. But of course she would not write. She probably wanted no more to do with me, the man who had hurt her in so many ways.

My mother had probably never even mentioned she was writing.

> *Dearest Devon,*
>   *I pray this missive finds you well. You have returned to one or both of your brothers, I assume.*

My brothers. She did not mean Harold, but Tudder and Joseph. Wisely, she omitted their names. Aye, my mother was sly.

> *I should hope very much that you chose to visit both. You need friends now.*

My fingers tightened around the letter as my other hand rose to my chin. I rubbed my jaw and glanced at the ceiling, then read on.

> *You also need rest. If you have not yet fallen ill, my son, do take care of yourself. When you left, it was clear to me that you had driven yourself to exhaustion in order to rescue the poor girl. Do not drive yourself too hard.*

I smiled. She knew me far better than I knew myself. Hungry for news of Gwyn, my sisters, and even Cade and Margried, I turned my attention back to my mother's curved handwriting.

> *I know your next question will be for her. The dear girl is*
> *strong, but she suffers, Devon. I know if she were writing this*
> *now, she would tell you otherwise. I, however, tell you true. She*
> *needs you. She misses you. Her love for you is no small thing.*
> *She cries. She tries to hide it, but she weakens in her grief.*
> *Do you remember what I told you of a woman's heart?*
> *Hear me now when I ask you to return to us. Your mother is*
> *resigned to losing you forever. But Gwyneth is not, nor will she*
> *ever be, I fear. Come back. Leave again if you must, but take*
> *her with you this time.*

My hands shook. Gwyn. Weeping. Weakening. I tossed the letter to the
bed and lunged for the porthole, looking out over the scant view. I could
hear the rush of the waves and see sunlight vainly trying to pour through
the fog, but my eyes could detect naught through the haze.

My mother was a sly woman, but sometimes she failed to understand.
Could she not see? I could not give what she asked of me. I dared not.
Pressing my hand to my eyes a moment, I gathered my strength to finish
reading her words. I sat once more and retrieved the letter.

> *And, Devon, a visitor has come from Lansberry.*

I shot to my feet and pulled the letter closer to my eyes. Lansberry?
That meant…

> *He seems a kind man, but do you recall your sister's*
> *reservations about your beloved? Those, I am quite sure, are*
> *unfounded. Do not grow angry with me for bringing them*
> *up—Millicent's heart is good. I mention them for this reason:*
> *I hold the same reservations about him.*

Him.

> *Mayhap I am merely becoming suspicious in my old age. Do*
> *not frown at me; I am becoming old. Even so, something about*
> *Lansberry does not set right with me.*
> *That is all the news I have, I am afraid. Do send me news*

of you. Take care of yourself. And come home.
Your mother

How like my mother to sign her name without leaving her name at all. That was not slyness on her part, I knew. Rather, she would not sign any other way. Why leave her title or even her name, she would ask? All that was important was that she was my mother, I was her son, and the letter was ended.

But what a letter it was.

I squeezed my eyes shut for a moment, but the words surfaced in my mind, bolder, blacker, stronger in my memory's vision than in reality.

Gwyn weakened.

And Lansberry had gone to her. Anders Revelin. I remembered him well. He had not had cause to visit Godfrey Estate often when we were young. In fact, I could not recall the last time I had met the man. But I knew him, and his reputation preceded him. Or rather, a second form of it. His reputation appeared pristine to the upper crust of England's nobles. It crumbled below the surface, however.

Yet I only knew that because mine had sunk until no veneer at all remained. Revelin was nowhere near the rogue I had once been, that was true. Nonetheless, he was capable of deception. Which made him very dangerous, indeed.

I refrained from throwing a fist through the porthole.

He was with Gwyn. And there was naught that I could do about it, save trust in Cade and God to protect her.

Gwyneth

Chapter Twenty-Four

I told no one save Thomas where I was really going. I asked Rohesia if I might go into the marketplace, if she minded if I take Thomas with me. She looked at me, and my red traveling gown, with suspicion. But the dear woman did not inquire. I knew she would disapprove of my true destination. I did not even tell Thomas where we were going until halfway there. He seemed surprised to discover we were going to the magistrate's office but confirmed my suspicion that the office was not far from the marketplace.

So I had not *truly* lied to Rohesia.

The marketplace reminded me somewhat of the Dutch one we had traveled through on the way to Tudder's ship. Merchants hawking their wares perked up at the sight of me riding in on Char with Thomas on his own mount in front of me. Though forced to adopt a slower pace to traverse safely through the crowd, we finally made it to the magistrate's.

Thomas helped me dismount, and I brushed dust from my skirt. Head held high, I entered the door he held open for me.

This was my chance. If my words had once before destroyed Dirk's reputation, my words now might reverse the entire situation. I swallowed my eagerness; could it really be this easy? I was the sole witness. Surely my testimony was the only thing holding my parents' murders over Dirk's head—and the only thing needed to reverse his alleged guilt.

When I entered, a young man looked up from a pile of papers and blinked twice before rising from his crude wooden desk.

"I must speak with the magistrate." I used the tone *Moeder* taught me to employ in the direst of circumstances. When the man scurried down the hall, I could have laughed. If I could intimidate him with a simple request to see his employer, surely I could convince the magistrate of the

136

truth.

The man returned and led me down a long corridor, at the end of which he lifted the latch on a door and allowed me to enter. Thomas remained behind.

"Good morrow, Lady Gwyneth." The magistrate rose to receive me, then swept a hand to the horsehair couch across from a dusty bookshelf. "With what matter can I assist you today?"

I lowered myself to the couch and waited while he arranged his overlong coat in the seat he chose nearest me. A slender man, he possessed a hawkish nose and close-set eyes. He appeared less intimidated than his associate, more curious about my requesting an audience with him. For a moment, the fact that he might be nonplussed by my title disappointed me; but intelligence might also prove to be in my favor.

If he were shrewd, he would see the absurdity of continuing to hold Dirk accountable for a crime he had not committed.

"I have come to set straight the matter of my parents' murders."

The man nodded solemnly but did not blink.

"I made a mistake."

He blinked. In fact, he fidgeted for a brief second before learning forward in his chair and folding his hands together. "Milady, everyone knows who murdered your parents. You yourself identified the man as Devon Godfrey months ago."

"I have since learned of my mistake. Devon Godfrey is not the murderer; my uncle was."

His brow rose. "Your uncle *was*?"

I swallowed the musty air in the room; I had not intended to announce my uncle's death so soon in the conversation but saw no other recourse than to tell the truth. So I did. All of it. How I had been wrong the night of the murder. How my uncle had later confessed all to me. How Dirk was innocent.

The magistrate waited patiently, brow furrowing deeper, frown lowering further as I went on. I prayed silently as I spoke, and, when at last I had come to the end of my tale, I waited for his response.

"But how do you *know* all this, milady?" he asked.

"My uncle said he did it and told me why. He wanted to marry me off, but he knew my parents would never allow it." I fingered the pearls at the bodice of my gown, trying to appear nonchalant. In truth, my heart pounded, the weight of this moment settling in. This man had the power to set in motion Dirk's absolution. It would be a long hard fight to set all right in the eyes of England, but if Dirk could come and go in freedom… we could be together.

The magistrate shook his head. "Daughters are married all the time. And what do you mean your uncle *was*? Where is your uncle, the alleged murderer, now?"

I swallowed my frustration and acknowledged he would not let this go until I gave him the admittance he sought. "My uncle is dead."

He sat back in his chair. Waited a moment before he spoke. "By whose hand?"

"The gatekeeper's." My gaze found the small window in the opposite corner of the room. The only view the portal provided was of the branches of trees arcing from the mouth of the forest at the back of the building.

But the magistrate seemed to recognize my reluctance to say more. "Why did your uncle die?"

"Because Dirk came back for me, to rescue me from the marriage my uncle had arranged for me."

Realization lit in his close-set eyes. "He came back for you? Why would he do that?"

Pulling in a breath, I knew the time had come. That this man might guess that my motivation for absolving Dirk of a crime I had said he committed was bound by more than integrity. I searched for words that would tell the truth without giving away my love for him. I needed to say something impartial yet convincing.

The clap of the latch on the door afforded me precious few seconds to decide. The young man who had led me back here poked his head in, and the magistrate waved him in. Silent, the man approached with a letter in his hand, which he then passed on to the magistrate. I considered what to say next and simultaneously watched the magistrate unfold and read the missive. "From Talan?" he asked the young man.

At his man's nod, the magistrate folded the letter and motioned for the other man to go.

Who was Talan? I knew no nobleman by that name. Whoever he was, he must be important, if the magistrate would accept a letter from him when a noblewoman sat across from him.

The interruption over, the magistrate drew in a breath and fastened his gaze on me. "I have a letter here asserting that Lord Godfrey is indeed a murderer."

Lies! Who was this Talan who sought to sully Dirk's name? I fought the urge to surge to my feet and demand to read the missive. I knew how that would seem, though—suspicious. And the magistrate already seemed suspicious of me. "I can assure you, he is no such thing, despite the lies that have branded him so."

"So you lied that night?" The magistrate returned.

"As good as such. I made a mistake, judging Dirk's posture and possession of the knife as proof of his guilt. In fact, he tried to save my parents' lives. It was my uncle's dagger that killed them." There. With that explanation, I in no way gave away how I felt about Dirk.

"Do you love him?"

Or perhaps I had given away everything.

As I walked down the hallway of the second floor of Godfrey Estate, I let my heart grieve.

The magistrate had believed this mysterious Talan over me. What was worse, he had seen straight through me, to my love for Dirk and his for me. So he had shaken his head, accusing me of lying for Dirk, and had me shown out of his office by the younger associate, no longer intimidated. I forced my mind to Rohesia's words. Was patience my lesson to learn now?

November had dawned. I had not seen him in nearly two months. Two months. Was that not long enough to be patient? It was long enough to form a friendship with the orphaned stable boy. Long enough for Anders to come and go from Godfrey Estate twelve times—and for me to send twelve letters. Long enough for me to begin to see Cade and Margried drifting apart.

I turned the corner of the hall and found myself with a view of the stairway that led to the second floor.

Millicent stood at the top of them, against one wall, not leaning—her posture far too perfect for that. Her gaze remained captured by one of the tapestries on the wall.

A deep breath in my lungs, a corner of my skirt in my palm, I ascended the stairs, watching her. When at last I reached the top, I let my skirt billow to the ground and looked at the design that had caught her eye.

Dark colors swirled in an endless sky. A breathtaking view of night stretched from corner to corner and back again. The pinpoint brightness of stars captured my attention at once. Less noticeable was the gold woven throughout. Only after several moments of staring at it did I realize the flecks of gold collided, if one looked long enough, to form the outline of a beautiful bird. The bird, somehow both serene and strong at the same time, had its wings outstretched and its head tilted back, chest bare. Open. Vulnerable.

I decided to allow that bird to inspire me. "It is beautiful," I whispered, loud enough so Millicent could hear. She did not answer. Turning to her, I asked, "Would you tell me about it?"

She glanced at me. "Why do you wish to know?"

"Because beauty like this deserves to be known." A blush approached, for how poetic and overly romantic had that sounded?

She blinked, unmoved.

Annoyed, I swiveled on my heel and stared at the tapestry again. Though what right did she have to remain silent? I was a guest in her home, nothing more. Not anymore. At one time, true, I had been her brother's betrothed. But that time was long gone. As was he.

Another crack in my heart chose that moment to split wide open.

"You are the reason he left." Her cold, clear words cut deep into that very crack.

I turned, slow, controlled. "What did you say?"

Her gaze moved from the tapestry to stare back at me. She must have inherited her brown eyes from her father, as Dirk had. Rohesia's gray ones always looked so kind. So, in fact, did Dirk's. But Millicent's eyes revealed pain. And anger. "I said, you are the reason he left. It is your fault he is gone."

A door opened and shut from somewhere behind us. I did not bother to look. I stared, my breathing quickening. "He left because he feared he would be followed."

"And he did not want *you* to be put at risk if it came to that."

"Us. He did not want *us* to be hurt. He left to protect us all."

She put her hand to her stomacher, splaying her fingers over the dark fabric. Like her mother and Susan, Millicent wore the shades of mourning. "We lost Harold not half a year ago. Now we have lost Devon forever, too."

I clenched my teeth. On the other point, she had been wrong. About this, I feared she was all too correct. "I am sorry for your loss."

"And I should reply that I am sorry for yours. But I will not. I am not."

Footsteps below us called my attention, but I ignored them and watched Millicent clasp her hands in front of her. Her fingers failed to shake; her wrists did not so much as flinch. Her movements looked controlled, almost planned.

"I should reply that I am sorry you dislike me," I said. "But I will not."
She blinked as if I had surprised her.

"I am, however, sorry that you blame me." I turned away, finished.

"You went after him." Her words called me back.

I did not so much as turn my head. "I did."

"What did you say to him?"

My pride abandoned me. "I begged him to take me with him."

If she had scoffed, I would not have been surprised. Instead, she remained calm and merely said, "As I thought."

"What would you have had me say?"

"He is my brother and the heir of this estate now. He should be here. You should have begged him to return."

"I would not have been successful." I hid my wince. I had not been successful, regardless.

"Because he is so intent on protecting you." A note of ire invaded her voice despite her best efforts.

"Us." I turned only my neck so I could look straight at her. "Because he is so intent on protecting *us*. And Millicent?"

She made no reply.

"I miss Dirk, too."

Her wrathful eyes snapped to mine. "His name is Devon."

I let her have the final word, and what a word it was. His name. I slipped my hand onto the banister and walked down the stairs. Cade waited for me. So he had been the one to enter the keep, his the footsteps I heard. I took his arm and let him lead me away, trying to ignore the fact that my hand shook.

I sat in the library and waited. Dusk had fallen on the day, sending shoots of the sunset through the few windows in the room. When the maid had entered to light the candles, I made my request. As a result, I now waited in semi-darkness. An abundance of books surrounded me, and, unbidden, the memory of my conversation with Joseph arose in my mind. How confused he had made me feel—how infuriated I had been after I learned he was not Catholic.

How confused I still was over so many things. I had not dared to voice my concerns with Rohesia yet, of course. I knew the answers she would give me—Protestant ones. Was I ready to receive them? I thought not.

My hands trembled in my lap. To distract myself from that telling sign, I rose and walked to a bookshelf. I fingered the spine of book after book without truly reading the titles of any. What I did notice was the variety of languages. All of which I could read. *A learned woman,* Joseph had called me. Mayhap, but in what? The tongues of the world and the thoughts of great men?

What good did it do to have figuratively sat at the feet of scholars when I knew little about sitting at the feet of the Lord as Rohesia said Jesus' followers had literally done?

I clenched two books in my hands and let my head fall forward. *Maddening. This is maddening, God. And it feels entirely too heretical to even be praying this honestly.*

But that was the way Rohesia had instructed me to pray. The Lord was interested in honest hearts, she said. *What about confused ones, God? Are you interested in that, in me, broken as I am?*

I knew the answer to that, but still I struggled to believe it. *God, am I Catholic anymore or have I converted? What do I believe?*

The door to the library opened behind me. I swiveled as the shuffle of footsteps announced the entrance of the person I was expecting. Only when I latched eyes with the visitor, disappointment flooded me. 'Twas not the person I had asked the maid to fetch.

Sister Agnes gestured to the bookshelf. "Are you choosing a tome, Lady Gwyneth?"

I flicked a gaze to the books I had pulled slightly free from the rest. "*Nee,* merely…thinking." If I confessed I was praying here, without my rosary, without kneeling in a proper chapel, I could not expect Sister Agnes to respond reasonably.

Sister Agnes stepped forward. Her eyes roamed the high shelves.

I pushed the books I had treated cruelly back into place. "Are you looking for a book?"

Her hand fluttered in front of her habit before resuming its place at her side. I squinted through my glasses, wondering if I truly saw the deepening color in her cheeks or if I imagined it. She shook her head, then hesitated. "I wondered if perhaps the family had a collection of the works of Hildegard of Bingen."

I sucked in a thoughtful breath and turned to the shelves. "Mayhap." Though I would be surprised if they did. For a Protestant family to have the long-dead nun's books of visions and music would be unusual. Still, I studied the spines, intent on finding the woman's words for Sister Agnes if indeed they were here.

She came to stand beside me but a few feet away, her gaze roaming the books to my left.

"You admire Hildegard, do you not?"

Sister Agnes looked askance at me. "Do you?"

"Her music is beautiful." 'Twas Hildegard's songs I had heard Sister Agnes humming when I told her Margried had come to God in the garden at St. Benet's.

Several moments passed. I assumed she did not wish to speak and had thrown my full attention into finding a book of Hildegard's works when Sister Agnes spoke again. "It was because of Hildegard that I became a postulant."

I schooled my features. "I did not know that."

"I have never told anyone."

I smiled. "How is it that Hildegard inspired you so?"

Sister Agnes smiled back. 'Twas a rare occurrence, and I found myself wishing it happened more often. Her face—and that was all her habit allowed me to see—shone when she smiled. "Her faith was so great that she…"

Her head tilted to the side, and she stared at the bookshelves as if remembering fondly, not a woman who had been gone for centuries and whom Sister Agnes could only have encountered through books, but an old acquaintance. Her voice turned wistful. "She achieved so many things, did so much good, and set an example for us all."

A new understanding of Sister Agnes touched me. "You know a great deal about her for having read only books by her."

The nun's face surrendered her smile, but her eyes still sparkled with joy. "Within the pages of books one's heart can be revealed."

I returned to studying the shelves at my fingertips. How heartily I agreed with that thought. Joseph would, too, I imagined, but I bit my lip before mentioning the reverend's name to Sister Agnes.

The door behind us opened once more. I turned swiftly, hoping it was him whom I wished to see, and hoping it was not at the same time.

It was.

Anders stepped closer to me with a grin slowly overtaking his face. "You wished to see me?" His voice had an unusual lilt to it.

I nodded. "I did. I wondered…" I glanced over at Sister Agnes. With one hand on the spine of a dusty-looking tome, she stared at us with unashamed curiosity.

Anders, ever the gentleman, assumed a serious expression and bowed his head to her. "How do you find this evening, good sister?"

Sister Agnes nodded. "Pleasing. And you, milord?"

One corner of his mouth quirked. He looked to me, then back to her. "The same." His gaze rose to examine the shelves. "Are you looking for any book in particular or merely browsing?"

"Have you heard of Hildegard of Bingen?"

He brought out the full force of his smile. "My dear mother claimed that she nearly entered a convent because of that German nun."

Sister Agnes's eyes widened. "I daresay I would like your mother very much."

Anders's smile dimmed. "Alas, we lost her three years ago."

I reached out and laid a hand on Anders's arm, remembering that dark time when he had lost his mother, and I my grandfather and aunt, to the plague outbreak. He had taken his mother's death hard. Hence why he empathized so well with me after my parents' deaths.

He covered my hand with his own. Unsure what Sister Agnes's reaction to this might be, I peeked over at her, but the nun only nodded, not looking at all concerned. "Forgive me."

He waved away her words. "You did not know. I do hope that you find one of Hildegard's works. Shall I send for Lady Godfrey to assist you?"

I expected her to refuse, but instead Sister Agnes's brows drew together. She glanced at the bookshelves again, as if gauging how long it would take her to study the titles on each of the hundreds of spines, and how much easier it would be to just ask. "I would be grateful," she said.

Anders tucked the hand I had laid on his arm into his elbow and nodded to Sister Agnes before leading me from the room. "You wished to speak with me," he whispered into my ear.

"I have a question to ask of you. Let us find Lady Godfrey first."

He nodded, but we soon passed a maid in the Great Hall. Anders crooked his finger, and the girl scurried over from where she had been lighting candles. "The sister requests Lady Godfrey's presence in the library."

The maid nodded, curtseyed, and scuttled away.

"Come." Anders led me in the direction of the door. We entered the twilit courtyard and stopped. I swallowed as the chill air bombarded my face, the only uncovered inches of me.

We surveyed the view of the stable, second kitchen, well, and armory for a moment. A few men walked here and there. "I do not wish to talk here, Anders."

He nodded, silent, and led me to the stables. I balked. As much as I would love to see Char again—I had only made time to visit him sparingly, as being in his presence reminded me that I could not take him and leave to go find Dirk—I did not wish to speak to Anders inside the stables, either.

The memory of Dirk finding me within Char's stall, my hair flowing free, his eyes darkening, and what happened after filled my mind. For some strange reason the stables meant Dirk to me. I could not be with Anders within those walls—even though these were different walls entirely.

Anders stared down at me. He dared to put his hands on my shoulders. "Where, then?"

I glanced around. As tempted as I was to suggest that we return inside to the comfort of the Great Hall—or even to the library as I had originally planned, if Sister Agnes had found her book and gone—I knew Anders had brought me outside for a reason. But why? I tilted my head to look up at him. "You wished to speak out here?"

"I wished to take you to see Char. I know he has not seen you in several days."

I swallowed at his thoughtfulness and at his choice of words. For he had not mentioned that *I* had not seen my friend, he had said my friend had not seen me. The loss was mutual; I appreciated that, thus I relented. "Very well."

Anders led me to the stables, shooed out those within, and allowed me to lead the way to Char's stall. Alfie peeked out of one stall and grinned at me. I lifted my fingers in a wave Anders would not see.

Char whinnied when I put my hand on his nose. I leaned to open his stall, but Anders's hand got there first. I entered and laid my forehead against Char's neck, breathing deep of the scent of hay and horse that permeated this place.

Then I looked up at Anders. He had always had a sensitive nose, and his compassion in bringing me here brought a smile to my face as I noted the way he breathed through his mouth now.

He cleared his throat. "What did you wish to talk to me about?"

"Do you know of a man named Talan?"

Anders's brow furrowed and he thought a moment, but it was clear he had never heard of the man of whom I spoke. I turned away from him, closing my eyes as Dirk's face appeared in my mind. *Oh, Dirk, I wish you were here.* He would know what to do, where to search for the man who

145

claimed he was a murderer.

Going about restoring Dirk's reputation with Anders's help had kept me occupied somewhat, but I still felt like I was floundering without him. None of the noblemen Anders had approached were inclined to speak for Dirk. No replies to my letters indicating any changes of heart had arrived. The visit to the magistrate—I royally failed at that.

"I can see you do not know him."

"Where did you hear that name?"

"At the magistrate's. He wrote and claimed Dirk is a murderer." I spoke before I thought better of it.

Anders's eyes hardened. "Gwyneth, we are doing our best. There is no need for you to go—"

I exploded. "*Nee*, we are not! Surely there is something more we should be doing."

"Gwyneth, I—"

I slashed my hand through the air, quieting my voice for Char's sake. "I do not want to hear platitudes, Anders."

He sighed. "I have none to offer. I have been thinking these past weeks—"

"You have been doing too much thinking and not enough convincing." Silence settled over us in the wake of my hurtful words. My eyes closed. I had not meant that. Anders had been working hard on Dirk's behalf, but the frustration of it… "I am sorry, Anders. I do not believe that."

His eyes were gentle. "I know you do not. But I am realizing I do not believe this can be achieved."

I glared at him. How could he say that? And what would I do without his help? With his contacts—he was an earl, after all—Dirk could have no better man advocating his innocence. But it was not just the convenience of having Anders's assistance—it was having a friend by my side as I fought for the man I loved to be able to return to me.

He sighed, his gaze boring into mine. "I do not believe this is for the best."

My mouth dropped open. "He is innocent."

"I understand why you feel that way—"

"I do not merely feel it; I know it is true. He did not kill my parents." The irony threw me; not a year ago, I believed the exact opposite of that statement with equal passion.

But now I knew the truth.

Anders saw his opportunity and took it. He grabbed my hand. "But *I* do not know it is true. And I cannot help you any longer."

I recovered my hand and put it to Char's neck. I threaded my fingers through his mane, wishing it were Dirk's hair I touched. "He took me on a Sea Beggar ship. Did I tell you that?"

I had shocked him. "Nay."

"We boarded at midnight the day after he rescued us from the riot." I deliberately skipped over my fall into the stormy sea. "We sailed to Portland and disembarked at the docks there the next morn."

Anders's eyebrows hit his hairline.

"I spent a night and half a morn on a Sea Beggar ship. My mother's language spun all around, spoken by the crew, the captain, even the captain's son." One corner of my mouth flinched. "Those were my countrymen, men with whom I share a heritage, a bloodline."

He found his tongue. "Gwyneth—"

I held up a hand, and he stopped. "Those are my people. And the English are my people. And the Spanish are my people. All my life I have sworn allegiance not to a land or a monarchy, but to a Lord I only thought I knew. And people despise me for that. The captain of the *Rich Soul* disdained me for not being true Dutch and not supporting the riots that nearly killed me. Uncle Oliver threw me in a dungeon for not swearing fealty to the Spanish king he wished me to marry. Here in England, I am not free to practice the religion with which I was raised."

His gaze flicked between my eyes as if he struggled to make sense of what I was saying. My voice rose in pitch. "Who I am has always been dictated to me. I was the girl who loved to ride across the land, reckless, headstrong. I was the young woman who sought her mother's approval. I was the Catholic so set in my beliefs I ignored the fact that I could very well die for them if I stayed at the convent."

Anders had heard enough. He gripped my face in his hands, his thumbs stroking my cheekbones. "You are not any of those things. You are Gwyneth, one of the strongest women I have ever known. You are a lady and a saint."

My heart sank into my shoes, and I pulled away. "*Nee*. I am not who you think I am." Had I ever been? "I am none of those things. Truly, I am not sure who I am except that I am the woman who ruined Dirk's life by assuming the worst of him."

"You thought it was true."

"It was not."

"I am not entirely convinced."

"Then trust me. Because I have never known myself as surely as I know this: Dirk did not murder my parents, and I must save him from a life spent running from the undeserved punishment for that very crime."

Anders stared down at me, his expression nearly unreadable in the dim light of the stables. But I thought I saw him wavering. I was winning him back to belief in this cause.

"I do not know if I believe Dirk is worth this."

I smiled. I could not discern the layers beneath his gaze, but I knew that sound in his voice. 'Twas surrender. I took his hand. "Then trust me on that count, also. For I *know* he is."

"Then *you* are worth this to me."

When I failed to respond, Anders blew out his breath, looked up and away from me, then stared down into my eyes with that charming smile I knew so well.

"You always get what you want, Gwyneth." No note of resentment dripped from his words as he squeezed my hand. I hid my smile's death in Char's mane and mourned that Anders was wrong. I did not always get what I wanted.

For more than anything I had wanted that fool man to stay with me, and he had sent me away.

Dirk

Chapter Twenty-Five

A silver coin in my hand, I leaned over the railing as a red and orange sunrise bathed the sky. Staring at the gleam of the shining circle reminded me of the glint moonlight always gave her hair.

I had sent the letter a fortnight ago. In the days since, Ian and I had acted as inconspicuously as possible. The *Rich Soul* had stayed in port to welcome winter's wind. We bunked in Tudder's crew's quarters at night; we exercised our limited seafaring skills by day.

I studied the docks laid out before me now. The uneven heights of the various buildings—more taverns than not—rose and fell as the slow but steady slap of the water forced the vessel to rock beneath my boots. The streets waited sleepily as dawn bade the people inside to rise and roam them. Times like these, when the morning sang of newness and the quiet reigned over the noise, were when I felt her best and missed her most.

I pressed my hands to my eyes and breathed deeply, trying to stifle the memories. But they bled through. As if there had always been cracks in me meant for her—then, when we had finally found each other, her soul somehow was broken in all the right places so that she fit inside me. She dwelt within, I was never free of her, and I would not ever choose to be free of her even if I had that choice.

This pain kept her close to me, so I deemed it worthy of suffering.

The ropes and rigging cracked above me, but I ignored the sound of the ship swaying on the morning tide. The chill breeze of the Channel announced November's arrival. Tudder had announced he would be setting sail soon. The currents were right, he claimed, for a trip to the Low Countries.

I looked up at the sky and sighed. *Lord, will You not work here? I ask not for anything for myself; I am long past that. But...* I broke off my prayer and put my head in my hands once more.

Tudder came up beside me and laid his arms across the railing. I pulled back and gripped the wood with my calloused hands, hard hands, unworthy hands that had held her face and wiped away her tears. I stared into the water.

Tudder remained silent for a long moment, but news hung on his shoulders.

"You set sail soon?"

He nodded slowly.

"To pillage and plunder?"

He turned his torso and looked up at me. "I have received news."

A moment passed. "Do I need to pry it out of you?"

"The Governor-General, Margaret, has written Philip. He sees the need for a harsher hand."

I stared back at him, not liking the look in his eyes as he spoke of the Spanish king's regent communicating with the Low Countries' technical sovereign. "Who does he plan to send to take her place?"

"The Duke of Alba."

The name hung in the air a moment before falling into the water below us and disintegrating. But the threat lingered still. Alba, a determined general, would not hesitate to be vicious. The outcome for the Low Countries, and those supporting the Dutch cause, seemed bleak in the light of his coming.

"There is more." Tudder blew out a breath. "William of Orange has retreated to his estate. All those involved in the Beeldenstorm are aware they may pay."

My palms clenched around the railing as I wrestled with my reaction to that. A small part of me wanted those involved to realize the wrath they had given vent to, however well-motivated it might be, had endangered innocent lives. But some of the rioters who had dared endanger Gwyn and her friends had perished that night at my hands and the hands of Ian and Cade—the ones who had hurt the ones I cared about had been given swift justice.

"What will you do?"

"The only thing I can do." Tudder rose to his full height and looked me in the eye. "Stand with my countrymen. Declare my allegiance. Be there when the worst comes."

My voice lowered. "What of Titus?"

He worked to control his expression.

Tudder's son had served beside Ian and me during our time on the *Rich Soul*. A quiet lad, he did as he was told without complaint or thought of disobedience. Little drew him out as Gwyn's immediate affection had.

"I am sorry, Tudder."

"I have no options save to trust in God. There is nowhere else to take him, no safe place he can stay."

"Let me take him with me."

Tudder's eyes met mine, the shock in his gaze mirroring that which pooled in my stomach and making me swallow hard. A dry laugh loosened his tongue. "A fugitive is asking me to send my son on the run with him."

I breathed deep. This scheme seemed to have plopped into my mind before it was fully-formed. *God, if this is You, we are both going to need some confirmation.* "I will take him to St. Benet's."

Tudder guffawed. "I am not entrusting my son to you only to have you take him to a monastery."

"Former monastery."

He just laughed harder.

"Fine, then." Though Tudder would never believe Joseph was hardly the staunchest Catholic, I did not even try to convince him. "I will take him to Godfrey Estate."

"You just came from there. 'Tis a miracle you made it safely there and back once. How can I ask you to repeat the trip?"

"Because we both know the God who gave the first miracle. He can give a second."

The man eyed me. "He is a young boy."

"As was I, at one point."

"He can be too quiet and unassuming."

"I will take good care of him, Tudder. You know that."

He slapped a hand into the rail. "I am his father. I should be the one taking care of him."

"Mayhap this is how." 'Twas all the confirmation I needed. Would it be enough for Tudder?

A glance askance at me revealed the agony in Tudder's expression. He looked up at the sky, blue and beginning to welcome the morning light. The fog that plagued the port most days seemed to have taken the day off. "What would Mary say?" Tudder whispered.

I closed my eyes. I had only met Mary twice, soon after Tudder left Cade and me and our wandering ways to marry her, and soon after Titus was born. She had been a beautiful woman, full of laughter and lightheartedness and love for her husband and child. She had died after a fire consumed their home a day before Tudder had returned from a voyage. Tudder had told me she had saved Titus's life that night. "She would say you are doing what she did: protecting him."

Once again, Tudder fought for control. In one swift move, he swiveled and clapped a warning hand to my shoulder. "He may die if I take him with me, but he may die if you take him with you."

I could not confirm otherwise, so I stayed silent.

His hand fell away. "You will do your best to see him to safety?"

He knew the answer to that, but if he needed to hear the words, I would oblige. "I give you my word."

Tudder took one step away. "I am grateful to you, Dirk."

"No more so than I am for the times you have saved my sorry hide."

One corner of his mouth lifted, then fell. "He is not going to like this. We may not be able to tell, if the boy keeps his mouth shut as is his wont, but he will be upset."

"I would expect no less of a boy wishing his father farewell for a time."

Shaking his head, Tudder stared out over the water. "You should leave on the morrow."

"We will, then."

The light in his gaze seemed false. "I want you to know that I am not entrusting my son's life to you, Dirk. I am entrusting his life to God."

For a moment, my gut wrenched. I turned my gaze on the roiling water below us. The scent of salt rose.

But he continued. "If anything happens to him, I will not hold you responsible. Do not go and collect more guilt than you have earned."

I raised a brow. "Meaning?"

"Meaning I see that haunted look in your eyes. 'Tis more than missing her that dogs your every step. I recognize the feeling, for I feel it, too. You hold yourself responsible for putting her through what she endured."

"Just because you were away when your Mary—"

He held up a hand. "Just because you were looking the other way when your Gwyneth—"

"Sleeping. I was not looking the other way. I slept."

He stared at me with an expression that said *point made*. "Just you remember how you saved her."

"How is that?"

"You saw her safely from the convent to the coast, from the Low Countries to England."

I shook my head. "Not without mishaps."

"I watched you jump in after her, Dirk." He let that sink in for a moment, then, "I am expecting you to take a small boy across half of England—I do not expect a smooth journey, but I do expect you to do your best to see him safely to your home."

I clasped his outstretched hand, agreeing. The time had come for another mission.

After Tudder left the railing, Ian stepped to stand beside me. The wind tossed his brown hair in the wind. I rubbed a hand down my chin. Though it was the fashion of the day, I had never before been a bearded man. I wondered what Gwyn would think of the beard I had let grow since I left her. *Gwyn.* My eyes widened. I would see her soon. "We leave on the morrow."

Ian nodded. "Tudder sets sail soon?"

"The day after tomorrow."

"What is his destination?" A blink revealed he noticed the discrepancy—we would leave the next day, Tudder the day after. We would not be going with him.

"The Low Countries. The situation is set to heat up soon. Philip is sending a new general to assume the current governor's duties."

Ian looked at me. "And Tudder is going back?"

"He feels it is his place. The Dutch will need every available vessel, and his friends are there."

Ian's gaze never wavered. "There is something else."

I dipped my chin once. "We will not be traveling alone."

His brows rose.

"We will bring Titus with us. Tudder fears for his safety if he takes his son back to the Low Countries. 'Tis not exactly the safest place to be with the current state of events." I was filling the air with empty words, hoping Ian would not bring up the obvious.

"With you is not exactly the safest place to be, either."

I ran a hand through my hair. Ian could always be counted on to bring up the obvious. "The lesser of two dangers."

"What is the plan?"

Meeting his gaze, I wavered. The thought of seeing Gwyn again caused me to want to leave that same second. But how would she receive me? She had not returned my letter. And Revelin might still be there. "We will take him to Godfrey Estate."

Ian leaned his elbows on the railing, lacing his fingers together and staring out over the waking port. People occupied the roads now, and the din of their dulled voices drifted over the water and into my ears. The sounds of life. The sounds of community. Sounds were important to Gwyn. She would love to listen to them and try to dissect their meaning.

Soon I would see her.

Ian lifted his gaze to tug on mine. "It will be different, traveling with a child."

"We extended our journey to get here. We will be faster this time, regardless."

"You realize we are creating a circle now."

From the coast to Barrington to Godfrey. From Godfrey to the coast. And now from the coast directly to Godfrey. "I am aware."

Ian cracked a smile. "Sometimes God calls us to walk in circles, eh? Like the Israelites of old around the Jericho wall."

I grinned. "Only we carry precious cargo each time we circle." First Gwyn, now Titus.

"Have you grown that beard to try to conceal your identity?" Ian and his randomness.

"Does it?"

"Nay."

"Then I'll shave it." Eventually. I had other things to concern me now. Like assuming care of Titus. Like returning to Gwyn.

"It draws further attention to your red hair, methinks."

Laughing, I socked him in the arm.

"It does!" A chuckle lined his words.

I sobered. "You do not have to go with us, Ian."

He expelled a ruffled sigh and turned his gaze back to the bustle of people. "Ah, this again."

"I am serious. You could leave, return home—"

"I have no home to return to."

"You said that before."

"I repeat it because it is true." His eyes glinted with anger.

Staring out over the water a moment, I gathered my words. "'Tis true for me, as well."

Disgust ran over his features. "You have a home. You choose not to return."

"For their own good."

"And yours."

I tilted my head back, reminding myself he was my friend, and friends do not break friends' noses. "I do not mean to offend, Ian, but how can I avoid it when I do not know the circumstances that brought you to Cade and me?"

A shadow fell over his face, blocking out even the glint of anger. Sorrow entered his eyes, weighed down his mouth, and trembled in his hands. "You wish to know what happened to me before you found me in that back alley?"

Cade and I had come upon him lying prostrate in the darkness, bruised and bloody. He had never told us where he had been, though we could guess well enough what he had been doing. "Only if you wish to tell me."

His brows drew down as he kept his gaze on the water roiling below us. "I not only have no home to go back to, I have no family to go back to."

"I am sorry." At least, though I knew I never could, I knew my mother and sisters would always welcome me should I choose to return for a time. But I could not. I would take Titus to their care, and I would leave again. My chest splintered.

He glared at me. "If you listen, you listen in silence, without apologies." I waited.

"'Twas just my father and me after my mum died. When he died, I tried to keep the stables steady, but there was little loyalty to the Barrow name."

He stayed silent for so long that I thought he had finished.

"I refused to take her as my wife because I knew she would be marrying the poverty, too."

I swung my gaze to his. Ian Barrow, the pup, had been in love? My respect for the man grew. Too often had Cade and I teased him, when in fact he had known love and loss as we had, mayhap more.

When he did not speak, I prodded. "What happened?"

The sound of his inhale stung the air. He stared up at the sky. "Jane's father considered her above me, and he was right. She was a seamstress— the miracles that girl could do with a needle and thread." He put his face in his hands for a moment as if seeking composure. Finding it, he looked up at me. "On the very night she begged me to take her with me when I ran away, her father announced her betrothal to another man."

My chest clenched. He had been forced to watch his beloved marry another. 'Twas a horrible fate.

Revelin's face entered my mind, and I sucked in a breath.

"The winter before the wedding, she took ill. I went to her house and stood beside her window every day. I knew her father would never let me in, but her mother did not say a word, though she knew I was there. Jane cried endlessly. I think she gave up because, if she had lived, she would return to a life she did not want. And I could not give her what she asked."

His eyes glistened. "After she died, the man she was to marry was furious. We brawled, and I ran, but I was in a bad way."

"That is when Cade and I found you."

We stayed like that a long moment, the weight and release of revelation between us. I laid a hand on Ian's shoulder, wishing I could do more. It was then that I realized I would not only be leaving Titus at Godfrey Estate. I would be leaving Ian, too.

Gwyneth

Chapter Twenty-Six

Alfie readied Char for me while I waited. When he had finished, he stroked Char's withers once and led him out of the stall and to me. "Here you are, milady."

"Thank you, Alfie. How are you getting on?"

"Well." The boy beamed. "No one hides the pitchfork here."

I mustered a small laugh and nodded. "Glad I am to hear it. You will let me know if you have need of anything?"

His gaze dropped, and his shoe shuffled in the dirt between us.

"What is it, Alfie?"

In the weeks since he had come here, he seemed to have grown several inches. Was that possible? I could not be sure, but I made a mental note of where he leveled with the stall door and determined to keep track in the future. Whatever future that might be.

When he insisted on silence, I stepped back. "When you are ready to tell me, I am ready to listen."

He smiled at me, and I smiled back.

Char and I rode free for at least an hour. At the sound of the blackbird, I called Char to a stop. Sliding off his bare back, I let my shoes sink into the ground. Yesterday's rain had softened the frozen earth, so a sucking sound punctuated my every step. But the cold still seeped in and chilled my feet. I lifted my hair off my neck; the pins had long since surrendered to the tugging fingers of the wind and the force of Char's gallop. They no doubt lay within the frostbitten blanket of leaves covering the forest ground. Lost forever, like Dirk was to me.

My hands dropped to my side. With surprise, I lifted them once more and examined my fingers. They trembled. I laid them against Char's warm, lathered mane and stroked. "Did I run you too far in this cold?"

I glanced around, at the open space Susan had said I would find northwest of the keep. She had been right: it was one of the most beautiful places on God's earth. And I had a wealth of places to draw from to compete for that title.

Barrington Manor would always be one of the first places I thought of when *beauty* came to mind. The abundance of fields to run and roam through beckoned me on every bright, brilliant day.

The openness of the Low Countries was synonymous to me of flight, freedom, and fear. Such a wide scope of emotions and experiences connected to that grand land. I could see why *Moeder's* heart longed for that place until the day she died. But if I never returned, I could not see myself being sorry.

Uncle Oliver had always spouted the loveliness of España as unequal to anything else. Though I doubted his lack of bias, I did not wish to test his opinion.

If I stayed in England for the rest of my days, I would be content with the beauty found here. Not happy, but content. *Nee,* I could not be happy as long as Dirk stayed away.

But did he stay away? Or did he force himself to go? What had really happened that day I had run after him blurred more and more in my mind. Had I begged hard enough, cried loud enough, clung to him tightly enough?

I spun in a circle to try to coax warmth into my chilled body. While Char had carried me through the woods and open vales across Godfrey land, his sheer speed and the power of the wind had warmed me through and through. But as I stood at his side, I cooled too quickly. I would not be able to stay long.

I would have to make this quick.

I wanted to reread his letter today. Privately. Even though I had complete privacy the first time I had caressed his words with my gaze, 'twas different now, a league away from all in the keep.

The doubts barricaded around my heart lately, taunting me. Had Dirk ever really loved me? Had I really loved him? Had I been capable of enduring love, having only truly known love for such a short time? This emptiness where my heart had once been reassured me I had.

I clutched the paper and the silver piece that had miraculously accompanied it. When they had arrived, at first I had feared this letter was from Talan. On the contrary, from Dirk. And he had chosen a most trusted messenger, whom we had rewarded handsomely, to guarantee the coin made it to me instead of being stolen. I closed my eyes, and it was as if the words had imprinted themselves on my eyelids.

A fortnight ago, the missive had arrived. A solemn-faced Rohesia had brought it to me, along with the single silver piece that had traveled with it. "A letter from Dirk," she had said. She could have called him *my son* or *Devon*, but instead she used the name I knew him by. I loved her all the more for that.

Dirk Godfrey, by the grace of God to Lady Gwyneth Barrington of Barrington Manor, Northampton, presumed Godfrey Estate, his most kind greeting.

Gwyn.
My pen hesitated to call you by the name by which I love you, but I know you would slap me if you could if I called you anything else.

I am sorry. I am so, so sorry. I stare up at the stars and fling those words into the sky, hoping they make their way to your heart and soothe it somehow. For I am sorry. I will always regret leaving you behind, as I will always regret that it was the only choice I could have made that could ensure your continued well-being.

It is not prudent that I reveal to you my location. Nevertheless, I give it to you. I am on Tudder's vessel, the Rich Soul. *He remembers you fondly.*

As do I. I remember the way your hair shines silver in the moonlight. I remember the way your eyes spit fire when you are angry with me—which is too often, I fear. Are you angry with me now, Gwyneth-mine? Do not be. Please. I deserve it, aye, I know. But do not be. Remember me with fondness. But now I am begging, something I told myself I would not do. I am praying, too. Every day I lift up your name to our heavenly Father. I will not lie and say I understand all He is doing in our lives, but I know He does, and that will be enough for me for now.

I pray you are well, heart. I do not deserve this, either, but I will beg once more: write back to me. I beseech thee, use Tudder's ship as the address and send me word of you.

Yours, Dirk

Sinking to the ground, I let the shackles around my heart fall away. The letter fell from my hand. The silver piece remained lodged in my palm—what did it mean?

My ribcage contracted and expanded as a sob stole my breath. Tears plopped onto the winter ground. Once this place must have been beautiful. Once this place must have been an oasis, a sanctuary of sorts. Now all that was left were brown leaves and dormant grass.

Godfrey Estate had been a refuge for me when I had first arrived. I had not wanted to accept it at the time. The tension between Dirk and me and my short-lived, unfounded fear of what his mother might think of me had temporarily blinded me to the safe haven to which he had brought me.

But, while it was still a sanctuary in some ways, my staying here seemed more and more like a banishment—the exile of the orphan and her broken soul.

I gave in to my grief and flung myself to the ground, staring up at the pale blue sky. He had been away for so long now. So long. *Dirk, come back to me* rose to my lips as it had so many times before, but screaming the words at the sky would do no good. And now the letter, written as if he were never coming back.

He was gone. I had lost him. Though so much truth these days seemed thin, this truth bound me round the ribs like an invisible cage. If I tried to flee and find him, I would fail. He had left no trace of where he was going—had he set sail on Tudder's vessel?—and, wherever he was now, he would not stay long. I would remain forever one step behind him, if that close. Never near enough.

Rising to my knees, I buried my head in my arms and surrendered to the agony of knowing I'd never see him again. I loved him. If there had ever been a question, none remained now.

And I would never be able to tell him. When I had penned my reply, the words had trickled onto the page, but they were stale, lifeless, meaningless without the answer in his eyes, in his kiss.

Drawing in shuddering breaths and furiously swiping at my tear-stained face, I rose and turned back to Char. The time of mourning was over. There was only one thing I could do now: clear the name of the man I loved until every trace of the crime of which I had accused him lay shattered at my feet.

Along with the pieces of my broken heart.

I passed Sister Agnes on my way in from the stables. Pasting a smile on my face, I turned to her and nodded in acknowledgment.

"Where were you?" she asked.

"Spending time in prayer in the meadow."

Her expression shifted. "The chapel is no longer good enough for you? You must seek out the cold of winter to pray?"

I blinked. "That is not it at all."

The thin line of her mouth softened. Eyes that had blazed a moment ago cooled. Her anger seemed to abate all of a sudden. "Then what is it?"

Unable to answer, I shook my head. How I longed for the proper words to help her understand. Faith was no longer about empty rules to me—it was about a love that saw me through even losing Dirk.

"You are…" She hesitated. Swallowed. "You are welcome to join me in the chapel sometime should you wish it."

Was this grace? I nodded. "I will."

My answer seemed to surprise her. I smiled and walked on.

She did not follow me up the stairs, even though a small part of me wished she would. Stopping outside the door of the chamber Margried and I shared—we had not lasted long in separate rooms—I grasped my hand to my chest. This sorrow resembled physical pain in a way that grief for my parents and grandfather never had. They had died; Dirk was still very much alive. He was out there, somewhere, but he was not here. He could never be here.

Steeling my shoulders, I shook it off. Mayhap I was merely weak. The early cold and downcast sky suggested this would be a hard winter—mayhap that was what caused this ache in my chest.

Lies.

I pushed open the door and stopped on the threshold. Margried lay across the bed, above the blankets, her gown cinching her legs.

"Margried?" I inched close, hoping she merely slept, dreading she did not.

She moaned. I sat beside her and eased the tousled black tendrils of her hair from her face. Her fingers clenched the blankets tighter, and her eyelashes fluttered shut over glistening cheeks. *Oh, God, what do I do?*

Hesitant at the thought of praying aloud, I settled for beseeching the Lord for peace silently. For both of us, selfishly.

As I continued to stroke her hair, Margried did not open her eyes. "Where did you go?"

"Tell me what pains you first."

"Where did you go?"

I sighed. "Susan told me about a little meadow a league from here."

"Did you find it?"

"Easily. Now I wish I could find what bothers you and throw it out that window."

She smiled.

"Char and I could not stay long, though. 'Tis too cold. But I am glad I am back. Tell me what is wrong."

She opened her eyes. "What were you doing?"

I stared at her, unveiling the emotions I kept ever hidden beneath my face now.

A tear trickled down her cheek. She rose and put her arms around me. I hugged her back, fiercely, as I might have if she had been my sister. Then I hugged her tighter, because I realized, in every way that mattered, she was.

"I miss him." I half-laughed because my voice sounded so strangled.

"I do not understand him." Margried drew away.

"What do you mean?"

"He left you here. If Cade did that to me…" Her lips settled into a thin line. "*That* is what pains me today."

I took that in. Must I explain his actions to her, too? I shook my head. Naught I could say would change Margried's mind; I needed to show her. I slid off the bed and went to the corner. Pulling a small box from beneath a chair, I smiled. Then I laid the open box in front of Margried.

She put a hand to her mouth. "Did he…?"

"Aye." I fingered the dried and crumbling remains of the wildflowers he had left for me that morning long ago. "He gave me these on the day he left. No farewell. Just these. Wild, unruly, in a bouquet made by a man's hand—so lovely."

Margried burst into tears anew.

I reached for one hand while she used the other to swipe at her cheeks. "You must tell me what is wrong, Margried. I do not believe that it is my grief alone that drove you to this misery today."

"'Tis Cade."

"What did he do?"

She coughed. "We are both at fault."

I raised a brow. "Not if you are the one crying." That earned me a smile.

"He wants to marry me."

My eyes narrowed. "I know you have been keeping something from me lately, but I have been aware of *that* fact since I interrupted you after he first asked you for your hand."

She blinked. "How did you know I have been keeping something from you?"

"You open your mouth sometimes only to snap it closed again. You look at me then look away when I return your stare. You moved in here with me." I swept my arm about the room.

"Because I wanted to be near you. You are grieving."

"My grief only makes yours more apparent. Let me bear it with you." *Except I am not grieving anymore. I am not.*

She studied her hands.

"So…what is it you want to tell me?"

"Cade wants to marry me. When we first arrived, Lady Godfrey discovered our betrothal and offered us her estate for our wedding."

A brief flash of an image entered my mind: Rohesia, Cade, and Margried, deep in conversation, leading the way into Godfrey Estate mere moments after we first arrived. Had they been discussing their upcoming nuptials even then? Margried had indeed kept something from me. "That was weeks ago, Margried."

She nodded up at me, a guilty expression on her face.

I covered her hand with my own. "Why did you not tell me?"

"That night, you were…indisposed. Then it was easier not to tell you. I did not want to cause you pain."

Because Dirk had left me. "I do not fault you. I daresay I might have done the same had I been in your position."

Shock colored her face. "Oh, I had not thought of it in that manner." She shook her head. "I would never wish you to withhold sharing your joy with me. I have been foolish, Gwyneth. Can you forgive me?"

"Can you forgive me for being so focused on my own loss I failed to see your pain?"

"There is no need."

There was every need. But this was Margried. "Thank you for being my friend."

She hugged me again. Then I remembered. "If you and Cade were talking of marrying that long ago and Lady Godfrey offered you her home, why are you not yet wed?"

Margried's expression turned as close to exasperation as I had ever seen on her sweet face. Her bright blue eyes lifted to the ceiling and stayed there. "We meant to wait until winter."

My eyebrows rose. "Winter has long since come."

When her gaze dropped to mine, she nodded. "I know."

"And...?"

She forced me to wait a long while for her reply. "I am angry at him."

I flinched. "At Cade? Wh—"

"Nay!" She shook her head. Her hands clasped together. "Nay, not Cade. I am angry at Dirk, quite bitter with him, actually."

My eyes closed. The unexpected mention of him blind-sided me, taking me by surprise and ramming a dagger into my heart—or, better yet, a dirk. I slammed the door on that thought and looked at Margried again. "For leaving?"

"Not for leaving. For not taking you with him."

"For a while, I was angry, too."

Her eyes widened.

"You have not been the only one hiding something." My smile held sorrow.

"Cade has not hidden from me how angry it makes him that I am angry with Dirk."

I struggled to imagine Cade, always so gentle with her, angry with Margried.

"He agrees with him, you know. He thinks Dirk's leaving was the best thing, the only thing he could have done."

I wanted to ask if she thought the same and just hated the injustice of it—and *that* was why she was angry—but held my tongue. Hearing her answer might not be the best thing for me now. Besides, Margried's story needed no such clarification.

"We have fought about the matter every few days since he left."

Astonished, I swallowed.

"I have asked him to write to Dirk, to fetch him, to take you to him. He refuses each time. I cannot marry the man I love with this hanging over us."

My wince made my eyes close. When I opened them again, I looked straight at her. "Do not do this. Not even for me. Do not give up the love God has given you and Cade because of a matter that is between Dirk and me."

"But, Gwyneth—"

"*Nee.* Please. Go to him. Straightaway. Tell him you will marry him. On the morrow." I leaned back. "It will do me good to have your wedding to look forward to."

Margried pressed her palms against her eyes. "I wish I could. I would, if only this fear did not strangle me even now. Do you not see, Gwyneth?

I argue with Cade not only about Dirk, but about himself. He agrees with Dirk that protecting you is a priority higher than taking you with him. What if the situation were reversed? What if he were faced with the choice of protecting *me* from those who seek him… or making a life with me?"

My mouth dropped open, snapped shut, and twisted to the side in a grimace.

Tears filled Margried's eyes. "That he supports Dirk in this terrifies me. Because I have watched you grieve for the man you love, Gwyneth, and I do not believe I am that strong. But Cade…" Her voice failed, and she collected herself. "I think if he deemed it necessary, Cade would do the same to me." She tucked a long ebony tendril behind her ear and cast her gaze downward as if she dared not meet my eyes.

"Because you fear losing him, you push him away?"

She gasped, looked up, straightened her spine, and stared at me. "Of course n—"

"Aye, that *is* what you are doing." So many things seemed unclear, but not this. Clarity rang. I grabbed her shoulders. "Go to him. Even if he were to go away one day in order to save you, would you not rather have the days before that terrible one to hold onto? I would, Margried. I would."

When once again Anders returned, he looked aged, worn. Weighed down, he came to me in the library. At once, I rose from Rohesia's company, begging for her understanding with a glance. She smiled in return and then looked down, returning to her Bible reading while she waited for me. I met Anders outside the library door and waited to speak until it had closed. "What is wrong?"

He sighed. "Did you miss me?"

I rolled my eyes. "How did Lord Mauldin accept you?"

Not well, from the tired look in Anders' eyes. A second sigh told me that he had guessed rightly. I reached out a hand and touched his sleeve. "I thank you for the effort you are making."

He seemed pleased at my gratitude; he had earned it. After all, he had taken it upon himself to visit these lords and ask them to reconsider their opinion of Dirk. All I had done was write to them afterward—as well as meet with the magistrate and fail to persuade him.

"This one was different, Gwyn." Anders shook his head, as if reluctant to tell me more.

Of course I would not let him get away with that. "How so?"

"Talan wrote to Lord Mauldin before I arrived."

I nearly staggered back, but Anders caught me with one hand. Then his other hand rose to cup my other elbow and I stood, buoyed and broken all at once. We were failing. And we were failing because of this Talan. Someone with no status but better timing. Someone with lies as his only ammunition but who wielded his power with more persuasion. Somehow this unknown Talan was undoing all the work Anders and I had invested.

I needed to find him.

Dirk

Chapter Twenty-Seven

The morn was still young when Tudder arose from below, his hand on Titus's shoulder. Titus's pale face and wide eyes turned up to me from my place at the railing. I stood tall and met his gaze, trying to appear kind and determined at the same time, as if to convince him I would see him safely across England and he need not be frightened of me.

In my peripheral vision, I saw a boat with a single passenger row up to the side of the *Rich Soul*. One man. No threat.

I focused on Titus as he strode up to me, detecting a man's walk in those short steps. But his confident gait and squared shoulders could not compare to the way he stared at me with his hands behind his back, a posture inherited from his father.

The sound of voices swung through the air and into my ear. Though I could not discern the meaning beneath the Dutch words, I thanked God the man from the boat and his business had naught to do with me.

I met Titus's gaze without tipping my head to look at Tudder—somehow I knew the young lad would equate my breaking eye contact with breaking faith, and I wished to avoid that at all costs. "Your father has told you his plan?"

"Aye, sir." His English rolled with a Dutch accent also acquired from Tudder.

"Will you be ready to leave in an hour?"

"Aye, sir."

"Do you have any concerns, Titus?"

At this, his age showed in the way he glanced at his father before quickly latching his gaze on mine again. His features remained steady as his legs balanced at every rock of the ship in the choppy water. "Will I get to see the pretty lady again?"

I swallowed. Tudder interrupted by stepping to my side and pressing a piece of paper into my hands. I took it. Surprise slowed my fingers, but when I turned it over, it said Tudder's name. I flipped over the seal Tudder had obviously already broken, unfolded it, and found my own name on the letter.

"You may wish to go below, man." Tudder's prompting proved enough for me. I bounded down the stairs and into his cabin.

A lock of hair fell out of the letter as I unfolded it. Rubbing them between my fingers, I read.

> *Gwyneth Barrington, by the grace of God to Dirk Godfrey, via Captain Mathieu Tudder of the merchant vessel* Rich Soul, *presumed Hemsby, her most kind greeting.*

> *How dare you reveal your location to me, idiota? 'Tis a foolish thing to do when so many seek your neck. This letter could have you killed.*

> *But I write anyway. Because you asked me to. An old friend once told me that I get what I wanted.*

My stomach clenched. Could Lansberry be the "old friend"?

> *He was wrong. I miss you. I am well, though I miss you. But do not fret about me. And do not ever call me anything save Gwyn. You are right; I will slap you.*

> *Your apology does soothe my soul, in some impossible way that cannot be put into words. Would you like to soothe it more? Then come back to me. Right now. Jump from Tudder's despicable—I use the word with fondness—ship and run home, or take a horse. I do not care.*

> *Except I do care. I have always cared for you. Even though at one point I confused that caring with loathing and later called it anger. Oh, Dirk, you fool, you stole away my heart as easily as you stole me away. Then you gave it back. But I do not want it. I want you to have it. Come and retrieve it?*

> *I wish I could write more. I long to tell you what is truly on my heart, what consumes the few thoughts in the day that are left after so many are consumed by you. But that will have to wait until our reunion—make that word not fall from my pen*

in vain—for this missive is dangerous enough.

I pray for you and—my pen bids me not to write this, but I must—I am afraid.

I jerked and stood. If Lansberry had so much as—

I am afraid you are never coming back, that our parting will be the last memory I have of you, that I will never again hear the song of the silver I tucked into your pocket, the song that made me believe true restoration was indeed possible.

Prove my fears unfounded, my knight. Stay well. Pray hard— as I do. Keep Ian close. Run. Run home. Come back to me.

Yours, Gwyn

I refolded the paper, pressed the two halves of the seal back into place, and tucked the missive into my breast pocket, wishing that putting back together the two halves of our hearts could be as easily accomplished.

Titus rode on my horse with me for the first few hours. I kept him wrapped within his coat and mine lest the cold numb him as it was numbing me. Ian rode before us, scouting the way, charting the path, and taking the brunt of the falling snow.

Tudder's farewell to his son had touched a place deep inside of me that I had tried to keep well hidden for these last long months. He had clasped Titus close, then kissed his curls and put his son from him with Dutch words flying between them in a pace worthy of Gwyn's Spanish.

Titus tugged on my arm. I switched my grip to hold the reins in one hand and looked down at him, eyebrows raised.

His own eyebrows had a few ice crystals on them. I brushed them away and leaned down, keeping my gaze on the path Ian trod.

"Is it nighttime?"

I shook my head. "Nay, not yet."

'Twas no wonder he asked that; the sun had long since failed to penetrate the thick storm that had come upon us not long after leaving the docks and the small coastal town just south. The wind I had grown accustomed to while on Tudder's vessel—the very wind I had looked forward to leaving behind—had followed us. Not only that, but small snowflakes had joined the ranks of the wind not an hour ago.

Decision made, I hailed Ian. We stopped, and I brought my horse shoulder to shoulder with his. When I opened my mouth to speak, Titus squirmed. He pointed into the woods. After I let him down, I watched him walk into the trees, seemingly unfazed by the swirling flurries.

Ian stared down the path. When he turned back to me, his grave expression confirmed what I already knew. "We are heading toward the storm, not out of it. If we continue on this way, it will only grow worse."

"As I thought. We change course, then."

"For where?"

"St. Benet's."

A smile hovered on his face. "We are taking a Protestant boy to what was once a monastery."

I appreciated the irony, but it did not concern me. "Tudder would recognize that we need to seek refuge now. Besides, Joseph is converted; he will not taint the boy's beliefs."

Ian nodded. "Challenge them, mayhap."

"As he does with us all." I peered into the woods, trying to see through the falling snow for any sign of Titus. Should I have allowed him to traipse into the cover on his own like that? Did the snow seem to fall more swiftly now?

Just when I would have gone in, Titus came out. The ice crystals on his hair and eyebrows stood out in contrast with his hazel eyes.

"Do you want to ride with me for a bit, lad?" Ian reached out his hand.

Titus shrugged, emphasizing his shivering, and grabbed for Ian's fingers. I saw the icy tinge on both their hands then and directed my horse to take the lead. St. Benet's was still a ways off, and seeing us all safely there in good time—before the storm became even more vicious—consumed my thoughts.

For the next few hours, we battled blinding winds and snow to make it to the monastery. At last, we stood before that imposing structure. 'Twas no time for dawdling and examining the difference between the intimidating edifice and the welcoming shelter it housed. We ran straight in and found ourselves alone.

Gwyneth

Chapter Twenty-Eight

The temptation to drag my glasses off my nose and toss them away pulsed strong. I would have, too, if I did not need them so much. But I did. And they had been causing me fewer headaches lately. So I left them. I examined again the tapestry on the wall that had held Millicent so transfixed. There was beauty, but there was also mystery. Why did the bird appear ready to fly? What did she see that inspired her flight?

My mouth twisted to one side. Or was it something that she heard?

My fingers reached for my neck for the first time in a long time, but I found no rosary there. I did not wear it anymore. It sat within the confines of the small box that housed Dirk's flowers and his letter. All trinkets given by people who had loved me and left, witnesses to promises broken.

No matter. I needed not the sound of hope. What good would hope do me now? My thoughts went to the sound of the silver I had given Dirk. His mother had intended for it to buy us passage to a safe place, but the promise I had heard ringing within that pouch had deceived me.

Instead of sentiment, I needed action. Something to do, anything that might change the course of these lives I cared about. Cade. Margried. Sister Agnes. Alfie, too. Even Rohesia and how her mother's soul mourned.

I spun away from the wall and descended the stairs on silent feet, clasping a corner of my skirt in one hand lest I fall. For no one here would catch me. Dirk's absence wrenched through my stomach and strangled my heart.

On my way to the library to fetch pen and paper, voices in the Great Hall caught my attention. Rohesia. She and I had talked more about the apostle Paul today…and what it meant to die to the flesh. My head still hurt with the idea. What would such truth look like if lived out?

I crept closer and heard another voice, also one I recognized.

"Your hospitality has been most appreciated, Lady Godfrey." Anders's voice sounded smooth and calm.

"You have been a welcome guest, milord. I hope you know that you are welcome to stay through Christmastide, as well."

I sauntered closer, intent on gliding by the entrance to the Great Hall and leaving these two to their niceties.

"I believe I may take advantage of your invitation. Lady Gwyneth…"

My steps came to a halt. For a moment, I believed he had called me, but I stood suspended in the center of the open entryway just shy of the Great Hall. He could not see me. He could not have heard me begin to approach. I should leave, yet…

"Does something cause you concern, milord?" What in Anders's expression gave Rohesia cause to ask him that?

Anders's sigh punctuated his next words. "Not something. Someone. I fret about Lady Gwyneth's health."

I touched my cheek, remembering Sister Agnes's worried remark from yesterday about my pallor. Yet it *was* winter now; the sun hid. And it had only been yesterday that Margried had spent the afternoon in our chamber with naught but our tears to keep us company—she had refused to seek out Cade. They were not to be married today.

Rohesia's somber voice interrupted my thoughts. "You have known her for most of her life. Could you tell me what some of her favorite dishes are? I have noticed she does not seem to eat much at table."

I smoothed my hand down my stomacher, feeling the looseness of the fabric. As Anders named a select few dishes I had expressed favor for in the past, my appetite failed to take notice. "There is something more." Anders sighed again. "I worry about her well-being. She seems agitated, restless somehow."

Restless? How could I not be when even now Talan schemed against us and Dirk and I had no idea how to stop or even find him?

Rohesia remained silent. I wished to see her face and discern which emotions crossed her features, but I dared not. I stood frozen, willing Anders to go on, to reveal what he had not revealed directly to me.

That hurt—that he had kept from me how I worried him.

"Have you noticed her changing moods?" Anders continued as I had wished him to, but as he said the words, my eyes closed. Mayhap I did not wish to hear this. Still, my feet remained rooted to the floor.

"You should talk to Gwyneth—" Rohesia's voice sounded hard.

Shuffling ensued. Anders had risen, then. The shuffling continued.

THE SOUND OF SILVER

Did he pace? I pictured him, hands behind his back, head down, gaze examining the rich rug covering the floor. He always made a handsome thinker, but the image irritated me now. Why had he not just approached me?

"I fear for her, to be honest with you, Lady Godfrey. I do not mean to offend, but I cannot help but believe her attachment to your son is unhealthy for her."

Rohesia's voice sounded even and cold. "You do offend."

Anders gave a short laugh devoid of humor. "Forgive me. How horrid of me. You must know that I do not mean to throw your son's unsavory reputation in your face; it is his absence. Gwyneth needs someone who will be there for her."

My feet found wings. Mayhap this was how the bird on the tapestry felt, emotions aswirl, ready to take flight. I stepped into the Great Hall and watched Anders's face tighten.

Rohesia sat facing Anders, her back to me. She must not have been gazing at Anders, so she missed the look on his face and, therefore, my arrival. She rose, her head held high, regal in her fury. "My son is an honorable man who would never twist a knife in a mother's heart by speaking unfavorably about her children to her face."

When she turned and saw me, her hand rose from her side in invitation. But I could not take it. I could not take another step without flying into the man who dared speak ill of Dirk.

"Anders." I pierced him with my gaze.

"Gwyneth, I—"

I held up a hand, willing it not to shake with my fury. "How dare you."

He gestured toward Rohesia, his gaze flicking in her direction briefly before settling upon me again. His features hardened. "I do not know what came over me. I overstepped, and I am sorry."

"Are you?" To me, he did not look apologetic.

A vein pulsed in his cheek. "You are making a mistake, Gwyneth. Do you not see that?"

My brows furrowed, and my hands rose to my hips. "I do not see. How can you speak so of the man you are working to absolve?"

He remained silent a moment too long, refusing to engage me.

"Do you care to enlighten me, or would you rather speak to another of my friends behind my back?"

When his head fell forward, that lock of hair I knew so well sprang over his forehead. Oddly, what before had always made him look so boyish now made him look foolish and immature. When his eyes flashed, I knew what I had been waiting for had finally happened: Anders's patience had run thin.

He stepped toward me. Rohesia came to my side. My gaze did not waver from Anders's eyes.

"I am worried about you, Gwyneth. You are unwell, yet you refuse to see what is causing your distress."

"I am not distressed." I prayed God's forgiveness for my lie.

"You are. And you know you are. Yet you cling to that which is causing your lack of peace." He glared, something he rarely did. It caught me off guard.

"Now that I know God, I have never been more at peace." I bit my tongue lest it betray me again with another lie.

Anders let out his breath as if he struggled to control himself. "You are seeking after this foolish scheme to restore his honor—"

Rohesia gasped, and her whisper rang in my ears. "What?"

She probably had not even intended to ask, but I turned to her. "'Tis the only way I can love him from afar. I want to see him free. I am working to make that happen—and Anders has been helping me. He is not just visiting; he leaves here to plead Dirk's cause to neighboring noblemen. And I send letters—"

His face colored. "You what?"

"You heard me, Anders. I write to the noblemen after you visit them, adding my voice to yours where Dirk cannot speak for himself." My voice sounded sad in my ears, and, though I had hardly been able to process the emotions raging through me in the last few minutes, that one I understood. Sorrow had been too faithful a friend in the last few years—indeed, in the last few weeks.

He stepped closer, his chest heaving.

Rohesia's attention fixed on me. "Gwyneth, I—" She shook her head, and tears shone in her eyes. "I know not what to say. Do you believe it will work?"

I had my doubts. Could I hold to hope, as Dirk had once said? "I believe it will." I looked straight at Anders. "But I could still use the support of a certain earl."

"To whom are you writing?" His volume and pitch rose higher with each word.

"All of them. The Earl of Cushborough—"

"Gwyneth!" His shout stung my ears.

Out of the corner of my eye, I saw Rohesia leave us to ourselves. Glad,

I stepped closer to Anders. He was reacting stronger than I had expected him to when the truth of my letter-writing came out. "What did you expect me to do? Sit back and wait for you to do all the work for me?"

"I thought we had talked about this. I agreed to help you in spite of my misgivings, in spite of my concerns."

"And you have, Anders. But I cannot help, is that what you are saying? Well, I am no longer the spoiled lady you once knew. I take matters into my own hands."

He reached for my hands, then, jerking them up between our faces, highlighting the comparison between his hands and my own as if to show me my own inadequacy. "You should have trusted me, Gwyneth."

Trusted him? Why had supplementing his efforts seemed to him like distrust? I winced at the pressure his fingers laid on my wrists and tried to pull away to no avail. My teeth gritted together. "Anders—"

"Unhand her, Revelin."

My neck swiveled to see Cade in the doorway. Rohesia stood behind him. My ears had failed to hear either of them approach. I studied Rohesia's pale face. She stared back at me with a determined expression. Then my focus was stolen as Anders wrenched me closer to him even as his stare remained on Cade. "This is no business of yours."

Cade came forward, eyes locked with Anders's.

I struggled against him. My arms were thin beneath his huge hands. "Anders, you are hurting me!"

Cade needed nothing more. He threw his fist into Anders's face.

The crack of bone against bone with only skin as a thin intermediary slapped my senses. Anders released me. I stood frozen while he swayed to one side, his hand reaching reflexively toward his jaw.

"Cade!" Margried. My gaze found her standing in the doorway, her palms cupped over her mouth. But Cade did not look at her; he stared at Anders like a hunter studies a deer, ready for whatever he might do next, muscles screaming to spring into action.

"Anders." I gripped my elbows in my shaking hands. "End this."

He looked away from Cade, down at me, into my eyes. Slowly, slowly, reason returned. He stared at me with an expression of surprise, but he did not step away from me. At last he straightened, the surprise in his face vanishing as resolve took its place. "You should have trusted me."

"You said it yourself: I need someone who will be there for me." The sharp clip of my words sounded harsh even to me, but I was powerless to stop the truth.

He continued as if he had not heard me. "You can trust me. You can always trust me." He took a step closer.

I stumbled away. Cade, standing beside me, reached for me, but Rohesia had come to my other side and was faster in catching my right hand.

She helped to steady me, then she leveled a look at Anders. "I believe you should go." The absence of his title hung in the air.

I breathed shallowly, the air in the room seeming to suffocate me.

Anders looked at Rohesia. "Forgive me for speaking out of turn." Then he gave me one last long look and strode from the Great Hall. Cade snorted and said something under his breath that I probably was better off not hearing.

I closed my eyes. I was learning that the absence of something can be felt just as well—or better—than its presence. Dirk's absence hung on me like a shroud. The lack of Anders's title after Rohesia's words spoke volumes. And his choosing to apologize to Rohesia but not to me had the same effect as a slap across my cheeks.

I opened my eyes and lifted my chin. Margried came forward with slow steps. She touched my arm, and I nodded, trying to assuage her concern for me. Her gaze went to Cade. They stared at each other for a long moment.

If I had had my way, today they would have been wed.

Rohesia rolled up my sleeves, took one look at my arms, and steered my shoulders toward the door before I was ready to stop studying my friends. "Come, Gwyneth. Let us apply some salve to those wrists."

My footsteps slowed to a halt at her words. I turned my hands over, my lips twitching as I saw the bold bruises on my forearms and wrists. Flower petal shaped, they whispered of the imprint of Anders's fingers. Looking away from them, I winced.

Rohesia clucked reassuring nonsense, and I let her lead me. Before we fully left the Great Hall, I looked back. Instead of the tender embrace I hoped to see, however, Cade stood stony-faced to one side, and Margried strode toward me.

She took my other arm and examined it as we walked toward the kitchens. When her haunted eyes met mine, I remembered how her arm looked that night at the riverside, with one handprint mark at her elbow.

We arrived at the kitchens. The maids all looked as pale as Margried and Rohesia. I wondered if I shared their pallor. A cook clucked at my bruises and produced her supply of crushed and stored violets. Silently, she mixed it with oil in a bowl. Then she pressed the oil from the herbs, stirred the mixture together once again, and applied the mash to my arms.

I recognized the recipe as one of Hildegard's. After my sleeves had been rolled back into place, I begged them all to secrecy. No need to worry Susan or Sister Agnes—or even Millicent—with the events of the afternoon. Anders would no doubt soon be on his way home to Lansberry, anyway, fuming from whatever had made him so furious with me today.

And I would be left on my own to plead Dirk's innocence with the noblemen we—and hopefully Talan—had not yet contacted.

I hardly slept at all that night, which was both a relief—for the nightmares could not invade whilst I stared out the window at the silvery moon—and a curse—for guilt and worry could.

Dirk

Chapter Twenty-Nine

"Reverend Joseph!" My shouts failed to produce my friend. I looked at Ian and bade him take care of Titus in my absence. A storm raged outside the thick walls of the monastery, promising certain death if I led Ian and Titus back into its cold embrace.

Then I found Joseph. The door to his room swung wide beneath my arm's command, and I rushed to his side after a second of shock-stricken staring.

Ill.

A muscle in my shoulder twitched. At the same time as a storm poured outside, an invisible storm surged all around us within these very walls, threatening danger. No sword could defeat a fever, though God's power could overcome any foe. And it was God's power we needed now, as I rushed into action, shouting for Ian, praying to the One I trusted most.

Joseph's forehead poured sweat, and he thrashed in his bed. The image of Gwyn in this state flashed before my eyes. Was this monastery haunted that one of our number always fell ill within its walls? Had I left Joseph with my illness, undefended?

Lord, what have I done?

Ian came, shooing Titus out the door when he saw. "What can I do?"

"Out!" I waved him from the room. "I need towels, water, broth, but do not enter."

If Ian and I fell ill as well, who would see Titus to my mother's?

What if Titus became ill? *Lord, the fever took my father and nearly took Gwyn from me. Tudder has already lost Mary…. Please, do not allow Titus to succumb to this illness.*

My gaze swung to a corner of the cell. The light failed to penetrate the darkness there, but it flickered in its attempt. The scent of tallow spun into my nose as my boots carried me out of the doorway and to the candle lodged in a hollow in a wall.

"Dirk?" Titus stared up at me.

I closed my eyes, Tudder's words coming back to me. *I want you to know that I am not entrusting my son's life to you, Dirk. I am entrusting his life to God.* Had Tudder had some horrible premonition that something like this might happen, that a situation might arise when all my knowledge of stealth and swords would cease to serve me in good stead?

Or had his words been a warning to me? *If something happens to him…* What had he said? He did not wish for me to collect more guilt than I deserved.

I turned away from the door. I had no intention of doing anything of the sort; Titus would survive this.

I backed away from the boy, the candlelight wavering at the shaking in my hand. The storm pulsed outside the walls in which we stood, and here I had brought him where fever threatened my friend's life. "All will be well, Titus."

But I knew from the look on his face that he knew I was not sure.

When I woke three days later, my head on my folded arms on his bed, Joseph studied me with patient eyes. "Good morrow, friend."

Wordless, I lunged forward and put a palm to his forehead. Broken. Praise God. My eyes closed in relief.

"How long have I been ill?" His cracked lips faltered on the words. I poured him some of the wine Ian had brought me to fuel these sleepless days.

"Three days since my arrival. I do not know before that. You really ought not to live alone here." The thought that had haunted me while I feared for days I would lose him was that he could have died before I even arrived.

"God looks out for me."

I shook my head and laughed as I had not laughed in too long. "I cannot argue with that."

"What brings you here to visit me?"

"I did not come alone."

"Ian accompanied your return?" He coughed.

"And Titus."

Joseph raised a brow.

"Do you remember my telling you of my captain friend?"

He nodded. "He used to run with you and Cade, but God drew Him to Himself—and through this friend, He drew you."

"You have an excellent memory," I said.

"This is Titus?"

"His son."

"How old is the boy?" He coughed lightly.

"Six years. You must rest, not talk." I reached for the blanket and drew it higher upon his shoulders.

"Is he a hearty lad?"

"Healthy enough, albeit quiet in temperament."

Joseph gave a curt nod. "Temperament notwithstanding, that he is healthy bodes well. I trust you have kept him away from me?"

"Ian has seen to it he has stayed away." I had gone from promising Tudder my utmost care of his son, to taking him out of a storm and to a fever-wracked friend.

He reached for my arm, looking at me with a solemn expression. "We are in God's hands, Devon. We can trust Him."

I nodded and turned toward the corner with his cup in my hand. Refilling it with water from the clay pitcher, I acknowledged that I trusted God. It was myself I did not trust.

Ian looked up with a somber face when I entered the kitchens. He and Titus sat at a table with two steaming bowls before them. The sight reminded me so much of the morning Gwyn had sat in this kitchen that my jaw clenched. Then I saw the expression on Titus's face. His light-colored brows drew together as he frowned. He allowed his spoon to rest in his bowl as I came forward.

"Reverend Joseph is well," I told Ian, who sighed his relief.

I sank into a chair opposite Titus, laying my elbows on the table and my head on my folded arms so that my eyes would be directly across from his. After three days and not catching the fever myself, I trusted we were safe. He stared back at me, waiting. I could remember little about being his age, but I knew I had never been as quiet or still as Titus was every day.

"What do you have there, Titus?" I nodded at the bowl.

He touched his spoon. "Soup."

"What kind?"

"'Tis thick."

I nodded. "Do you like it?"

"Aye, sir."

I decided to ignore the fact that he most likely said that to appease me. In time, I was determined he would know he could be completely honest with me, that he would incur no wrath if he disagreed with me or expressed displeasure of any sort. Truth mattered.

Running a hand down my face, I focused on the boy again. "Do you like this place?"

"It is warmer here." He pointed toward the fireplace.

Ian pushed his spoon around his bowl. "When he asked why we had come, I told him we would be warmer here."

I chuckled. "It was cold during that storm. I am glad to be by the warmth of the fire, as well.

That Titus had asked Ian why we had come made me smile. Mayhap the lad was opening up, after all.

"Titus, do you know where we are?"

He shook his head, and his blond curls bounced across his brow.

"This is an old monastery, where men used to live...so they could have more time to pray." I ignored Ian's chortle behind me. "But only one such man lives here now. He is my friend. Thank you for being brave while I helped him get well again."

For the first time, I saw the boy grin. "Can I meet him?"

"He rests now. He is still regaining his strength." I hesitated, then rose and motioned Titus from his chair. A hand on his shoulder, I led him down the hall and into the doorway of Joseph's sickroom. Before I even asked if Joseph was up to this, he caught sight of the boy and smiled. How long had it been since the man had seen a child?

"Good morrow, Titus. I hear you have been quite brave."

"I am brave. I am going to be a brave sea captain, like Papa."

I dipped my chin in a quick nod, fully confident of that fact. "You will make a fine captain, Titus."

But first I had to see him safely to Godfrey, without losing him to sickness or a snowstorm or any of the other dangers that could befall us en route to my home. Then I had to leave him there along with all the others that I loved—and resume my exile.

Gwyneth

Chapter Thirty

A figure leaned over the stair rail as I entered the keep. I squinted, straining to discover who it was. Then she smiled at me, her straight, white teeth gleaming in the light of the evening's candles. Susan. "Is that you, Gwyneth? I can scarcely make you out in this dim light."

Her gentle voice made me suspicious at first, as if mayhap she knew something. Had Rohesia confided in her why I had favored my wrists these last few days?

Nee. She had promised she would not.

I returned Susan's smile—albeit, with effort—and cocked my head to the side. "It is I, Susan. Will you not join me?"

I hugged my arms as I watched her descend the stairs, trying to will warmth to return to my cold limbs. The snow fell faster outside the keep now; the flakes that seemed so fragile and innocent from my window sank straight through my sleeves once I had stepped outside. I had not minded. I had needed only to see Char and Alfie.

Susan somehow made bounding down the stairs and skipping to stand in front of me appear graceful. She giggled. "I fear one of these days my clumsiness will join forces with my excess energy and get the best of me."

I allowed her to loop her arm through my own, ignoring the possibility that she might bump my wrist and aggravate the healing bruises. "But it is not this day."

"Nay." She giggled, her eyes meeting mine. "Your arm is cold."

I looked around, trying to appear innocent and aware that I was failing. "Is it?"

"Does this mean you were visiting your favorite horse again?"

I smiled at her. "And if it does?"

Susan gave a melodramatic sigh and placed her free hand at her collarbone. "I suppose it means you must confide in me as you confided in Char."

My smile died. If only I had not revealed to Susan that half the time—especially when winter's bitter cold forbade me from riding out for long—the reason I visited Char was because I needed to talk to someone who would listen without judgment or comment. Since my grandfather had died, Char had been the only one who listened.

"You look sad, Gwyneth."

My gaze went to our feet. I watched us walk, the hems of our skirts whispering over the stone and our shoes. The scent of the rosewater Susan loved teased my nose.

Then Susan stopped. "You are sad." She released my arm so she could spin and face me. Her features drew into an expression of concern. I had no doubt she would have placed her hands on my shoulders if not for the fact that she might have trouble reaching them. No matter. Her face gave away her disquiet just as well as a tender touch. "Tell me?"

I swallowed.

Susan's smile could never leave for long. It reappeared, although colored with apprehension. "Come." She swiveled and stepped toward the staircase. She looked back at me, and her smile grew. "Sister Agnes!"

I turned to see my nun friend walking toward us. "Lady Susan. Lady Gwyneth."

This awkwardness between us had never faded—not since I had told her of my surrender. Or conversion. Or whatever it had been. In truth, what it had been still plagued me. Was I now Protestant or could I still claim to be Catholic?

Did it matter?

I sought for something to say to her. "Were you in the chapel?"

She nodded, smoothing her hands down her habit. "I plan to retire now that my prayers are said."

For as long as we had stayed at Godfrey Estate, a Protestant home, Sister Agnes should have been snappish and eager to leave. Yet she stayed just as she had said she would. Exuding all the while a calm, cool control that reminded me of Anders. Mayhap the woman was more truly Catholic than I knew, or her prayers did her good.

I quite wished my prayers had the same effect on my own heart. "Susan and I were just about to retire, as well—"

Susan clapped her hands together. "What if we all go the Great Hall, instead? Mayhap there are some of those delightful scones left."

I could not even remember the foodstuff to which she referred; if it had been on my plate at dinner, I had picked at it without tasting the flavor for which Susan now expressed affection.

With a glance, Sister Agnes deferred to me. Nodding, I forced a smile for Susan's sake. She continued to chatter as we made our way to table. I tried to listen, but mostly I was grateful I did not have to exercise the lessons *Moeder* had drilled into me about how to be a good guest. Susan spoke; I remained silent. It was as simple as that.

Weariness drifted over me as I sat with Sister Agnes and Susan and put small bites of the fruit-flavored scone into my mouth. The dried berries defied my teeth. Could we not have the real thing? But it was winter. Ah, pointless questions; I was weary. Rising to leave, I mumbled a goodnight to Sister Agnes and Susan.

Susan blanched. "Gwyneth, are you well? You look pale."

Sister Agnes stood and came to stand beside me. "You wish to retire now?"

I nodded, willing a reassuring smile to replace whatever on my face had caused such a reaction from them both. "I am well, merely tired."

The events of the last few days revolved in my mind. Anders's inexplicable eruption. Cade's altercation with him. Margried's refusal to bend—even after I begged her to reconsider again, even after her love for Cade shone through that frightened shout she had given when he had struck Anders.

"Aye, Sister Agnes." Pulling away from her, I straightened the mask of emotionless calm that I kept ever on my face. "I will leave you two to it, then. Thank you for the lovely conversation this evening." Even as my energy seeped into the floor, proof of tutelage bled through.

I managed to walk from the room with a sedate, regal pace, but as soon as I found myself at the foot of the stairs, my legs weakened beneath me. I reached out to the rail, but before I could cling to it...

He caught me.

At once, I stiffened and turned in his arms, loathing that I swayed even as I did so. I tossed a hand behind me. My fingers touched the rail, and I leaned away from him and into it for support. "What are you doing here?"

Anders grimaced at me. "What do you mean?"

I allowed my disgust to show. "I assumed you had left already."

"Already?" He tipped back his head and laughed though his eyes never broke free of mine. "I am not going anywhere, Gwyneth."

"Fine, then. I will." I swiveled and started climbing the stairs.

But he followed. As I knew he would. I turned back, but before I could say anything, he put his hand to my cheek and whispered, "You need someone who is going to be there for you."

I shook my head, dislodging his hand, even though I agreed with him. Partially. *I need Dirk.* Loneliness crashing down on me, I kept silent.

He sighed, his fingers dropping to his side. When he looked at me again, his eyes brimmed with brokenness.

I recoiled even further away.

"You are beautiful." His whisper spun around us, taking my surprise with it, until I was banded by the weight of the sorrow in his voice and the shock in my soul. "You have always been beautiful."

I touched my glasses. I was not beautiful. I had never been beautiful. "I am cross."

"About what? My being honest with you?" Anders flung his arm to the side. "I was protecting you, Gwyneth. From yourself. You can trust me."

"You bruised me." I had not meant to tell him that. Somehow, the admittance made it even more real, a failure on my part. I had let him hurt me.

He paled. Well, he already knew. I yanked up my sleeves and held out my wrists. Aware we stood on the staircase with people sleeping above us and Sister Agnes and Susan still in the Great Hall below, I lowered my voice to a whisper. "You did this."

He took my hands, and his touch had changed, gentled. Turning over my arms, he shook his head. Did his breathing quicken? "I am sorry. I never meant..." His words fell to the floor.

I shoved down my sleeves, hiding the ugly marks from his tortured expression before they caused him further grief. "I know, yet you did."

His chest rose and fell as he pulled in a deep draught of air. "Can you forgive me?"

My shoulders relaxed, and I gave in. "Of course, Anders." Once again, the boy I had grown up with stood before me. Since he stood on the step beneath mine, we were the same height, eye-to-eye. "What I cannot do is fail to see your hypocrisy here. You ask me to forgive you and obviously expect me to grant your request. But you want me to withhold forgiveness for Dirk's failings."

He stared back at me with a blank expression.

"Do you not see? Both of you are imperfect men who sometimes hurt me and need my forgiveness."

He remained silent in that patient way of his that so irritated me. "I meant what I said, you know. That you are beautiful."

My eyes narrowed. Back to that again.

He leaned forward and touched the arm of my glasses. Why did he insist on touching me? "The day I arrived, you took these off."

My brow furrowed. "They give me headaches; sometimes I carry them for a time, but I always put them back on." That had not been the reason Anders had seen me without them that day, and we both knew it. As well as we both knew he already knew about my headaches; after all, we had grown up together.

That first day, I had taken off my glasses because my trust in Anders had been so great, my blindness had paled in comparison.

Because we had grown up together, I trusted him so much that the one thing I wanted more than almost anything else—Dirk's honor restored—I had entrusted to him. But all my trust in Anders had gotten me was weeks of waiting on him to return with unfavorable reports.

I had battled to remain content with that. For a time. After all, acting rashly had once landed me in the middle of the Beeldenstorm. Acting rashly recently had failed to win over the magistrate. So even though I considered visiting the noblemen *myself*, I knew I would most likely ruin with my snappishness and lack of diplomacy any chance Dirk had of being proven innocent.

He tapped my nose with his finger. "Thank you for forgiving me."

I scrunched my nose and leaned away from him, but not out of fear now. Out of annoyance. "Did you even hear me?"

Something in his face changed. It was barely discernible. Almost imperceptible. Somehow, his eyes told a story I did not care to know.

He took me by the shoulders, then, and slid his hands around my back until I was tucked against him. My cheek met his chest. My eyes closed without my permission.

A moment passed and then he said, "I have something to ask you. Not yet. But soon."

I opened my eyes and looked up at him. He had trampled a piece of my trust when he had given in to his fury. He had bruised me in more ways than one. But this was Anders. He had always come when I called. I had always been able to depend upon him. *You can trust me,* he had said.

When I finally pulled away, he kissed my brow. I smiled softly before I turned to climb the stairs.

Because right then I needed a little always.

Dirk

Chapter Thirty-One

Our boots crunched in the snow as Ian and I passed through the monastery's outer grounds. Titus's laughter followed us from within the walls. I had left him and Joseph building a tower. On our second day, Ian had worked to whittle the blocks; Titus had since not let half a day pass without playing with them.

Ian and I scoured the snow on the forest floor for twigs and branches felled by the storm. Then we freed our axes.

The snowstorm had passed, heading west, the day after Joseph recovered. Ian and I agreed to stay a while longer. After all, if we left, we would be following the snow's path. It would be best to allow it to settle and give the storm several days' lead. I entertained the idea that the storm would continue to forge a path west and assault Godfrey Estate, but the images of the storerooms and the keep itself rose in my mind. Godfrey Estate would weather the storm's fury as well as St. Benet's could.

Ian stood a few feet away, axe in hand, intent on creating his own pile of firewood. I turned back to my own. I swung, lobbed the branch—as thick as my waist—in half, and deposited both halves in the pile by my side. Glancing over at Ian, I swiped my brow. Winter kept the snow at our feet alive, but its power stopped there and failed to counteract our exertion. Sweat rolled down Ian's forehead, too. Even the wind could not prevent us from perspiring whilst swinging axe-heads above our shoulders and down into the wood marrow.

After the pile beside me reached the height of my knees, I looked over at Ian. His back met my gaze. His shoulders slanted. My head cocked as I watched the man seem to rock. Then he heaved a silent breath.

I stuck my axe in the trunk I had claimed as my base and strode forward on noisy boots. His hand lifted to cover his face when he heard me approach, but I did not mean to pry or intrude, only to support. My hand rose to rest on his back.

Long, quiet moments we stood there, bound by invisible strings of grief that kept our innermost selves shut off to even each other. Only God knew the pain we had both experienced.

Something happens in a man's heart when he loses someone. It sits heavy, indeed.

"She was nineteen when the fever took her." Ian's voice pulled me from my prayer.

"Jane?"

"Jane Thomason. She was the prettiest lass in all London." Ian turned to face me, a smile on his face. "Did I tell you the miracles she could do with a needle? I had never seen anything like it."

I studied him. "Did she ever know you stood outside her window?"

"At first she did. It grew harder to tell toward the end. Then, at the very last, she knew nothing at all."

"It was the same with my father." And it very well could have been the same with Joseph had we not come upon him when we did.

Ian stepped toward me, snow crunching beneath his boots. He gripped my shoulder all of a sudden. "I regret letting her die, Dirk."

"You could not have—"

"Nay." He slashed a hand through the air. "Jane died because her heart was broken and she saw no reason to go on. If I could live last year over again, I would never have allowed her father to pledge her to another man. I would have taken her with me the night she begged me to."

My jaw clenched.

"Do not make the same mistake I did, Dirk."

I raised a brow, surprised by the ferocity in the younger man's gaze.

He took a deep breath. "I do not mean to insult you."

"Yet you do." My voice lowered. "You are telling me I made a mistake."

"I mean only to say you have something I did not have—a second chance." His words, full of fire, burned straight through me. "We are returning."

"To bring Titus." I hefted my axe again and turned away slightly, to face the white-capped trees and icy chunks of wood we needed.

"To see her." He stepped in front of me and his gaze dared me to deny his words.

I let my axe slide gently to my side, ran a hand through my hair, and bit back a growl of frustration. I had not even wanted to think of what returning to Godfrey Estate might mean, but I acknowledged now that it meant what I at the same time longed for and loathed.

I would see Gwyn again.

Or would I? Would she even see me after what I had done to her? My fists clenched and unclenched as I struggled against the pain of that possibility.

"Dirk." Ian watched my face, anxious at whatever he saw there.

My heart hardened. I respected the man's grief, but…I shook my head. "Ian, you know not into what you pry."

"I do." Tears glistened in his eyes now as he looked around the snowy forest in which we stood. "I know that a good woman loved me, I loved her back, and we could have been happy together. But I let her go."

I fought to keep my expression under control. "You thought it was the right thing." Did I give voice to that thought in order to comfort him… or myself?

"I did." Ian nodded once, a quick chin thrust weighted with regret. "And you think that this is the right thing—leaving Gwyn behind." He gripped my arm. "But it is not. 'Tis a gift, the love you share. Do not squander it. Make right the way you have hurt her."

His words hung in the air between us; I left them there, shouldered my axe once more, and filled my other arm with chopped wood. I tromped back through the wind to St. Benet's. Throughout the many trips that transported my pile of wood to the monastery, I prayed. For us to have finally evicted the lung fever, for us to remain well. For safety on our trip back to my father's land.

And for Gwyn. I prayed for her well-being, that since the letter I received from my mother, she had strengthened once again. For her heart and continued renewal in her relationship with God. But I dared not pray as I wished to pray. I dared not ask God for Gwyn's favor on me when she saw me again, for her to even consent to seeing me again.

Back within the warmth of St. Benet's, I took a moment to pull the lock of hair she had sent with her letter out of my pocket. My thumb and forefinger held it gently even as my eyes remained tightly closed.

Four days later, I burst into Titus's room and found him rearranging a tottering tower. "Ian has whittled you a few more blocks, I see."

Titus nodded, staring at me curiously. "I made my tower higher."

"You have done an admirable job. If you wish to work on it further, you may; however, it may have to wait until we arrive at Godfrey Manor. The last of the storm has released its hold."

His mouth formed an O. Then the grin on my face found a mirror in his. He yelped and jumped to his feet, putting the tower to death. He did not even spare it a glance, but barreled from the doorway as if intent on diving into the snow that no longer posed a threat but promised play. As if I had released him from prison. Mayhap I had. I looked around the small room.

As I listened to him clomp down the hall in his boots, I smiled for the first time in days. Weariness tugged at my eyelids. When had been the last I had slept? I looked to Titus's cot in the corner. *Too long.*

When I came to dinner that night, Joseph grinned up at me from his place across the table from Titus. "There you are."

Titus turned and looked up at me.

I rubbed my hand over my face. "How long was I out?"

Joseph laughed and shook his head. "Not long enough, from the looks of you."

"Where is Ian?"

"He stumbled into the first bed he saw, too."

I raised my brows and laid a hand on Titus's shoulder. "And what have you been doing all afternoon while your guardians slept?" Sleeping while responsibility rested on my shoulders had resulted in disaster before. Fighting the wince, I felt relief when the boy smiled.

Mumbling a response to Titus's account of the escapades Joseph had led him on this afternoon, I sat down. A bowl appeared in front of me, and I ate, actually tasting my food for the first time in days.

"We made it."

My eyes met Joseph's smiling ones. "Indeed we did."

"I could not have done it without you, Devon. I thank you for putting yourself at risk for me."

I shook my head. "After all the times you have put yourself at risk for me?"

He sobered.

My spoon clinked into my bowl, oddly reminding me of the silver Gwyn had given me. "What is it?"

He glanced at Titus, who seemed to be nodding off into his bowl. I smirked at the boy, surprised at the burst of joy it gave me to see the child, healthy and out of danger, at peace.

"Would you mind creating us a new tower, Titus?" I asked.

Titus blinked up at me with heavy eyes, but a spark of joy entered them at the mention of his block creation. After he left to fetch his blocks, I laid my elbows on the table and waited.

Joseph sighed. "He was looking for you, Devon."

"Who?" Though I had my suspicions.

"The man who came and cut short your last visit. He stayed for three days. I think he thought you were hidden in a barrel or secret corner somewhere and he would be able to just wait you out."

I merely laughed at that.

Joseph did not. "He asked questions."

A flashback surfaced of my standing on the docks in the Low Countries, Tudder before me, Gwyn behind me, the decision of whether to tell the truth or speak falsely on my shoulders. "What did he ask?"

"If I knew who you are. If I knew what you had done. If I knew where you were going."

I waited.

"You know him. And he knows you."

No. It could not be.

"I told him I knew your name, that you were an honorable man with a crime pinned to your reputation, and that I did not know your destination."

My eyes closed. "Such speech could see you swinging, Reverend."

He glared, annoyed. "They do not hang monks."

"Former monk."

The glare dissipated. "True. Even so, I would not lie."

"Which name did you give them?" The small dining area in which we sat seemed to shrink around me. I rubbed my hand down the rough wood of the table and suddenly recalled sitting in this very chair, only across from Gwyn. My nose conjured the sweet scent of the porridge with which we had broken our fast that day. When I looked up at Joseph again, his face remained solemn.

"Devon, of course."

"Most know me by Dirk now."

"That name does not fit you."

I leaned back slightly. "Some would say it is not violent enough."

Joseph looked straight into my eyes. "It is Talan."

And suddenly my past caught up with me and sunk its claws into my shoulders. The demons on my back breathed down my neck.

I looked again to the wooden table beneath my hands. Then one hand lifted and rose of its own accord to the scar beside my right eyebrow, the one Gwyn once inquired after. I had refused to give her the story then. Mayhap I would never have the chance to tell her.

But one man knew the events of that night, and he had vowed we would meet again. Not long after, on the night my father died, I had given up that lifestyle and hoped Talan would stay in my corrupted past. I had been wrong.

Talan did not seek money. Neither did he seek justice. God knew we had operated outside of it that night. Talan's motives sprang from a far more dangerous source: the thirst for revenge.

Gwyneth

Chapter Thirty-Two

My knife speared the piece of meat on my trencher and carried it to my mouth. I looked across from me and found Margried's eyes on Susan, sitting to my right. Following her gaze, I discovered Susan smiling at Cade, beside Margried, who was making some kind of remark to Rohesia.

Rohesia smiled, nodded, and said something pleasant in acknowledgment of his compliment. The table fell silent once more, save for the sound of knife blades finding root in our food and wine swirling in glasses. I reached for my goblet to wash down the bite of food that I did not truly taste—I forced myself to eat more out of concern the others would notice if I did not—and took a larger swallow than I intended.

Since the night I drank too much wine, I had lost my fear that I might imbibe too much, but this was more than I could handle. I choked, trying not to sputter.

"Gwyneth?" Margried leaned forward. Concern washed over her face, as well as that of Sister Agnes beside her. An echo of my name came from beside me as Susan relieved me of my goblet.

Anders, to my left, put down his own goblet and turned toward me. One large palm reached for my back but stopped short when I managed to swallow and regain control. "All better?"

I nodded, unable to speak just yet, but trying to project with my eyes to all around me that I was fine. This bath of attention was exactly what I had wished to avoid. Pasting on a smile for everyone's benefit, I reached for the hunk of bread at the corner of my trencher.

Everyone relaxed and resumed eating, their gazes returning to their own food. This tension had overtaken us the day after the altercation in the Great Hall.

Seven days later, the letter had come, and the strain grew even worse.

Even Rohesia's excellent hostess qualities could not soothe the tear that Tudder's words had made. His missive had been brief, but his meaning had echoed through my innermost heart and soul with the force of a storm.

Captain Mathieu Tudder, by the grace of God to Lady Rohesia Godfrey of Godfrey Estate, his most kind greeting.

By now my brothers should have arrived with my son, dear aunt. I write to thank you for your care of him. I am most grateful for your compassion. Will you please tell Titus I love and miss him? I pray for all of you.

Yours, Tudder

Rohesia had nearly tossed me the letter yesterday afternoon in the library and begged me to explain. I had read it, hurried and flushed, and looked up at her with my heart in my stomach. Titus, I had said, was Tudder's boy. I knew Dirk had been with Tudder, but not why Titus would be with Dirk.

By now my brothers should have arrived.

But they had not. The only guest intruding upon Rohesia's hospitality—besides Anders, who seemed to see no need to leave Godfrey Estate after he had offered an apology for his atrocious behavior—was the storm that blanketed the land in snow, denying me the privilege of taking Char out to that meadow again.

Only that one letter of Dirk's had arrived. No more word had come from him. What had happened?

And why had he been retracing his steps to Godfrey Estate? With Titus in tow?

Unless this was a trap of some sort. Mayhap someone who sought to apprehend Dirk was trying a new tactic—that of bringing me into the fray. But who knew that the best way to hurt Dirk would be to hurt me?

Talan. The man who sought to see Dirk remain a murderer in the magistrate's—and others'—eyes. The man who had somehow turned the magistrate against me with a stroke of his pen in a single letter.

Yet what did Talan hope to accomplish by forging a letter in Tudder's hand and alerting me that Dirk might be near? None of the meanderings of my mind made sense.

Our meal over, we all rose to retire to different rooms—Sister Agnes to the chapel, Anders with her, Cade to the library. Watching the tortured look in Cade's eyes shutter as he looked at Margried—and her turn away from him—I moved to her side. My intent? To ask her to come with me and then meander to the library where I knew Cade usually retired after the evening meal.

If I could not have my love, I would see to it they had theirs.

Then Rohesia smiled and spoke before I could. "Gwyneth, would you accompany me to the boudoir?"

I hesitated but could find no suitable excuse, except for the fact that Millicent glared at me from behind her mother. And how would that sound? *I beg pardon, Lady Godfrey, but I would rather retire to my chamber, where I will not have to suffer the company of your older daughter.*

"Of course." I fell into step beside Susan. Margried walked behind me.

We had just settled into seats—Millicent across the room from me, a blessing and a curse, for she was both at a distance and able to continue her glare—when Rohesia turned to me. "I know you may not wish to share, dear girl, but I…" She pulled in a deep breath and looked at me with her heart in her eyes. "I do so want to hear your plan."

I swallowed. Though a part of me wished not to involve her, lest the rejections hurt her, she deserved to know what I was doing on her son's behalf. "You already know that Anders has been seeking out lords with whom he can speak who might be receptive to Dirk's innocence."

Rohesia nodded. "How many support him now?"

"Yes, how many?" Susan perched on the edge of her couch now. "He has come and gone so many times."

I swallowed. "None. But I have written each one, asking them to reconsider. I—"

"This is ridiculous." The scoffing voice brought my gaze to Millicent. The young woman's eyes darkened with her anger. Her cheeks flushed.

Margried's hand landed on my shoulder.

"Would you care to explain yourself, daughter?" The light in Rohesia's eyes had dimmed.

Millicent stared straight at me even as she answered her mother. "This foolish plan will only serve to exacerbate the state of my brother's reputation."

"He is not only your brother, but my son, Millicent." Rohesia reached out and laid a hand on her daughter's knee.

I bit my tongue before I could say Dirk was the man I loved.

Susan spoke up. "Why do you not want Gwyneth to do everything she can to help Dirk?"

My eyes remained on Millicent as I wondered the same.

Millicent huffed. "She will not help him; she will worsen his situation. If we only sit quietly, his past indiscretions will be forgotten."

"His indiscretions, mayhap," Rohesia said. "But he has been accused of murder. Or have you *forgotten*?"

I flicked my glance to Rohesia. I had never heard her voice so hard.

Millicent stared at her mother. She stood, pulling away from her mother's hand. "I have most certainly not." Her tone lowered. "I daresay I remember far more often than any of you that he should be here with us now."

I closed my eyes as the force of her words slapped my senses. She thought I did not remember every waking moment—and the sleeping ones, too—that he should be here? "Then why would you find it troubling should I write to Her Majesty herself?"

"He should be at table with us. He should be walking the halls. He should be…" Millicent's voice broke.

"Millicent." Susan's tears brought her sister's gaze to hers.

Rohesia, her face showing her shock, reached out to her daughter, but Millicent only ignored her and strode straight toward me. "And you."

It took everything in me to stay seated and allow her to tower over me.

"You are the reason he left, the reason he had to. You are the reason everyone believes him to be a murderer, because he was at *your* home, with *you*, when your parents died at the hand of *your* uncle! All of this is your fault." Her shouts calmed to a deadly whisper. "I will never forgive you for that."

I could not stand, not breathe, not speak.

"There is no reason he should have been at your home—except for you!" Millicent screamed. "Did you seduce him?"

"Millicent, that is quite enough." Rohesia shot to her feet, surprise at her daughter's behavior written in the worried wrinkles on her face.

Susan wrung her hands in front of her.

"No!" Millicent swung her gaze from her mother to me. "You deserve to be thrown out of here, but, nay, instead we allow you to stay. We treat you as our guest. When it was you who stole my brother's reputation from him, and him from his family."

"Millicent!" Rohesia came forward.

I faced Millicent again, unflinching, my stare hard. "As I said before, I am sorry."

She had the audacity to look triumphant.

"I am sorry I said he was the one who murdered them that night. He did not deserve my judgment, my rushed allegation. I am also sorry for *our* loss. Your mother knows a mother's sorrow over his departure, I a woman's broken heart. Just because we do not allow ourselves to drown in our pain does not mean that we are not tempted—or that our pain is somehow inferior to your own. Never think that you miss Dirk more than any of the rest of us."

Millicent glared. "His name is Devon."

She swept from the room, once again claiming the last word. And again what a word it was. His name. I summoned a deep breath into my lungs, hearing his name deep within my soul.

Then I heard more. Rohesia asked if I was well, Susan echoed her question, and Margried whispered my name. But I ignored them all and brushed away their gentle hands.

Stumbling from the room, I swallowed the sobs, and, for one moment, for one agonizing moment, I gave in to the temptation that had plagued this household for weeks. I succumbed to pain's outstretched claw and drowned in the sorrow of losing him whom my heart loved. I felt what Millicent felt.

Then I opened my eyes and walked up the stairs to gaze at the bird on the tapestry. Mayhap she could teach me how to break from these bonds that bound me. Mayhap she could impart some ancient secret about how to fly when one's wings are ripped.

But I found no answer, no truth, in the beauty of the tapestry. *God, help me. I cannot bear one more day apart from him, knowing I caused it, knowing I may never succeed in seeing his name cleared, his honor restored.*

As much as I longed to flee to the stables, I knew I would find no answer in Char's mane. *God, I need You. You were once so close. Why do You stay away now? Why does everyone stay away?* So I secluded myself in the room Margried and I shared, burying myself beneath the blankets with the box that held his letter and those crisp, crumbling flower petals—his farewell.

After the tears were spent, I remembered something I had said in anger's fire: *"Then why would you find it troubling should I write to Her Majesty herself?"*

I rose from the bed, closed the box, and reached for a pen.

Later, when the knock came, I did not think twice about answering it. Did Sister Agnes have a question? Did Rohesia want to speak to me further? I opened the door, surprised to find Anders waiting on the other side.

"Come with me." His three words arrowed straight to my soul and lodged there.

A sigh pulled down my shoulders. "Anders…I." *I cannot.* "You know I cannot." What if Dirk really were out there, waylaid by the storm, wounded and weak but making his way to us? I could do naught but wait for him here. Leaving now, with Anders, was impossible.

"Listen to me. He is out there, is he not?" His eyes looked wild. Wide and intent. Almost…impulsive. And Anders was anything but impulsive.

I think it was that look on his face that made me step outside my bedchamber and close the door behind me. "Dirk? Tudder's letter certainly seems to suggest so." Never mind that Anders should not know the contents of the letter; I had certainly not shared them with him.

"Rohesia left the letter on the library table."

"What?" How could she have been that careless? Unless she had intended to leave the man's words—words that seemed to promise her son was near—where she could view them easily, reread them regularly. And that certainly seemed like Rohesia. So unlike me, who kept Dirk's letter in a box with crumbling flower petals.

"Let us be away tonight."

My eyes narrowed, sick that my friend would suggest I abandon the hope of seeing Dirk again. "He might be coming, Anders. I must stay where he knows he can find me. You know that."

Anders shook his head. "I mean, let us go find him."

Immediately, my wings knit and my soul flew to say yes.

"But why?" Why would Anders want to do this? Reunite me with the man he disapproved of?

Anders's expression faltered as he processed how to answer me.

Was this what he had spoken of that night? What he had needed to tell me, only the timing had not been right?

Margried's wariness of him, Rohesia's warning about his character when we had talked about patience, Sister Agnes's blind trust in him—all these wrestled with the silence he maintained, bidding me not to trust him.

But I would never know his true intent if I did not at least pretend to play along.

So when he said again, "Come with me."

I said, "Yes."

The snow had ceased falling, but still it crunched beneath our horses' hooves as we departed from the gate to the sleepy, suspicious stares of the guards. Anders immediately led us east, and my shivering eased. I had not been cold, just anxious that mayhap he planned on absconding with me to somewhere Dirk could not possibly be.

But Dirk's traveling back from being with Tudder at the coast would have brought him from the east.

An hour passed with silence arcing between us, and slowly I realized how foolish and impulsive this had been. At least when I had fetched Alfie, Rohesia had known where I went, and Cade had come along. At least when I had gone to see the magistrate, Rohesia had known the general direction, and Thomas had accompanied me. At least she had known I was leaving both times!

This night, Anders and I had left without telling a soul, although the guards surely had reported our absence now.

"What are we doing?" I pulled up on Char's reins to force Anders to rein in his own mount and circle back to me.

To my surprise, Anders did not only come back to me, he dismounted. Then he reached up to help me down. I let him, aware of the way his hands lingered at my back even after I stood on the ground, steady. "I just have to know," he whispered.

I tilted my head. "Anders?"

The lack of moonlight denied me insight into his expression. Darkness swathed the sky and the forest around us. There we stood, in the middle of trees with the forest folk skittering around us. An owl hooted. A shiver raced across my back; I tugged my cloak tighter, a subtle signal Anders was to remove his hands.

He did not.

Instead, he pulled me into an embrace, and what once had been brotherly suddenly was no more. He leaned to rest his head on my shoulder. I drew in a breath, unwilling to hurt him by pulling away, but unwilling, too, to see what he meant by *having to know*. "Anders, whatever are you doing?"

"You feel nothing, Gwyneth? Nothing at all?"

As gently as I could, I pulled back slightly until I was eye to eye with him. "I am sorry. I love Dirk."

"But have you always? Were you ever mine?" It was as if he laid his heart in my hand with that last question.

How I wished I could do something more than merely hand it back to him. "No." I could have given him a thousand reasons why we would have never worked. I viewed him as a brother. When I ran to him the night my parents died, he saw me to the coast but did not go with me. He was Catholic, too, and would never have challenged my faith as Dirk had.

He was Anders and never meant to be mine as Devon Godfrey always had been.

He held me close for one more moment…then let me go. I did not force it, just let him be the one to step away.

"We are not actually going to find him, are we?"

"Do what you wish." He moved to stand beside my horse. "I go with you wherever you go."

My eyes closed. "Do not say that, Anders. You cannot. You should not."

"Now, where to?" He lifted me to Char's back, and I saw just a glimpse of how my choice had affected him in the glistening of his gaze.

My heart lunged for my throat as I realized I held the chance to go after Dirk right there. I could tell Anders we would seek the man I loved until we found him. Anders offered me all of England in that moment. Anywhere I wanted to go, we could go.

I wanted to go with all my being.

But I could not. 'Twas not right. If I went after Dirk now, what would that say to the God to whom I had given him up? The God who had saved me when all seemed impossible, when my very heart had been hardened against him? And if Dirk really were on his way to me, I needed to be where he could find me.

This was not a night for running, as much as I wanted it to be. And how I wanted it to be.

"Let us return," I whispered. Surprise stole across Anders's features, but I refused to explain. I could not even explain this decision to my own heart. I just knew Dirk was not coming back to me, and naught I could do would change that.

Dirk

Chapter Thirty-Three

Hours after I had seen Titus to sleep that night, Joseph found me kneeling in the chapel. He interrupted me just before I lay down prostrate on the floor. The sound of his footsteps behind me stilled my movements, and I stayed on my knees. Looking down, I realized my knuckles had turned white after clutching the lock of Gwyn's hair during the hours I had been here. But I refused to let it go, refused to let *her* go.

What would she be doing right now? I smiled. Mayhap sleeping. A frown killed the smile. Did she still suffer from the nightmares?

Did Revelin know she knew no peace from sleep? I trusted Cade to protect her, but more and more often, Revelin's shady reputation broke into my thoughts and churned my stomach.

Joseph's voice preceded his presence at my side. "You pray."

I nodded.

"You have knelt here for hours, Devon." His tone was gentle.

"Have you been watching?" The small window that allowed the moonlight to drift down onto the altar on which my numb knees sat would allow him the perfect view. I studied the slender rope of her hair between my fingers. It turned silver in the light.

"Aye, and I do not care for what I see."

"Will you finally disagree with me on matters of religion, then?" I winced at my biting tone and tucked my chin to my chest as I closed my eyes. I certainly did not act as if I had been in the presence of God for the last two hours.

"I expect you and I will ever disagree on matters of religion, Devon. Such trifles are easy to argue over."

"What are you getting at?"

"I thought we agreed on matters of *faith*."

I turned and glared at him.

"You have been praying for two hours. Why?"

"I do not know what to do." Actually, I did. I should send Ian on to Godfrey Estate. With Titus. And I would finally be free of all responsibility. Nothing—more importantly—no one would depend on me. No more mission. No more chance of seeing her again.

But I had no peace. I put my head in my hands.

Although, I conceded, I deserved no peace at all. Who was I but a condemned murderer? And if I did not fully deserve that title, I did deserve the title of rogue, rake, and rebel.

Joseph knelt beside me. "I think you do, in fact, know what to do."

My fingers curled into my hair. "Has God spoken to you where He has not spoken to me, then? How impolite of Him. After all, I am the one seeking His answer tonight."

Joseph chuckled. "You should be glad this is not still a monastery. These walls would have surely cracked had they heard such things years ago."

"Blasphemy. Another sin some would be eager to add to my list. One more blot on a long, dark trail."

"And mine, as well. What is one more?" Joseph's flippant tone pulled my gaze to him.

"Do you remember when you called Ian and I into your armarius and asked us to pour out what was on our hearts?"

His eyes lit up.

I could smell my demons' breath on my back, but I was no less eager to face them. "I am still not ready to tell you."

He looked at me. "What *are* you ready to tell me?"

"Why do I have to tell you anything?"

"You do not. But you said you do not know what to do."

"Mayhap that is all I wish to say." I sounded younger than Titus, who slept now with a block in his hand.

"But I can tell that it is not."

I sighed. He was right, of course. He always was. "I know what I should do."

"And that is?"

"Send Ian to take Titus to my mother, to my sisters, to Gwyn."

A ruffled sigh spewed from Joseph's mouth. "Then why have you not informed him he is leaving on the morrow?"

My hands fell away from my head, and I glanced at the cross above us. The form of the Christ stretched out upon the wooden crucifix, reminding me of the sacrifice my God had made willingly, even eagerly, on my behalf. How could I not now make a sacrifice for Him?

"He loves you, you know." Joseph whispered the words. "And He is near."

I nodded. "I know."

"Do you?" Joseph's whisper grew more forceful. "Do you, truly?"

"Do any of us truly know a love like that?"

He chuckled.

I looked at him. "He gave His all for me. How can I not give my all now for Him?"

Joseph's grin widened. "I once stood where you stand."

I glanced down at my kneeling position and smiled ruefully at him. "I thought it would be too easy to become what I once was."

"A monk?"

He nodded. "I entertained the idea of going into law, like my father before me. But what I wanted was to join the order."

"How did you decide?"

Joseph smiled up at the cross. "I did not. I asked God for wisdom and followed the peace."

My sigh sounded frustrated. "I have no peace."

Joseph murmured something I did not catch.

"Speak up, brother." I stood on sore legs and swatted at my knees even though I knew they had accumulated no dust or dirt. It was almost as if I avoided looking at the cross, but that was ludicrous.

"Devon, I believe you do know what you are to do, but you do not wish to do it."

"You are right about my not wanting to do what I know I must." Sending Ian and Titus on to Godfrey Estate would not only stretch what little soul I had left, it would tear it from my body. I feared I would no longer be the same.

The need to leave England forever swamped over me, and I almost fell to my knees again. Caught in the trap of my own anguish, I missed Joseph's rising. He stole my attention by grabbing my shoulders. "Listen to me. I do not mean the fool plan you have concocted. I mean the plan that gives you peace."

I swiveled away, my boots pointing toward the door. "Did you hear me? There is no peace for the likes of me."

He wrapped a hand around my shoulder and tugged me toward him again. "You are listening to lies now. That is not truth. You can have peace. You are a child of God, after all."

I stared into Joseph's eyes. He was right. Again. I *was* listening to lies. Well, no more. Somehow the God who had seen me through everything else could see me through this one last surrender—but would He? I blinked, etching on my heart the faith that He would. I would just go on saying it to myself until I finally believed it. "Thank you. I needed that reminder."

"And you need this one. I am not finished. Think."

"I am thinking. I think I shall rouse Ian and tell him he is to leave on the morrow."

Joseph shook his head, his expression revealing exasperation. "Are you always so thick where she is concerned, man?"

I raised my eyebrows.

"I see I shall have to spell it out for you. These two hours, while you knelt at this altar and prayed, did it ever occur to you the Lord was giving you the desire of your heart?"

I crossed my arms over my chest and studied first the altar he pointed toward, then his face. "The desire of my heart is to see her safe."

Joseph stared into my eyes. "Mayhap the Lord is trying to pound through your thick skull that He wants *you* to keep her safe. Mayhap the reason you have no peace about sending Ian and the boy ahead and leaving here for good—and do not tell me that was not your plan, for I saw that very scheme revolving in your eyes—is because that is not what you are to do."

He spoke nonsense.

"Mayhap what you truly want—to go to her—is where the peace lies."

I closed my eyes, drew in a breath, and raised a hand to my hair, struggling to hold onto my patience. "The way to keep her safe is to stay as far away from her as possible."

I was the only reason she would not be safe. Oliver was dead, but Talan was after me.

Revelin's image spun through my mind.

I looked down at the lock of her hair in my other hand. It suddenly seemed heavier than before.

Joseph sighed. "Consider it. For a moment. Right here. Ponder returning to her."

Against my better judgment, I obeyed. The rope of hair shining silver in the moonlight lightened against my palm.

"Do you have peace?" Joseph asked.

I stared at the strands of silver in my hand.

He grinned.

Eyes wide, breathing fast, I clasped a hand to his shoulder. "I will be putting her in danger."

"No one is more intent on keeping that woman safe than you."

"I will only have to leave again." And rip out my own heart once more by doing so.

"Will you?" Joseph glared.

"There is no other way. I could not possibly take her with me. A vagabond's life is no life for a lady."

"You are not a vagabond. You are a lord with an estate."

My lips tightened.

"I know you to be a fighter." Joseph looked at me, compassion and conviction combining on his face. "You fought against God, then fought to let Him change you. You fought your father, then fought to get to his side and say farewell. You have fought for her since the moment you met her. Why are you giving up your future without a fight?"

I steeled my expression. Crisp words fell from my mouth. "I am not giving up. I am giving *her* up. I am doing what is best for her, for my family."

"Are you?" He shook his head. "I know I am pushing you tonight, but hear me out. You *are* giving up. You concocted a plan once before to restore your reputation."

"A foolish plan."

"Mayhap. But one that saved the woman you loved."

I swallowed. "Are you telling me to go to the law and try to make this right?"

He smiled. "I am."

A dry chuckle escaped. "Do you know how foolish that is?"

Joseph turned to face the cross. "I once contemplated my options, as you do this night, Devon. I thought the smoother path—converting so I could stay—would dishonor the God I loved, so I planned on pursuing a life of sacrificing what I truly wanted as a sort of penance for my sins."

Staring up at the cross, I mulled over his words and the striking disparity between us. This former monk spoke of sinning. Surely, he had some small idea of what black deeds I had done. Yet mayhap he merely forgave me of them even without knowing. Gratitude for a friendship such as that filled me.

"But I was wrong," Joseph continued. "Just because we want to walk one path does not mean we should turn away and choose another out of some misguided sense of duty, honor, or sacrifice. Instead, mayhap the very path we desire most is the one God seeks to lead us down, in order to teach us holiness, trust, and even joy."

My chest constricted with a full gamut of emotions. Desperation. Despair. Resignation. Hope.

And now, determination.

For I did indeed know what I was to do: I was going back to her.

Gwyneth

Chapter Thirty-Four

Three nights after Anders and I had ridden away, I slipped from bed, down the stairs, and into the courtyard. It seemed fitting somehow: three days Christ had been in the grave. Three days I had wrestled with the ramifications of my decision in the forest with Anders. The decision to surrender.

The bitter cold seeped into every pore, even through the many layers of my gown and cape. A nightmare woke me this night—a nightmare more horrible than any before. Dirk had died in my arms. I sat straight up in bed, a scream clawing at my throat, but I denied it the freedom to wake the keep. Instead, I rose on trembling limbs and dressed quickly, sloppily, without the maid to help me with the buttons.

Silence bathed the inner bailey of Godfrey Estate. I looked behind me once. The towering expanse of the castle seemed intimidating in the bright moonlit night. Then I turned around, intent on my destination. Although no light emanated from the stables, inviting me in, I entered anyway. For I knew here I could cry and mourn and pray until, if need be, daybreak.

This just might take that long.

In that meadow, I had declared the mourning over. Had that proven true? I knew not. Tonight, though, my heart was breaking anew.

For he was not just not coming back. I was giving him up.

My snow-covered boots scudded across the hard ground between the stalls. I stomped once, twice, to relieve my feet of the snow accumulated during my walk from the door of the keep to the creaking stable portal.

A part of me hoped Alfie would appear tonight and somehow coax a laugh out of me as he was wont to do. Or even confide in me whatever consumed his thoughts when that thoughtful expression took over his face—what I had first seen the day he told me no one hung the pitchfork too high here.

But another part of me wanted Alfie tucked somewhere warm…and solitude for myself.

Darkness cloaked my trembling body. Shadows leapt all around. I reached for the lantern near the entryway, grateful for the height that allowed me to easily unhook and claim it in my already frozen hands. Tremors wracked my fingers, but I succeeded in lighting it with a bit of flint I had stored in my pocket before venturing out here.

A few of the horses glanced at me, their eyes round discs of curiosity. One neighed as if to express disapproval of my making noise at this time of night.

Swift steps carried me over straw, hay, and other matter I did not care to think about until finally the flickering firelight revealed Char in his stall. He put his head over the barrier between us as if sensing my need for companionship, for a listening ear, for him.

I petted his nose then laid my head on his, grateful for his presence, even as the sorrow of having known a greater love than this and lost it washed over me. The scent of the stables washed over me, too, breaking into my need for a moment to myself.

Raising the lantern high, I opened the stall and slipped inside, then laid my head against Char's mane. I had left my glasses behind, but no blurs bothered me; I stood too close to my horse for that. I stroked the long locks of his mane with my free hand.

"I dreamed he died tonight, Char."

His breath rumbled through his chest and thus through my fingers.

"My knight. I dreamed he was lost to me forever." My voice cracked. "And I know now that is true, even so, even without that dream coming true." *Oh, God, please do not ever let it come true!* Even if Tudder's mysterious letter was supposed to mean that at one point Dirk had turned his footsteps toward this place, he must have turned around again for unknown reasons.

And even though I was surrendering him this night, I wanted him to live. I wanted him to live free. That was why I had worked so hard—going to the magistrate, enlisting Anders's help, writing the lords whose support we needed, writing that foolhardy letter to the Queen herself I had not yet sent. I wanted him to be free of the consequences of *my* false accusations.

I had failed in my cause. The magistrate had not believed me because of that villain, Talan. Anders and I had not found one nobleman willing to support Dirk. I knew not if the Queen would even read my letter.

My hand stroked Char's mane. Until tonight, I had imagined I felt the tethering of our hearts across the many miles. Whatever the distance, I had always felt the mystery of Dirk's living soaring within and around me. Save my love for the God who had delivered and redeemed me, I had needed only that, needed only Dirk, his love for me, my love for him, unfulfilled though it may be.

I still needed it.

Oh, God…how can You ask me to surrender even that?

Putting the lantern down behind me, I squeezed my eyes shut then opened them again and turned back to Char. My fingers pressed into his back. "I would take you out tonight, Char. If the snow did not warn me it would be foolhardy and dangerous, I would ask you to take me back to that meadow." I smiled softly and glanced up at his face.

He turned his head and nodded slightly.

"Aye, see, you agree with me; 'tis a perfect night for a moonlit ride. The light is quite bright tonight, actually." I would not have needed the lantern if I had not chosen to come into the stables.

Pulling in a deep, shuddering breath, I gave in to the temptation to sit at Char's feet. My grandfather had often told me 'twas perilous to sit in a horse's stall. But I trusted this horse with my life. How often had we flown over Barrington land? How often had he led me exactly where I needed to go?

How often had I come to him on a night such as this, my heart heavy, my eyes full, my hands shaking?

I gathered my knees to my chest and stared up at his large body. Ensconced in the heat emanating from Char and settled into the circle of light cast by the lantern beside me, I knew I was safe. Protected, even.

But I did not wish to be here, safe, not without Dirk. Allowing my head to fall back against the stall, I closed my eyes. "I wonder where we would be right now, you and I, if Dirk had allowed me to go with him. Would we be sailing on Tudder's ship, off to some impossibly exotic location? Would we have already arrived? Would he have wanted to take me to France or the Americas or Iceland or someplace I do not even know exists?"

Where would I have wanted to go? Anywhere. Anywhere, as long as he went with me.

"We would have been wed by now, I have no doubt. He would probably have taken me straight to St. Benet's and seen to that." A smile rose. "Mayhap Reverend Joseph would have bound us to each other."

I would have worn the diamond rosary my parents had given me, reveling in the fact that their pledge to me—that I would marry the man I loved—had come true.

Sobs piled in my chest, and I breathed through my nose to keep them at bay. "I miss him, Char. I miss him more than anything else. I fear for him, out there, constantly having to stay one step ahead of those after him. And what of Tudder's letter? Why would Dirk have Titus with him? And why did Tudder say he should have arrived by now?"

My eyes closed. If he had been on the path back to Godfrey, what kept him and what caused him not to come?

My head ached from the questions, and, though I knew I was tired, I knew too that these questions were not pointless or futile. They were justified. But I had no answers for any of them.

Mayhap I would never have answers.

I make my peace with that, God. I do not need answers. I just need… The word *him* rose to my heart, but I swallowed it back. *I need You. I have always needed you. You gave him to me to lead me to You. And when he went away, You used that pain to bring me to You, too.*

I could rejoice in that for the rest of my life. God's love had found me. In that, I *would* rejoice.

Touching my cheeks, I sighed. I had been crying without realizing it. And for a while, for the tears had nearly frozen to my face. "Char, it is so cold out here. I know I should not stay, but I do not think I can move. Nor do I wish to." I reached over and put out the lantern. Darkness swathed the small space and covered me.

I knew I should pray, too, that God would bless my plan for his restoration, but tonight I had no strength to waste.

A lance of pain shot through my chest, so that I gasped and looked up in anguish.

He was calling me to surrender that, too?

The sobs began in earnest, but I forced myself to calm them. "God, that, too? Must I surrender that? You have already asked me to give him up, but must I give up the hope of making restitution for what I did to him, as well?"

Pushing my fingers into my hair, I shook my head, the sobs coming harder despite my best efforts. "I cannot do it. You must help me…"

The tears ceased. A sweet knowing spun all through me until a strange, unearthly peace dwelt where pain had clawed at me just a moment before.

"I give him to You, God. I give him up. And I give up the plan of seeing his name cleared, his honor restored. I give it all to You." He could do with it what He willed.

Well, then, there was only one thing left to say.

Tears laced my whisper as I spoke the words I had not been able to give voice to in the two months since he left. "Dirk, I am so sorry."

I brought my hands up to cover my face. "I wish I had never blamed you that night. I will always regret ruining your honor in that way. I did not mean to, but I feel responsible. And I know I once said you possessed no honor, but, in truth, you are the most honorable man I have ever known."

My fingers could not hold back the teardrops. A strange evenness invaded my voice. "My heart is yours and has been since you took my hand by the river that night you came to carry me away, when I could not even see you. But I saw your heart; I knew you then, though I tried to deny it. And I love you."

I surrender you.

"I love you, Gwyneth-mine."

I gasped, but air refused to enter my lungs. Instead, it pressed all around me, surrounding me with the pressure his words left on my chest. My hands fell away, and I looked up. There, standing just outside Char's stall, stood Dirk.

Dirk

Chapter Thirty-Five

I needed to touch her, to convince myself she truly sat in Char's stall, but a few feet away. My fingers shook as they sought to find the stall door's latch, but I did not look down to guide their way. I could not free my gaze from her beautiful face, shocked expression, wide eyes, and open mouth.

"Gwyn." Pushing away the need to ask about the 'confession' I had just heard, I stared.

When she stood, I gave up on the latch. All grace, she floated to her feet. For one heartbreaking moment, she did not move, did not blink, did not speak.

I swallowed, desperate for the sound of her voice. "Will you not say something, Gwyn?"

"What shall I say?"

I shook my head, at a loss. So striking in the moonlight cast from the stable door, she held me spellbound, enchanted. Then she moved, crossing the last few feet of distance between us. All those miles, all that distance, down to just a few inches...at last at an end. She stood shoulder to shoulder with Char, who had moved his head over the stall door toward me.

When she stopped, my stomach sank, for she yet remained out of reach. "You left me."

Pain. Just pain. "I am so sorry, Gwyn."

"You stayed away." Her even tone denied me even a glimpse into her heart, but her eyes spoke of how much she hurt.

I drove my gaze into hers. "I made a mistake. I pushed away God... and His answer."

Sweet confusion stole over her face. "What was your question?"

"Never mind the question."

"What was His answer?"

"His answer was you, only you, always you. The truth of your love drew me back to you."

"But you left me behind." Her face took on such sorrow that I was helpless to do anything but fumble for the lock again. This time, I dropped my gaze, wishing for more light so that I could see what I was doing. In truth, I could not meet her eyes. She was rejecting me; I could feel it. And it broke me.

The sound of her strangled sob pierced the night at the same time as the lock gave. I looked up, rendered immovable by the look in her emerald eyes.

"I thought you were never coming back to me." Hesitant joy entered her wobbly smile. Tears glistened in her gaze.

I thought the same. "God led me through sickness and a snowstorm to get to you." My whisper was choked. I threw the stall door out of the way and came close.

"Dirk?" She reached up a trembling hand, but hesitated.

"It is I." Hearing her say my name again made me want to scale a mountain for her.

"I thought..." Her words faded into the darkness.

I clasped her hand in mine and put it to my cheek. I started at the touch of her icy fingers. "You are cold."

"Then warm me."

My eyes widened and searched hers.

For one blinding moment, it was enough. To share the same space. To drink the same air. I watched her, loving without touching. Then she touched me. She took one tiny step, and her delicate fingers rose to rest on my chest. Suddenly it was enough no more.

She launched herself into my arms, and I crushed her to me, hoisting her high. Her gown tangled in my arm and her shoulder bumped mine, but I gave neither heed. I was kissing her brow, her hair, her cheeks, wherever I dared reach.

Her arms encircled my neck so tightly I stopped breathing. But why did I need air? I had Gwyn in my arms once again. It would take so little a movement to pull away slightly, close the space between us again and claim her lips. I breathed in the scent of the hair swirling about her shoulders.

She pulled in a shuddering breath, almost as if afraid to believe I truly stood before her. Gathering her against me, I convinced us both with a long kiss that I was real, really here, with her. Together again.

When we opened our eyes, her smile slowly grew. "How I have longed for this moment."

"No more so than I."

"'Tis not exactly as I would have imagined."

"Would you like me to leave and come back again?" I knew the moment the words fled my tongue they were the wrong ones.

Her smile froze, then vanished. Her brows dipped down in anguish. "*Nee, idiota.*"

I had never heard her speak both Dutch and Spanish, before. Sad and angry at once? "What if I stay with you forever? Would you forgive me then?"

The expression she gave me was stone, and the fear I had felt upon reading my mother's words of concern for Gwyn's health resurrected. Never had she been able to hide her heart from me before. When had she learned the art?

And how could I convince her to discard it?

Of a sudden, her mask melted before my eyes and her heart on her face lay open for my perusal. I feasted on that look, those eyes. Then she trembled, and her skin was ice...

"Are you well?"

"You are here. How could I not be?" Her laugh fell across my ears, a song. She pulled away slightly, to my grief. My hand went into my pocket and pulled out the lock of hair she had sent me. She stared at it before her fingers reached up and touched it. "You kept it."

"You doubted?"

"I have doubted much these last months." Her gaze met mine. "And I wondered if you even received the letter."

"I did. On the ship."

Her head tilted to one side in an adorably, achingly lovely fashion. "Why did you not write back?"

"I was already on my way here."

Her mouth formed an O. "Tudder was right, then."

"Tudder?" It was my turn to be confused.

"He sent a letter."

My brow furrowed. "What did he say?"

She shook her head and closed her eyes. A single tear escaped and traced her cheek. I caught it on a fingertip. That single touch proved too much. Her presence—after so long an absence—pulled me in. I cupped her face in one hand then replaced the lock of hair to my pocket with the other. My right hand rose to join the other, and I held her there, reveling in the sight of her. "You are not wearing your glasses."

She opened her eyes. "I do not need them. Everything I want to see is near. At last."

"Aye." My hands captured her waist, and I laid my head on her shoulder. "At last."

Her fingers tunneled into my hair. Then I was kissing her shoulder through the fabric of her gown, moving upward, leaving kisses on her neck and on her cheeks, wet from her tears. They started anew in a torrent now, but she was kissing me back. "I thought I would never see you again."

"I am here now." I grasped her to me, quieting her tears, whispering soft nonsense in her ear, wishing I could quiet her fears as easily. For the truth was I had no idea what I would do now, where God would lead. Could I stay here, if only for a short time? Or would I leave again just as suddenly as before? How to go about fighting for my honor as Joseph had urged me to do?

Either way, I knew this time I was not letting this woman out of my sight.

If she would have me. Ice trailed down my back at the thought.

Tossing it away, I held her. When at last she calmed, I wrapped my arms more tightly around her, relishing the feel of her head on my chest. My fingers bumped over the buttons at her back and around to her sides.

"I have much to tell you."

She had already revealed much to me as I stood, unbeknownst to her, listening at the stable door. "Not now, Gwyneth-mine."

When I had asked about Tudder, she had shaken her head. I would not ask her to talk now. She needed time to get used to the idea of my being here. Shutting out the ways my mind wandered to a certain guest within Godfrey Estate, I let the joy sluice through me at my next thought: I would be privileged to get used to the idea of being beside her once more.

She stiffened in my arms, and fear coiled within me. Her head lifted, her gaze searing straight into mine. "Will you truly stay?"

I hesitated, for she had found the one question I could not answer.

Understanding in her eyes. Two footsteps took her away from me. "How long until you leave again?"

I strode forward and laid my forehead on hers, closing my eyes. "I know not."

She tore away. "Dirk?" Betrayal laced her tone.

Eager to reassure her I would never again leave her side—as long as she would have me—I said, "God did a work in my heart, Gwyn."

I watched her watch me with wariness, eager for her to understand, eager for that look of complete trust she had given me when she first saw me return tonight.

"He taught me that my way is not always best."

She hugged herself. A deep breath shuddered into her chest, hope cascading on her features. "What are you saying?"

I reached for her, sliding my hands down her arms, encased in that thin coat, until I held her hands in mine. "I do not know where I will go from here, but I want you by my side whether I leave or stay."

Emotions crossed her face in quick succession. Shock. Disbelief. Doubt. Hesitant joy.

Each look burned my heart. "Can you ever forgive me? For leaving you behind?"

A smile quirked at one edge of the mouth I wanted to kiss.

I settled for bringing her fingers to my lips. "Gwyneth-mine, you are turning to ice and it is past midnight. I should see you inside."

Joy lit her eyes. "Your mother will be so happy to see you!"

I shook my head. "I will not wake her until morning. 'Tis far too late."

She gave me a droll look. "She will be upset with you for not waking her."

"Then I will go to her chamber after I see you to yours." I scooped her up.

"Already?" Wistfulness captured her voice.

My grin stretched. "I will see you in the morning."

"Oh, I like that." When her head found my chest, she sighed. Her hand trailed from my chest to my shoulder. "Did you hear me speaking just now, to Char?"

All. My footsteps carried us over the now empty courtyard. Ian must have silently seen to the horses and taken Titus inside. I discarded every temptation of pretense, deciding not to hide that I knew to what she referred. But I would not tell her just how much I had heard. "You fell in love with me in the Low Countries, at the side of the River Rhine, when you held out your hand to me, so bold and brave, and could not see mine outstretched to you."

She smiled, tears filling her eyes once more.

"You were late." I finagled the door open and saw us inside to the warmth of the keep.

She cocked her head still further. "What—?"

"I already held mine out to you. Long, long before." The stairs ascended beneath my feet.

"Explain."

"I fell in love with you first..." I stopped and kissed her cheek. "On the first night I saw you." Kissed her nose. "You were a vision, and you looked down at me like I was unworthy of your regard." Her eyelids. "You have entranced me ever since."

Her throat worked as she swallowed, her eyes still closed from where they had fluttered shut a moment before. "Way back then?"

"Aye." My lips found the corner of her mouth.

"Before you even followed me to the Low Countries and rescued me from—"

Chuckling, I forced some self-control and resumed walking. "From many things. We do not have time to list them all."

Her eyes popped open. "Why do we not have time?"

"Because, milady..." I covered the distance to the door to her chamber too quickly and set her down reluctantly. "...you are weary, and I must let you sleep."

"What if I do not wish to sleep?"

I stared down at her, a strange sense of power travelling through me. This was new. The distrustful Gwyn had left long ago, but now even the mourning Gwyn had gone. In her place stood a stronger woman, a woman who wanted to be near me as much as I wanted to be near her. I leaned down and kissed her cheek. Pulling back, I resisted temptation and touched the door, almost begging her to step inside before reason deserted me. "You will need your rest if you are to accompany me tomorrow."

Her spine straightened in excitement. "How do you mean...?"

"You and me. Together." Before I let her close the door, I pressed a single silver piece into her palm.

Gwyneth

Chapter Thirty-Six

When the first touch of dawn slanted across my eyelids, sorrow, my constant companion, dove in. My lungs sucked in the first wakeful breath of the morn, filling my stomach with life-giving air. Only I felt anything but alive. My eyes opened as I pressed a hand to the pain hidden inside my chest and sat up. Swinging my legs over the side of the bed, I waited until the last vestiges of the nightmares swept away in the pale light pooling on the stone floor before me.

But then the weight in my palm reminded me. I opened my hand and saw the silver flash.

He had returned.

Had that really happened? I turned the silver over in my other hand. It must have. During the nights, nightmares came, not such glorious dreams as that. Amazing joy drowned my sorrow at the same moment as I caught sight of a straggly bouquet beside my glasses on the table. The air froze in my lungs. Where had he possibly found wildflowers in winter?

And why?

A single thought pressed hard. *He did this once before.*

Reason abandoned me, but I did not care. My feet found the floor, and I ran for the door. Ignoring my state of undress and the fright that was my hair, I plunged down the stairs. My heart clawed into my throat, my stomach, my shaking legs, all of me, all at once. How could fear strangle so many places, tangle so many limbs?

The pounding of my footsteps filled my ears, intensifying the debilitating dizziness. My hand slid down the railing and my gaze, the stairs. But the second I descended them, my eyes lifted.

And I saw him.

I mouthed his name and ran. Launching myself into Dirk's arms, I closed my eyes against the sting of tears that pricked eyelids so recently imprinted with the images of my nightmares. He spoke my name, and the sound of his voice set off a torrent inside me. Against my will, sobs tore from my throat with all the raggedness of grief deferred. I held on tight, relishing the feel of his arms coming around me, wrapping me up as securely as a swaddled babe.

My tears bled into his shoulder, dampening his shirt. He smelled of woodsmoke and hay and himself. His palm brushed my hair, and I never wanted to leave the safety of his arms. I had thought those flowers meant farewell, but they meant something else entirely...

He was here.

To run to. To embrace. I turned my face into his neck, my weeping quieting at last. To love.

Dirk

Chapter Thirty-Seven

She lifted her head from my shoulder and turned dazed, damp green eyes to me. I smiled. How I had missed that barely-awake look, the faint creases on her cheeks that said she had hugged her pillow hard. "I am here, Gwyn."

Snuggling in again, she sighed. Then with a small cry, she pulled back, although I did not let her free herself completely from my arms. Her thin nightdress fluttered around my legs as she whirled away.

Cade's smile echoed in the lines around his eyes as he gave me a look. My mother had one hand pressed to her mouth. Ian and Joseph had probably taken Gwyn's nightgown-clad, weepy appearance the best. They waited patiently, small smirks on their faces.

Gwyn's shoulders lifted and fell as she breathed deeply. Then she nodded to each person in turn, ending with Joseph. When she saw him, she turned and blinked at me.

"It is good to see you again, Lady Gwyneth," he said.

She swallowed and swiveled to look at him again, but not before I spied the expression coming across her face. 'Twas pure lady. As if his use of her title had sparked the noble upbringing in her, she spoke to Joseph as if she were the Queen holding court. "I trust your journey was a smooth one, Reverend Joseph."

"Rather snowy for my taste, milady, but what awaited us at the end of it more than made up for any inconvenience."

"And what, pray tell, could coax you from your warm former monastery in the middle of winter?"

Joseph flicked his gaze to me. That was one of the things we had been discussing before Gwyn had flown down the stairs.

My mother stepped up to Gwyn then. "Dear…" The rest of her words fell into Gwyn's ear but not my own. Pink rose in her cheeks before she bade us each a polite farewell.

But that would never be enough for me. I reached out, and she returned the gesture. Squeezing her hand, I watched her eyes widen. For into her hand I pressed one more silver piece.

Moments later, sedate footsteps carried her up the stairs. Never had a woman looked more regal with a nightdress swaying around her bare ankles.

I ignored the sudden hike in my pulse and turned back to Cade, forcing my thoughts to our prior discussion. "She said what?"

As if Gwyn had never interrupted our conversation—although what a welcome interruption—Cade continued. "She refused to marry me."

Joseph's brows hid in his hairline. "I do not understand. Were not you and Margried betrothed when you left St. Benet's?"

"We were."

Blowing out a breath, I let the compassion pooling in my chest bleed into my look. "We will get to the bottom of this, Cade. There's got to be a reason why Margried—"

Mother came toward me and put a hand on my arm. "That is what he has been trying to tell you, son."

I glanced back at Cade. When I had asked him what was wrong with Margried after she had given me a cold stare upon my request that she take Gwyn the flowers, I had never expected Cade to divulge that there was tension between them, much less rejection.

"She is angry..." His head ticked toward his shoulders.

"What did you do?"

"Agreed with you."

"Agreed with me?"

Mother swept away from me in a wash of rosewater-scented air. She must have borrowed the perfume from Susan. "Reverend Joseph, will you join me in breaking the fast?"

The man looked as if he wanted to stay, but he offered a quick smile and followed her toward the Great Hall.

Cade's tone betrayed his discomfiture. "She saw how you hurt Gwyn by leaving."

I winced.

"She said...she was not certain she could weather the same if I abandoned her."

"Why would you do the same to her?" Incredulity thickened my voice.

"Your reputation is intact. You are not wanted for murder."

"That is what I told her."

"So what is the problem?"

"She knew I felt the same way you did. That you and I were of the same mind when it came to your needing to leave to draw the lions away."

I nodded. Cade's support had meant a great deal to me. Why had Margried taken offense?

He mauled his face with his hand. "Then she asked me what I would do if it were me."

I raised a brow, not liking where this was going. "What did you say?"

His eyes lidded. "What do you think I said?"

"You said you would do the same." The very words he had given me the night before I had left. The very words that had cemented my decision in my mind had driven a wedge of the same strength between these two people I loved. "When was this?"

"The day Revelin confronted Gwyneth."

All thoughts of Margried and Cade fled my head. My gaze lifted painfully slowly to stare at Cade. "What did you say?"

His expression faded to concern as his voice faded to a whisper. "I should allow her to tell you."

"But you will tell me now, as I would if it were Margried of whom we spoke."

Clouds of pain darkened his eyes, but I could not stop to reassure him that everything would be well between him and the former postulant. Revelin had *confronted* Gwyneth?

"Cade." His name came forth in nearly a bark.

"I came upon them in the middle of it. He had her by the wrists."

My jaw tightened. "He was accosting her?"

"I do not believe so. Merely…furious." Cade's sigh echoed in my mind. "I saw the look in his eyes, the expression on her face, and I lost all self-control. It was as if I could see Margried being struck by those raiders at the convent—I will never forgive myself for not rescuing her from that. I tore him away from her."

"How?" My fists clenched at my sides, hating that I had not been the one there to defend Gwyn. *Why, Lord, did You allow my stubbornness to keep me away?* She had needed me, and I had not been there. Again. Would I ever stop failing her?

"I landed my fist in his jaw."

"How did he react?"

"He did not fight back, if that is what you are asking."

That did not surprise me. Revelin had never been the type to dirty his hands. Not with brawls and blood, like had once attracted me. Revelin dwelt with far more gentlemanly sins—namely, gambling debts. "Thank you. For doing what I should have, Cade."

We exchanged a look. No need for words. I would have done the same if it had been Margried, and we both knew it.

I forced my fists to relax and dragged my hands through my hair. "I am grateful to God you were here to protect her while he stayed."

Cade blinked. "He is still here."

"Why would he remain after humiliating himself in such a way?" Why had he not crawled home to Lansberry? My fingers curled yet again.

"He is an odd one. Too patient. Cannot seem to act quickly even if it costs him."

"Are you insinuating something?"

"Aye. Are you not getting my meaning?"

I waited, suspecting what he was about to say had something to do with Gwyn and that I was not going to like it.

"My guess is he has feelings for Gwyneth. And, though he may not realize it yet, he waited too long to tell her."

Disgust that a ruined man such as Revelin would show regard for Gwyneth rattled me.

But in the next moment, my stomach clenched. For I was a ruined man, as well.

Gwyneth

Chapter Thirty-Eight

After the maid left the room, I put my hands over my face. Even though I had splashed water on my skin until the girl helping me dress gently warned I would drown myself, the blush persisted in staining my cheeks.

I had flung myself down the stairs and jumped straight into his arms.

Right in front of his mother.

And a clergyman!

Cade and Ian, too. Oh, if *Moeder* had seen my performance! An involuntary moan escaped, but I lifted my chin, knowing I needed to descend the stairs—at a normal pace—and enter the Great Hall, if not to restore my good standing in their eyes then to calm the nervous rumbling in my stomach.

For the first time in days, I had an appetite. *Thank You, God, for bringing him back to me.*

I walked over to the door. My hand landed on it before I froze in shock and fright. *God, did I do it wrong? Did I not surrender Dirk wholeheartedly? Is that what brought him back? I meant to give him to You. Completely. Truly, I did.*

Nee. Of course not. If there was anything Rohesia had taught me, it was that God was always sincere. He never threw sorrows in His children's faces just to see them break.

But…

Pulling in a deep breath, I closed my eyes. I had indeed surrendered Dirk in that stable stall last night. And God had, in His infinite mercy, been the One to bring him back to me. Tears piled in my throat.

I shook off the emotion and walked down the hall. Head held high. Shoulders back. Steps measured, even. Just as Moeder had taught me. Skirt hiked in one hand, I started down the stairs, the click of my heels the only sound in the keep.

Releasing the lip I just realized I had been biting, I strode across the entryway and set my course for the Great Hall. Where was he? Had he retired here as well to break his fast and laugh with his sisters?

His sisters. I stopped. Millicent. *Oh, God, mercy.*

Low voices met my ears as I stepped into the sunlight shining from the Great Hall windows. But I failed to identify to whom they belonged because my feet froze to the stones and a smile sprang to my lips. He sat directly in front of me, hands motionless on the table, the seat beside him empty.

He waited for me.

He grinned at something Cade said, his gaze resting on mine. Or was that his reaction to my reappearance? He rose and came toward me.

For the third time, the miracle of his presence threatened to sweep me away. Forcing my eyes closed, I struggled for composure. He was here. At last. After so long without him, I could scarcely take it in. The way I had embarrassed myself this morn ceased to matter. The blush leaked from my face.

A hand slipped in mine, and I opened my eyes to stare up into his. A gasp stole my breath. His other hand reached up to cup my cheek just as mine reached for his. The scruff of his face tickled my palm, but I could still tell he had not been eating well. *Oh, Dirk.*

"Gwyn." My name a whisper on his lips, he studied me with concern in his eyes.

What was it he had said last night in the darkness? *God led me through sickness and a snowstorm to get to you.*

I stroked his beard. "Have you been ill?"

At the same time, he asked, "Are you well?"

My gaze fled to the floor, suddenly remembering the comments I had brushed off these last few weeks. Sister Agnes telling me I had thinned; Rohesia asking after my favorite foods; Margried's praise of the food as she pushed the choicest bites over to my side of the trencher we shared.

"Come. Eat." The look in his eyes reminded me of his rescuing me from the Low Countries. Memories assaulted me, but I forced them back.

"*Wacht.*" I tugged against him. "Answer me."

He smiled, even though the intense expression did not so much as flicker. "I have not been ill."

"But you have not been eating."

"'Tis the beard."

"*Nee.* I can tell even without that bear's coat on your face."

One side of his mouth lifted before he released a chuckle. Oh, the sound of his laugh. "I trust you wish me to shave, milady."

I shrugged one shoulder and gave him a bored look. "If I said I did, would you?"

The smile filled out and became wolfish. "With all due haste."

Unable to resist the laughter any longer, I allowed him to lead me to the long wooden table. My gaze fell on Rohesia, who nodded at me as I passed her. Swallowing, I let Dirk seat me beside him. His empty trencher had already been arranged between our seats. He *had* been waiting for me. Indeed, the whole table had.

I looked up and across from me. "It is good to see you again, Ian."

He nodded and echoed my words. "I am most glad to be here, milady."

On Ian's other side, Susan smiled. I raised my brows then schooled them again. Those two? My smile resisted my efforts to be only subtly pleased.

Margried, beside me, touched my hand, her eyes curious. I gave a delighted smile, wishing I could tell her all was well with me today—in fact, had never been better. She no longer needed to worry about my mourning Dirk.

Rohesia, ever the hostess, beamed at all of us. "Shall we begin?"

The servants came forward then and served each of us. A frown momentarily captured my mouth, and I shot a quick glance past Dirk. Where were Anders, Sister Agnes, and Joseph?

Replacing my goblet after taking a sip, I felt Dirk's eyes on me. He winked, and I knew he thought of the night we had arrived. That seemed like so long ago, but the look in his eyes transported me instantly back. A blush climbed my neck.

Only Millicent stared back at me from beside her brother. Her blank gaze arrested mine more for the surprise that gripped me than because of any malicious intent in her eyes. She had never looked at me with such a disinterested expression before.

Dirk bumped my shoulder with his as he reached for a piece of bread and whispered an apology. I smiled at him and took small bites of the food even though my stomach wished for more.

Mayhap her brother's arrival had cooled Millicent's passion for berating me. After all, she could hardly blame me for his absence now.

I glanced around the table, marveling at how different this meal was from yesterday's. Today I would not choke. Today Dirk was here. Ian, Susan, and Rohesia talked of the recent snows. I smiled, relieved to know that Dirk and Ian had been able to find refuge at St. Benet's during the storm.

A ruffled sigh pulled from me when I noticed Cade staring at Margried, and Margried avoiding looking at him.

Catching Dirk pushing the more savory pieces of meat and bread toward my side of the trencher, I countered by replacing them on his side. He scowled at me. I glared back. Not wishing to disrupt the conversation swirling around us, I remained silent. Apparently, he shared my sentiment, for he only laid his fingers over mine in an effort to dissuade me from further efforts.

I pulled free and resumed stashing the succulent bites on his side. He switched roles, dismantling the pile I had made. Inevitably, he worked faster than I. Our fingers fumbled together as our glares locked.

What was it about this man that encouraged mischief in me, to the point of playing with my food? Reminded of the way we had flung porridge at each other months before, I laughed first.

Rohesia's account of the way the snow had piled almost as high as the southernmost wall ceased as five sets of eyes swiveled toward me.

Dirk's wolfish grin reappeared.

The rescue from my embarrassment appeared from the most unlikely of places. Mayhap Millicent truly had forgiven me, for she spoke from her position flanking Dirk's other side. "Devon, surely you have kept us waiting long enough. We are eager for the story of your return."

My puzzled gaze met only Dirk's profile, for he had turned toward his sister.

Touching her hand with his own, he sighed. "It is a long story, Millie, best kept until we are finished breaking our fast."

"I am finished," Millicent said.

Rohesia pushed her trencher away. Susan put down her goblet. Ian, eyes wide, looked at Susan and stopped chewing. I caught Cade's eye roll and the longing look he cast the little food remaining on his trencher.

I placed my hands in my lap, eager to hear this story as well.

Looking down at the wooden table, I braced myself for what his answer might be. This had been what I had not wished to speak of last night when we had been alone. What would he say? He had said he wanted me by his side whether he left or whether he stayed...but a tiny niggling of doubt stole my appetite.

Margried put her hand over mine.

Dirk shook his head at Millicent, but I could not see if his look was brotherly and amused or actually annoyed. Knowing him, I guessed the former. Whatever Millicent's faults, Dirk was a good brother. "Mother told you she wrote to me." His gaze went to Susan, too.

I blinked.

Susan nodded. "Of course, of course, we know that."

I did not. Until now. Margried's hand tightened over mine. Had *she* known Rohesia had written to her son?

Susan waved a hand. "Skip that part. What made you leave the Dutchman's ship? And what took you so long to return?"

Dirk glanced at Ian. "We were entrusted with…a charge."

Every person at the table acquired a knowing look. My brows rose, surprise flashing in my stomach. How had I forgotten they brought Titus with them?

Dirk looked straight at me. "Tudder asked me to take Titus to safety."

My shoulders straightened. "But why is he in danger?"

"The Low Countries are in upheaval, Gwyn."

I raised a brow.

"Philip has promised to send the Duke of Alba."

My mouth fell open.

"Why is the child in danger?" Rohesia asked. "Your friend is in an English port, under Her Majesty's protection."

"Not anymore, milady," Ian said. "He set sail the day after we left."

"For the Low Countries."

"Why, Dirk?" I turned to him. "Why would he go back?"

He touched my cheek. "He felt it was his duty." Why did that sound less like Tudder's reason and more like Dirk's apology? "But he knew the risks, the danger. And so he entrusted Titus to me."

Warring emotions both tied me to my seat and threatened to force me to rise. I wanted to hear more, but I wanted to see the boy. The second call won out. "Where is he?"

"He slept in my chambers last night." Ian's words brought my gaze to him. "He asked for you several times, though."

I jumped from my seat and saw Dirk start to rise, but I laid a hand on his shoulder with a pleading smile. So he reached for my hand.

And I felt the warm weight of silver.

Too many minutes later, I found Ian's chambers empty. My heavy footsteps trudged down the stairs. Resignation about returning to the Great Hall—and Millicent's simpering—filled me. I knew I was being unkind; she had not so much simpered as staked a claim on Dirk she considered me below possessing. Still, her treatment rankled. All too akin to what Rohesia shared she had experienced with her late husband's sister.

At the base of the stairs, I heard it. A child's laughter. A little boy's joy. A grin splayed across my face as I made my way to the library. So Dirk and I both had taken charges during our separation. Mayhap because we were lonely for each other. Mayhap because we saw ourselves in these children. Alfie echoing my orphan's pain. Titus speaking to how Dirk felt displaced.

For just a moment, I stood in the doorway, unseen, and watched him.

Joseph knelt on the floor, but he was not praying. Neighing noises expelled from his mouth. He caught sight of me, and his eyes widened.

Titus crouched in front of him, laughing at Joseph's impersonation. He noticed the man's reaction and turned around.

He saw me. I saw him. Unlike our first meeting on his father's ship, I did not open my arms. He did not run into them. Instead, this time, he rose on legs that had grown longer since I had last seen him, and we walked slowly toward each other.

"Good morrow, Titus Tudder." It seemed perfectly natural to speak to the boy in his native Dutch.

A grin split his face. "The knight told me I would see you again."

Dirk, you rogue. "Did he now?"

His head bobbed up and down as he broke into English. "He told me to always call him the knight to you, too."

Dirk would definitely laugh when he learned I had brought here the first lad who had taken to calling Dirk a knight—after I had called him such.

Male laughter broke out behind Titus. I looked at the man recently arisen from the floor. "Reverend Joseph."

"Good morrow, Lady Gwyneth."

The question that I had never received an answer to earlier this morn came to my lips. "You never told me why you are here."

His expression gentled. "It would be best if I allowed Dirk to tell you that."

I blew out a ruffled sigh and glanced down at Titus. My smile reappeared, and so did my Dutch. "I missed you."

He grinned up at me. "And I you. Would you like to play horses with Reverend Joseph and me?" Such a little man and a boy all at once.

Joseph cleared his throat before I needed to answer. "I believe I may venture into the chapel, young lad."

Titus frowned. "Why?"

Joseph smiled. "To pray."

Titus looked up at me and said in a loud whisper, "Reverend Joseph's from a mon'stery. Men there have lots of time to pray."

I nearly choked but managed to steel my features. The former monk seemed to have less success than I did, for he hurried from the room as if his cassock were on fire. Chuckles filtered back from the hall. To muffle them, I spoke. "Titus, what say you we read?" I took advantage of the opportunity to venture toward a bookshelf to pacify my expression. "What shall we read?"

When I turned back to him, I noticed the wrinkles on his nose. He came to stand before the bookshelf that had gathered my attention. Staring up at it with an analytical look, he bound his hands behind his back in a stance I knew must be Tudder's. *God, please keep this little one's father safe. And help us to do our best by him.*

"I would rather play horses, but we can read if you would like." The way he spoke so respectfully baffled me. At six years of age, I'd had quite a rebellious streak. However had Tudder managed this miracle before me?

For the next half hour, we engaged in a modified version of the game of horses. Titus played the horse, I the lady. He scampered across the floor on his hands and knees, always staying within my sight, and I provided dialogue.

Then he hid behind the settee on which I lounged. "Oh, no! Where has my fair mount gone?" It had been too long since I had played like this.

Snickers. "*Handsome* mount! Or, or mighty or strong!"

"Forgive me," I whispered. "Oh, no! Where has my handsome, mighty, strong mount gone?"

Giggles met my ears, and shuffling ensued, then heavy bongs that could rival Dirk's boots. Titus could indeed make noise when he wished. Laying an arm across my forehead, I interjected desperation and drama into the English words. "Will he ever return?"

A strong hand cupped the elbow over my eyes. "Always."

I jerked my arm back, but too quickly. The smack of my elbow into his face drew a wince from me, painless though my part had been. "Dirk!"

He massaged his jaw, sank beside me, and grinned. "I had hoped you intended to stick with spewing Spanish when you were upset, milady."

All the sympathy that my accidental hit had aroused dissipated. "False hope."

An intense look invaded his eyes, and suddenly no longer did we speak of smacks and Spanish. My words, spoken as part of Titus's game, echoed in my ears. *Will he ever return?* He had. But not until after I had lost hope that he would. Inexplicably, that revelation made guilt rise in my throat. I should have believed in him. Even when he had not believed in himself.

Titus popped up from behind the settee and neighed.

The seriousness evaporated, and I giggled.

"Well, what have we here? A noble steed in the library?"

Titus locked intent eyes on mine. "I like noble steed better than handsome, mighty, strong mount."

I nodded. "Me too."

"Char may be upset with you for fraternizing with other equine friends." Dirk looked at me but tousled Titus's hair.

The boy's eyes widened. "Who is Char?"

"My horse."

"May I meet him?"

"Certainly." I rose. "In fact, there is someone else I want you both to meet."

Dirk helped me up, but his hands did not linger on mine. Did he think I meant Anders when I said *someone else?* I wondered if his invitation last night for me to accompany him—if invitation it could indeed be called— was now coming to fruition. When he caught my fingers in his again and tucked my hand into his arm, I was certain of it.

"We shall all go visit Char. Right after we return to the Great Hall and Gwyneth finishes breaking her fast."

Titus scuttled behind us as Dirk led me down the hall. And I could not help but think I could most definitely become used to his presence every day—both the child's and the man's.

Dirk

Chapter Thirty-Nine

She ate with an eagerness that suppressed my concern. Somewhat. In the time that I had been away, her cheeks had hollowed slightly. Her skin had grown pale, and her eyes seemed larger in her face.

Her beauty shone, but, beneath the smiles she tossed at the chattering Titus, I detected weariness. It gouged my heart that I had put that weariness there. I had caused the distress my mother had written of, the distress I now saw in the way her gown hung and her smile failed to fill out her cheeks.

Titus talked more with her than he ever had with Ian and me. Of course, it had been a long, cold journey here.

My gaze slanted toward the ceiling as I waited for Gwyn to finish. Home. I was home. Strangely enough, the place earned that title less by its location or its name, and more by the presence of the woman sitting beside me. Nevertheless, I would show her more of this place I had grown up in after she ate. I longed to tuck her into my arms now but feared that would impede her appetite. Wanting to shake my head at the way she had insisted on sharing the choicest pieces of bread and meat with me earlier, I determined now to do naught to remind her of my presence and make her think she had to offer to share with me.

When she had laid aside her knife for a full two minutes, her chin propped on one hand as she giggled at something Titus told her about the tower he had built at the "mon'stery," I touched her shoulder.

She did not turn, only released her chin and laid her fingers over mine. Warmth sluiced through me with the force of summer rain. *Lord, I will do all in my power to keep her safe, I vow it. Only let me succeed.*

I knew not how He would answer that prayer, but I poured every ounce of faith I possessed into believing He would.

Tender eyes turned toward me.

"Gwyn." My voice broke on her name, and I tried again. "I want to take you on a ride over the land." What had seemed like such a good idea the night before now appeared wanting in my eyes. A ride. Over the land. In the dead of winter. To do naught but give me the opportunity to enjoy her presence.

"I would love that." A happiness I had rarely seen in her eyes lit in her smile, too, and I would have given my oath right then to put that look there all the days of my life. I leaned, and her gaze dropped. Slipping my hand from her shoulder to the nape of her neck, I fingered the strands of her hair that had fallen loose. I wanted to see it free again, as it had been when she had caught me this morning.

"Can I meet Char now?"

Gwyn sucked in a breath and looked to Titus.

I slid my hand down her back as I stood and offered my other hand to help her rise. "Aye, Titus."

He grinned, and so did Gwyn. But then I watched her features freeze into a look that was both numb and resigned as her eyes locked on something behind me.

Cold knowing seeped into every pore as I stiffened and turned to face the man who wanted to stand where I stood in Gwyn's life, in her heart.

Revelin. A serious frown sat on his mouth. All about him seemed smooth and at ease, except for the weariness that pooled around his eyes. "Good morrow."

"Anders." Gwyneth stepped beside me, her chin high, her eyes soft. She called him by his Christian name?

He took several steps forward, and I counted each one. "You must be Dirk."

Mayhap she addressed him with familiarity because he had been with her for the last several weeks. He had seen her every day. A question pounced on the back of my mind…why? Why was he here? Why had he come?

He gestured behind him. "I met your friend outside."

Cade. Standing guard outside the Great Hall? Mayhap he had sensed that Revelin and I would meet this morning. If so, I wished he had shared the premonition with me. I had in no way prepared myself to see the man who had treated Gwyn with disrespect.

"I want to…" Revelin's words trailed into nothingness.

My silence cloaked us. I let it, hoping Revelin would choke on it. But he did naught but stare at me, returning my glare with a closed look.

Titus came to stand at my side, not oblivious to the tension that had threaded together the adults in the room and interrupted his plans to see Char. "Are we going to meet the lady's friend now?"

Working my jaw, I never took my eyes off Revelin as I replied. "Aye, Titus." I let my voice rest a beat so Revelin knew I did not refer to him when I mentioned Gwyn's friend. "Lord Revelin was just coming down to break his fast. Char awaits us."

Revelin's eyes widened. I swept past him, my hand on the small of Gwyn's back, listening for the sound of Titus's footsteps clomping after mine.

And that was the first time I met Anders Revelin in person instead of just by reputation. The look in his eyes reassured me it would not be the last.

Gwyneth

Chapter Forty

My lungs filled again once we were free of the tension thickening the air of the Great Hall. Dirk nodded to Cade, who stood outside the door, arms crossed. He looked at me, motioning for Titus and me to go on so the men could fall in step with each other as we gathered our cloaks and made our way to the stables.

But I had never been one to blindly obey. I ignored him, reaching for his arm so I could walk by his side.

He shot me an annoyed look. I conveniently looked away and smiled down at Titus. I had not expected to see the boy again. I had certainly never foreseen this, taking him to meet Char and Alfie with Dirk by my side once more.

And Anders behind me, standing in the Great Hall.

Swallowing, I matched my steps to Titus's as we left the keep and entered the courtyard. Clouds hung low in the sky, I noticed as I glanced up. The sun hid. How I wished I could join it and avoid the strain between Dirk and Anders. But I knew that was impossible, so I settled for praying to the God who not only had created those two men, but also knew them better than I.

"What is his name again?" Titus grabbed my hand and asked the question in Dutch.

"Char. Short for Charger."

His nose wrinkled. "I like Charger better. Sounds like a *noble steed*." His tongue tripped on the English words before he recovered. "What color is he?"

As we drew closer to the stables, I noticed Dirk and Cade softly speaking to each other. "He has a brown coat and a lighter-colored mane. But you will soon see for yourself."

"Is he nice?"

"Very."

Dirk grunted. Cade turned and started walking away. Alfie chose that moment to emerge from the stables. Dirk nearly dropped the lantern he was holding.

"Milady—" Alfie caught sight of Dirk. His expression of shocked delight was only mirrored on Dirk's face.

I laughed. "Titus, meet another friend of mine, Alfie."

"Gwyn!" Dirk looked at me. "When did you…?"

"Soon after you left," I whispered. "Something compelled me to go get him."

"I say, my good man." Dirk strode forward and clapped Alfie on the shoulder. "Titus, I imagine Alfie is excellent at building towers."

Where before Titus's expression had been hesitant, almost as if he feared Dirk's joy at seeing Alfie meant he himself might be replaced, at this news Titus perked up. "I'm Titus."

Alfie nodded. "I'm Alfie."

The two boys beamed at each other.

"Alfie, we were just about to introduce Titus to Char," I said.

Alfie led the way, the two new friends' chatter filling the stable. "This, Titus," he said as we approached Char's stall, "is Char."

Titus's eyes grew wide as he stared up the horse's height. I smiled and laid a hand on the velvety nose. "Char, meet Titus. He is my friend, as well."

Titus smiled, his eyes losing some of the fear. He reached up a tentative hand. Char leaned down his head even as Titus rose up on his toes. The result was that Char and Titus stared at each other eye-to-eye. Titus's hand stroked the horse's nose.

What we witnessed next put tears in my eyes. Char snorted as if in approval, and Titus flinched, laughing. He burst into Dutch, telling the horse about his father, the ship, the country of his birth, his mother. Alfie's eyes grew wide at the different language.

Dirk put his arm around me, and I looked up to find him looking as touched as I felt. I leaned into him and spoke in English. "He is telling Char his mother was the most beautiful woman. He knows that because Tudder tells him, even though Titus himself cannot remember." My voice caught. "He says that I remind him of her."

Dirk kissed my head.

"Dirk." Ian interrupted my translation by coming into the stables.

Dirk turned to him. Ian crouched at Titus's side. Titus flawlessly made

236

the transition between the language of his heart and the language Ian and Alfie knew. Dirk tugged on my hand, then, but I stared, watching the boys talk to both Char and Ian.

Gently, Dirk led me forward to another stall. I watched him position the saddle and reins. "Whose horse is this?"

"Mine."

"He's not spotted."

A snort and a smile. "We left that horse in the Low Countries." He finished readying the horse. "How do you say horse in Spanish?"

I blinked and studied him before answering. "*Caballo.*"

"Ca-ba-yo?"

I giggled. "*Si.*"

"And in Dutch?"

My head cocked to one side. "*Hengst.* Why do you wish to know?"

He gave no response but led his horse from the stall. I walked on the other side as we left the stable. Then, when I expected to see him return for Char, he mounted. My eyes flicked between the darkness of the stable and his smiling face. He reached out a hand. Recognizing his intent, I shook my head in amusement, but I let him clasp my hand in his own. I stared at it a moment. "Your hand is so much larger than mine."

His face sobered. "Does it frighten you?"

For the second time that morn I suspected some hidden meaning to his words. "Should it?"

"This hand has committed crimes." He spoke the words with calm, without hesitation.

"This hand is forgiven." With that, I stepped forward. He tugged, and I swung over the horse's back to sit squarely behind him. After arranging my skirt, I put my arms around him. "Where are we going?"

Again, he did not answer. Instead, he nodded to the man at the gate. The wooden slats lifted, the land stretched out before us, and Dirk coaxed his mount into a gallop. The icy wind of winter played with my hair, freeing it from its knot, and shivered over my skin.

I watched the open land surrounding the keep fall away. Thick wooded forest took its place. Towering trunks with peeling bark beckoned me to touch them. Spindly branches, naked of leaves, looked sorrowful. Yesterday I had known their barrenness.

But Dirk had come back for me.

When our speed slid my glasses down my nose, I let go of him to adjust them. At the same moment, the horse's muscles bunched beneath him.

Panic rippled through me, for I knew what that meant. The flash of a dead log rose in my sight.

Then the horse jumped before I could lash my arm back to Dirk's side.

We landed on the other side of the log. My glasses teetered on my nose, I lost my balance, and only the clamp of Dirk's hand to my other arm kept me seated. He drew the horse to a stop. "Gwyn?" His voice held concern. And amusement.

Annoyance sparked, and I chose to dismount first.

He dropped to his feet beside me. "Are you well?" My silence seemed to have infused more concern into his voice. His hands rose and fell along my arms, and I could not tell whether he checked for injuries or sought to warm me.

My words from last night drifted through my mind. *Then warm me.* I turned away before he could see me blush, pretending that I fixed my glasses. Such a mix of emotions he stirred inside me.

"Did I hurt you?"

I whirled. "What? *Nee.*"

His gaze flicked between my eyes before he reached for my hands. Gentle fingers pushed up my sleeves to reveal the bruises. They were faded but faintly visible. A cascade of different shades of blue to match the ice-blue shades of snow and sky all around us. His hands grasped mine even as his whisper grasped my heart. "I should have been there for you."

"Who told you?"

"Cade."

I nodded.

"I would hear the tale from your own lips, though."

I pulled down my sleeves. "There is no tale to tell. Anders apologized."

When I looked up at him, a vein ticked in his jaw at my mention of Anders's name. "How do you know him, Gwyn?"

"He is an old friend." I laid a hand on Dirk's chest to calm him, but that action only revealed the hurried heartbeat pressing against my fingers. "The brother I never had. I called him here to help me."

He stiffened beneath my hand. "You called him here?"

A moment passed before I found words. "You left. I needed his help." I paused, knowing my words surely sliced through him, but unable to admit to him just yet all Anders and I had done.

Dirk laid his hand over mine, his eyes hard. "How long have you known him?"

Months ago, I would never have allowed him to question me like this.

Now I only praised God he was here to do it. "Since I was but a girl. Years and years. I forget how many." Although Anders had known *me* for twelve, I still failed to remember the day I had met him.

Dirk stared down at me a moment before his other hand rose to brush my hair from my forehead.

I looked down, knowing the bruises must look frightful. "I have never seen him react like that before."

"He has never before hurt you?"

I shook my head. "Of course not."

His chest rose and fell beneath my hand. "What garnered such an unusual reaction then, that he marked your arms and Cade had to step in?"

A wince arose at the memory of Cade "stepping in." How much to reveal? I sighed. "We argued over you."

He quirked a brow. "Me?"

"Aye."

His chin rose as his gaze surveyed our surroundings. The horse blew out a ruffled breath, and I tossed a glare in the mount's direction. If it had not been for his sudden boldness in jumping that log, I would not have nearly fallen and incurred Dirk's concern—and his questions of that day nearly a fortnight ago.

Dirk took my hand and tugged me in the direction of the trees. I followed, wondering where he led. All around, all I could see were bare branches and snowy mounds. I slipped once, but righted myself before he had to catch me. I looked up, however, to his warm brown eyes on me, and I knew he felt that stumble as if it were his own.

"Why did you do it?" I whispered.

His brows drew together, but not in confusion. In pain. He started walking, leading me behind him once more.

"Why did you have to leave me?" We had been through this, but just once more I had to ask.

"I deemed it too dangerous to stay." Conviction rang in his voice. "I had to protect you."

I nodded and said the words I had never thought I would say. "Thank you."

He stopped again, turned back and blinked at me. "For leaving you?"

"*Nee.*" I let my annoyance show. "I will never thank you for the pain I have borne these past months." My feet kept walking until I was as close as could be to him. "But I do thank you for loving me that much, that you would put my safety above our love."

He swallowed, moved. Expelling a breath, he lifted one hand to my cheek and let his gaze drop to my lips.

I put a hand to his chest. And shoved. Hard. He did not lose his balance, but the shocked look more than satisfied.

"Now do not ever do it again."

Dirk

Chapter Forty-One

I chuckled and grabbed her hand again, vowing I would steal the kiss later. For now, I had something to show her. Leading her forward, I heard her giggle from behind me. Turning around to look at her would prove dangerous in this thickly wooded area. I did it, anyway, and was rewarded with the brightness of her smile.

Mayhap I should not steal that kiss later. I had never seen her like this. When I first met her, she had been cold. Then she hated me for a murder I had not committed. And when I left her months ago, fury and blinding sorrow had engulfed her.

Now she was almost happy. And she had brought Alfie to my mother's home. This was a new Gwyn that I both could not wait to know and who frightened me more than anything I had ever known. Up until now, I had been determined to make her see that delivering her from danger—or preventing her from encountering it—was my intent.

But her new trust in me, her openness… never had it occurred to me that I would need to protect her from myself. Yet I found that very much a need when she giggled again.

At last we reached our destination. I pulled her up beside me, sent her a smile, and pushed away the last branches. Her gasp was reward enough.

The small glade, perfectly enclosed, wrapped us in solitude. Pushing aside the thought that the recent turn of events—the recent turn in the woman I loved—meant seclusion held danger, too, I led her deeper in. Boughs arched above us, forming a canopy through which sunlight bled.

One glance at Gwyn convinced me the greater beauty lay not in the nature around us, but in her face. The sparkle in her widened eyes took my breath. The way the sunshine stroked her hair, calling out every golden hue, entranced. Her parted mouth made my teeth clench.

"Where are we?" Her whisper met my ears at the same moment as her gaze met mine.

"Susie told me she directed you to the meadow."

She nodded.

I pointed. "The meadow lies beyond."

She let out a breath. "Why did Susan not tell me about this place?"

"She said you needed the open space that day."

Her eyes flicked down to the snow at our feet.

"What did she mean, Gwyn?"

A careful breath, a glance upward, and she looked to me with eyes glistening behind her glasses. "I needed *you*."

"You went there missing me?" I swallowed.

"I went there prepared to cease missing you."

I came closer. "What did you do?"

"Read your letter."

One step more, and I touched her hand. "I have read yours so many times it has cracked."

A corner of her mouth lifted. "Yours, too."

My fingers threaded through hers. "Did you stop missing me that day?" I knew not what I wished her to say. If she said nay, I would hurt for her hurt. If she said aye, I would hurt for mine.

Her smile widened. "Did you stop missing me?"

Taking her other hand, I reveled in her nearness. "What think you?"

"I think not."

"And last night? When I found you freezing in Char's stall? Gwyn, you could have died from the cold." 'Twas a thought that had assaulted my mind as soon as I had heard her voice. Just before the words she spoke had assaulted my heart.

That smile I loved fled. "I went there to surrender you."

I bent to see her face more clearly. "Surrender me?"

"To God. I felt His call to give Him all. Of me. My whole heart. And we both know you are my whole heart, so that meant I must give Him you."

A swell of love took my soul from my body and spun it around until I could scarcely breathe. My head fell forward until my forehead lay on hers. I closed my eyes and spoke her name.

My name fell from her lips at the same time. On a sob. My eyes opened. My hands let go of hers to rise and catch the tears trailing down her cheeks. My fingers were too slow, so instead I kissed her tears away. "Tell me what is burdening your heart."

"Your honor." She gasped for breath. "Your honor is what we fought over, Anders and I. He and I have worked to clear your name. We have not done well, for no one believes us. I visited the magistrate. He visited every nobleman with whom he has even a casual acquaintance, and I wrote to them afterward."

I froze, brow furrowing, hands stilling even as they cupped her face. She had done all that? "Gwyn—"

"Do not." Her finger met my lips. "Do not say I need not have labored, for I owe you much more." She spoke in Dutch for a moment, then caught herself. "You know as well as I that it is my fault you look over your shoulder, my fault that you cannot rule the manor that is your inheritance."

I grabbed the hand at my mouth. "Gwyn—"

More Dutch. She only spoke Dutch when upset. Then in English, "I branded you a murderer."

I kept silent for a second too long, shocked she blamed herself with such vehemence. How could she blame herself? Her accusation that fateful night had been entirely justified; the blade had been in my hand!

She plucked her hand free and covered her face. "It is all my fault, Dirk. This vagabond life you live is the result of my mistake. That night…"

A groan pulled from me before I could think. Realization and dismay took the place of confusion. Suddenly all she had said in the stable stall last night made complete sense—and none at all. *This vagabond life you live is the result of my mistake.*

I had thought she understood all this time that I had never once blamed her. Time to make that clear. "An honest mistake, Gwyn. You saw me with his dagger in my hand." I stared into her eyes, unmoving, praying to God for a way to comfort her, to make her see.

She started to crumple to the ground. I caught her in my arms but only succeeded in breaking her fall. Settling her across from me, I watched her shoulders shake. Breathing silent prayers into the sorrow pouring from her, I gathered her close. "If Revelin has anything to do with this, I swear I will—"

She pulled back slightly. "This has nothing to do with Anders…and everything to do with my telling everyone what I saw that night." The deep breath she pulled in could have shattered her lungs.

"Be at peace, Gwyn." I touched her hair and worked to keep my expression clear. "That was not at all your fault."

She swallowed. "I hate that I caused you all this pain."

"Pain?" Frustration that I could not hold what pained her so—and that

I could not cure it—streamed through me.

If I could have kissed her quiet, I would have, but the look in her eyes said naught would satisfy her but to tell me what was on her heart.

I touched her hair. "You have brought me not pain but love. You are my whole heart, and my whole life, as well. I love you with everything I am—and always will. Nothing could ever change that."

She looked through me. "Mayhap you choose not to see the gravity of what I did."

I drew her into my embrace, relieved that she let me. "Tell me everything, exactly what happened that night. Then let me reassure you my love has not changed."

Gwyneth

Chapter Forty-Two

This was it. I was about to shatter his world with my guilt. The guilt he now knew I carried but did not know I carried so heavily. I longed to speak of something else. Anything else. Mayhap the silver pieces he gave me each time we parted from each other's presence.

Steeling my resolve, I closed my eyes. Would we ever get over the events of that fatal hour? I had lost my parents. I had sown the seed of hatred for the man I had thought did the deed. And I had laid the blame at the feet of an innocent man. The same man who now held me, who stroked my hair, crooned in my ear, repeating over and over that his love for me was enduring.

Something broke inside me. I steeled my features, shuttered my heart, and closed tight my eyes. "Dirk, I ruined you."

"I ruined myself."

"I blamed you."

He pulled away. "You saw me standing over your parents with a dripping blade in my hand, Gwyn! What else were you supposed to think?"

I blinked up at him, reeling from his raised voice.

He hung his head and cinched me to him. "Forgive me."

"*Nee*, forgive me."

"I cannot. There is naught to forgive." The stubborn man refused to see.

So I told him all. My heart a rock in my chest, I told him how after he had fled, leaving the knife behind, I had screamed until the whole keep had come crashing into the Great Hall. My uncle had been the last to arrive and the calmest of them all. The grief—which I now knew to be pretended—had caused his face to crumple, but he had held steady. At the time, I had thought his steadiness was for me. Now I knew better.

"I gave him your name."

"As well you should have."

I glared at him, wanting to slap him. "But you were innocent!"

He buried his head in my shoulder and spoke into my neck. "I looked guilty."

"But you were not!"

"And you should not blame yourself for what is not your fault."

Silence settled over us. I had expected him to rail and rage. I had expected him to rescind his love. I had never expected him to defend me. "My head tells me anyone would have done the same after seeing the same sight. My heart tells me you should not love me. I ruined your life. How can you even look at me?"

A tortured sound came from his throat, and he lifted his head. "Gwyn, you are everything good in my life."

I swallowed hard but refused to cave. Fine, then. At least let him appease my guilt. I dug my fingers into his shoulders. "Please, just say it. I will never bring it up again and hopefully this terrible guilt will go away if you just tell me. Tell me. Forgive me."

He kissed my forehead. "I cannot give forgiveness when none is due. It is I who should ask forgiveness of you."

"Dirk!" I hated the tremor in my voice. "Just say you forgive me."

"Nay."

"I blamed you for murder! Now everyone thinks you did it!"

"I did it."

"It is my fault that—" I stopped, opened my eyes, and stared into his. What had he just said?

"I did it, Gwyn," he whispered, cold as rain, still as stone, somber as a grave. "I committed murder."

"*Idiota.*" But the word was a whisper. "My uncle killed my parents. Oliver—"

"I killed a man two years ago."

The chill in the wind reached my bones. "Oh, Dirk."

He ran his fingers through his hair. "Is that all you have to say?"

"Why? Why did you have to kill him?" Sorrow for him filled me, even though just a moment ago I had closed myself off completely. Aghast at how the man could open my soul like no other ever could, I melted into him and listened to his heartbeat.

"A tale for another time."

The old Gwyneth would have pushed. She would have insisted on knowing the truth. But I sat there, feeling something akin to peace, content at last, breathing deeply of the forest's scent all around us.

He did not hold me responsible. Though I had held him so.

Long moments later, Dirk shifted and lifted me to my feet. "I need to know something about Revelin." Tension traced lines around his eyes.

"What is it?"

"Do you love him?"

Time ceased to turn. "You know the answer to that."

He leaned down and kissed me then. Not a kiss of joy, of love, or of farewell—thank God. A kiss of relief.

I broke away. "Why would you have to ask?"

He gathered my hand in his. "Because he loves you."

My lips pressed together as Dirk turned. He led us from the glade and helped me onto the horse, back toward Godfrey Estate. This time I paid no attention to the barren beauty of winter's touch all around us. I merely held on to Dirk and prayed.

It wasn't enough for Anders to say he loved me, or for another to observe the same. Did his love for me excuse his irrational actions over the last months? I did not know. I did not know if I could still consider him a friend. He loved me, so he had sought to help me in my cause to absolve Dirk. He loved me, so he had wished to persuade me away from Dirk. What should I do with the knowledge of his love for me?

When Dirk had mentioned the night before my accompanying him this day, I never envisioned an afternoon such as this. Having to wonder how I felt about Anders. Learning that Dirk would not forgive me *because he did not hold me responsible.*

Just as the gate came into view, I realized what Dirk had given me back in that glade. He might not have granted me the pardon I had been desperate for, but he had given me a far greater gift. Himself. His heart. His love. He did not blame me. He did not hold me responsible. He only loved me.

I nestled my face in the back of his coat and held on tight.

Dirk

Chapter Forty-Three

Oh, Gwyn. I hugged her arms tighter around me and held on. Lest she suffer another slip. Lest she for a moment lose her grip. Lest I forget she was mine, all mine, and she loved me.

She had thought what she had to share with me would hurt me, but had what I shared with her hurt her more? I kicked myself for once again letting the wrong words out of my mouth at the wrong time. Still, her resilience once again amazed me. She clung to my back as I rode into the courtyard, not trembling, not weeping.

She had blamed herself. The thought ricocheted through my mind for the thousandth time. It swirled in my stomach and threaded through my throat.

A man came forward to help her dismount. I followed her to the ground, jealous of the way the servant's hands circled her waist as he helped her down, although he immediately let her go. Before she could turn and walk away, I spanned her waist with my hands. She smiled shyly up at me.

The image of her face as it had looked in the glade assaulted me. Naught revealed the truth of her guilt like the way her face had paled and went blank as she begged me for the forgiveness I could never grant. She had held herself accountable. She had suffered guilt. As I did. The only difference was that her guilt was false, her crime against me ethereal. The danger I had put her in time after time, the way I had—over and over—not been there when she needed me most…my guilt surged anew at the mere remembrance.

'Twas I who should beg her forgiveness.

Yet when I opened my mouth to ask for that very thing, her gaze shot past my shoulder.

"Margried!" The bellow came from the opposite end of the courtyard.

My head jerked up at the sound of Cade's voice.

Gwyn released a small cry and surged in that direction. I followed, taking in the scene with one glance.

Margried, her back to Cade, walked toward the keep with a straight spine and lifted chin. Even from this distance, I detected the faint streaks of tears on her face.

Cade stepped after her, his face full of anguish and…fright. Never had I seen such a look of pure panic on my friend's face.

"Margried." Gwyn fell into step beside the woman, touched her arm, and called her name again. Margried gave no answer, just continued walking.

I came to Cade's side at the same moment as he looked my way and stilled. I clasped his shoulder. "Do not stop. Go after her."

"'Tis no use." His voice lowered. "Naught I can say will convince her now."

"What happened?"

"She said I remind her of her father."

I winced, for Cade had told me Margried and her father had been estranged ever since the man had pledged her hand to Gwyn's uncle. Looking up, I saw Margried disappear through the door. Gwyn glanced back at me, the expression on her face pleading and determined at the same time. I nodded once and held up a hand. I knew the moment she saw the flash of sunlight against the silver in my palm, for she smiled softly before following her friend.

I turned to Cade. "Why?"

"I would like to know the same," Revelin asked.

I turned slowly on my heel to see the man Gwyn called friend standing before me, a shadowed look on his face. My voice lowered. "I would like to know why you are still here."

Fake shock widened his eyes. "Will you toss me out on my ear?"

"Will you require such humiliation?" Never. Revelin would never stand for such a public disgrace. Not, at least, after he knew he had lost. And I planned to make him aware of that fact very, very soon.

Darkness entered his eyes and curled his lip. "I need to speak with you about Gwyneth. She…she is vulnerable right now."

I narrowed my gaze. "State your piece."

He sighed and glanced at Cade.

"Cade stays. He is as much a friend to Gwyn as I am."

Revelin let out a breath and lifted a brow. "Do you think I will believe that clever turn of words? I know you hope for much more than friendship."

Cade shifted to stand slightly closer to me. A warning. "Is that what you wish to discuss?"

I stared at the man before me. His tousled hair suggested an uneasy night. So did his weary posture.

Revelin glared. "I wish to discuss Gwyneth." He looked in the direction of the door through which Gwyn had left the courtyard. "Her heart is broken."

Forcing myself to take a breath, I fought to relax. This would be a lot easier if I could just lay him flat with one blow. Taste the victory Cade had known. Avenge the bruises Revelin had left on Gwyn's arm. Their image in my mind was nearly enough to send me whirling into the man, but I held back, by God's grace. Once I would not have hesitated so long to react in such a way. But I was a different man now.

"And you did the breaking," Revelin whispered, pain in the eyes that turned back to me.

Not as different as I would have hoped. I surged forward and grasped the fabric at his chest, pulling him up. "One more chance." Shoving him away as I let go, I waited.

He straightened, pulled in a fortifying breath, and met my eyes. "You left her."

His words twisted in my gut like a freshly-sharpened blade, but I could offer no counter strike.

"Do not think that your return will heal the wounds you created."

My shoulders dropped an inch as I struggled to breathe without showing the affect his words had on me. "What are you about, Revelin?"

"Her. Only her. I am concerned for her welfare." His expression softened.

Cade's hand on my arm held me back from breaking the man's nose.

"She needs time," Revelin said through his too-thin nose.

A lightning bolt struck my brain, but how to explain? "Aye. She does."

"Then you agree with me?" His eyes lightened, and the pretense fell away. The demeanor of the man I had heard of during my prodigal days vanished to be replaced by a look of genuine affection on his face.

"You have known her many years, Revelin."

His brow furrowed, though the guileless look of love failed to fade. "I have."

"You care deeply for her." A small measure of pity entered my stomach when I saw the truth in his eyes.

"I do." His voice was choked.

"Then you will know better than I that the manner of woman she is requires a manner of man better than either of us could ever be."

He looked down. "Then we should let her choose."

Gwyneth

Chapter Forty-Four

Susan entered the chamber before I had succeeded in prying half of what had happened from Margried. The woman simply refused to cooperate and tell me what had transpired between her and Cade.

Then the humming came, a knock sounded, and Margried sat up and called, "Come in." I shot her a glare but schooled it when Susan entered on a whiff of rosewater. She stopped humming, walking, and smiling when she saw Margried collapsed on the bed with me sitting at her side.

Margried sank down again. I merely continued patting her back and shrugged helplessly at Susan. What kind of a sweet soul was Margried that she would invite an interruption when it seemed as if her heart was breaking?

"Whatever has happened?" Susan flew to the other side of the bed and knelt down in front of Margried's face. Mayhap it was a good thing Margried invited her in; mayhap her more direct approach would work.

Margried mumbled something unintelligible that ended on a sob and flung her arm over her face. Or mayhap not.

Susan looked at me, dismay crossing her features, before a bright look of realization stole the sadness away. She winked at me then left with the same abruptness with which she had arrived.

"Margried, please."

"I cannot."

I squeezed my eyes together. "I liked it better months ago when we were happy in love together and did not realize what work men can be."

That earned me a smile.

I threw a hand in the air. "We were plopped on a bed much like this one, but we sighed instead of cried, smiled instead of simpered, laughed instead of..." I stopped because Margried giggled. I threw her a pointed look.

"I liked it better, too."

"We can find our way back to that simpler time." Though I did not know how.

She rolled over, plopped a hand to her stomach, and looked up at me. "Can we?"

I swallowed. "Always."

Her eyes filled. "But how can you be sure?"

"I am in love with a Protestant man. The man I thought murdered my parents. And he left me. Then he came back." I smiled. "I believe in impossibilities now."

She sat up and hugged me. "I am not going to be a nun. I am back in England. I am in love with a Protestant man, of whom my father would never approve." When she pulled away, her frown decried her words. "I suppose I believe in impossibilities, too."

"You suppose?"

A tear traced her cheek.

I rose from the bed, crossed the room, and rummaged until I found the beloved box that held my treasures. Clasping them close to my chest a moment, I marveled at how reminiscent and sentimental I had become since my parents' deaths. Until I had lost them, I had not recognized the significance of the diamond rosary they had given me.

And it had only been since I had learned life went on without them that I had fallen in love for the first time.

Returning to Margried, I watched her face. After I once again sat across from her on the bed, my skirts tangled around me, I laid the box on her lap.

"You showed me this once before."

"It holds one thing more since then."

She opened it tentatively, as if knowing the worth I assigned to the contents. She did not need to study the inside of the box long before she located it.

The silver piece enclosed in Dirk's letter. The one he gave me last night, when he returned. The one he gave me after I ran from my room and flung myself into his arms this morning. The second one, when I left the table.

"There are four."

I smiled. What she could not see was the fifth—the one Dirk had held high in the air for me to see right before I placed my footsteps in Margried's and ran after her to this room.

Why had he given them to me? I knew not. But, in some strange way, I did not need to know until Dirk felt it fitting to tell me. Which, knowing me and my finite patience, I would decide was very soon indeed.

"I asked his forgiveness today."

Margried lifted startled eyes to mine.

"He took me to a beautiful glade, and I broke. I confessed how I feel responsible for his ruined reputation."

She laid her hand on mine, her brow furrowing. "I never said you were responsible—"

"He shares your sentiment."

"'Tis no sentiment."

I sighed. "It may take time for me to agree."

Her eyes narrowed. "He will convince you. What did he say when you *confessed*?" She spat the word as if in disdain.

I smiled again. "He said that he could not grant forgiveness where none is warranted."

Margried blinked, and a small smile tugged at the side of her mouth. "He may just have made restitution for the hurt he has caused you these past months."

I closed my eyes. "Please do forgive him, Margried."

"I will try, if you will please forgive yourself."

Swallowing, I lifted my chin and met her gaze without flinching. "Agreed."

Her smile became a grin.

"Next please forgive Cade for agreeing with him."

Margried closed her eyes, pain written on her features. I reached to embrace her. A moment of serenity passed, then Susan burst through the door, a tray in her hands. "I brought berry scones to make you feel better! And a letter for you, Gwyneth!"

My first instinct was to believe it was from Talan. So I tore from the bed and reached for the missive on Susan's tray.

"Who is it?" Margried asked, sounding as breathless as I felt. She knew what anxiety Talan had caused me. But it was not from him.

"Lord Mauldin." Ripping into the short letter, I read:

Lord Charles Mauldin, by the grace of God to Lady Gwyneth Barrington of Barrington Manor, presumed Godfrey Estate, his most kind greeting.

I received your correspondence a fortnight ago and have

puzzled over it ever since. Curiosity compels me to write and ask, why send a letter defending the dubious Devon Godfrey? I also received a letter from a mystery of a character named Talan, his missive being in direct contrast to yours. I must say I am surprised about all this attention being paid to the murderer.

Satisfy my curiosity, milady. Why would you write such a letter, especially after going to such effort to send the Earl of Lansberry to speak of how the murderer cannot be trusted?

Yours, Lord Mauldin

The letter fell from my hands as the bitterness of betrayal slid through me.

Dirk

When Cade, Anders, and I entered the keep, it was to see Gwyn flying down the stairs. "How could you?" she screamed.

At first I thought she spoke to me, but it was to Anders she ran, stopping just short of bowling into him. She fought differently with him than she did with me. Her pointer finger did not land in his chest. No Spanish flew from her mouth. She only stared coldly into his eyes, enraged.

And lifted a letter into his face.

"What are you talking about?" Anders took a step back.

"This! Lord Mauldin told me what you did! You lied to me."

Anders' face paled. "Gwyneth, wait. Let me explain."

"Explain what? That you told all those noblemen that Dirk is not to be trusted? After you told me you went to them to explain his innocence? Lord Mauldin seems to have explained it all for you."

Quite a crowd had gathered. Servants lingered in the corners. Margried and Susan leaned over the staircase. Cade touched my shoulder. "Should we intervene?"

I shook my head. "She knows what she's doing." I did not. Despite my assurance to Cade, every inch of me wanted to surge forward, stand beside her. But I held back. This was her fight. This was her realization that the man who had once been a friend to her deserved the title no longer.

"Will you deny it?" Gwyn asked Anders.

He remained silent. His hands lifted toward her as if in a plea for her understanding. She countered with a downward slash of the hand that held the letter.

"I am sorry," he finally whispered into the deadly silence that reigned over us all, spectators to his betrayal.

It was in that moment that she looked to me, her heart in her eyes. I

256

almost expected her to approach me, but instead she stalked toward the staircase and passed Margried and Susan. They exchanged a glance when she disappeared from sight.

Hours later, the sun had set and Susan and Millicent had received far more than their share of tweaked noses and tugged hair. I had been certain that Gwyn needed time but would soon descend the stairs and join us in my mother's boudoir. Yet my glances at the door went unrequited.

When Mother walked in, her brows rose. "Why do you look so disappointed to see me, son?" But her twitching mouth told a truer tale.

I gulped and searched for a good answer. Alas, there was none.

Millicent's scowl and biting tone begged my attention. "He is waiting for her."

Shocked that my sister had seen right through me, I stared.

Susan laughed. "He has been since she confronted Lord Revelin."

Millicent's face noticeably brightened. "Lord Revelin seems most affectionate towards her, Devon."

Had Millicent not seen the altercation earlier? I shot my sister a glance, unsure of the game she played, before studying our mother's expression once again. My mother frowned at my sister. "I believe Gwyneth may be outside her chamber talking with Sister Agnes."

Then she flicked her gaze between me and the door. I rose and followed her out, taking note of the way Susan chided Millicent for her comment. I failed to catch Millicent's reply.

"Did he tell you?" My mother's words brought my gaze down to her. The candlelight flickered on the silver of her hair.

"Did he tell me what?"

"Cade. He defended Gwyneth against him. Not that she cannot hold her own." My mother's short laugh strung through the air on a series of snorts.

I allowed the smile to slip through, then answered, "He told me."

"He did well."

To tell me or to strike Revelin? "I agree." On both counts.

Mother shifted her weight. "I believe Revelin carries some affection for her, son. He has known her for much longer than you have. And he is a patient man."

"I see the way he esteems her, but his patience may have cost him his chance."

She smiled and touched my shoulder. "Her heart is yours. Do not give it back to her. Anders will only be too eager to lay claim to it."

"Do not fear, Mother. I have no intention of doing anything of the sort. In fact, I plan to never let her out of my sight again."

Her gaze probed deep. "Then you are staying."

I ran a hand through my hair. "All I know is that I am waiting on God to show me the proper path. That, and I wish to make Gwyn my bride."

Mother's grin stretched across her face as her hands rose to clasp in front of her. Her eyes brimmed. "I am happy for you, son. Most happy."

I kissed her cheek. "Thank you for helping me see the error of my ways, Mother. Over and over again."

Her smile deepened yet again. "What else are mothers for?"

Touching her shoulder, I said, "Praying."

Then I turned to go. If I were to find Gwyneth, as my mother had said, talking to Agnes, cornered by one of the two Catholics in the keep, I would indeed need all my mother's prayers.

Gwyneth

Chapter Forty-Six

If I were to see Margried reconciled with Cade, I needed to get those two together somehow. And I wished to turn my mind to that quest and away from Anders's betrayal. So I slipped from our chamber, intent on finding Margried and Cade and locking them both in the library if necessary. All they needed, I felt confident, were a few uninterrupted hours in which they could work through the argument that had arisen between them.

Instead of finding Cade, I found Sister Agnes outside my door, hand poised to knock.

I put a hand to my chest. "You startled me, Sister."

"Forgive me. But there is something I need you to know." She looked toward the darkened corner, and I followed her gaze.

"I am sorry." Anders appeared from around the corner. "I never meant to hurt you."

I did not hesitate, my anger from earlier not at all cooled. "But you did. You betrayed me. You told me you were helping me, but you were working against me instead. You are worse than Talan, for you are not a stranger. You were my friend." The words fell from my lips before I could bar them behind my teeth.

His eyes shadowed.

The sleeves of Sister Agnes's habit swirled in the dimly-lit hall as she crossed her arms. "What he says is true, Lady Gwyneth. He never meant to hurt you. But we have something we must share with you."

I fought the desire to cross my own arms and block out both of them. Sister Agnes had unknowingly brought forth a word that meant a lot to me lately. *True*. It seemed all I wanted was truth. Truth about Dirk's love. Truth about my own. Truth about God's love for me—and just what that meant.

What I wanted no more of was the *truth* Anders offered, the kind that conspired against me these past weeks but still for some reason offered to take me to Dirk in the middle of the night. His actions made no sense—not until I remembered what Dirk had said. He loved me.

Well, the man had a terribly inconsistent way of expressing it: working against the man I loved then volunteering to take me to him.

"I am sorry, but I must find—"

Anders shook his head. "At this hour? 'Tis most improper."

He sounded like Sister Agnes, and annoyance twinged. "It is improper for me to see *him*, yet here *you* stand?"

"Sister Agnes stands right here. And I care for you."

My eyes widened. "And he does not? He is the one who rescued me! The one who carried me from the Low Countries, from my uncle—"

"To where you would be sure to be influenced by his Protestant mother and sisters. Do you not see, he has forced you to fall in love with him, bribing you with rescue and safety!"

I stared, struggling to maintain the blank expression. "How dare you."

"How dare he?" Sister Agnes blew out a breath. "How dare *you* turn from your religion and fall for a heretic?"

My mouth fell open. "I need not defend myself or my decisions to either of you."

"But you recognize there is need for a defense?" Sister Agnes asked.

Anders smiled sadly. "All this can be rectified. Leave this place."

"I am staying. I have no wish to *rectify* anything, nor is there any need. I love him, not because he saved me but because of the man he is." Releasing a breath, I looked between them. "I had not realized such a friendship had been forged between you."

The look the two then exchanged cemented in my mind that their relationship was stronger than I suspected. And why not? The only two Catholics in a house of, in their estimation, heretics.

Sister Agnes looked at me again. "We see the situation in the same light, Lady Gwyneth. You of all people should know why."

Of course I did. "You are both Catholic."

"True children of God."

I shook my head. Now there was one use of the word *true* that merely irked me, though I had used it many times myself. "I once counted myself among you. I still do, but in different fashion. I am a true child of God not because of what I have done, but because of what He did."

"What you say makes no sense," Sister Agnes whispered.

A wry smile turned my lips. "I know. Oh, how I know. For once it made no sense to me, either. In truth, it still does not sometimes. That God loves me."

"You speak in riddles, like the rest of them," Anders said.

"The *rest of them* are wise, even when sometimes their wisdom is hard to comprehend. I have learned more from Lady Godfrey these last weeks than during my lifetime in the church."

Sister Agnes shook her head and crossed herself as if to protect against my heresy. It stung. But once I had been there, too, so I could not be offended. Only saddened that they did not yet see—and that they wasted thought instead on thinking that Dirk had somehow forced me to love him.

Anders merely said, "Yet you struggle to believe it."

I blinked. How could he possibly have known that? I worked so hard to render my features unreadable, to give naught away. In doing so, I must have given everything away to the man who had known me the longest.

"It is time you return to your religion, Gwyneth." Anders's eyes drove straight into mine. The pleading, the pain in his expression sank into me with all the force of a blow.

The bruises on my wrists ached of a sudden. My words were whispers. "That is impossible. I can do nothing but what Christ leads me to do. And right now He leads me away from you."

I had only taken one step when Dirk strode from the shadows with his brows knit together, his gaze fierce—and focused squarely on Anders.

Anders drew up to his full height. "You suffer from the same madness that took your uncle."

I could not breathe.

"You overstep. Yet again." Dirk glared at Anders. Hearing his voice infused me with renewed confidence.

This was one of the reasons I loved Dirk—he made me better than I could be alone. Yet another reason I loved him was for that wolfish grin he now gave me as he asked, "Do you wish to return to Catholicism?"

I shrugged flippantly, though I did not feel so. "Not tonight."

He turned back to Anders, standing in front of me just enough to send a message. "Be away before I throw you out."

Sister Agnes threw her hands in the air. "Lady Gwyneth, your consorting with this man endangers your soul."

I shook my head. "One day you will be proven wrong."

Dismay written on her every feature, she walked away. *Please, God, one day, teach her to stay and listen so she may know the truth.* For I knew now what the truth was—true love, both Dirk's and God's, was unpredictable and enduring.

When I returned my gaze to Anders, he stared at me. Sadness reigned on his face. "Are you certain, Gwyneth?"

Long years had I known him, but never had I felt him more a stranger. For so long I had counted him a dear friend, the brother I had never been blessed with, but the years had changed him. *Nee,* I amended that thought. The years had not changed him.

This last year had changed me.

I looked to Dirk. His strong, steady gaze never wavered.

"I am certain," I told Anders.

And for the first time in a long time, at long last, that was true.

Dirk

Chapter Forty-Seven

Watching Anders walk away, a warrior's whoop rose up in me. I stamped it down, and it transformed into trembles as I turned back to Gwyneth. Something significant had passed between her and Revelin just now. I hesitated to believe it.

"Are you indeed certain, Gwyneth?"

She smiled up at me, real joy shining in her eyes. "Of all things save one."

Dread sank like a stone to my stomach. "Me?" *Us?*

"Silver."

My lungs emptied. Her hand reached for mine. My fingers threaded through hers, but that was not enough. So I gathered her close and cherished the look in her eyes as she gazed up at me. "Silver?"

"Aye." She knew then. That I knew exactly to what she referred. The silver pieces.

I plucked another from my pocket and gently stretched her palm open to receive it. "You gave these to me."

"They were from your mother. She meant for us to begin a new life with them."

I watched her study the silver piece, watched her eyes widen and her mouth open. "You mean…?"

"One for believing in me before you knew the truth and stretching out your hand at the riverside. One for believing in me once you knew what happened the night your parents died and trusting me thereafter." I kissed her forehead. "One for believing in me when I left and for telling me to come back to you." Kissing her cheek, I tasted her tears.

"Dirk."

"Let me finish." I kissed her nose. "And one for believing in me after I returned and for running to me this morn."

She buried her head in my shoulder and whispered, "I love you."

I whispered it back into her ear and waited for her to realize.

When she did, her head lifted. "But that's four."

I kissed her other cheek.

"You gave me one in your letter, one on the night you returned, one this morning, one in the Great Hall, and one now. And you held one up in the courtyard earlier. That is six!"

I smiled. "My mother's pouch holds more than four or six." I kissed her ear, delighting in her shiver. "I would give you one each time we part, to remind you of the truth."

"The truth."

"Aye, the truth. Though once I left your side for far too long, never again will I leave you behind." I cinched her tighter to me and kissed her brow. The vague thought that she would ask again about the scar above my own brow entered my mind, but I pushed it away to be dealt with at another time. "Do not think for a moment that I plan on letting you go."

Gwyneth

Chapter Forty-Eight

I smiled. "I asked you to in my uncle's dungeon. You refused to let me go, then, too."

He cleared his throat, and the sound filtered through my ears—the sound of nervous happiness. "Gwyneth-mine, I am a man with a marked past."

"That matters not to me. It once did, but no more."

His gaze was intent. "I know not where we will go or if we should seek to stay here for a time. Only God knows His plans for me, but…if you would have me, I will ask you to go with me wherever He leads."

I ceased breathing. "Then ask."

He released me—all but my hand—and knelt. "I know I asked you this once before…"

I giggled. "Actually, you did not ask me the first time."

His head lowered and lifted again, a sigh pulling from his chest even as he smiled at me. "Gwyn?"

"Aye?"

"Do not make me kiss you before you agree."

"You assume I will." I tilted my ear to my shoulder and watched his gaze fall to the hair that cascaded to my waist.

He rose and kissed my chin. Pulling back, he had the audacity to grin at the way I blinked.

"You missed your aim."

A growl pulled from his chest. "If you wish me to kiss you properly, then allow me to ask…"

The breath froze in my chest.

"Will you be my bride?"

Dirk

Chapter Forty-Nine

She tugged me to my feet and nestled close. The scent of her hair swirled around me, intoxicating. Thanking God for this woman, I waited, knowing she must hear my heartbeat galloping like Char across the meadow.

Tilting her head, she stared at me, adoration in her expression. One day I would be worthy of that look. "A very important question hangs in the air, milady."

"I just wished to hear you call me milady once more." A beat of silence. "Aye."

I cupped her face in my hands. "Is that *aye*, there is a question? Or *aye, you will marry me?*"

A teasing light entered her eyes. Or had been there all along, hiding like the moon behind a cloud. "Aye." Her smile lit the night.

Gwyneth

Chapter Fifty

"Mar—" Bursting through the door, my gaze fell on my sleeping friend, and I smiled. The lashes fanned across her cheeks made her appear younger than our shared nineteen years. Margried mumbled in her slumber, and I tiptoed to the window, wishing not to disturb her, even though a part of me longed to shout the news.

I was to wed Dirk, the one whom my heart loved.

But another part of me wished to relish the strangeness of the truth to my heart alone for a moment more. He loved me. And I loved him. And, despite the danger and risk of it all, we were to be wed.

I spun from the window and the light of the moon to fetch the box that held the tangible things I treasured most—and the letter to the queen I had left unsent. Opening it, I stared down at the glittering diamonds. Then I shut the box's lid—hard. Half of my parents' promise was coming true, while the other half never would.

Slipping beneath the blankets, I forced that fact from my mind and focused on his face.

Mayhap I simply would not wear the diamonds on my wedding day, after all.

Dirk

Chapter Fifty-One

Two Months Later

I hovered outside her chamber door and waited for her to emerge. When the portal opened, I pounced and only narrowly avoided attacking Margried. The poor woman threw a hand to her throat. I garbled air and apologized profusely.

She just smiled at me. "She still sleeps."

Expelling a sigh, I nodded. I could wait. Although the sun had risen hours ago and I had already waited a lifetime. Wait— "She sleeps?"

Margried nodded. "She did not wake once during the night."

"The nightmares?"

"Seem to have left her alone for one night."

Forever, if I had anything to say about it.

It already felt as if it had been forever since Gwyn had accepted my betrothal. Since marriages could not take place during Advent or Christmastide, we had spent a quiet holiday while the Banns had been cried. Three Sundays in a row, a minister who knew and respected my family coughed or garbled my name so as not to arouse undue attention. A meager safeguard but one that would allow Gwyn and I undisturbed entrance into holy matrimony.

An hour later, the door creaked at my back, and I swiveled in time to see Gwyn's green eyes widen and a smile light them. "Dirk."

The way she said my name could both bring rain to ashes and put fire to the ocean. "Gwyn."

After a moment of silence passed, she laughed. "May I come out?"

Realizing I blocked her path, I sidled my gaze down her nightgown-clad form and tossed her a grin. "Must you? I prefer you here, right in front of me, where I can feast on your beauty."

She blushed to the roots of her hair.

Enjoying it, I stepped away, but only slightly. "Marry me today."

Her smile grew.

My tone became serious. "The past is behind, the future uncertain. But today, today I long to give you forever."

Her step brought us together, but it was I who leaned and pressed fervency into the kiss. When she pulled away, her narrowed eyes latched on mine. "What are you not telling me?"

I sighed. "Revelin is gone."

The blood drained from her face as quickly as it had arisen. The man had waited, as he always waited, to obey my command to leave this keep. He had spent Christmastide with us, as tense as that had been. But even with the added tension, I had preferred knowing where he was to his running off during the night, as if to gleefully turn me in to the magistrate Gwyn had told me failed to believe her.

She stepped into my arms, and I gladly fastened my arms around her. "Will you be all right?"

"I had thought he would stay and see me married to you."

We both remained silent, and all I could think was how it would kill me to do the same if the situation were reversed. Thank God it wasn't. But, for once, I did not blame Revelin for letting Gwyn down.

I cradled the back of her neck and swayed. "I do not fear what he may do, Gwyn, but I do fear staying."

"We must wed and leave?"

Pulling back to kiss her forehead, I nodded. "I will understand if you want to—"

"*Idiota,* of course I do not wish to wait until it is safer."

I grinned. "I was hoping you would say that."

Gwyneth

Chapter Fifty-Two

"Today I am to be married." I spoke the words into the mirror, marveling. "On the 19th of January in the Year of Our Lord 1567."

Margried put her arms around me again. "I could not be happier for you, Gwyneth."

I looked into her eyes. "I could be happier for you."

"Let us not speak of that on the day of your wedding."

"But we shall speak of it. Soon." Then I stopped and smiled at Susan, who stepped around me, having finished fastening the buttons at my back.

She smiled back. A box lay in her hands. "Are you ready?"

I shook my head and reached for the box. Tears brimmed as I pulled out the diamond rosary my parents had given me. As my father had clasped it around my neck for the first time, they had promised they would not only allow me to choose the man my heart longed for, but that they would be there when I wed him.

Oh, Moeder, Papa, though you may not be here with me today, Dirk is all my heart longs for and more.

The diamonds rested at my throat with an old familiarity and a new significance. A sob broke free, and I felt Susan's and Margried's arms close around me.

A click caused me to look up. Rohesia closed the door behind her. Her gaze rising from my hem to my eyes, she clasped a hand to her mouth. I watched her walk forward, already trembling inside at what this all meant. The end of my maidenhood, the beginning of the rest of my life.

She hugged me close, then took my cheeks in her palms. "It is an honor to gain you as a daughter."

In that moment, I knew healing.

Dirk

Chapter Fifty-Three

"You must leave after you are wed." Cade's mouth tightened into a thin line. His low tone caused Titus and Alfie to look up from where they built a tower on the Great Hall floor. The irony that both Gwyn and I had taken these two boys into our hearts did not fail to rouse compassion in me. The line between Alfie's status as stable boy and Titus's as captain's son had never come between them; I had arranged for Alfie's duties to be largely dispersed so that he had more to time to spend with Titus.

Seeing the boys' widened eyes, I glared at Cade.

Revelin's departure had been swift and sudden—albeit not unexpected. My dread that he might disclose my whereabouts was only overshadowed by the fact that Talan could very well be on his way to Godfrey Estate now.

On top of those threats, because of the allegations against me, we would not fulfill tradition and ride to church with friends singing before us and family following behind. Instead, I would escort my bride beneath the cover of nightfall to the parish church, where the bishop loyal to my family would look the other way while Joseph performed the short ceremony. I wished I could give her more, but it gave me joy to know she did not care how we were married, only that we would be.

Ian nodded and whispered, "There is naught else to do but leave."

Yet my spirit rebelled against the very thought. *God, is that You telling me to stay? I need wisdom.*

Then footsteps announced a woman's entrance to the Great Hall. Margried kept her eyes trained on me—purposefully avoiding Cade, I felt sure.

I rose, toppling my chair. "What is it?"

"She must see you."

Without another thought, I vaulted from the Great Hall and to the foot of the stairway. Gwyn, a vision in the palest blue, traditional bridal array, smiled at me. Sleeves that hugged her arms furled out from her elbows in a waterfall of lace. A belt at her waist accentuated her beauty, but the embroidery above drew my eyes to her face. My tongue lodged at the top of my mouth. For there was nothing traditional about this—this beauty before me.

Her smile slipped slightly. "Are you pleased, my knight?"

"You look lovely." If I possessed a poet's soul, I would have expressed myself with honor, but all I could do after those insignificant three words was grovel in speechlessness.

She flew down the stairs, but, unlike yesterday morn, a smile captured her face. Straight into my arms she came, and she fit perfectly. "No matter what happens," she said, "I am proud to be your wife."

I swallowed. "The honor is all mine, milady."

Gwyneth

Chapter Fifty-Four

There was no one to give me away.

Where traditionally my father would place my hand in Dirk's, no one was present to take his place. The pang of sorrow quickly swept away when Joseph moved on in the order of ceremony. I was grateful. And speechless. A quick, dark ride to the church's door and we were here at last, pledging ourselves to each other. I treasured the look in Dirk's eyes and the solemn, joyful way he said, "I take thee as my wife."

Then, to my surprise, Rohesia stepped forward. She took her wedding ring from her finger and placed it in Joseph's hand to be blessed. Dirk had tears in his eyes when he slipped it onto my finger.

Next I whispered, "I take thee as my husband." And we knelt together in that dark parish church; I almost laughed. I would never have believed I would be married at the door of a Protestant church.

Finally Joseph blessed us both: "May God bless, preserve, and keep you; the Lord mercifully show his favor whilst looking upon you; and so fill you with all spiritual benediction and grace, that ye may so live together in this life, that in the world to come you may have life everlasting. Amen."

After our marriage kiss, my hands laced at Dirk's neck and I leaned back in my new husband's arms, relaxed, joyful. A flash of memory, of finding him in my adopted nun's cell, in the convent so many months ago, contrasted with his grin now. "I cannot get enough of you," he whispered. "You are radiant."

And we were wed.

Silence cloaked us as we made the quick journey back to Godfrey Estate. Owls hooted, and the sounds of the forest serenaded us. At the gate, we separated. Margried, Susan, and Rohesia swept me away and, to my surprise, escorted me directly to Dirk's room.

"We will have the celebratory meal tomorrow," Rohesia reminded me. All of them smiled and fawned and laughed, joy in their eyes, as they helped me lay out the pale blue gown and slip into a nightdress the purest shade of ivory.

I started to tremble when the last button was fastened.

Susan twirled me into a hug. "I am so happy to have you for a sister."

My grin drew a matching one from her. "Mayhap you will be the next wed." I whispered in her ear, "To Ian."

Her blush drew raised brows from her mother, and I smiled.

Rohesia wrapped her arms around me and whispered "Daughter" in my ear.

Margried embraced me next, only pulling back after breathing the most beautiful prayer.

Then they left, and I spun, examining this chamber that had belonged to my husband for longer than I had known him.

My husband.

The bed dwarfed the room, of course. It had to if it were to hold the warrior I loved. Turning quickly away from it, I traced the frosted window with a fingertip. The view had changed, since his chambers sat in a different wing of the estate than my own. I looked out over the meadow in which I had given up mourning for him. My shoulders relaxed and my smile widened at how fitting that was. *God, You are so good.* And true. And faithful.

My breathing seemed loud in my own ears as I gave Dirk to God yet again. His life. His reputation.

Then I squinted and saw the faintest hint that the glade Dirk had shown me sat at the corner of the meadow.

"Do you see it?" His voice at my ear made me jump and turn.

My hands met the wall below the window. He stood close, but the barest of spaces separated us. He maintained it, and I did not dare breach that gap. "See what?"

"The glade."

I nodded, smiling. "I do."

He grinned.

I tipped my head down, feeling shyer than I ever had before. But then he took my hands and put them on his shoulders. "Do you like the view?"

Swallowing, I stared up at him. "Of the glade?"

His grin melted into something more meaningful. "What else would I mean?"

My hands curved around his neck, clasping there firmly, without hesitation. "Indeed?"

He leaned forward until his forehead met mine. "You are beautiful."

Then he reached up for my glasses. Freeing them from my face and folding them carefully, he never looked away. "Do these still cause you headaches?"

I blinked up at him. "Interesting you should ask. Not nearly as much lately."

He grinned but did not say a word.

One brow rose. "What did you do?"

"The night I left, I loosened them for you, hoping I would not break them."

A soft smile slipped onto my mouth just before he claimed it with his own. Pulling back, he called me lovely. "Truly?" The question slipped out before I could think.

His brows drew together as he grasped my elbows. "You are the most beautiful woman I have ever seen." His arms came around me, and he held me, just held me, for one long moment.

His hands slid up my back to my shoulders as he lowered his head. He kissed me once, twice.

And, when he pulled back again, he whispered against my lips, "Anyone who even thinks otherwise needs glasses."

My chuckle died as he kissed my throat.

"I love you, Gwyneth-mine." The same words he had spoken on the night God had given him back to me.

"And I you, Dirk." Love sung through me on a melody both haunting and lovely. A melody that contained both of the sounds that I loved most—the sound of diamonds and the sound of silver. Hope and truth.

Dirk

Chapter Fifty-Five

I rose up on an elbow so as to better see my wife's sleeping face. *My wife.* Golden lashes fluttered against creamy cheeks. No worried wrinkling dared disturb her pert nose as she lay on her side. Her shoulder rose and fell beneath the blanket as if she slept peacefully. I dared to hope she did. Not a nightmare had intruded upon our night.

A second knock at the door reminded me why I had awakened. Annoyed, I made quick work of making myself presentable and striding across the chamber before a third knock could introduce the possibility of waking Gwyn from her serene slumber.

When a third rapping sounded, anger thundered through me. I nearly plucked the door from the wall, then slapped it to one shoulder so as to conceal Gwyn. My whisper rang out loud, "What is it?"

Cade stood in the doorway, looking both sheepish and serious.

"Cade, by all that's holy—"

"Revelin has returned."

Historical Note

In 1563, the plague really did sweep through London. In addition to Gwyneth's grandfather and pregnant aunt, an estimated 20,000 people died. So, at sixteen, Gwyneth lost two people close to her—and three years later lost two more, her parents. Of course, her uncle's death meant she was entirely alone in the world. And women could not inherit in Elizabethan England, though a woman had inherited the throne. So Gwyneth's home, Barrington Manor, passed to the Crown.

Though Barrington Manor is not a real place, St. Benet's really is. Once a monastery, it was stripped of its Catholic association when King Henry VIII—Elizabeth I's father—enacted the Dissolution of Monasteries when he split from the Catholic church and founded the Anglican one. St. Benet's was the only monastery left standing, and only because it was absorbed into the Bishopric of Norwich. The bishops still maintain the site today, preaching there once a year.

During the years 1559-1574, "Marian priests" were the only Roman Catholic priests in England. After their model, I fashioned Reverend Joseph, the converted monk turned Anglican clergyman. Marian priests maintained Catholic practices. Additionally, some parish clergy stayed in their posts but retained Catholicism in their churches, continuing Catholic activities among the people. Catholicism might have been technically illegal during Elizabeth's reign, but she was far more lenient about religious affiliations than, say, her sister, Mary, who sentenced Protestants to death.

Life was hard, which is one of the things about this time period that first drew me. Politics, religion, poverty, and rebellion define the era, but daily life centered around less tangible things: like hope, love and going on after grief. Thank you for reading this second book about Dirk and Gwyn's journey! I promise (spoiler!), the happy ending is coming soon, but it might take one more tragedy to convince them both that theirs is a love steadfast…

Acknowledgments

I am so grateful:

To Jesus: for loving me and daring me to dream.

To Mama: for saying in the bookstore that one day my novels would be on the shelves. You are always right.

To Daddy: for closing the cabinet doors when your absent-minded writer daughter leaves a trail of open ones (most often to the Oreos).

To Grandpa: for asking me, at a book fair you and Grandma took me to, where I wanted my one-day book table. I miss you. I was thrilled when I had the idea of giving Dirk and Gwyn your and Grandma's wedding anniversary—399 years early.

To my clan of a family: for supporting me.

To Sarah Fisher: for all the book and Netflix recommendations. I could *never* measure how much I have learned about Story from you. I am so glad you forgave me for calling you by the wrong name when we first met.

To Meghan Gorecki: for forgiving me that the epilogue to *Diamonds* became *two* more books. And, always, fangirling.

To my Journey Church friends: for calling me *author*. Especially Leah, for that face you made in the Woods' kitchen when I told you I signed a contract! And Chelsea Bouknight, for taking *notes* of all the things you liked about Book One.

To Chelsea Mauldin: remember, eat my dust. And now everyone who reads this thinks I'm being mean to you! Thanks for letting me name a lord after you (surprise!).

To Linda Gooding: for saying publication was in the works for me.

To Amber Stokes: for being the first to edit *Diamonds*.

To Stephanie Morrill: you first told me I had voice. GTW has been invaluable on my writing journey.

To Joanne Bischof: for your friendship and all the advice!

To Tiffany Titus: for letting me use your name!

To Susie Vahala: for believing in me.

To Kim Branham: thanks for the name Cade!

To Kim Howell: for calling me your author friend!

To Tiffany Briley: for being such a treasured friend.

To Rachel Blom and Jennifer Bishop: for all of your translation help! (Readers, all mistakes are mine.)

To Laura Anderson Kurk: for writing *Glass Girl*, because Meg reminds me of Gwyn.

To Roseanna M. White and everyone at WhiteFire: I said this last time, but it still holds true: I am so glad to get to work with you.

To Disney: for all those movies where dreams come true. You're right.

And, finally, to the reader who made it this far... *Be daring*.

See how the adventure began in Book 1 of the
Steadfast Love Series

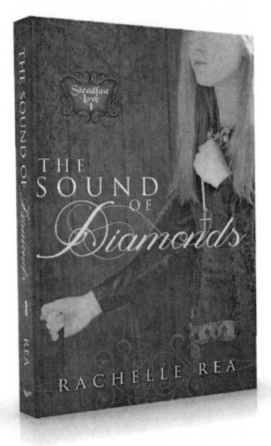

And don't miss the exciting conclusion,
The Sound of Emeralds

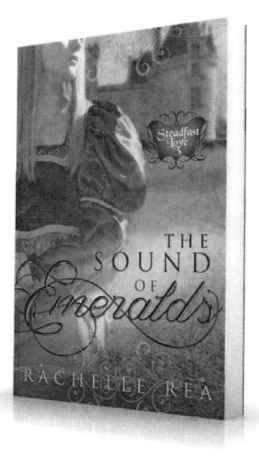

You may also enjoy these other titles from WhiteFire Publishing

October 2015

A Fair to Remember
by Suzie Johnson

During the Pan-American Expo of 1901, a Kodak girl's life is in danger when she documents the assassination of the president.

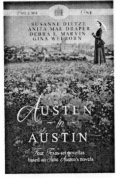

December 2015

Soul's Prisoner
by Cara Luecht

1890s Chicago - She'll fight for her future...but can she escape her past?

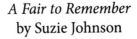

January 2016

Austen in Austin
(Volume One)
Dietze, Draper, Marvin, & Welborn

Discover four heroines in historical Austin, TX, as they find love—Jane Austen style. These novella-length re-tellings of Jane Austen's novels are sure to make you smile.

CPSIA information can be obtained
at www.ICGtesting.com
Printed in the USA
LVOW12s2222130716

496174LV00010B/985/P